ITHACA BOUND

by Kirsten McKenzie

CHAPTER 1

THE ACCIDENT

Attending a Halloween costume party in a town where her lawyer was the only person she knew was, as expected, an unmitigated disaster. Lillian Arlosh had not factored in the possibility that she wouldn't be able to identify Darren Saunders amidst a pair of human-sized pea pods, scarily realistic versions of Michael Jackson and Prince, as well as a veritable army of Roman centurions and at least four King Henry's. Of the lawyer, there'd been no sign.

A newly arrived resident of Hexham, in Northern England, Lillian Arlosh spent two torturous hours regretting her life decisions before deciding to leave with three glasses of warm chianti under her belt, and a stomach lined with soggy canapés and dry sausage rolls. As she drove the narrow laneways out of Hexham, through an eerie late autumn mist blanketing the countryside, Lillian chanced another look at her GPS before returning her eyes to the road.

A dark figure emerged from the mist. Lillian slammed on the brakes, swerving violently to the left, the brakes squealing with the sudden engagement. The car grazed the ancient stone wall lining the narrow country road, scraping the length of the passenger side before careening headfirst into a shallow ditch, the engine whining in agony.

. . .

With no airbag in the ancient vehicle, Lillian's head hit the steering wheel, only the seatbelt saving her from certain death. Blood gushed from the wound, running into her eyes, staining the steering wheel.

The revving engine pierced the deathly silent night air.

The car door opened, and a face loomed over her, one which was both familiar, and yet unknown.

'Did I hit you?' she asked, before slipping into an unconscious fugue in his arms.

'*Ego adsum,*' he said in Latin. '*I am here.*'

Lillian didn't stir as the stranger carried her from the car, her blood staining the leather of his ancient uniform, but her laboured breaths slowed until her chest returned to its familiar rhythmic motion.

Unbeknown to her, the soldier brushed the hair from her face, and wiped the blood from her face.

'*Ego adsum. Experietur quicquam mali tempus,*' he said. 'I am here. You are safe.'

He laid her on the ground, before a sound in the distance caught his attention. Casting one more glance towards her, he disappeared, just as Lillian came to.

Groggy, Lillian used the stone wall to push herself up, her mind full of her father's warnings about never swerving for an animal. But it hadn't been an animal she'd swerved to miss. It was a man. A man who'd appeared from nowhere. Had she hit him?

Lillian wiped the blood from her eyes, her head agonisingly sore. Everything was a blur. She didn't even remember getting out of the car. Confusion and fear fought for dominance. And although she'd never vocalise it, she'd swear that the man she hit had been dressed as a Roman soldier.

'Hello?' she called out.

No answer. Was it a Halloween prank?

Lillian stood in the road, her heart pounding and hands shaking. There was no sign of the man. The lane was too narrow for him to have vanished, or for her to have mistaken his shadow for anything other than that of a man. A blurred memory tugged at the edges of her mind. Had he helped her out of the car? Lillian couldn't remember opening the door, let alone climbing out of the damaged car.

A glint in the moonlight caught her eye. Bending down, she pulled at the metal, still attached to what looked like a blanket. A brooch snagged on a woollen cape. Part of the man's costume?

As Lillian examined the tubular brooch, another car appeared, its headlights glaringly bright. At first glance, it looked like it wasn't going to stop, and Lillian pushed herself up against her car.

It slowed to a crawl, then stopped.

'Do you need a hand?' the driver asked, unfolding himself from the Fiat. At almost six feet tall, he loomed over Lillian.

'It's stuck in the ditch,' Lillian replied, her voice quavering. 'There's nothing you can do unless you've got a tow rope?'

The driver shook his head, his black hair with a distinctive white streak obscuring his eyes. 'Sorry, no rope. Are you okay? It that blood?'

'I thought I... I swerved to miss someone,' she said, conscious of a car full of eyes watching. 'But I can't see any anyone, it was probably an animal.'

'Do you need an ambulance?'

Lillian touched her head, still sticky with blood. 'It was a man,' she said. 'Like one of those reenactment guys, dressed like a Roman soldier,' she mumbled, turning away, pacing the road, her cheeks infused with red. Focussing on her phone, she tried dialling the number of Roadside Assistance. Anything to deflect her embarrassment.

'It could have been a deer? We get them here. Although, on All Hallows Eve, you never know what might be stalking these fields,' he laughed, but must have seen the unimpressed look cross her face, because his laughter cut off like the electricity after a terrible storm. 'Ah, you won't get any cellphone connection here, not until you're up the top of the hill.'

'Come on, Badger!' yelled a girl from the car. A chorus of complaints from the backseat joined in. 'We can go the other way.'

'Cellphone coverage here is as useful as a sieve in a boat,' he laughed, his lame joke diffusing the tension. 'I'll call them when I'm in range. My name is Badger. It's really Andy, but everyone calls me Badger, on account of my hair,' he said, tugging at the prominent white streak.

'Lillian Arlosh. I only need a tow up to Ithaca Farm.'

'Ithaca Farm?'

'I just moved in.' How she came to own the place was too much for a roadside conversation with a stranger.

Badger looked like he had something else to say, but one of his passengers sounded the horn. 'I'll ring Roadside Assistance, and they'll be here soon enough. But you should see a doctor too, about your head.'

Badger seemed to hold her eye for a moment longer than necessary before jogging back to his car, throwing a casual wave behind him.

Badger's car reversed up the lane, pulled into a driveway, and drove off the way it had come, plunging the lane back into its unnatural darkness. Lillian shivered, and not from the night air. The mist seemed thicker now, amplifying the sounds of the night which had returned—owls, the snuffling of woodland creatures, running water, marching boots.

Lillian twisted her head, trying to locate the source of the sound. Snatches of muted conversations drifted towards her, too far away to decipher. A laugh. The metallic jingle of a horse harness. A cry, followed by another one, then another, full of anguish perhaps? Then just the heavy beating of an owl's wings.

The broken pin of the brooch in her hand pricked her hand, leaving a tiny smear of fresh blood on her skin.

CHAPTER 2
ITHACA FARM

After jumping down from the frigid cab of the tow truck, Lillian trudged across the unpaved driveway into the house she now called home. To her, it was anything but. It was in the wrong country to start with.

Her face flamed as she remembered the hostile stares of the passengers in Badger's car and the lack of warmth from the tow truck driver. He'd seemed less than impressed with her predicament, only agreeing to tow the car because of its proximity to the farm. She'd been warned that small towns weren't all church fetes and kindly neighbours. But more a hotbed of decades-old feuds and anger at big-city dwellers and all things government. Strangers and foreigners were as welcome as an infestation of deathwatch beetles.

The door swung open without her even turning the key. The lock hadn't engaged. Anyone could have come inside and robbed her blind, not that she cared if the family silver went missing. It wasn't as if she spent hours buffing the stuff to a mirror-like sheen. A half-formed memory of her mother polishing a tea set toyed at the edges of her mind, the pungent smell of silver polish heavy in the air. When she'd passed on, the silverware had come to Lillian, and for some reason she'd insured it, packed it, and carted it all the way to England.

Now it sat accusingly on the sideboard, neglect turning it blacker and blacker. Burglars were welcome to it, and the memories it held.

The wind had picked up as Lillian waited for hours until the local tow truck arrived to rescue her. And outside the kitchen window, an old farm gate hung off its post, the wind crashing it into the stone wall. She added mending the gate to her long to do list. A list she hadn't intended ever to write. But life moved in mysterious ways.

Chilled to the bone, despite the found cape she'd hung around her shoulders, Lillian stomped upstairs, slamming her bedroom door, uncaring as to the age of the hinges. Throwing herself onto her bed, she rolled to her side to stare at the wall so she didn't have to look at the unfamiliar room filled with unopened boxes and furniture which wasn't hers.

Moving to Ithaca Farm hadn't been part of her life plan. Taking the traditional route after completing high school, she'd gone straight from school into university, where she'd bumbled through a degree in zoology, primarily because she didn't know what she wanted to do and liked animals. A good enough reason to become a zoologist, especially when the earth's fauna were disappearing faster than an ice cream at the beach. After graduating, she'd fallen into a conservation role with the local council, the sort of role one does for a few years before marrying and producing two-point-four children. That's the life her parents had raised her to expect, and although Lillian was living it (apart from the marriage and procreation side of things), she didn't love it. And then her parents had died. Not a memory she enjoyed dwelling on. Bad things happened to good people. That was life. But it had derailed her life. And just when it felt like she couldn't cope anymore, Ithaca Farm had fallen into her lap. An unexpected inheritance from a grandfather she didn't know she had.

Clutching her battered toy panda bear — the one she'd gone to bed with every night as a child, Lillian cried for the life she'd left behind, grieving for her family. Moving to England wasn't the answer to her problems. Working a Northumberland farm seemed so far beyond her skill set that she felt paralysed every time she dared think about the mammoth task ahead. But deep down, she knew what she wanted to achieve at the farm. Selling it was the easy option.

But where would that leave her?

Working for some not-for-profit but with a comfortable cushion of cash behind her. No, she planned on returning this tiny sliver of England back to nature — to rewild it.

Lillian nuzzled deeper into the threadbare fur of Panda, wishing her father was here. He'd have turned the crash into a joke, and everything would feel better. Even his lame dad jokes used to make her smile. But he wasn't here and never would be. She had no one to confide in. She had seen someone in the middle of the road. He must have dashed out from the hedge, his arms outstretched, like he was appealing for help or maybe warning her. And he had run off after she crashed.

He hadn't been a figment of her imagination; he was real. The cloak at the end of her bed was evidence. She didn't know why he'd run off, but she'd never forget his face. A face she swore she'd hit, despite the complete absence of evidence. There would be words when she saw him again.

CHAPTER 3

AN ENCOUNTER IN TOWN

With no serviceable car until the garage rang her back, Lillian hiked into town, the stunning landscape more than making up for the punishing hills between Ithaca Farm and Hexham. She paused to catch her breath and to check the map on her phone.

A steady stream of school students flowed around her, accompanied by the easy patter of conversation between kids who'd spent their whole lives together in the same small town. Their uniforms echoed the post-war aesthetic, when the only available fabric was a dour grey wool combined with a surplus stock of blue air force style shirts, and she could only imagine the chafing of the shirts and the scratchiness of the woollen skirts. The town had not embraced the move into the twenty-first century.

The map showed that Hexham's public library was another two blocks from the school. Almost two blocks too far for her city-raised legs. When the lawyer had explained that a serviceable vehicle was in the garage at Ithaca Farm, she hadn't imagined a car almost as old as the farm. Held together by wishes and good luck, it usually took several attempts, and much swearing, to get the thing started. But she'd sell her soul for the old thing to be operational now.

. . .

With a deep breath, Lillian readjusted her shoulder bag and trudged through the cobbled streets, conscious of the crispness of the air and the absence of fumes. So different to Auckland. If she knew what she was looking for, she wouldn't have gone to the library. But she didn't. So an actual librarian was what she needed, before she ploughed into the unknown and set about trying to rewild an area she knew nothing about.

Focussed on her map, she kept her head down, lifting it only to orientate herself against the street signs. Not the best of strategies. She walked into a solid immovable object — the man from the accident.

Despite it being a literal impossibility, Lillian prayed for the ground to open up and swallow her.

'What the hell?'

Lillian's knock had spilt his drink down his front, leaving an unsightly wet patch blooming on his trousers.

'I'm so sorry,' Lillian said.

'Watch where you're going,' Badger said.

'Or you might see another Roman soldier,' added a melodic voice.

A blonde goddess appeared, with her arms crossed and a smile on her face. A smile which didn't reach her icy blue eyes. Holly Corben. Every town has one — desperately popular, and horribly mean.

'What did you say your name was? Vespasian or Hadrian, I get so confused with my Romans? Was it Nero? Nero also left a trail of destruction behind him, a bit like you,' Holly laughed, tossing her hair and resting her manicured nails on Badger's arm.

'It's Lillian. And like I said, I'm sorry,' Lillian repeated, her cheeks flaming red.

'It's just water, it'll dry,' Badger replied. 'I probably shouldn't drink and walk. The Health and Safety guys would deem that a hazard,' he added. His smile infusing his face with a warmth wholly lacking in Holly.

'You seem quite adept at crashing into things, *Nero*. Is that normal where you come from?' Holly sneered.

Lillian opened her mouth to answer, just as Badger laughed.

. . .

'Don't bother answering that. We're teasing. And don't get too upset about Holly calling you *Nero*. She has nicknames for everyone, so welcome to the club.'

Badger might not have heard, but Lillian couldn't mistake the huffy sniff emanating from Holly's pink-lined, gloss-encrusted lips, and the subtle tightening of Holly's fingers. What was the saying? Possession was nine-tenths of the law?

'Anyway, nice to meet you again. We have an appointment to keep. I just hope they don't think I've wet myself!' Badger laughed again, and strode away in the opposite direction, Holly's high heels clattering behind him.

Lillian shook her head. Of all the people to bump into, again. She'd barely even waved to her new neighbours, and her lawyer was the only other person she'd had an actual conversation with in Hexham. But to bump into Badger, literally, after what had happened at the scene of her accident, she couldn't help but blush.

CHAPTER 4

THE WHEELBARROW

Lillian stood outside the library, rereading the notice on the padlocked door. *Closed*, permanently, with the addresses of the closest Newcastle-based libraries displayed in bold type and underlined. As if that made it any better.

Hexham Council had decommissioned the library the previous summer. Decommissioned. News imparted with a shrug by a passerby who'd found her standing openmouthed in front of the abandoned building. The woman at least had the grace to look apologetic, explaining that the council had voted to sacrifice the library in order to establish an information centre for the tourists and a new technology hub, because everything was online these days, making libraries redundant. Redundant? Could Lillian's life get any worse?

It could.

Without being able to access any archived data about Ithaca Farm and the surrounding area, Lillian had to attend her scheduled appointment with the council's town planner without any data to support her request to pull down the farm's stone fences — fences which had separated that farm's paddocks for two hundred years, give or take.

. . .

The council had made it abundantly clear that she wasn't allowed to deconstruct the stacked stone walls on her own land without jumping through all the hoops, and then some.

Lillian wanted to attend the meeting armed with the information she expected to find at the local library — old land deeds, boundary lines, the rules and regulations related to land in the shadow of Hadrian's Wall. Without that data, she'd felt naked walking into her meeting with the planner, and left feeling even worse afterwards. Especially when she couldn't ignore that she'd overheard someone in the office mention the name *Nero*, followed by a hearty laugh. She, of course, could have been mistaken... but she'd left with a weak acknowledgement that they'd look into her request, and a warning not to undertake any work until after hearing back from them.

What a bureaucratic nightmare, and not one she was prepared to abide by. It wasn't as if she planned to dismantle Hadrian's Wall. Just a farm fence.

Back at the farm, and wielding a sturdy wheelbarrow, which looked in better condition than her car, Lillian spent the afternoon prising rocks from their ancient mortar and stacking them into the barrow. With her focus on the job at hand, she slipped into a routine. After a couple of overloading mishaps, she'd taken to layering the rocks on the base of the barrow, stacking them three high, then wheeling about and trudging the twenty feet to the barn wall, piling them neatly for potential reuse.

The work was mindless and laborious, and Lillian's mind wandered as she tugged stubborn stones from the old farm wall. It was crazy to think that they'd once been part of the engineering miracle which overshadowed Ithaca Farm - Hadrian's Wall. Someone, at some stage in the distant past, had systematically removed pieces of Hadrian's Wall, brick-by-brick, to reuse it as fencing to corral stock. Stock Lillian hated with a passion. There would be no milking of cows or shearing of sheep at Ithaca Farm, not while there was breath in her lungs. A vegetarian since the age of eight, Lillian would no more farm cattle than she would carve a turkey at Christmas. One day, the planet would thank her.

· · ·

An hour passed, but the farm wall barely looked any different from when she'd started. Lillian collapsed on the long grass and closed her eyes. The sun's position changed, and Lillian turned towards it as it sank into the horizon. The stones held a little of the sun's warmth, and after the day she'd had, sitting and dreaming was all she wanted to do.

Her moment of respite fled as quickly as the sun disappeared. Faced with a full wheelbarrow, Lillian stood. Blowing on the angry blisters in the middle of her palms, she hefted the last load, her shoulders complaining at the effort.

As Lillian stepped forward, the weight of the rocks shifted, forcing the entire load to tip. The barrow's wheel slipped into a rut left by generations of cattle rubbing themselves against the rough stones. Lillian pushed harder, and the ground disappeared beneath her. If anyone heard Lillian scream, no one came running. No crowd gathered around the yawning hole in the ground, marvelling at the power of nature, and no one offered to pull her from the void. Instead, there was total silence, partnered with a complete blackness.

Lillian wasn't sure which way was up or down, uncertain if she'd survived the fall. Lacking any sensation in her body, her pulse raced as she considered the genuine possibility that she'd broken her back.

Whispers replaced the silence — the sound of a nearby conversation competed with the roaring of blood in her ears, and the far off barking of a dog.

'Hello?' she yelled, blood filling her mouth as she adjusted her position.

The voices seemed closer now, near enough for her to understand nothing they were saying. Tourists. Since moving to Ithaca Farm, she'd had every man, his dog, his mother and his neighbour traipse across her land. She'd given up pointing out that the walkway didn't cross her fields, that it meandered behind the farmhouse before skirting around an ancient stand of trees her neighbour hadn't yet culled, despite cutting down every other stick of wood in the vicinity.

. . .

The dogs were the worst. They terrified her, and too many ramblers let their animals roam free.

'Help,' she tried, coughing on the metallic tang in her mouth. 'Help, I'm down here!' she called out. 'I'm down here.'

Through a murky haze, she caught sight of the owners of the voices. They'd lowered their voices to a whisper, their shifty eyes taking in every direction except hers. Despite the frigid temperature, the men wore only sandals and leather skirts with worked-leather vests covering rough-spun linen shirts. The moonlight picked out the subtle shade of gold and silver on the coins they were counting.

She swallowed her call for help just as the sound of panicked dogs swept through the night. And then all hell broke loose.

CHAPTER 5

THEFT FROM THE PAY CHEST

'Marcus, are you sure no one will check?' Darius asked.

'We'll be long gone before they audit the pay. They won't notice until it's too late. What was that noise?' Marcus said, lifting his head.

'Just an animal,' Darius replied, licking his lips, his eyes probing the darkened landscape.

The moonlight disguised Marcus's scepticism. He'd heard something louder than any beast. In this country of strange gods and stranger people, evil spirits walked the land. Stories abounded of centurions stolen by tribes north of the wall who had returned as pale imitations of their former selves. Even in their own cohort, there was a man who'd escaped the barbarian's clutches, reappearing at the fort's gate. His hair turned white by what he'd seen, speaking gibberish about monstrous beasts with wheels for legs.

Marcus swallowed, checking for any sign of the northern savages, or the Roman guards, as he helped Darius drag the pay chest from the vault.

'By the time they notice the pay is missing, they won't suspect us,' Marcus said, panting. He wiped the sweat from his brow and straightened.

· · ·

The moon cast an unearthly light across Marcus's face, highlighting cheekbones the girls swooned for, and lips better suited to a high-born maiden. A physique Atlas himself envied, and an easy way with words, regardless of who he was talking with.

In contrast, Darius was unremarkable. Of average height and build, he was neither strong nor weak. His beard grew in patches, giving him a mottled, unkempt look. He wasn't rich or poor. His family sent additional funds to supplement his army salary, so no one came to him for loans, and he owed no one any money. There were no significant achievements in his name, nor that of his family. They too were unmemorable — dutiful citizens of Rome, but averagely so. Despite a family connection to a minor senator, his family lacked ambition, and therefore the senator ignored them as he awarded favours and bestowed rewards. Darius and his family were and would always be unmemorable. Their greatest shortcoming was that they were too dim to recognise that their lack of achievement was entirely their own doing, and so bitterness ate at Darius, as it did his father, and his father before him.

Theirs was an odd pairing — the enigmatic Marcus with the dullard Darius, but it was a partnership of convenience — more for Marcus than Darius, although that reality escaped Darius's notice. He was more than happy dealing with Marcus's female castoffs, consoling them, sometimes with more force than a better man would use, but the allure of reuniting with Marcus was too great for the girls to complain. And as for what Marcus got from their peculiar union? He had a fall guy if his plan came to a sticky end.

Marcus removed a key from his leather satchel and slipped it into the lock on the strongbox. It had taken more than a month to befriend the soldiers responsible for guarding the pay. Half a year they'd been in this godforsaken place. Six months of nothing. No sorties, no raids, no raping or pillaging. Just endless drills and the mindless manning of lonely outposts along the border.

The men stared at the contents — hundreds of coins lay in tidy lines, like soldiers lined up for inspection. Coins filled every inch of the box — silver, gold, bronze. A mixture of coinage from Rome, and local currencies they traded with the villagers.

'How many do we take?' Darius asked.

Marcus stared at the man he'd chosen to aid him, swallowing the contempt threatening to envelop him. Darius was an idiot.

'The gold and silver ones. Help me empty the top. We need to get to the older coins underneath. Quintus told me they only count the top layer; that they don't bother counting the bottom layers.'

He emptied the bulging coin purse at his hip and a tumble of stones fell out, each fashioned like a gaming counter, but larger, the size of a gold denarius. For months he'd sourced and shaped the perfect stones. Anyone who found him hard at work assumed he was making gaming counters. A common enough practice, and a convenient lie. The fake coins would ensure the strong box remained as weighty as it had with the gold coins. His ruse would go undetected for at least a week, hopefully longer. Especially with the added entertainment he had arranged for tonight. Something Darius knew nothing about. Trust only went so far. By the time anyone discovered the theft, he would be far away from this bitter landscape, and Darius would be visiting his ancestors.

Darius emptied the top layer, his oddly delicate hands perfect for ensuring he made no noise, shuffling the coins from the chest to the bag.

A muffled cry startled them, and Darius dropped a handful of coins. They *tink tink tinked* their way down the stairs to the open strongroom.

'Idiot,' Marcus hissed.

'But I—'

'Hurry,' Marcus hissed, scanning for any disturbance among the guards.

Darius wiped his hands on his tunic and peered into the dark stairwell.

'What are you doing? Finish transferring the coins before the sentries come,' Marcus said, fists clenched.

'There's someone down there,' Darius said, shrinking back from the void.

'How can there be anyone there when we've just been down there?' Marcus said through pursed lips.

'We should check.'

Marcus sucked in a lungful of cold air. He had timed everything to the last minute. Months of planning, of surreptitiously bribing his fellow soldiers, surrounding himself with the right people, manipulating the roster so the incorruptible and conscientious were away from the fort — on manoeuvres or at an outpost, far, far away. He'd even invested some of his own money in supplying libations for drinking and for offerings to the goddess Meditrina, to make sure something more pressing would cover their theft...

'Fine.'

Marcus ducked his head as he descended into the darkened vault, his height as much of a hindrance as the night. He had no torch, but even in the dark, it was obvious the room was empty of anything other than the cohort's standard.

'There's no one there. You're dreaming,' Marcus grumbled, climbing the stairs, his jaw aching from working with such an idiot. 'How many did you drop?'

'I got them all,' Darius replied.

'Apart from these,' Marcus snapped, dropping half a dozen coins into Darius's hands. 'We don't have time for mistakes. Make the switch and get the chest back into the vault.'

From here, he could see the rest of his cohort celebrating the Meditrinalia Festival around a huge bonfire, the drunken laughter carrying on the wind. The firelight hid his activities, ruining whatever night vision the sentries might have had, although Marcus had taken great pains to ensure the make up of the patrols tonight — weak men, drunkards, all of them, and incapable of patrolling properly. They deserved what was coming. The dolt behind him did not know the legwork Marcus had put into this endeavour. Once he was flush with his newfound wealth, he'd start afresh with an assumed identity and a fine home in the city, surrounded by servants and a beautiful wife from a respectable family. He planned to reinvent himself as a man of stature. He was nothing like Darius. He had no money behind him, nor was his family aligned to a senator. Marcus only had his looks and his wit to trade with. And whilst he'd done well using the skills he had, he wanted more. He deserved more.

'It's done,' Darius said, distracting Marcus from his musings.

Marcus took the leather bag from Darius, checking its weight. He'd had it designed by a woman in the *vicus*, the village, to his exact specifications. The bag would hold, despite its unusual weight.

'Good,' he said, placing the bag on the ground and locking the chest. He slipped the bulky key into his satchel as he checked the moon's position. If his calculations were correct, they had ample time left to get to safety. 'Come, let's return it now.'

The men heaved the chest into the vault, marvelling at the inconsequential weight change. Both consumed by their separate dreams of what they'd achieve with the gold.

With the vault door locked behind them, Darius grunted with the effort of hefting the bag of gold. He fumbled as he tried sliding the pouch into his own satchel, swearing under his breath.

'Hang on,' he called out to Marcus, changing his hold on the bag.

But Marcus ignored him, walking behind the strongroom.

'Marcus, we have to get out of here. Marcus!' Darius hissed.

'I told you there was a noise,' Marcus said. And he hauled a young woman up by the scruff of her shirt. A white shirt, of plain construction, adorned with round buttons. Plastic buttons, in Roman Britain, on a white Esprit shirt.

A girl, Lillian Arlosh, struggled under Marcus's hand, her eyes wide with terror.

She screamed.

Within seconds, Marcus had his arm around her throat and mouth, choking off her cries.

'You deal with the girl. I'll return to the barracks and hide the bag as we planned,' Darius stuttered.

Marcus spat at Darius's fleeing visage. Saving his own skin clearly trumped any loyalty to Marcus. Marcus would not forget that.

'Who are you? Why were you spying on us? What did you see?'

The girl stared at him, confusion on her face. She was a stranger, and not one he was expecting. Had the gods abandoned him?

'How much did you see?' Marcus hissed.

The girl struggled under his arm, before she surprised him by stepping backwards and punching him between his legs.

The shock loosened his grip, and she wrenched free, flying across the darkened landscape.

Marcus had no time to chase after her. There were worse things out there than him, and they were close. Very close. He needed to make himself scarce and return to his bag of coins before it was too late. And then there was the Darius problem, but one easily sorted. All part of his complex plan. Already he could hear the far-off cries of the Iceni warriors and the clash of metal on metal.

CHAPTER 6

CHAOS

Julius tipped his wine over the marble base of the altar, the vintage far too young on his tongue to enjoy. The wine from this country tasted nothing like the sun-kissed wines from his homeland, a home he wondered whether he'd ever see again.

Celebrating the Meditrinalia Festival in Britannia wasn't the same. At home the village gathered to harvest the grapes and to prepare that year's vintage, before making the required offerings of both the new and old vintages to Meditrina, the goddess of health and wine. All around him, his fellow soldiers were participating in the part of the ritual where they sampled the different vintages. Some sampling more than required.

Whilst he had taken part in the Meditrinalia Festival in his first year of deployment to this forsaken island, this year's celebrations seemed to go beyond what a supply outpost on the edge of the empire needed. Organised by Marcus, and part paid for from his purse, the celebrations were stretching long into the night, leaving men slumbering on the ground where they fell, incapacitated by the strong liquor. Julius had no time for such unbecoming behaviour.

. . .

If they had any *Primus Pilus* — First Spear, other than Titus Caelius Castus, he doubted that such dedication to the goddess Meditrina would have occurred.

Julius propped up one woozy comrade when the fort's dogs began barking, their howls filling the frigid air with warnings of an imminent threat. A warning worthy of Jupiter himself.

'Rouse yourselves,' he yelled, kicking the nearest man.

His warning came too late. Panicked voices drowned the sound of the frantic dogs, as men raced past, their drinking vessels flung to the ground, drenching Meditrina's altar in wine from a dozen different vintages.

The first cry of pain came from someone to his left. Impaled by a long tapered spear, there was nothing Julius could do to save him, other than to remove the spear and close his empty eyes. There was one Roman soldier who would never see his home again.

They'd been fools, celebrating, thinking themselves immune from attack. They'd gone so long without so much as a stone thrown at their walls. And now they were paying the price.

In the chaos, it was futile trying to discern friend from foe, only the guttural war cries differentiating the combatants.

With his cohort scrambling to defend the fort from the attack, Julius almost missed the slip of a girl sprinting out of the fort, catching his eye as she ran. She looked familiar. A girl from the village? Before he could dwell on that thought, a horde of Ician warriors crested Ithaca Fort's wooden walls, and fell upon the ill prepared, and inebriated Roman soldiers.

Swinging the spear from side-to-side, Julius fought his way to the armoury, where harried men handed out weapons. Soldiers ran back towards battle, dressed in whatever was at hand. This wasn't how a Roman fort operated. This was chaos in its purest form, and people would die.

Exchanging the spear for a *glades pugnatorius*, a fighting sword — a weapon much easier to wield than an Icean spear, Julius waded into battle, only to find that the Iceni had wrought their damage and were fleeing the scene. It was blood, Roman blood, not wine, which anointed Meditrina's altar.

He fought to hold down the contents of his stomach as he surveyed the carnage. The Iceni had been armed with more than just wooden spears, slicing through the necks of the ambushed soldiers with swords sharper than most Roman weapons, leaving headless corpses as macabre offerings to the goddess, before disappearing into the hills. It made no sense for the Iceni to abandon such a successful rout of the fort.

'How could this happen?' asked a bewildered soldier, blood blooming from a wound in his shoulder.

Julius shook his head. This should never have happened. The wanton carnage was beyond all comprehension. For the Iceni to have breached the fort's defences, they must have had help. It was impossible to have happened in any other way, regardless of the inebriation from the festivities.

Roman soldiers should be prepared for any eventuality. That was the point of the endless drills and mindless practices. They were better than this. Someone had betrayed them.

CHAPTER 7

THE VISITOR

Lillian woke with a jolt, confusion flooding every fibre of her being. The ground beneath her felt softer than expected, the light brighter, the noises more familiar. Her hands brushed over her thighs and the coarse cotton weave of the gown covering her legs. A woman in a white dress stood at the end of the bed, concentrating on pages clipped to a chart.

'Where am I?'

'Welcome back,' the nurse said, abandoning the chart.

'Am I in hospital?' Lillian asked.

'Hexham Hospital, and you're lucky to be in a private room. You must have done something right. How's your pain level?'

The nurse looked as exhausted as every other nurse Lillian had seen on the news over the past couple of years, with deep lines scouring her face, but she could still feel the depth of caring emanating from the overworked woman.

'In my head? About a seven.'

'Hmm. They're keeping you in overnight to monitor that, but here is the best place for you, especially with the circus you've left behind.'

Lillian stared at her.

. . .

'The Roman altar you knocked your head on. Every man and his dog are crawling over it. Because of the skulls.'

'I don't know what you're talking about.'

'The altar they found in the ruins you discovered, and the human remains.'

'I'm still not following. I fell down a hole, down an old stone staircase, and a hiker pulled me out, I think. He was wearing sandals. I can't remember anything else.'

This time, the nurse stared at her.

'Oh, sweetheart, it's so much more than a hole. Your farm is famous. It's in all the papers. After the farm wall collapsed, a hole opened up, revealing ruins and a Roman altar surrounded by human skulls. That's what you hit your head on, or so I'm told. Anyway, it's whipped the archaeologists into a high state of excitement. If it wasn't for Badger driving past, you'd still be under the pile of rubble.'

'But there was a group of hikers wearing sandals and kilts. And then the man, I remember, he had, maybe, a walking stick...' she trailed off, unsure of what she remembered. There wasn't much difference between a walking stick and a spear.

'You think you remember, sweetheart, but that knock to the head will confuse things. Now, is there someone we can ring for you? Some family?'

Lillian shook her head and turned away. She couldn't shake the feeling that she'd seen the man with the spear before, regardless of what the nurse said. A wedge of dread settled in her stomach. What would the discovery of Roman ruins do to her plans for Ithaca Farm? That concerned her more than the question about her family.

Badger poked his head into the hospital room after the nurse left.

'Hey, is now a good time? Or should I come back?'

Lillian turned around. Badger. Concern written all over his face.

'Hi,' she said.

Badger slipped into the room and poured himself into the nearest chair. 'How are you feeling?'

'Sore and stupid.'

Badger laughed. 'You look better in bed than you did covered in stones,' he laughed, before blushing at his verbal faux pas. 'Ah, I meant, you look—'

'It's okay. I know what you meant. I'm told you found me, thanks,' Lillian said.

'I couldn't leave you there. You looked like the witch under the house in the Wizard of Oz!'

'But without the striped stockings?' she said.

Badger's blush returned, and he laughed. At least he had a sense of humour.

'How did you find me? I didn't realise you could see that field from the road. Was it your dog who found me?' she asked. The memory of the barking dog so real she could almost still hear it.

'I... ah, I'd come by to say sorry for what happened today. And when you didn't answer the door, I figured you'd be out the back. On old friend used to stay at your farm with his grandad, so I jumped the fence like when I used to come over to Seb's place. And that's when I saw your legs...' he tailed off for a second. 'I saw your legs, and there was a stack of rocks covering the rest of your body. And I froze, sorry. Just for moment, though, and then I couldn't move those stones fast enough... It bloody hurt, too.'

He turned his hands over, and Lillian couldn't count of the number of gouges and scrapes to his skin, there were so many.

'Seb? Do you mean Sebastian Arlosh?'

'Yeah, his parents moved his grandad out of Ithaca Farm when he got too old to look after himself, and then they moved away, and we lost touch. You're related right?'

Lillian shrugged, 'I never met him, but he was a relation. He and his parents died in a car accident overseas. That's what the lawyer said. The farm should have gone to my dad, but... well, that's how I ended up with it.'

'I never knew,' Badger said.

'Sorry for being the bearer of bad news,' she added, noting the sadness on Badger's face.

. . .

'Seb was a good guy and his grandad always made life interesting. I hadn't seen him for ages. You don't expect people our age to die so young. But at least that friendship meant I found you, so I'm glad I came by when I did. They're falling over themselves at your farm, so you'll have to watch out for night hawkers.'

'For what?'

'Night hawkers — metal detectorists who come out at night. Thieving maggots who skirt the rules, but the most dangerous ones come out of their holes at night.'

'The nurse said it was an altar, a slab of stone. So what would any metal detectorist want with that?'

'It wasn't just an altar. Where you find altars, there are usually other things—coins or rings, offerings to the Roman gods, made two thousand years ago.'

Lillian processed the information, a range of emotions crossing her face. 'I should go home. God knows what they're doing to the place. Am I allowed to access the farm?'

Badger shrugged. 'It'll take them a couple of nights to sort themselves out, but there won't be much you can do to stop them short of standing guard. Night hawkers are slipperier than eels dipped in grease. You could get some dogs, they work.'

'I need to go home,' she reiterated. 'I'm feeling fine.'

'You don't look fine. You need to rest,' he said. 'At least the accident will give them something else to talk about at in the village...'

'That's something, I guess.'

'I've gotta go, but I could give you a lift home tomorrow?'

'Um, sure,' she said, confused by what she thought was hope in his eyes. It made no sense. She barely knew him.

'Okay... well, see you tomorrow,' he said, hovering in the doorway.

Badger stood in the brightly lit hallway. He'd overheard Lillian telling the nurse about the hikers, and her mumblings had reminded him of what Seb's grandfather used to say. He'd talked about Romans still rampaging through the English countryside, bristling with swords.

Seb's family had used that as an excuse to have him packed off and placed into a care home, leaving Ithaca Farm untenanted, until now. So Lillian's words didn't sound as fantastical to him as they had to the nurse, and now Badger wasn't sure if Seb's grandfather hadn't been talking the truth, as unbelievable as it seemed.

CHAPTER 8

THE REPORTER

Jasper Fletcher refused to budge from his position beside the farm wall. It hadn't taken the big city media long to appear with their superior equipment and international reputations, but he'd been arrived first, nabbing a prime spot and spreading his gear as wide as possible. This was his scoop, his byline, and he would not let a flash blonde from Newcastle muscle her way in, especially when the suede heels on her tiny shoes kept sinking into the boggy soil surrounding them.

'Seriously, can't you move? You don't have the monopoly on Roman ruins,' the reporter moaned through pursed red lips.

'You didn't say please,' Jasper replied, adjusting the focus on his old-school camera.

'Come on, Jasper. Move over half a foot, so we can get a better shot of the thing—'

'The thing? The thing, Charley? You don't know what it is.'

Charley Scott huffed, her manicured hands brushing flecks of dirt from her tailored skirt.

'All we need is a foot. The big boys won't ask.'

'You didn't ask, Charley. You never do. But because it's me, you think you can flirt your way into me giving in. You've done that too many times for me to fall for it. So the answer is no.'

The arrival of Ayla Raposo, the local Finds Liaison Officer from the Portable Antiquities Scheme, cut short their circular argument, and each of the reporters turned on their professional personas and waited.

Ayla Raposo, wearing sensible knee-high waterproof boots and a heavy raincoat, stood next to Lillian, who was dressed in entirely unsuitable clothing given the environment was known for its unpredictable weather.

Lillian watched Ayla's eyes roam over the partially dismantled wall, the gaping hole, before stopped at the stone altar — protected for three hundred years by the wall Lillian had been dismantling. The woman's eyes widened at the cache of human skulls. The unnaturally decapitated human skulls.

'Amazing.'

'For you,' Lillian said. 'But what does it mean for me, this stuff in my field?'

'It's incredible, isn't it?' Ayla said.

Lillian flinched at Ayla's enthusiasm.

'Normally I spend my days cataloguing Roman coins and broken fibula brooches. But this... this is incredible.'

'Hmm,' Lillian replied. 'When are you taking it all away so I can carry on dismantling the wall?'

'Take it away? No, not yet. We need to investigate the site to see if there is any context to the altar, the remains and the stairs,' Ayla said, shrugging as if it was as plain as day. 'I'm sorry I can't give you a solid timeframe.'

'Are you saying I have to stop what I'm doing because of a gravestone?'

'It's not a tombstone, Miss Arlosh—'

'Please stop calling me that. Lillian is just fine.'

'Sorry, it's not a tombstone, it's a Roman altar, full of historical information. And the stairs, well, we don't know about where they lead to, and what they were for.'

. . .

'The positioning of the skulls throws up more questions than answers. We can guess, but when the team gets here, they'll—'

'Fine, I'll just start in a different field,' Lillian replied, her face devoid of any emotion.

'I don't recommend that, Miss Arlosh—'

'Lillian.'

'Sorry, Lillian, but the team will need to do a complete analysis of the area before you can undertake further work on the farm. Until then, maybe something indoors? And besides, the police still have to do their thing. They are human remains after all.'

'Indoors? Are you joking? You can't waltz in here and shut me down. This would never have happened if I was keeping the place functioning as a regular farm, would it? You are all against me returning the land to nature, too afraid that I'm messing up your picturesque postcard scenery. You don't give a damn about it being a piece of history. You and the council and the bloody Historic England people are all in cahoots. Fine, do whatever, I'll be inside.'

Lillian storm off, slamming the kitchen door so hard a pane of glass, loosened by years of frost and snow and inadequate maintenance, fell from its frame, shattering on the old cobbles.

With his car engine revving dangerously high, Jasper screamed back to Hexham. He had to get his story out first, and what a tale it was. Although in his mind, finding a Roman altar with some skeletal remains was secondary to Ithaca Farm's new owner returning the centuries old grazing pasture to the wild.

With one hand on the wheel, and the other gripping his phone, he called his contact at the council, almost driving off the road himself as he heard about Lillian's grand plans for Ithaca Farm. That story was more important than Roman ruins, bigger than just another incompetent hobby farmer. He expected this story to rock the establishment, and he was more excited than he could remember.

.   .   .

'Rewilding? She called it that?... No walls and free ranging what? You're joking?... No, I won't tell anyone where the info came from... yup, good. Catch you later.'

Jasper pulled into the carpark behind the offices of the Hexham Herald, his place of work for longer than he could remember. After walking through the doors as a nervous acne-covered teenager, the only scars he sported now were of the emotional kind — the kind nurtured over countless years of missed promotions and mediocre assignments covering the annual Hexham Hoedown and reporting on the removal of historic pavers for urgent road repairs. His ignominious existence made worse by the veritable merry-go-round of beautiful bright young things who'd walked through the Hexham Herald's doors after him, and who wrangled the glory jobs, catapulting them to newsrooms in Newcastle, or in the case of Lorna Milroy, to the dizzying heights of the BBC in London. Sometimes he fancied he could still smell her perfume lingering in the lunchroom amidst the aroma of microwaved tomato soup and cheap filter coffee.

No one bothered him as he made his way to his desk and slid into his stained seat, hidden by a wall of file boxes documenting decades of local events. He'd found it helpful adding historical information to his articles, not that anyone cared. Half the time, his editor culled the additional material to *keep the word count down*. The worst five words ever uttered by the man who claimed the title of Editor, Hexham Herald.

Jasper emptied the negative thoughts from his head, thoughts which normally consumed him, day and night, but not today, not with this story. This story was a headline worthy of the Newcastle Chronicle, or even The Guardian, and potentially his way out of this town. A town the tourists thought picturesque but which suffered from a festering underbelly. After covering the affairs of the locals for the past two decades, Jasper knew more of their secrets than their parish priest, including all the hidden skeletons. People shared more with a journalist than they did with their own family, and he'd found that most people over shared if it meant garnering fifteen minutes of fame and a headline in the local paper. And he was sick of it.

. . .

It was time to move on to the city, any city, and the planned development at Ithaca Farm was his ticket.

Jasper's fingers flew across the keyboard, his well-bitten nails massaging his words into some of his best work despite being more used to typing up the results of the Haydon Bridge High School Rowing Competition and detailing the disallowed soccer goal in the weekend game against Prudhoe.

'You happy to lock up tonight, Jasper?' asked John Revell, scratching at the eczema on his arms.

Jasper looked up from his screen to see Revell, golf clubs in hand. Monday afternoon was golf day, always had been. Over the years, Revell's golf days had stretched to include Tuesday afternoons, then Wednesdays. Friday too was a big day for golf, and on most Fridays, none of them saw their illustrious editor until it was time for Friday afternoon drinks. Then, like a genie, he would appear, swigging back a pint or three before tottering home, his clubs left languishing in the corner until the following Monday — Mrs Revell didn't allow golf on the weekends.

'Sure, I'll be awhile working on this piece.'

'Is that the story on the Bellingham Tea Rooms?'

Jasper shook his head, regretting his honesty as Revell's brow furrowed.

'The last thing we need is another B&B. It is our responsibility, as the only local paper of note, to inform the public of what is happening in their town and how it will impact on the other hospitality providers.'

'Meaning you and Mrs Revell,' Jasper muttered, thinking about the holiday cottages the Revell's owned out by Hadrian's Wall, the cabins the newspaper advertised for free every week.

'Pardon?'

'I said I should interview Mrs Revell. She would be a marvellous spokesperson for the accommodation industry, with all her experience and contacts.'

'Yes, yes, I'll check with her tonight. Might not work for her. We try keeping our lives separate, as you know. I'll see what she says.

. . .

It's good you're working on it. I want to run that piece in the weekend edition. So, you'll lock up then?'

Jasper nodded, relieved that his misdirect had worked as well as usual.

'Good, tomorrow then. Oh, and there's an email waiting for you from the local metal detector group. They want you to pop along tonight to their AGM. I replied on your behalf, said you'd be there.' And with that, John Revell sauntered away, golf clubs clanking behind him.

Jasper glared at the retreating back of his editor, swallowing his anger. What this town needed was an injection of fashionable B&B's. Modern enough to entice well-off tourists to Hexham, over and over, instead of the dated pub rooms and lacklustre hostels which choked the town, run like a cartel by locals such as Revell's wife. Woe betide any outsider who dared encroach on their turf. He may as well pen his resignation letter at the same time, if he wrote that article.

With his fingers bashing the keyboard, his thoughts strayed. All he wanted to do was... *thump thump*... write the article about... *thump thump*... the bizarre rewilding of Ithaca Farm... *thump thump*... and it was not without a measure of glee that he imagined the reactions from various interested parties around town... *thump thump*... but now he couldn't work on it because he had to attend another damn AGM - Another Ghastly Meeting... *thump thump*. The minutiae of the town's local clubs was enough to send the sanest person into the clutches of alcoholism. He was nearly there himself.

Jasper opened the email from the Hadrian's Heroes Metal Detecting Club, the one Revell forwarded him. Of all the places they could have held their meeting, they'd chosen the St Oswald Church hall, one of the few venues who forbade alcohol on their premises because of the large Alcoholics Anonymous group who used the hall, where even the merest sight of a bottle top or an empty wine glass could send the ex-alcoholics into a tailspin of epic proportions. Knowing that tonight would only end with tea and biscuits — the cheap biscuits, not the good iced ones from Tesco — instead of a pint and a packet of crisps set his teeth on edge and his pulse rate soaring. Fuck Revell and his small town mind.

Pushing the print button, Jasper's notes on Ithaca Farm poured from the printer. He stuffed them into his bag together with note-books, chargers and a bundle of last weekend's papers (Revell loved giving away copies of the paper — free advertising). After locking up, he clambered into his car for the drive to St Oswald's, for a night filled with fun and frivolity, where men his father's age would slurp their tepid tea whilst reminiscing about a cache of George V half crowns found in the ditch next to the A69 motorway, or rehashing the story of their detector pinging on Cheryl Visor's lost wedding ring (she'd been very insistent that the story include that it came from a London jewellery shop) in the grammar school's field. He'd written half these stories a thousand times over, and tonight would be no different.

CHAPTER 9
TRESPASSERS WILL BE PROSECUTED

Lillian stared out the kitchen window, the sight just as disappointing as it had been when she'd first arrived. At least the horde of archaeologists and media, eager for a glimpse at the newly discovered ninth wonder of the world, had left, leaving behind a churned mud filled driveway, and a laneway as barren as Ithaca's fields. A green landscape devoid of life, of heart. Where were all the trees? The ancient hedgerows?

The farm's old stockyard stood awash in outdated machinery and wooden pallets stacked at the edges. An immense roller sat squat in the corner, immoveable by hand but worth a fortune in scrap metal if she could ever move it. The house, whilst resplendent in stone thieved from nearby Hadrian's Wall, had an air of neglect hanging from its window sills and missing gutters.

Barking dogs sounded outside, interrupting her thoughts. Lillian eased open the back door. Now the dogs sounded like they'd made it into the field behind the big barn. When Badger had suggested she get some dogs to keep the night hawkers away, she hadn't wanted to tell him she was terrified of dogs.

It hadn't always been this way. When her mother had been alive, they'd had a dog — Erin, who'd been a constant presence in her life.

Walking with her to school, running the length of the beach and back again, snuggling in bed together. But then life had changed, and now Lillian couldn't even bear to be on the same side of the road as a dog. Let alone have one in her house.

A frenzied barking seemed to fill the house. From the safety of the kitchen, Lillian scanned the empty fields. No dogs or walkers, yet she could hear the faint yelps of an animal, and even to her terrified ears, the dog sounded like it was in trouble.

Lillian tried whistling through the open door, which sounded more like a smoker's rasp than a melodic flute. She had memory of her grandfather whistling complex tunes through his pursed lips as he beavered away in his shed, restoring furniture, the tang of varnish thick in the air. He'd tried teaching her how to hold her tongue behind her teeth to manipulate the noise, but she'd been a poor student, more interested in hammering nails into offcuts of wood than whistling operatic pieces.

With no sign of the animal, Lillian ventured outside and clambered over the nearest wooden style, worn smooth from thousands of pairs of booted feet traversing their land, following the line of Hadrian's Wall. Stomping through the rock-hard paddock, searching for the injured mutt, she didn't notice the pockets of disturbed earth, until she stumbled into one, sending her tumbling to the ground, the motion shooting rockets of pain through her head.

With the wind knocked out of her, Lillian lay on the ground, cursing her life and nursing her grazed palms. Deciding that she'd sustained no further injuries, she pushed herself to sitting. From this position, the fresh damage to the pasture was obvious. It was as if an army of moles had taken up residency in the field, systematically burrowing through the earth, leaving clods of earth marking their search for a new burrow.

Lillian ran her eye over the crumbling piles of fresh earth, her brain defying her initial assumption that an animal was to blame. The piles of dirt were too systematic. Was that how moles operated? She'd never seen one. They didn't have moles in New Zealand.

A movement in the field's corner caught her eye — a man wearing headphones, with a metal detector strapped to his wrist.

As she watched, he dug with an adapted spade in his other hand, turning over the pile, before sweeping his machine over the freshly turned earth. It was so fluid that his stride never faltered as he swung his attention to the next patch of undisturbed pasture.

'Oi!' she yelled.

Head down, he didn't turn, intent on his task. Even the barking of the dogs didn't affect him, the howls now mixed with a high-pitched whine, as if someone had tied it up and left it to die.

Lillian scrambled to her feet. She'd see this parasite off her land, but the pain in her head overwhelmed her and she more stumbled forward than strode. She reached for the wall to steady herself, scraping her palms on the rough edge. A loose stone jiggled under her hand. Lillian pulled it free, took aim, and fired it towards the metal detectorist. She'd never enjoyed ball sports of any kind, choosing to hide in the changing room instead of participating in school sports, but her aim was true.

The rock fragment fell short of hitting the trespasser but bounced on the hard earth, hitting the back of his shovel. He spun around, his eyes widening as he clocked sight of her before he melted away, bounding along the line of the wall, vaulting over the style at the end, and vanishing. A field of holes was the only evidence that he had been there.

'Bastard,' she muttered. The dog's howls vanished as if the animal itself had run after the man, hounding him from the field.

Lillian's headache was too bad to consider what he was searching for. That was someone else's problem. The police, hopefully. As she turned towards the house, the sun caught a glint in the soil. A fraction of a flash, but enough to draw her eye. Bending threatened to split her head into a million fragments, so Lillian nudged the object with her toe, dislodging it from its slumber, before bending like a geriatric with a double hip replacement and dicky knees. A coin.

Lillian cleaned the coin on her jeans and a burnished brass appeared beneath the filth, as shiny as new. Warm in her hand, the metal featured the profile of a man with a firm jaw. She rubbed it again, mixing the blood from her grazed palms with the damp soil clinging to the surface of the coin.

It was pure chance the detectorist had missed it, and she had a measure of satisfaction that she'd scared off him off before he'd pocketed her treasure despite knowing the last thing she needed was the discovery of more Roman artefacts on her land. One altar and a handful of skulls were causing enough of a ruckus, so this coin would be her secret.

Safe inside, Lillian set about looking for a first aid kit for her hands. After a fruitless search of the downstairs bathroom, she caught sight through the window of a long-legged man striding up the lane, his jacket unusually bulky. She watched him turn into the driveway, pause for a moment, before stepping out of sight. A knocking told her where he was. Lillian ignored the hammering on the door, deciding to pretend that she wasn't home. She raced upstairs to hide, and was halfway to her room when she heard the front door open, and the telling squeak of the floorboards in the entranceway.

Lillian peered through the old wooden railings on the landing. A fine smattering of dust lay in tiny piles beneath the railings — a telltale hint of resident woodworm consuming the ancient wood.

The intruder looked into the kitchen before backing out and loitering in the doorway. He looked as if he was about to step through before guilt, or something else, made him hesitate, his hand resting on the hall stand. If he was planning on robbing the place, he was doing a fine job of leaving fingerprints behind.

He took a step, moving out of Lillian's sight. She pressed her face harder into the railings to get a closer look. And then they gave way.

Weakened by years of voracious feeding by generations of tiny woodworm, the railings splintered under her weight. Parts of the balustrade plummeted downward, crashing to the ground. Lillian only just avoided the same fate by hooking her arm around the newel post — the only part of the structure untouched by the woodworms.

Lillian screamed. The intruder ducked. And the wood shattered on the ground below, sending up plumes of dust. Halfway dangling above the yawning void, Lillian struggled to hook her legs back over the edge of the landing.

'Stop struggling,' the intruder said. 'I'm coming.'

He vaulted up the stairs, hugging the wall, the whole balustrade now in danger of giving up its hold on the ancient staircase.

'Grab my hand,' he instructed, his deep voice full of authority.

Lillian glared at the stranger, resisting his help. He'd let himself into her home. How did she know he wasn't about to manhandle her into a room and rape her?

'Grab it,' he repeated, leaning forward, proffering her his hand, his other arm secured around the nearest door frame.

'How do I know you aren't here to kill me?'

'If I wanted you dead, I'd be pushing you off this landing, not offering to save your life. Now grab my hand before the whole thing gives way.'

Lillian took a deep breath and reached for his hand. With no apparent effort, he hauled her up, his jacket belying the muscles he had.

As the pair lay slumped on the floor, Lillian stared at the man. He looked younger up close. She'd thought him much older than her mother, but he wasn't far off her own age.

'Why are you in my house?' she asked, shuffling backwards until she was leaning against the wall, as far away as possible from the gap at the top of the stairs.

'I'm here to see Mrs Arlosh,' he replied.

'There is no Mrs Arlosh. Just me, Lillian Arlosh, so you were already barking up the wrong tree before you broke in—'

'I didn't break in—'

'Yes, you did. I was watching you.'

'I let myself in. It was unlocked, which is standard practice round here, with farmers—'

'It's not standard practice where I'm from.'

The man shrugged. 'I was looking for your mother, sorry, I mean you, and assumed you were in the kitchen, unable to hear my knocking. Look, I saved your life.'

'You wouldn't have needed to if you hadn't broken in,' Lillian retorted.

The conversation could have carried on in circles, with neither one of them making any headway, but the intruder unfolded his lanky body, towering over Lillian.

'Can I bandage that for you?' he asked, pointing to her bleeding hands.

Lillian looked at the raw scrape, reopened by her almost cataclysmic tumble.

'I'm fine,' she lied.

The faint sound of barking dogs leaked inside.

'I don't mind,' he said, stepping closer.

'I said I'm fine,' Lillian said, distracted by the sound of the dogs.

'That's a bulky jacket, isn't it?' Lillian said, changing the subject, her level of unease creeping upward under his stare.

'I feel the cold. You'll feel it soon enough, with the weather turning. Best you stock up on firewood. Most of us have got ours laid in already. And you'll need a good generator. If you're not up for a chat now, call me later because we have a lot to discuss. I'll leave my card.' And with that, he sauntered downstairs, threw a card on the hall stand and strode out the door, leaving it wide open, and the chaos of the broken balustrade behind him.

It was only then that Lillian breathed again, the incident a surreal moment in what was turning out to be an unbelievable year. The missing railings were the reason she couldn't blame the experience on a bad dream stemming from her concussion. Two near-death experiences in less than thirty-six hours. Surely a record?

The temptation to go to bed was high, but she should tidy the mess downstairs. She'd win no awards for Housekeeper of the Year, but she could clean up the rotten wood, which she could at least use for firewood. Blessed with three separate fireplaces, she would need the wood.

First she closed the door, snibbing the lock. No more leaving it unlocked for all and sundry to walk in. Next, she picked up the intruder's card. Pearly white paper stock, thick with golden print, it felt, and looked like a banker's card. She'd seen enough of those strewn across her father's huge roll top partners desk over the years. But the type on the card destroyed that assumption. It was for Anson Darby, Archaeologist, Tyne River University. Only here about the bloody altar. She dropped the card onto the hall stand.

There were too many things to worry about. The metal detectorist, the altar, the archaeologist. Her visions. At least the barking dogs had disappeared. She'd ask around in case they belonged to a local farmer, but for now, she had to lie down. Her headache was killing her.

CHAPTER 10

THE IMAGINED LIBRARY

'I can't believe this town doesn't have a library. Who made that decision?' Lillian commented to the woman sitting across from her.

Jesha Martin chewed her chicken burger and took a sip from her tea before answering. 'They shut it ages ago. There was a petition asking the council to reverse their decision, but then the newspaper said there were better things for the town to spend their money on, so the closure went ahead.'

'Better things?'

'Getting more tourists in, you know, that sort of thing.'

Lillian mulled over Jesha's answer as the pair sat together, the rest of the cafe empty, the floor sticky with spilled kombucha. It didn't seem like the council's prioritisation of the tourist dollar had kicked in. Jesha had been the only friend she'd made to date, literally bumping into her in the Sainsbury queue. The first local who hadn't narrowed their eyes and called her 'Nero' under their breath.

'What happened to the books?'

'The books?'

'The books from the library? They must have put them somewhere. Stacked them in a basement, or attic, or wherever?'

Jesha shrugged. 'It doesn't matter, everything's on the internet.'

Lillian didn't agree with her, but would not jeopardise their burgeoning friendship over a difference of opinion about the priceless nature of a library.

'I know where they are,' said a newcomer.

Lillian checked out the new arrival and had the uncomfortable experience of thinking someone had slipped a gauze mask over her eyes. The girl was albino white — her white/blonde hair indistinguishable from her pale skin. Only the pink rims around her watery blue eyes gave any depth of colour to the girl.

'You living at Ithaca Farm, right?' the watery apparition said.

'Yes,' Lillian said.

'This is Apple Collings,' Jesha said, her consonants short and sharp.

'I live down the road from your farm.'

'Sorry I haven't been over to say hello.'

'You haven't missed much. It's just me and my dad. And he's not the welcoming type unless you've lived here for the last four hundred years.'

Lillian clocked Jesha's grimace, her mouth full of limp salad.

'Anyway, I can show you where the books are. It's not an ideal location, but at least they didn't chuck them in the incinerator,' Apple said.

'Who throws books in an incinerator?'

'Happens all the time,' Apple replied. 'How about I meet you outside when you're finished? It only takes a few minutes to walk there. Everywhere is only a few minutes away.'

Before Lillian could reply, Apple was up and away, her white head bobbing unhindered through the still empty cafe.

'Are you going to go with Apple to look at those books?'

'I guess so. I don't have anything else to do until I get the archaeologist's approval. And there's a chance I might find something useful from a historical context.'

'I'll give you one piece of advice. If you're seen with Apple, there won't be anyone else you could hang out with. Just giving you fair warning, most people think she is weird, and you're already suffering a little from that tag too, if I'm being honest.'

Jesha's phone shrilled, capturing her attention, signalling the end of her warning.

'I have to go. I'll see you later,' she said. 'Remember what I said about Apple.'

Lillian was still recovering from Jesha's astonishing comments and quick exit, when a familiar face appeared at the table. Badger.

'How was lunch?' he asked.

'Filling,' Lillian said.

'I saw you talking to Apple.'

'And are you going to tell me not to talk to her, either? Are we in high school?' she snapped.

Badger threw up his arms. 'I would never say that, I was just making an observation.'

'I was just leaving. I've got a meeting to get to,' she said.

'Hello *Nero*. Seen any more Roman soldiers lately?' sang a voice from behind Badger, and a pair of painted talons snaked around Badger's waist and Holly slithered into view, her smile as fake as the Cartier watch on her wrist.

'Got to go,' Lillian said.

As she walked away, she glanced back and saw Badger removing Holly's hands from around his waist, and the resulting look of malice on Holly's face.

Lillian shivered as she stood outside the cafe waiting for the ghostly Apple. The temperature had dropped at least ten degrees since the day before, and she hadn't come prepared for the low afternoon temperature. Wrapping her arms around herself, she pushed herself into the corner of the portico, out of the wind.

'There you are, almost didn't see you,' Apple said, before laughing at her own joke. 'Mostly people say that to me, "*Oh Apple, we didn't see you there. You blend into the walls so well.*"'

Lillian blushed. She'd been thinking something similar — that Apple was the same colour as the white pillars framing the cafe's historic entrance.

'Come on, I'll take you to Pram's place,' Apple whispered, her eyes darting around.

'Pram?'

'He's the guy looking after the books.'

They crossed a road featuring the original pavers from hundreds of years ago, re-purposed from the stones forming Hadrian's Wall. The chill in the wind lowering the temperature even further.

'It's only autumn, and I'm already freezing,' Lillian said through chattering teeth. 'I can't imagine how I'll cope with winter.'

Apple, wearing a bulky anorak, didn't answer. She had her head down and hood up, avoiding the gawping pedestrians on the street. How could adults behave like that? But Apple didn't seem to notice. Lillian assumed she was used to it, sadly.

'We're here,' Apple announced, pulling up outside a small church set back from the road.

'The library books are in the church?'

'No, in the hall behind St Marks. We have to go in around the back. There's no front entrance.'

Lillian followed Apple through the graveyard, picking her way through the haphazard arrangement of headstones smothered by creeping vines and wayward brambles.

'I guess they haven't buried anyone here in a while then,' she joked, trying to keep an irrational panic at bay.

Apple ignored her again, ploughing through the Victorian graveyard.

'Okay,' Lillian muttered. Maybe following this strange girl was a mistake? Maybe Jesha and Badger were right, that it didn't pay to hook up with the outcasts in a new town because it tarred you with the same brush, marking you as weird for the rest of your life.

'Here we are,' Apple said, knocking on a weathered wooden door.

As the door opened, the pungent aroma of knowledge drifted out. A scent tainted with dust and delicate paper, well known in libraries and book stores everywhere.

The person who greeted them was as far removed from what Lillian could ever have expected. As old as the books he protected, his wrinkled skin was parchment thin, with limbs barely able to support his anorexic body and tiny head.

. . .

'Ah, Miss Apple, you have come back, and with a friend. Come in, come in,' he sang, putting aside the small animal he'd been whittling before they arrived, delicate wood shavings decorating his woollen vest.

Apple motioned Lillian to follow her in and Lillian smiled at the old man, still marvelling at the apparition before her. Not only did he look out of place in the library, but he looked like he was in entirely the wrong century.

Lillian stepped into a wonderland, a forest of tottering books, obscuring every window and every inch of wall. The floor was reduced to a narrow galley-like space where no stroller or wheelchair could ever navigate. Despite the cavernous space being filled with a mishmash of wooden shelves and cast off aluminium carcasses, not a single inch of shelf space remained. Half of the spines wore protective plastic covering — lovingly dressed by a librarian in a prior life. Some were naked, their spines suffering from various stages of sun damage. One impressive tome perched fat with water damage, its buff pages and glue swelling from beneath the now inadequate binding.

'What is this place?' Lillian asked.

'Heaven,' Apple replied, moving effortlessly through the stacks on the floor.

'How'd they all end up here?'

'Most of them we moved ourselves when the council turned the library into a tourist information centre. They said we didn't need a library, as there was a bigger one in Newcastle. They'd planned to incinerate all the books, so we moved them here. Word got out amongst those who care about books, and now the locals leave boxes of book donations at the door for us, but sometimes the weather gets to them before we do. We have to keep it quiet, though. Not everyone approves of what we're doing...'

'The church offered to build a cupboard for us outside, to protect any donations, but they haven't got the funds since a storm damaged their roof last winter. So...' the old man said.

'Lillian, this is Pramod Sharma, head librarian of the *unofficial* Hexham Library.'

'Nice to meet you,' Lillian said.

'You're the girl from Ithaca Farm?'

'According to the lawyers, yes.'

The man appeared to appraise her, staring into her soul.

'It's a special place, your farm. Plenty of history, or so I've heard.'

'What's new this week?' Apple interrupted, and the pair disappeared off behind a partition, leaving Lillian to her own devices.

She wandered through the narrow aisles, her fingers brushing against the spines of the rescued books. She noticed an ad hoc form of order to the chaos. Although space was an issue, the librarian had done his best to shelve like with like, positioning Dan Brown up against Jeffrey Archer and Clive Cussler, leaving Harper Lee to rub shoulders with Cormac McCarthy on one side, and William Faulkner on the other.

'Is there a local history section?' Lillian called out.

'Keep going towards the back, and on the left before the big black cabinet, you'll see the shelves of local stuff. It's fiction and non-fiction, but from around here,' Apple shouted back.

Lillian picked her way past cardboard cartons spewing books from their collapsed sides, avoiding an avalanche of yellow post-it notes peeping out from the covers of hundreds of books waiting for their new forever homes. Notes with suggested categories for shelving crossed out and rewritten, sometimes more than once, and in half a dozen different hands.

The cabinet was monstrous, originally from the library of a stately home, where its shelves caressed expensive leather-clad folios. But now, with its doors removed and its edges scuffed by decades of wanton duty in a building far beneath it, it was now a repository for books of dubious morals — books by Nalini Singh and E. L. James seared the shelves together with erotic novels by Sylvia Day and Jackie Collins.

Turning left at the cabinet, Lillian found what she wanted — a treasure trove of discontinued local tomes and remaindered works of fiction from a bygone era, rescued from being pulped and sold at railway stations and school book fairs and car boot sales, living out their days at the makeshift Hexham Library.

· · ·

Dry academic books detailing the local ecology, books about Vindolanda fort and life two thousand years ago, and a series of walking guides detailing the best way to walk Hadrian's Wall. Lillian flicked through the Countryside walking guides, not because she had any interest in hiking through miles of cow dung and festering swamps, but more for any mention of Ithaca Farm.

A pink child-sized stool sat dusty in the corner, and despite the stool's stature, Lillian sat on it, deciding that sitting was better than standing given the headache lingering at the back of her head.

With a stack of reference books at her feet, she checked the indexes for any mention of the farm. After powering her way through several dozen books, she found three likely candidates, leaving the surrounding space looking as if a tornado had torn through the ancient floorboards. The mess was so bad, that when Apple reappeared Lillian blushed, and stammered out an apology.

Apple waved away her words. 'It looks like you're separating the fiction books from the nonfiction, although who knows what's true and what's not? It could all just be alternative facts,' she laughed. 'Don't stress. Pram is more than happy for us to file the books anyway we think makes sense. We can tidy it up later but we should get going cause it's getting dark and Pram needs to lock up.'

'How do I check these out?' Lillian asked, gesturing to her three books.

'You don't. You take them and bring them back when you're finished. Or bring back different books to replace them if you want to keep those. We don't operate as a normal library, more like those little free libraries you see on the side of the road, but on a bigger scale.'

Apple walked Lillian out of the de facto library, and they waved their goodbyes to Pram, leaving him sitting on a matching pink stool, paging through an old National Geographic magazine. In the failing light, he resembled a muted watercolour, sun-faded and slightly out of focus.

The girls promised to catch up later and Lillian started walking back to her car, the extra reference books heavy in her bag. To lighten the strain, Lillian took one out to read as she walked along the narrow lane.

Finding a parking space in the historic town was almost as hard as navigating the arcane council planning division, and she had to back track several times after forgetting where she'd left the ancient Land Rover.

Speeding cars forced her into patches of wild blackberry, their thorns plucking at her shivering legs, drawing thin lines of blood. The weather had turned, with the mild autumn giving way to a wintery chill, which caressed her legs and snaked its way down her collar to settle on her chest.

A filthy lorry thundered along the laneway, belching black smoke, only inches between its scarred sides and the rock walls lining both sides of the road. With the driver's head buried in his cellphone, he didn't see Lillian, obscured as she was by the lowering dusk. Screaming, she scrambled towards the wall, desperate to escape the menacing vehicle.

The driver looked up from his phone, shock flooding his doughy features. He had no where to go. There was no room for evasive manoeuvres, no vacant space for him to veer left or right. His brakes squealed, the heavy lorry lurching to a stop, burnt rubber staining the road — the brakes well past their use-by date.

Billowing in the wind behind the lorry were the torn pages from a book first published in 1937, Digging Up The Past by Sir Leonard Woolley. Of Lillian, there was no sign.

CHAPTER 11

WE'VE FOUND A SPY

Lillian stumbled, falling to her knees, before scrambling up again, her sense of direction warped by the strange vista around her.

Her farm boasted one old oak standing guard over the house, and that was it. Earlier generations of farmers before her had pruned, cut, dug up, pulled out, or poisoned everything unprofitable at Ithaca Farm, without realising that true wealth came from the symbiosis between the living creatures and the land which hosted them. And this field was not a manicured pasture suffering from decades of chemical fertiliser and overgrazing. She was not in Kansas anymore.

The shouts were louder, following her. A group of men lit by torch-light. Not battery powered torchlight, but flaming torches, like those from Bram Stoker's Dracula.

Eyes wild, Lillian spun straight into the arms of a stranger. No, not a stranger. The man with the gold.

'Come here,' he snarled.

There was no time for to run before the men with the torches reached them. These weren't lorry drivers, or refugees escaping from people smugglers, but men dressed as Roman soldiers, as centurions. Had the world gone mad?

'Let me go. The police are on their way,' she bluffed.

'Ho, Marcus, did you catch a spy?' called out a burly man, his broad shoulders encased in thick leather pads.

Her captor appraised her under the torchlight. 'I'm not sure who she is, Gaius. She could be a spy for the Iceni?' he responded to the giant. 'This could be the bitch that let them into the fort. The guards said that they'd seen a woman fleeing just as the Iceni attacked.'

'Take her to the Commander. He'll know,' Gaius said, his giant hand never straying from the short sword at his hip.

What language were they speaking? Latin. Latin of all languages, and for the first time in her life, she thanked her lucky stars that she'd worked so hard in her Latin classes. Old Mrs Shears would be so proud of her now.

'Where are we?' she rasped, her throat hoarse.

Marcus jabbed at her side. 'Don't you play dumb with me. Mention the gold, and I'll make sure they display your head on a pike for everyone to see. Where the ravens will pluck out your spying eyes and the maggots will feast on your pagan brain,' he whispered, pinching the soft skin on the underside of her arm.

She stumbled alongside her captor, bewildered by everything she saw, and heard, and felt. Had she strayed onto a film set, a remake of Braveheart, or Spartacus? A set where they'd employed an entire army of extras and ponies, after teaching them a dead language? The snuffles and snorts of uneasy horses filled the air, and old manure fermented underfoot. The men seemed unbothered, joking amongst themselves, making lewd comments about Lillian and their intentions after the Commander had seen her.

'You've gone too far,' Lillian said. 'So much for the sexual harassment stuff Hollywood is meant to be addressing.' Her voice quavered.

'Hollywood? Is that your tribe? I already said to stay quiet. The Commander will question you. You will pay for the blood on your hands,' he said, his voice only loud enough for her to hear. 'We're here,' he said louder, pulling her to a stop outside an impressive stone building.

Marcus left Lillian left outside the building, with Gaius for company.

. . .

She cringed as Gaius stared at her, his meaty hand rubbing at his worn sword handle. Lillian shivered, the icy wind exacerbating her shock.

'Bring that torch nearer,' Gaius instructed, waving over another guard. 'Stand there,' he ordered, pointing to a spot next to Lillian. 'She's cold.' He nodded at her.

Lillian gave a small smile. The heat from the torch lent a touch of camouflage to the arctic night.

'He'll see her now,' said Marcus, poking his head through the door. 'I'll take her from here, Gaius. Get back to your post,' Marcus added.

Gaius grunted. As the giant heaved his bulk away and lumbered back to his post, Lillian couldn't help feeling she was safer with Gaius than with the better looking Marcus.

Marcus grabbed her by the arm and pulled her into a world she couldn't have ever imagined.

The notion that she'd found a secret film set vanished as she walked into a sparsely decorated room lit with candles in sconces on the walls and containing little more than a cot and a desk. This was the apartment of the Primus Pilus, the leader of the cohort, which included Marcus, Darius, Gaius, and the others.

'Sir, this is the woman who was in the fort when the Iceni struck, the one who escaped,' Marcus announced to a man seated on a plain wooden stool behind a simple desk.

A man with a snowy head of hair and a brutalised nose lifted his head to gaze at Lillian, his shrewd eyes narrowing as he examined her.

'I told the others, I've rung the police, they'll be here soon,' she said, faltering under his unwavering gaze.

'You do not dress as a Brigante woman, and your speech suggests you are from a different tribe. How did your men breach our defences?'

'Look, I don't know who you are or what this bizarre Hollywood stuff is, but I want to go home. This isn't funny.'

'I am Titus Caelius Castus, Primus Pilus, the senior centurion leading the cohort of Batavians. You have the luxury of knowing who I am, yet you speak in circles when I ask you to explain yourself.'

Who are you, and how did you come to be inside the walls of Ithaca? Do you know how many of my men your tribe murdered?'

'Ithaca?'

'Ithaca Fort.'

'This is Ithaca Farm, my farm. I just moved in. Look, sorry that I disturbed your filming, but don't you have studios in London for this? I'm not about to alert TMZ or the women's mags,' Lillian replied.

'Why are you wasting my time with a foolish village girl?' Titus said, flicking his hands at her as if she were nothing more than a fly in his wine. 'She is of an addled brain, and she had nothing to do with the slaughter. My time is better spent writing to Rome to ask for reinforcements, instead of dealing with this stupidity. Send her home, and I mean home. I don't want some indignant villager claiming that Roman soldiers raped his daughter.'

'But she was there when the Iceni attacked. She escaped,' Marcus started saying.

'Concentrate on fixing our defences, and double the guard for the next seven moons. She is an imbecile.'

Lillian had no time to react before Marcus pulled her from the room and had no words to describe the fear gripping her. Every rational thought screamed that the situation was fake, a farce, a dream. But everything physical, the sounds, the smells, the touch of the man beside her, told a different tale. A story of reality. And as fantastical as it seemed, she knew in her heart of hearts that she wasn't on a modern day Northumberland farm, but that somehow she was in a Roman fort, on land which would one day be her farm, Ithaca Farm.

She wrenched free of Marcus's hand and turned back towards Titus. 'But I don't know where my home is,' she blurted, terrified of being turfed into the night with nothing but a cotton shirt and shoes more suited to carpeted floors with central heating.

Titus was already conferring with another man who'd entered through a side door, a roll of parchment in his hand. A peculiarly familiar man, someone she'd seen before — the man from the road, from before all this.

Lillian touched her cheek, a faint memory surfacing. 'It's you,' she said.

'Wait,' commanded Titus. 'You recognise this man?'

The man standing at the desk looked at her and shook his head imperceptibly.

'No, yes. No, I don't,' Lillian stuttered. 'I was mistaken.' Why had she said that? Why was she protecting someone she'd never met? She'd persuaded herself she'd imagined him, his face leaning over her after her accident. Had it been him appealing for her help when she'd seen him in the middle of the road?

'Julius, do you know this girl?' Titus asked the other man.

'No,' he said, his eyes burning into hers.

'But you—' Lillian said, confused about what was real and what she'd imagined.

'Silence! Speak boy, come now,' Titus said, his voice rising.

'I don't know her,' the man said, looking the senior centurion in the eye.

'Good, then you won't care if her head adorns a spike,' Titus said, the whites of his eyes wider than the yawning pits of hell. He turned his attention back to Lillian. 'Was I wrong to think that you were just a lowly village girl?'

Lillian's grasp of Roman nomenclature extended as far as Shakespeare's plays, which would have mortified her English teachers, especially when the only phrase she could think of was "*Et tu, Brute?*", but it was the best response to the unbelievable position she found herself in. She looked at the young soldier before realising that she was on her own. And she fancied that everyone could hear her heart break, just the tiniest bit.

CHAPTER 12
SOLD TO THE HIGHEST BIDDER

Marcus marched Lillian from the Primus Pilus's rooms into the night air, his mouth a thin line, his hand a vice around her arm.

'I said nothing about what I saw,' she said, scrambling to stay upright as he pulled her along the paved road.

'There was nothing to see. We were doing our jobs,' Marcus replied, increasing the grip on her arm.

'Where are you taking me?'

'To the vicus, where you belong.'

'The vicus?' Lillian repeated, the word strange on her tongue.

Marcus stopped, grabbing Lillian's chin.

'I cannot tell if you are playing the fool, or if you are one. But I am not the sort of man to cross,' he said, his dark eyes boring into hers. 'You aren't from the village, I would know. Tell me where are you from? Castus is a fool to let you go. He should have slit you from ear-to-ear.'

'I told the truth, I'm from Ithaca Farm, from here.'

Marcus seemed to consider her words before snorting.

'Ithaca Farm, we'll see. I have somewhere in the village for you to stay, where I can monitor you,' he said. He muttered further under his breath as his long legs carried them both across the straight flagged paths of the Roman fort and into the sleeping village.

Dogs congregated on the street ahead of them, scuttling away from Marcus's boot. The mournful cries of a baby filtered through an uncovered window. The hushing coos of the babe's mother smothered the cry as Lillian considered calling for help, but what good would that do? She was as much an oddity here as she was in Hexham. At least at home, there were rules to follow, including the one forbidding the council from displaying the decapitated heads of their ratepayers.

Stopping in front of a long skinny building, it was impossible for Lillian to discern much other than it looked like a shop front, closed up tight for the night. Marcus slid back the wooden door and pushed Lillian into the inky interior before sliding the door shut behind them.

'Where are we?'

'Belongs to a friend of mine,' Marcus said, channelling her further inside. 'Yo, Metella?' he called.

A strip of light appeared before it filled the room when a far door opened.

'We're closed, Marcus,' came a woman's voice.

The lantern illuminated a woman of indeterminate middle age, the robe covering her body obscuring any sense of her shape.

'I'm not here to buy, I'm here to sell,' Marcus said, lowering his voice.

The woman's demeanour changed from the angry visage of someone woken from her slumber to that of an entrepreneur assessing the potential profit.

'Selling, eh? And who's saying I'm buying what you're selling?'

'Come, Metella, I see you calculating the worth of this one. Have a closer look. I'd wager she's still a virgin.'

Whilst the conversation had alarmed Lillian, Marcus's last words terrified her. As her brain processed his words, it was as if lava flowed beneath her feet, forcing her to flee.

Lillian spun on her toes, and in one fluid movement, flung aside the sliding door and fled into the village. She heard Marcus swear as he gave chase and curse even more when he tripped over the threshold. The woman followed behind, the dancing light of her lantern destroying Marcus's night vision. Lillian heard the echo of his roar as he smashed the lantern from the brothel keeper's arms.

And Lillian ran. Away from Marcus, the brothel, and the soldiers. Away from this living nightmare. She ran until no breath remained in her lungs and the strength in her legs failed and she stumbled down a river bank, ripping her hands on gorse and brambles. Lillian splashed across an ankle-deep stream, her inadequate shoes slipping on the mossy stones. She didn't think her legs could take her any further, but still she tried, her run morphing into the stumbling gait of a drunk, carousing their way home from a night on the town. Until she stopped, spent, terrified, alone in the dark. And a long, long way from home.

The dawn brought no relief, and Lillian remained hunched under an outcrop of stone on the edge of the river, her feet wet, her teeth chattering. A week ago, there would have been a sliver of warmth in the autumn sun. Today there was none, just an arctic breeze direct from the North.

The bird chorus awoke with the sun, a chorus of so many voices, a sound impossible to imagine in today's barren environment, their habitats destroyed by the incessant encroachment of humankind. Tracks of dirty tears streaked her face, with her hair resembling the tangled roots of the trees on the riverbank opposite her hiding hole.

With cramping limbs and a rumbling stomach, Lillian eased her way into the open, cautiously poking her head from under the rock. Perhaps Marcus had given up looking for her? She was nothing to him. She had no one to tell about the gold she'd seen him stealing with his friend. Had she really seen him steal it? She'd hit her head. It could have been something she'd imagined. None of this was real. Was it?

Regardless of her reality, at this precise moment, there was no police force to call or newspaper to alert. She was on her own. And the only other person she knew, or thought she knew, had disowned her.

Her legs aching, she climbed the bank, her body a mess of cuts and scrapes, and wrapped her arms around her body. Where to now? She needed to find something to eat. She'd slurped water from the stream below, satisfied that in this day and age it remained unpolluted by industrial run off or agricultural fertilisers.

Food was a different story, especially when the wind carried upon it the unmistakable scent of wood-smoke, and meat of some description — the scent enticing her, toying with her hunger. What did she have to lose? A hundred different things — her life, her freedom, and her future.

Lillian took an unsteady pace forward, towards the streak of smoke beyond the trees, before changing her mind and turning in the opposite direction, away from the food. The last thing she needed was to throw herself into the lion's den by stumbling into a group of soldiers searching for her.

With one foot in front of the other, Lillian forced herself to walk away from the mouthwatering scent and along the edge of a hard-packed road surrounded by thickets of bush bustling with bird life and the scurrying of small mammals... animals she was more used to seeing on television and on the lists of the world's top endangered species. Animals such as the red squirrel and humble hedgehog. At least that's what she hoped was making the rustling noises in the undergrowth — hedgehogs hurrying home from a busy night out. Back in New Zealand, hedgehogs were more commonly found smeared across the road, so it amazed her they were on the endangered species list in England.

While Lillian pondered the fate of Beatrix Potter's Mrs Tiggy-Winkle and her spiky offspring, she shoved her hands deep into the pockets of her jeans, where her hand curled around a coin nestled in the seam. The coin she'd picked up in the field behind the metal detectorist — a Roman coin, a gold coin. One lost in the hurried theft from the soldiers' pay chest by Marcus and his accomplice.

Lillian's worries vanished as the coin transported her back to Ithaca, to the farm, not the fort. To the modern day, to broadband and Brexit. Where the landscape was artificial and the media ruled the masses. To a time where the law said she had to pay council tax, and drive on the left whilst wearing a seatbelt, and where the food at the supermarket came wrapped in plastic for freshness and for hygiene. But now that she was back, she wasn't sure she wanted to be here.

CHAPTER 13
STRANGERS AREN'T ALWAYS ENEMIES

'Where are they?' Marcus asked, tempering the anger in his voice.

'Where we discussed?' Darius answered, oblivious to the other man's tone.

'Under the altar?'

'Buried deep, and I moved the other offerings to cover the fresh dug earth.'

Marcus sniffed. At least one part of the plan had gone right, but the rest was a disaster. The missing girl was the least of his worries. The Iceni raid was meant to have been a quick in and out, with minimal loss of life, creating enough confusion for Darius to sneak out of the fort, hide the bag of coins, and return.

'Good, I have some taskings which demand my attention. I'll see you tonight.'

Marcus watched Darius wander off, his gait as loose as his morals. Sadly, Darius wasn't for this world much longer. He would soon join his ancestors, not that he knew that. And with any luck, the girl would join him.

With thoughts of his golden future filling his head, Marcus made his way to the headquarters, the *principia*, with a stack of tablets under one arm and a smile on his face.

The smile transformed his hard visage into one worthy of the gods. For Marcus was a beautiful man, by any standard, and knew how to work that in his favour.

Nodding at the guards, he made his way into the study of Castus, a man who radiated despair. As useless as tits on a bull, just the way Marcus liked his commanders. The more pliable and incompetent, the better. And Castus had been the most useless one yet.

'They'll strip my command,' Castus said, raising his head. His unshaven face a picture of abject misery.

'It was a raiding party, nothing more, nothing less. They got lucky. It won't happen again. There won't be any repercussions for you, Rome understands.'

'I have to prove to Rome that my appointment wasn't in vain. That I'm a loyal son of Rome. And as such, I've ordered punishments for all the guards on duty that night.'

Marcus had to stop himself from smiling. 'Punishments?'

'I could have crucified them, but I am a lenient man.'

Marcus froze. 'If not crucifixion, then what?'

'They're all about to lose a hand, their choice which one.'

'But...'

'I will not have drunkards in this legion. The attack has made us the laughingstock of the empire. But it was a festival, and they were showing the due respect to the Goddess. I hardly think that she'd look fondly upon a phalanx of crucified worshipers.'

Marcus scrambled for an answer. He'd handpicked the worst performers in the legion to be on duty, expecting Castus would apply the standard punishment for dereliction of duty, which was crucifixion. That way, there would be fewer opportunities for any link to be drawn between the attack and Marcus's potential involvement. But men losing their hands, that meant that they kept the power of speech. And thought.

'Crucifixion would send a better message?'

'Are you questioning me, Centurion?'

Marcus shook his head. Of all the times for Castus to find his balls.

'Are those the daily muster reports?'

. . .

Marcus handed the stack of wax tablets to his commander and took his leave, his steps a thousand times heavier than they had been upon his arrival at HQ.

The horse whinnied in complaint as Marcus tugged on the straps of the saddle.

'Shut up, you stupid beast.'

Leaving now was a risk, but one he had to take. Fortunately, he'd already established a well-recognised routine of nighttime visitations to Metella's house of pleasure, that the guards at the gate wouldn't blink an eye. They'd never know that he had no intention of going there tonight. Instead, he spurred on his horse, dashing across the darkened valley towards a figure waiting for him in the cleft between the hills.

'What are you playing at?' Marcus hissed, swinging himself down from the saddle, his hand already on the hilt of his short sword. 'It was meant to be a quick attack, not a slaughter.'

'My men were hungry for blood. You promised us blood.'

'In time. My promise still stands, but I only meant you to provide a distraction. That's what we agreed.'

'My men wanted blood,' Gar repeated.

'Damn what your men wanted. You'll get your blood, and the coin that we agreed upon. But you have to follow the plan.' Regret tainted every word out of Marcus's fine-lipped mouth. Rome would remove his head from his shoulders if they discovered his deal with the barbarians. But the payoff was worth it. A new life, away from these accursed isles, and out of the army. Somewhere warm, under a new name, with a houseful of willing women. That's the life he deserved. And he would do whatever it took. If that meant dealing with the painted Icenian devil, then so be it.

'When does my steel get its next taste of Roman blood?' Gar asked, the whites of his eyes glowing in the moonlight.

'When they deliver the next pay. On the next full moon.'

'Too long.'

'No, not too long. It is the way it is. You and your men wait until my signal. The gates will be open and you attack the convoy delivering the pay chest, killing as many men as you like. I meet you here and we both go our own ways.'

'They'll find you,' Gar said.

'They'll think me dead,' Marcus replied, already planning to sacrifice the hapless Darius in his escape, dressing the fool's headless body in his own tunic and decorated sword belt, Marcus's pride and joy. They were similar enough in body shape that no one would question whose body it was, not with his waist cinched by Marcus's ostentatious sword belt.

'Humph,' Gar said, spitting into the hedgerow. 'You play with fire, Roman.'

Marcus agreed with him, but refused to say so.

'On the next full moon, then?'

'It will be a blood moon,' Gar laughed.

Marcus paled. 'And as we agreed, you'll spare the vicus, yes?'

'There are women in your village, Roman whores. Blood and women, that's what my warriors want.'

'Not the village, we agreed.'

For all that Marcus wanted rid of the Roman yoke around his neck, the villagers didn't deserve what Gar and his tribe would inflict.

'Blood for Gar's help. That was our agreement, Roman.'

Marcus nodded. To push for the safety of the vicus would risk everything. He could warn Metella and her girls. He might not be a good Roman, but he wasn't a monster.

CHAPTER 14

TREASURE IN THE SHED

The chill in the air was as sharp as it had been moments earlier, and the feel of the ground as solid. But there, the similarities ended. Diesel fumes filled the air as a truck thundered along the road. The horizon boasted uninterrupted views of power lines and church steeples, with a far away chimney belching white smoke into the air. Bird calls were intermittent instead of the constant cacophony serenading her just before. Somewhere a phone rang — her ring tone — the old-fashioned ring tone which still amused her.

There was no mistaking that she was back in the present day. Standing on the opposite side of the wall, hidden from view, Lillian could hear but not see the cars passing by — the drivers oblivious to her presence. What would they say when they heard her story?

The phone rang again, prompting Lillian to search the overgrown field edge for her handbag, as she tried to recall where she flung it in her haste to escape the lorry who'd almost run her off the road.

Lillian spied her bag and clambered through the bracken to retrieve it, the morning dew crunching under her shoes, soaking her already damp socks. The bag vibrated in her hands as she struggled with the zip, her hands shaking.

Two missed calls, both from unknown numbers.

Lillian checked the time. By the time she got home, showered, changed into something dry, and filled her empty stomach, the day would be over.

At some point during her adventure, her keyring with her car key had become separated from her bag, so with her bag over her shoulder, she climbed back over the wall, and limped home, praying against all hope that it was too early for anyone she knew to drive past. On this one occasion, her prayers weren't in vain, and she stumbled up the unpaved driveway unmolested by any curious commuters.

Lillian turned the doorknob, pushing against the ancient door simultaneously. To no avail. Her house key was with her car key, somewhere in a field in Roman England, or modern-day England.

'Damn it!' Lillian yelled, kicking the peculiar square of perspex screwed to the bottom of the door.

The door rattled in its frame, but didn't open.

Lillian stomped round the back. From here she could see a tent erected over the site of the altar, but this early in the morning, no one was there. No one was there to see her try the back door. Locked. She jiggled the windows in their frames. Locked tight. The only solution was to break into her own home, and she cast around for a suitable stone to break the glass of the door to reach the flimsy lock on the inside.

With her arm snaking through the jagged hole, Lillian unlocked the door and stepped over the shattered glass and into a house which echoed with emptiness.

Dumping her muddied bag on the table, she swiped a shrivelled apple from the fruit bowl and made her way upstairs, keeping to the far side of the staircase. An unnatural chill accompanied the emptiness of the house as wind whipped down the chimneys, ruffling the decaying curtains, making them seem as if the village busybody was twitching them aside to spy on her.

Lillian tugged the ancient curtains shut, wrinkling her nose at the blood-like maroon colour. Replacing them wasn't anywhere on her financial radar.

Usually the dismal water pressure of the old-fashioned shower sucked the joy from her mornings, but not today.

Drenching herself under the hot water flowing from a not-so-ancient shower head was a delight. Dirt swirled down the drain, vanishing in a miasma of soap and blood.

Lillian closed her eyes, the steaming water massaging her head. Her wound stung under the pressure, but the pain was less of a problem than the confused thoughts rushing around inside her brain. Her narrow escape from the surreal chaos of the night before pulsed against her eyes as flashes of fire and swords, armour and anger, running men and flaming torches, forced her heart to race and her breath to quicken. None of it could be real, but the bruises on her body told a different story.

Turning the water off, Lillian stepped over the edge of the clawfoot bath, kicking her clothes out of the way. A metallic clunk pinged on the tiles as the gold coin rolled from her jeans pocket.

Lillian froze with her towel clasped to her body. Her wet hair dripping down her back was not the cause of her sudden chill. The coin caused every terrifying moment she'd experienced. Inextricably tied to the Roman altar, and the skulls, covered by the tent outside her window. She knew what she'd experienced was real. That it wasn't a figment of her imagination or the results of the knock to her head.

Tearing her eyes from the coin, she checked her reflection in the foggy mirror and touched her cheek, remembering when Julius had stroked her face after the accident. She fancied she could feel the remnants of his touch on her skin. But then he'd refused to recognise her. His actions almost sending her into a lifetime of untold horrors. Impossible to forgive.

Somewhere a dog barked, quickly turning into an angry howl. Lillian dried herself. This time, despite her fear, she'd find the dog and lock it up until someone from the council came to pick it up.

And in her haste, she left the coin lying on the bathroom floor. Forgotten and abandoned in a corner, like everything at Ithaca Farm. Like her.

The barking in the front yard intensified as Lillian dressed. She couldn't see the yard from her window. Her room was on the other side of the house, with a view of the action around the archaeologist's tent.

. . .

A Land Rover was parked next to the tent, with a farmer's hardy quad bike parked next to it.

Anger filled her. These people had entered their property without asking and had driven vehicles over her land. Like every other day, she wished her father was here. He wouldn't have allowed these parasites access. But then if he was there, she'd still be living in New Zealand, and she'd still have all her friends, and her books, and her mother...

No, she didn't have time for her grief, and anger. She needed to get the stray dog sorted. The trespassers she'd deal with later.

Using the spare key on the hook in the hall, she unlocked the front door and stepped outside. The farm gate stood wide open, left that way by the archaeologists. Apart from that, everything looked unchanged from the day before, save that her car wasn't there. Left somewhere in town until the spare key turned up. The barking grew louder.

A flash of memory swept through her as she remembered the sound of hounds barking amongst the mayhem of the battle. The memories weren't clear, just fragments and moments too ethereal to grasp. But there had been dogs. And death. So much death.

She whistled, hoping that would be enough to encourage the animal to appear. Nothing. She followed the dog's barks. It sounded close. Maybe it'd crawled into one of the multitude of dilapidated farm buildings which surrounded the house and couldn't get out. That would make things easier.

Lillian whistled again. She moved further away from the action under the tent, the voices of the interlopers fading away. She couldn't deny that at least the archaeologists sounded happy, ecstatic even, with the discovery of an altar and previously unknown Roman remains on the farm. If only they knew how violent the deaths had been as the soldiers placed their offerings at the very altar the archeologists were salivating over.

What had she seen? She'd seen death, lots of death. There were screams and yells, and running, and torches and trumpets blared, and more soldiers. And her soldier. The one from her dreams. Or where they dreams?

The barking stopped as Lillian drew parallel to an old shed.

The door swung on its hinges, creaking in the wind. She pushed it open and whistled again. A slight rustling inside greeted her.

'Hey there, come on out,' Lillian called out.

Nothing happened.

'Come on.'

Still nothing. No rustles, no squeaks, no sound. She walked into the shed, propping the old door open with a brick on the ground.

'Where are you?' she called, swallowing her fear and hoping against hope that the dog was small.

The remnants of mildew, wheat, horse-feed and engine oil competed with the dust and decades of neglect. Pieces of old farm machinery stood idle, leant against the walls. Walls older than the house, built with stones stolen from Hadrians Wall, and held together with the same lime mortar used two millennia ago. But none of that interested Lillian. Her brain didn't work that way. Despite everything she'd been through, or thought she'd been through, her attachment to history only went as far back as her father, and that grief alone was enough for her.

'Where are you?' she called again, using her toe to nudge away a toppled over sack.

A flurry of feathers and a flash of sharp talons greeted her as a wayward hen took fright, scuttling out of the shed into the daylight. Lillian watched the hen shoot her a disgusted look before it settled down outside to preen itself in the daylight.

There was no dog in the shed. The stupid thing had run off again, instinctively knowing she was on a mission to capture it.

Lillian stooped to tidy the sacking the hen had disturbed, and her hand froze. She pulled the sacking away, discarding it on the floor, where a second sack joined it, then a third, as Lillian exposed the pile of stones concealed by the hessian. They weren't just stones. They were gravestones. Roman gravestones. Haphazardly stored arse-about-face next to each other, on top of each other, parallel to each other. There must have been a dozen of them jumbled underneath their sacking cloaks. Some weren't even whole, cleaved in two, clean through the middle.

How did no one know that they were here?

They weren't hidden well, barely covered by old sacks reeking of eons of old grain with a hint of molasses. Or maybe everyone knew, but didn't care? What was one gravestone when every museum within a hundred-mile radius had a dozen or more of their own? But then why was so much fuss being made of the altar hidden under her farm wall?

Somewhere outside, the dog barked again, so close it could almost have been right outside the shed.

Lillian scrambled to replace the hessian sacks, an indefinable caution filling her lungs. Covered in dust, she rushed out of the shed, smack bang into a stranger. The pair toppling over into the muddy yard.

The barking stopped.

CHAPTER 15

THE FOURTH ESTATE

'Lillian Arlosh?'

Lillian wiped the mud from her hands onto her jeans, smearing the dust from the shed until she looked as though she'd just emerged from working in the mines.

'What are you doing in my yard?' she replied, staring at the stranger.

'Jasper Fletcher, from the Hexham Herald. Is now a good time to talk about the ruins in your field?'

Lillian blanched, glancing behind her. She kicked the brick from the doorway and tugged the door shut and dropping the latch into place.

'Have to keep the chickens out,' she explained, already distrusting the appraising look on the reporter's face.

'You've got chickens?' the reporter asked, bounding about and peering around the yard, the wind messing his mop of red hair.

'Someone does,' Lillian replied, moving away from the shed. What a stupid question to ask, when a true flesh and blood chicken was pecking at the bag the reporter had left on the ground.

'Eggs, chickens, I've never been able to work out which one came first, have you?'

She stared at him, categorising the man as an idiot.

He shooed away the hen to rescue his bag. 'Shall we go inside?'

'Excuse me?'

'Inside, to have a quick chat about the skulls in your field?' Jasper asked.

Lillian panicked. The last thing she wanted was to be interviewed by anyone, least of all this man who'd been wandering around her yard. Her skin prickled. It was almost as if the dog had warned her the reporter was snooping.

'I don't have time for an interview,' she said. 'I'm heading into town to pick up my car before a meeting,' she made up, massaging her head, which had started thumping again.

'Oh, it's a good thing I'm headed that way, then. I can give you a lift, and we can chat in the car, and get to know each other and I can point out some sights, being that you're new to town.'

Lillian had no appropriate answer. He sounded sincere, and she couldn't backtrack, not now that her own lie had tripped her up. Despite planning on spending a quiet day at home recuperating, now it looked like she'd be spending an uncomfortable half hour in the company of a reporter giving her a lesson on Roman history and where to buy the best coffee. Excellent.

'I need to get changed,' she tried.

'Happy to wait. I'll be in the car,' he replied, smiling.

Lillian cast one last glance towards the shed door, checking it was still latched before trudging inside to get changed for the second time in one day. The trip to town might be preferable to spending the day here, jumping at every noise. Waiting to be flung back into the past.

The drive to town was a jumble of disjointed comments about the environment, the history of the area, the reporter's tenure at the paper, all of them flowing over Lillian's head like a river in flood. Too many words, and too much information. She couldn't take it all in. And she had the distinct impression that every question served to elicit a soundbite from her, to be twisted into something worthy of publication. Raised in the world of online disinformation, Lillian was well versed in the proliferation of fake news.

. . .

She wasn't someone who revelled in talking to the media and she knew not all reporters were trustworthy. And she suspected that Jasper Fletcher couldn't be trusted. In it for the glory, and bugger the poor soul he trampled to achieve his wish. And so she gave him nothing, instead staring out the window and nodding, occasionally adding in an appreciative hmm when necessary.

'And this is where it's reported a massacre of almost an entire Roman cohort took place. Details are of course sketchy, they didn't record it in stone you know, or write books about it. But they found a fragment of a report on the tablets at Vindolanda. You've been there, of course?'

'Pardon?' Lillian whipped her head around to face the reporter.

'Vindolanda, the old fort. Magnificent ruins and a world-class museum.'

Lillian shook her head. Visiting local tourist sites wasn't high on her to-do list.

'That is a shame. I bet they'd love to get their hands on your altar, being so close and all. Have they been to see it yet?' he asked, innocence dripping from his tongue.

She shrugged, 'No idea.'

Jasper returned his eyes to the road. If her monosyllabic answers discouraged him, he hid it well.

'Do you ever think about how all those skulls ended up being buried under your land?'

This time Lillian stared at him, her mouth open, incredulous at the blasé words he was using to describe the dead.

'No, never. Look, just drop me off here. I'm fine walking, honestly,' she said, unease snaking up her spine.

'No, no, I'm happy to drop you off at your car.'

She was stuck with a man discussing the decomposition of dead bodies as if he was discussing the roadworks on the A69. As soon as he parked beside her ancient Land Rover, she wrenched the door open, slamming it shut without looking back, praying that the key she found in a drawer in the kitchen would work.

Lillian watched him drive off and slumped in her seat, wondering how he'd report their interaction. It wouldn't be good.

But what bothered her the most was that her newly sourced reference books lay on a side road, ruined. There'd been more local history books at the hidden library, and given what had happened, today was as good a day as any to visit. She doubted that any of the books would cover the logistics of time travel, but there might be a book on Romano British history which could shed some light on the wholesale slaughter of men worshipping. And the theft of the gold from the pay chest.

Lillian closed her eyes, trying to remember what she'd seen. The men had stuffed the gold into a bag, with one of them running off into the night. She did not know if the attackers had caught him, but she assumed he hadn't been. He'd gone in the other direction, into the darkest part of the night, away from the camp fires, and the torches and the other worshippers. So there was a chance he'd escaped. She knew the other man had survived, the man called Marcus. That meant two of them knew what she looked like, and that worried her.

A rapping on the car window startled her.

'Hey,' Apple called out.

Lillian wound down the window. 'Hi.'

'Wanna grab a coffee? I'm parched and we're out of milk at home.'

Lillian sipped a small latte. Counting her pennies seemed the prudent thing to do given her current circumstances. At least there wasn't an over-hyped Starbucks in town to drain her coffers.

'Look at that,' Apple whispered. 'That there is something more commonly served to prisoners of war in Westeros.' Apple gestured towards a plate heaving with mushy peas and baked beans, suffocating under a cheesy spread being delivered to a nearby table.

'Westeros?'

'Game of Thrones.'

Lillian laughed, her mood lightening against the babbling of the girl at her side. Nothing beat having a friend, albeit a ghost-like girl, whom everyone else avoided.

. . .

Lillian hadn't contacted Jesha since the other woman had made the disparaging comments about Apple. No one needed friends like that.

Over their (decent) coffees, they discussed the weather, the goings-on in town, the developments at Ithaca Farm and Apple's lofty goals for reinstating the town library. Lillian did not raise the spectre of Roman soldiers and gold coins. Their friendship hadn't quite reached that level...

'Have you talked to the papers about the library, to get them onside? Invite them to visit, to see what you and Mr. Sharma have achieved?'

Apple mimed choking on her drink.

'You've got to be joking? They were the ones who nailed the coffin shut when we were trying to save the library. They're worse than the mayor, and that's saying something.'

Lillian stirred the froth of her coffee and considered how to respond.

'I found a local reporter snooping around at the farm this morning.'

'Sounds about right. Which one?'

'Jasper Fletcher, from the Hexham Herald.'

Apple grimaced.

'He asked a hundred questions about my plans for Ithaca Farm and everything else.'

'Everyone's talking about your plans.'

'Why? I don't understand it. It's just one farm. It's not as if I'm planning to convert all of Northumberland to palm tree plantations or solar farms.'

'People here don't like change. When they've only ever grazed live-stock within the confines of their pretty stone walls, they can't understand why anyone would want to do anything different.'

'Because doing the same thing on the same bit of land and expecting the same outcome doesn't work. Not anymore. We're killing the planet.' Lillian blurted. Conscious of the swivelling heads at the tables near them, she lowered her voice before continuing. 'I wish they'd never found that bloody altar because then no one would care about what I was doing.'

'Oh, they would care, trust me.

When a group of us questioned what was going to happen to the old library building, which was an old Carnegie Library building, they shut us down faster than you can swat a fly. There was some deal with a hotel group who wanted to turn it into luxury accommodation for wall walkers to stay in. And I don't mean wall walkers from Game of Thrones, I mean the thousands of tourists who keep the money pumping through this town year in and year out. Anything to part the tourists from their money is fine, or anything to do with farming, but watch out if you want to do anything else in this town.'

'How do you know so much about it all?' Lillian replied, a frown marring her forehead.

Apple shrugged. 'I read. And I pay attention to the surrounding conversations. No one worries about a freak like me, so they don't bother whispering. It used to bother me that everyone thought I was dumber than a plank of wood because of my lack of melanin. Now it just amuses me.'

They left with a promise to meet at the church later that day after Lillian said she needed a reference book for the farm, while avoiding any mention of researching Roman history to identify the people she'd met or the battle she'd seen. She didn't want Apple to think she was losing her mind.

The rest of the day passed in a blur of bank appointments, registering at the local doctor's surgery, which all took more hours than was necessary in a functioning democracy. Upon her exit from the tiny Red Cross charity shop, where she'd spent a quiet few minutes pondering the shelves of paperbacks before settling on a pair of books by the Pakistani author Awais Khan, she spied the tall visage of Badger.

Badger waved and jogged across the road. He pulled a tattered book from his satchel and slid into her hands.

'What's this?' Lillian asked.

'I found it on the road to your place. There were a couple of other books, but they were too far gone. This was the only one worth saving,' he replied.

'How did you know they were mine?' Lillian's hands stroked the dusty copy of the English Tourist Board's Roman England book.

Printed circa 1983, it had been one of the books she'd taken home from the makeshift library Apple and Mr. Sharma ran.

'I was swinging by to see if you were okay, but then I saw you leaving in Jasper's car, and that's when I saw the books on the road. I couldn't think of anyone else who'd be interested in reading this sort of stuff, apart from you and Seb's grandad, so I stopped and picked them up.'

'You were at Ithaca Farm?'

Badger blushed. 'My father is the supervising archaeologist working at your place, so I also wanted to have a proper look at the skulls and stuff... We could go together and I'll introduce you? I know dad is looking forward to meeting you.'

Ah, the truth comes out. He hadn't been coming to see her. She should have expected that to be the case. Lillian pondered her reply. She had her appointment with Apple. Would Apple mind if Badger came with her before they drove out to the farm?

If only she'd known who Badger's family was, things might have panned out differently.

CHAPTER 16

A LITTLE LIGHT READING

If Badger considered the prospect of visiting a secret library in the heart of town peculiar, he didn't say. He kept up a witty banter as they hurried through the wind towards the church. He stopped once to buy them each a hot chocolate from a small cafe housed in the town's old flour mill. Although the place was clearly closing up, the proprietor's face spilt into an enormous smile when Badger walked in across the freshly mopped floors.

'She looked happy to see you,' Lillian observed, as the woman turned away to serve another couple.

Badger grinned. 'Everyone loves me,' he quipped. 'That's what happens when you've grown up with the same couple of thousand people your whole life, and when you've worked almost every part-time job in town. I helped when they were doing their renovations, just manual labour. They wanted to reuse all the old bricks. Man, that was a shit job,' he laughed. 'But I've never worked in the library,' he added.

'This isn't the sort of library where people work,' Lillian replied.

'I've given up work for now. I am meant to be concentrating on my studies, to become a big-shot archaeologist or politician like my parents, so I'm told.'

. . .

Walking the overgrown path between the gravestones behind the church whilst dodging the wild vines grabbing at their ankles, neither noticed Holly Corben sitting in her car, staring at their retreating backs.

Pramod Sharma didn't seem at all fazed by Badger appearing alongside of Lillian, letting them both in through a well-weathered door.

'Welcome back,' Pramod said. 'No Apple today?'

'She's on her way,' Lillian replied. 'Mr. Sharma, this is—'

'Badger. Yes, we know each other. It's a small—'

'A small town, yes, I am beginning to realise that,' Lillian replied, curious that Badger hadn't mentioned it.

Pramod vanished behind his screen, and Lillian could hear the gentle rasping of sandpaper against wood. A man of many talents, working away in his dusty corner of the makeshift library.

If Badger seemed perturbed by Pramod's revelation, he didn't say. Instead, he replicated Lillian's own wondrous initial walk through the towers of books.

'All these books,' Badger said, running his hands over piles of unshelved books.

'So you haven't been here before?'

'Didn't know it existed.'

'It could be something wonderful,' Lillian offered, watching Badger's face for his reaction.

'I guess,' he said. 'A lot of these are rubbish, though, outdated. Only good for the bonfire.'

'And that's why we never asked you to help move the books in the first place,' Apple interrupted, sliding through the door, straining beneath a carton of books.

Lillian watched Badger smother a flash of anger before he sprang forward to relieve Apple of her load.

'Always happy to help.' He smiled.

'You shouldn't have brought him here,' Apple said to Lillian, her pale hands on her hips. 'He'll ruin everything.'

'Hey, that's not fair,' Badger replied. 'I can't ruin anything if I don't know what it is,' he said, attempting a level of humour.

'He's going to run home and tell Mummy the Mayor. And together with her cronies, they'll shut us down citing fire safety, or unpermitted activity or something,' Apple hissed.

'I will not tell anyone, least of all my mother. You don't know me,' Badger retaliated.

Apple stormed off, knocking over a tower of books in her haste.

Guilt washed over Lillian. She should have asked Apple before inviting Badger to come with her, and now her only friendship dangled by a fine thread.

'I'm sorry,' Lillian said to Badger.

'Doesn't matter. I'm used to being tarred by the same brush as my mother. It's a hazard of her job. Don't worry about me.'

Lillian turned her attention to stacking the books into a more stable pile as she considered how to mitigate the fallout with Apple. A large folio caught her attention, its brown leather cover embossed with gold letters proclaiming it as a treatise on Roman history, printed in London by Thomas Vautrollier in 1586. She marvelled at the history in her hands, wondering at how such a valuable treasure came to be abandoned in a church hall in a small Northumberland town.

She checked to see if anyone was looking. Badger stood engrossed in a colourful souvenir book about the Tottenham Hotspur Football Club. Apple and Mr. Sharma were nowhere in sight, so Lillian slipped the treatise between two vertical stacks of old library books, with every intention of asking Apple if she could take it home to read when Badger wasn't with her.

'How long are you going to be here?' Badger asked, startling Lillian with his sudden appearance by her side. 'We'll be losing the light if we don't head off soon.'

'You don't have to wait for me. You can go whenever you like,' Lillian replied, before biting her tongue. She hadn't meant to be so short, but she felt guilty about hiding the book, and for bringing him here. 'I'm sure your mother and I will be well acquainted in no time.'

Badger shifted his weight, staring at her, making her feel even more uncomfortable.

'Right,' he said, drawing out the syllables. 'I've got a couple of other things to do, so I'll catch you another time?'

Lillian's heart sank. She'd ruined things again. 'Sure,' she said, and stood up to say goodbye, but Badger was already halfway to the door, his long strides swallowing the narrow passageway through the books.

'Inviting him was a bad idea,' Apple announced.

Apple stood behind Lillian, an armful of books clasped to her chest.

'He wanted to come and see the altar—'

'He wanted to get some inside gossip for his father, or mother. They're the same people,' Apple interrupted. 'Look, you haven't lived here long enough to know the ins and outs of who rubs who on the back, and who owns what. But when it comes to the library, and to the funding for the library versus funding for one of their pet projects, a lot of shit was flung around. It stuck to some people like mud to pigs, but some people it just slid off and they carried on doing that thing that they do when they know they're better than everyone around them. And for people like Badger's parents, they are impervious to shit, despite drowning in it. It's them you have to watch out for.'

Lillian shook her head. Apple's dire warnings made no sense. This was a small town. Yes, it was bad that they lost their library, but they weren't living in a war zone operating under a dictator. This was small town, rural England. Surely the residents only got upset about tardy snowplows and the price of cheese at the supermarket?

'Hopefully he won't come back, or remember to tell his parents. But we're screwed if he does.'

Lillian's heart couldn't sink any further. What an idiot she'd been to think he'd ever be interested in her, anyway. Because yes, that was exactly what had gone through her mind. There'd been too many accidental meetings, and she'd got her hopes up. But, he had Holly, and who in their right mind would break up with someone as beautiful as Holly to go out with some idiot girl from New Zealand who has hallucinations about Roman soldiers? Lillian rubbed her head again, the pain pulsing.

Apple thrust a box of books into Lillian's arms.

· · ·

'He's not worth the worry. He'll have forgotten all about us as soon as he stepped out the door. Come and help me sort these. Someone left a whole carton of craft books outside, and if we don't put the knitting books in the right place, I'll have a dozen old ladies calling for my head,' Apple joked, her pale face split open with a smile, diffusing the tension in the crammed room.

The pair spent a comfortable hour shelving books, joking about the odd patterns, and they decided that a seedy underbelly existed of grandmothers who designed handmade crafts to scare the living daylights out of small children everywhere.

'Look at this one!'

Lillian peered at the open page, where knitted in full technicolour glory stood a legion of Roman soldiers, helmets knitted in a buttercup yellow, with fire-engine red uniforms. Their woollen eyes were a deadly shade of violet. Each soldier held either a sword, a shield, or a staff with a misshapen eagle on top.

'Imagine knitting all those. There's someone with too much time on their hands,' Apple said, running her finger down to the photo acknowledgement. 'Ah, and here's who had so much free time, a Miss Loretta Hambly of London, back in 1986.'

Lillian turned to carry on shelving books as Apple continued perusing the knitting book, half listening as Apple read out passages related to Loretta Hambly's handicrafts, pausing in her work as Apple exclaimed at another photograph.

'Holy hell, knitted Roman altars.'

'Knitted what?'

'Altars, like yours. See here?' Apple shoved the book into Lillian's hands.

The photograph showed the same knitted Roman legion, but this time the soldiers stood posed around grey knitted altars. The shade of wool used varied, with the ancient Latin script picked out in contrasting colours. Lillian's blood froze as she read the first inscription. It was the same as the altar she'd seen in her dreams, in her nightmares. The altar where she'd watched a legion of men being slaughtered in the night.

. . .

Dedicated to the god Jupiter Optimus Maximus, the altar named the legion who'd commissioned it, and that of their commander, Titus Caelius Castus. A man Lillian never imagined was real. A man she wished she'd never met.

Either oblivious to the distress on Lillian's face or else choosing to ignore it, Apple pulled the book from Lillian's trembling hands and read the photo caption.

'Altars such as this one, once dotted the Roman Empire, up to its furthermost reaches. What's wrong? You look like you've seen a ghost?'

'Can I borrow it?' Lillian asked, gesturing to the book in Apple's hands.

'Look, I'm used to people not talking to me, so I've learnt how to read body language. Everyone gives off subtle clues when they think no one's looking. But I'm an observer. You have to be when you're treated like you're stupid, so I know more about what's going on in this town than any council employee. And I know something happened to you, something to do with the altar. Whatever it is, it's coming off you in waves. There's a type of... energy.'

'It's nothing—'

'It's something.'

Lillian felt her resolve crumbling under Apple's uncomfortable gaze, her pink-rimmed eyes unblinking.

'I can't say. I don't know...'

'I can wait. But know that we're here for you,' Apple replied, returning to her books.

'We?'

'Pram and I. He's... well, we're here for you when you need us. You should head home now. It'll be dark soon and it's a funny time of year. The Romans had a special name for it, which I've forgotten now. Anyway, go. Given your run of bad luck, you should be at home in bed already!'

Apple disappeared down the hallway with an armful of modern bestsellers in her arms. Lillian was about to ask about borrowing the old manuscript, but hesitated. She'd borrow it tonight, and return it tomorrow. It wasn't like she was stealing. She just wanted to see if it included anything relevant to Ithaca Farm.

Lillian slid the antique tome into her bag, together with the knitting book. The coincidence of the knitted altar was too impossible to ignore.

Mr Sharma was waiting for her at the exit, his face unreadable. Lillian's face coloured. Had he seen her take the books? His smile suggested otherwise.

'It's good you know your way here now. Anytime you need to pop by, I'll be here,' he said, inclining his head.

'Thanks,' Lillian said, slipping through the open door, her bag brushing against him as she stepped through.

Mr Sharma reached out with his bony fingers, bringing her to a sudden halt.

'But be careful, you're playing with fire. Don't let them through,' he said, his eyes shining with an intensity she didn't understand.

And then, like the sun coming out, a smile replaced the manic look on his face and he released her arm, patting her sleeve, before pressing a carved wooden animal into her hands. An exquisitely carved dog.

'A gift,' he said with the little wave, before closing the door between them, leaving Lillian on the front step, her heart beating just a little too fast for comfort.

CHAPTER 17

THE INDIAN TRAVELER

It was true that Pramod spent his days administering the secret library. He didn't do it for the pleasure of reading nor for the joy of helping the community, although those two things did play a small part. No, Pramod had selected this small invisible library, and the surrounding community, so that he could get his hands on as many old texts as possible without having to resort to breaking into the archives of the Hexham Abbey or Newcastle University. It aggrieved him no end, that valuable research materials were held in climate controlled warehouses but never saw the light of day. That despite all the advances in technology, the world over, millions of records in the north of England alone, had yet to be digitised. He didn't kid himself that he would have been any better off had they been digitised, but the electronic records may have sped up his research. They may have helped him pinpoint the exact moment in history when things changed.

It had been the arrival of an old tea chest. Old-fashioned stencils covered the sides, proclaiming it as belonging to the Horniman's Tea Company, a company long since subsumed by a foodstuff conglomerate that touted their small company beginnings as a way to pull the wool over the eyes of their consumers.

. . .

Too heavy to carry inside, he'd dragged the tea chest across the threshold, leaving it in the doorway until he could find a hammer or screwdriver to prise off the lid.

Pramod had expected to find it filled with user manuals for portable typewriters and faded microwave cookbooks, well-thumbed copies of Barbara Cartland novels, and a set of Reader's Digest books, the spines uncracked, and the pages unturned. Instead, what he found were two delightful leather-bound sets of Dickens novels and those of Arthur Conan Doyle, and the journals of James Arlosh — a coal mine owner, long since dead. A collier who'd dabbled in archaeology long before anyone had given archaeology a name.

And so Pramod started reading, struggling to decipher the spidery handwriting, guessing at possible translations for the collier's short-hand. The significance of the text hit him harder than a derailed freight train. He was reading the journals of the ancestors of Seb Arlosh, whose grandfather William had lived his life up at Ithaca Farm, once part of James Arlosh's sprawling estate.

The journals held irrefutable evidence of a bustling village servicing the Roman fort, a Roman fort that history had no record of. Until now. Pramod was no archaeologist, but still understood what a monumental discovery this was. For days, he'd pondered what to do with the infor-mation, making discreet enquiries on his daily walks around town. The townsfolk considered him an oddity as it was, so he hadn't raised any red flags when he'd asked at the Information Centre about undiscov-ered Roman ruins, and no one at the paper had blinked an eye when he'd shuffled into their foyer one day, asking about access to their archives. They'd said no, but his query hadn't tripped any alert system. There was no great scheme to keep the existence of a Roman fort from the public, any more than there was a conspiracy to inject nano tech-nology into the arms of billions of people disguised as a vaccine. No. Ithaca Fort was merely a place forgotten by time. Until now.

The point that Pramod could not move past was how one fort, surrounded by so many others, had ceased to exist. Unless the amateur archaeologist had misinterpreted their findings all those hundreds of years ago, but based on what he'd read, Pramod doubted that more than he doubted Boris Johnson's ability to lead the country.

Pramod had settled into an armchair, long abandoned by its previous owners, and repurposed into the library's only reading chair. The springs under the horsehair ticking, parted on strange angles, and it was a challenge to find a comfortable way of sitting, but he managed. Beggars can't be choosers, as the old saying went.

Time had sorted the chair's leather upholstery, which still carried a faint scent of tobacco and some spice. Cinnamon maybe? Or nutmeg? The chair always reminded him of Christmas, especially when the night fell early and he dozed off in the premature darkness, dreaming of winters long gone, with people long buried. It was in this chair that he'd first decided that he had to go to Ithaca Fort. The old fort, not the expanse of over fertilised, underperforming farmland that existed now. Barren of almost any flora or fauna other than grass. Acres and acres of grass, only good enough for cattle or sheep, with nothing for the butterflies or moths or field mice or badgers or moles or foxes and hares, or toads and frogs and fungi of every sort.

Pramod's preparations took longer than he'd anticipated. He hadn't anticipated how difficult it would be to source items from a fort no one knew existed. No one except Seb Arlosh's grandfather and his family. Would they even share that information with him? He didn't think so.

After a long walk along the Roman Road, all the way up to Ithaca Farm, and a night spent hiding in an unlocked outbuilding, Pramod had bided his time, waiting until William Arlosh had climbed into his Land Rover, seemingly a relic from the last world war, before pulling out of the driveway and disappearing down the road for his weekly shop at the local ALDi. People's habits were amazing. They shopped on the same days, usually at the same time, buying the same foods in the same quantities. They ate at the same cafes, ordering the same menu items, whilst sitting at their usual table. Pramod had seen it again and again — the angst flashing across the faces of regulars when they discovered some uncouth tourist sitting in their usual seat. In general, no one other than a Russian spy changed their routines. Which is why he knew that this was the day that old Arlosh drove into town, parked on the far left of the Safeway customer parking, after cautiously backing in.

Pramod knew that after William Arlosh had finished his shopping, spending almost fifty-four quid, sometimes closer to sixty pounds, he'd walk across the road to Costa Coffee for a pot of tea and a date scone, with the newspaper on the side. Consistent, predictable, and long enough to give Pramod time to find what he needed inside the unlocked house.

At first glance, any film loving visitor might have thought the decor of the house harked back to the props list for Elizabeth Taylor's 1963 film Cleopatra or Russell Crowe's Gladiator infused with a dash of Braveheart and finished with a nod to Lawrence of Arabia. To the untrained eye, the furniture and decorative pieces looked to be fairly competent copies of the genuine article. But to anyone who had even the smallest inkling, they were the real deal. Genuine antiquities. Priceless.

Pramod had been shuffling through time his entire life since that fateful thunderstorm in Jantar Mantar in Jaipur, India. He hadn't understood it at the time. No one could have. But he'd fumbled his way through eighteenth century London, through two world wars. He'd survived plagues and pandemics. He'd accidentally fallen through holes in time, disappearing from one life and creating another, all through trial and error and happy coincidences. And over time, he'd harnessed the magic. Yes, he'd made mistakes, losing keys he'd previously used to flit backwards and forwards to some of his favourite places, interfering in things which he had no business being involved with. And he'd lived to see the consequences of that. Pramod suffered no guilt for the change he'd affected, for the lives he'd saved. It had been tempting to try to avert some of the world's greatest disasters - Hitler, the assassination of JFK and Martin Luther King, the sinking of the Titanic. Chernobyl. He had power, but he wasn't all powerful. He could no more protect the American president than he could waltz unchallenged into a Russian nuclear plant. No. He'd saved children from dying from treatable infections. He'd helped a factory with their safety improvements so workers wouldn't lose a finger and then their livelihoods. He'd done his best to help, where he could, in a limited capacity, without causing too many ripples in the fabric of time. And then he'd met Metella.

As the bombs pummelled London, a young Pramod took shelter in the vestibule of the Bow church, hoping that in the absence of a Hindu shrine, the Christian god would protect him. He wasn't alone, a motley collection of Londoners too slow to find their way to one of the Underground shelters huddled next to him, including a woman with her hair in curlers and a toddler clinging to her dressing-gown clad legs, two sisters still in their teens, wearing dirty dresses and shoes two sizes too big, both with tiny leather satchels clasped tightly across their chests, a silent couple with faces full of the horror beyond the stone walls of the church, and a remnant of a man alone in the corner, his right leg somewhere in France. Pramod had watched the old soldier fill his Cherrywood pipe, calmly and precisely, tamping down the shreds of tobacco before lighting it and drawing the fragrant smoke deep into his mustard gas scarred lungs. And then there was the priest, his collar stained with soot and blood, his black robes torn, disheveled beyond all imagination, but holding up better than any of them, his prayers filling every corner of the vestibule and beyond. His prayers hadn't saved them. A German bomb had landed on the nave, plummeting down through the ornate ceiling, landing atop of the crypt, blasting outwards. Taking the curlers out of the hair of the harried mother, and the babe from her arms, divorcing the couple clinging to each other, and separating the old soldier from his remaining limbs and life. The valiant reverend had flung himself atop of the sisters, only for all three to be crushed by a falling pillar. In his efforts to save the girls, Pramod himself was saved by the pillar as more masonry rained down on them. He'd held the hand of the youngest girl, unable to move the pillar crushing her, and watched the life fade from her pale blue eyes until she saw nothing but heaven.

Once the dust settled, Pramod had checked the bodies of his companions for any sign of life, but to no avail. Just as he was about to leave, he spotted one of the girl's leather satchels. Checking inside for any form of identification for the authorities, he knew there wouldn't be any identification, or any need to inform the authorities. For inside the satchel, and Pramod assumed inside the other sister's satchel, were jewels and silverware and trinkets and other valuables that they'd obviously stolen from bombed-out houses in the better parts of London.

Scooping up both satchels, and with nothing more he could do to help the dead, he vanished into the night, like he'd done so many other times in so many other places.

With the satchels safe in his home on Fetter Lane, Pramod had fallen into bed, troubled dreams making sleep almost impossible. So it wasn't until daybreak that he finally tipped the contents of the leather satchels onto the kitchen table. Broken strands of pearls clattered across the wooden top, silver spoons and christening mugs clunked together, while circles of gold rolled onto the floor, sending Pramod onto his hands and knees to rescue the rings from oblivion in the gaps between the wide floorboards. The girls had been busy, the contents the obvious culmination of many nights of sneak thievery, or rather, opportunistic thefts. The spoils of war, if you like. And then it became clear what had led them to be in the church the previous night. Wrapped in a hand-knitted shawl, at the bottom of each bag, were a small collection of Roman era statues, probably Lares, the household gods. And as Pramod leaned forward to admire their ancient worn faces, and for the briefest of moments, he'd picked one up, forgetting the risk. Time whisked him out of London's war torn streets, placing him instead into the back room of the officer's mess in a Roman fort, somewhere on Rome's northernmost frontier, in the early second century.

Aside from the debilitating headache, Pramod had adjusted to his new location, his knowledge of history aided by the books and texts he'd filled his days devouring for moments just like this. He knew he couldn't stay in the fort, the soldiers would recognise him immediately as an intruder, and take appropriate, read deadly, action. He had to escape.

Slipping through the open door of the mess out onto a cobbled lane, he'd run straight into a cloaked figure. As the pair frantically tried disentangling themselves, Pramod had realised with a start that the other person was a woman, and that she was even less inclined to be caught in a Roman mess.

'Get away from me,' she'd said, tripping in her haste to escape.

Pramod had picked her up, as the sound of voices and boots and the rattling of swords seeped around the corner.

It was at that moment that realisation set in that neither of them should be there, so with no further discussion, the woman had told him to follow her, and like wraiths, they'd slipped through the starlit streets and out of the fort. When Pramod had looked back at the fortified walls, the sentries silhouetted by the leaking moonlight, he couldn't believe she'd smuggled them both out alive. He'd followed her back to her home, never once stopping to consider why she had been where she was at that time.

That was the beginning of their story, but not the end.

And now this girl, Lillian Arlosh. She had the gift, he could tell, but there was something more going on in the universe, something he couldn't discern. And although the risk to his health was immense, he needed to stop whatever was coming. He needed to go back. Metella needed him.

CHAPTER 18

BOOKS AND PAPERWORK

Lillian unpacked the takeaway containers on the bench, avoiding the kitchen table covered with an impossible pile of paperwork. A quantity of dirty coffee cups and empty biscuit packets accurately described everything about the trip to London she'd just returned from. A trip which had managed to push the strange experiences to the back of her mind, and which had provided some semblance of normality to a life which seemed to be unraveling. Inviting Apple over for a wine and a curry had seemed like the next most sensible option for someone who thought that they might be losing their mind.

Apple slipped into a kitchen chair.

'You've eaten a whole packet of biscuits?'

A smile swamped Lillian's tired face.

'I would have eaten a second packet if there'd been another one in the house,' she replied.

'Okay if I pour the wine?'

'Sure.'

'What happened on your trip to London? Did our reptilian over-lords have anything to say about your plans for the farm?' Apple asked.

Lillian didn't immediately answer. London had been fine, mostly. Other things were weighing on her mind.

She didn't want to tell her friend about the reporter, or draw her attention to the weirdly prophetic knitting creations in an old pattern book from the Eighties.

'Oh, they support my ideas absolutely. They couldn't have been more enthusiastic. But they just don't think it will work. Farming is apparently the lifeblood of the country. They reminded me a bit of the old war adverts, "Dig for Victory. Grow your own vegetables". They couldn't wrap their inbred Eton heads around the notion of fertiliser-free food and allowing nature to lead the way. They left a sliver of hope open. There's a fund I can apply to for support. And they're the ones who can sign off my plans. Hence,' she said, spreading more papers across the scarred table, 'this paperwork.'

'And what about the altar and the skulls? What's happening there?' Apple asked, staring out the window towards the tent covering the site of the ruins, its garish blue and white stripes a stain on the green field.

'I don't want them here, so I'm not making it easy for them. Hopefully, they've got the message that the sooner they remove everything, or go away, the better. It's complicated things. I can't touch anything in either of those fields until they have finished their inspection. People around here used hundreds of altars to help build almost every stone wall in this whole county. You just need to look at the church in town, made with dozens of bits of old Roman stonework robbed from Hadrian's Wall and all the other forts. What's one more altar and a set of stairs? They can have it.'

'I don't think you quite realise how important that history is to people around here,' Apple said. 'Sure, in the past they used the Roman-cut stone, but nowadays, that would be like someone using a strut from the Eiffel Tower for their loft conversion. It just doesn't happen anymore. And they have to treat the skulls with the proper respect. As weird as it sounds, their relatives are probably working at the local Tesco's.'

Lillian didn't know how to answer. History had been her father's passion. He'd have been all over himself helping the archaeologists, showing them the stash of history in the shed. But without him here, history held no importance in her life. It just complicated things.

· · ·

Part of her wanted to know everything about the Roman occupation of Ithaca Farm, and if there was any record of Julius and his service. Which was stupid. He was imaginary, and didn't exist, brought on by a blow to the head. None of it was real. None of it.

'You're right. It's just so frustrating.'

'Without the skulls, this would have all been sorted ages ago,' Apple said. 'For all the evidence of Roman occupation around here, a cache of decapitated heads is more unusual than an episode of the Jeffery Dahmer documentary.'

Lillian and Apple retired to the living room for a date with Strictly Come Dancing and the rest of the Pinot Grigio. It felt like years since Lillian had done anything quite so normal. She'd read about female friendships like this, but for one reason or another, she'd never had one. Not since school anyway, and that was a lifetime and a half ago.

With only a mouthful left in the bottle, and the travesty of the elimination decision thoroughly debated and chastised, Lillian waved Apple off into the night, the quiet hum of Apple's electric bike joining the last of the season's crickets.

As much as she'd enjoyed Apple's company, Lillian relished the solitude to look through the treatise and to examine the knitting book. She couldn't help but harbour the suspicion that one of the books held the key to uncovering what the hell was going on with her life.

There was no point in pulling the curtains despite it already being dark outside. She had no visible neighbours. The sheep on the far hills didn't count. And the road didn't run past this side of the house. In the last moments of dusk, all she could see beyond the house was the archaeologist's tent and the faint undulations of the field she hoped would soon be heaving with wild flowers and young saplings.

Turning away from the window, she missed the shadowy figure of a man slipping out from under the tent and heading off towards the bottom of the pasture where the ground was slowly reverting back to wetlands, undoing the Victorian efforts to drain the land. Nature always found a way.

The parchment of the treatise crackled under Lillian's hands. She might have taken a little more care if she knew the crackling was a sign of poorly prepared animal skin. The pigment on the pages was of much better quality, and the colours shone like a stained-glass window with vivid reds and blues and a glowing gold. The green on the page was deeper than the emerald in her mother's engagement ring. A ring Lillian now wore, a daily reminder of what she'd lost. Lillian tried not to give voice to the thought she had harboured deep inside her. But her tears watered it and her grief fed it. If she could travel back through time to the days of the Roman's, did it not therefore stand that she could travel to a different a time? A more recent time?

'No,' she said loudly, rubbing away the tears. 'No.'

It was truly black outside. With no stars nor moon, it was a night for dark deeds and darker thoughts. She shivered as she imagined how hundreds of men, far from the warmth of Italy, would have coped with the northern cold. How did they live? Did they love? Were there friendships and games? How did they escape from the noise of their companions? Was solitude even possible in the Roman army? She'd had enough trouble concentrating at school for six hours a day. Lillian couldn't imagine being deployed in a foreign country for years, away from their loved ones. It was no wonder they turned to the gods, any gods, for succour.

Lillian put aside the treatise — the ornate script was impossible to read without a magnifying glass. She instead opened the knitting book. If her mother could see her now, she'd split her sides with laughter. Lillian was the least crafty person in their entire family, so the concept of Lillian taking up knitting was as far removed as the idea that time travel was real. But still, she started at the beginning of the book, examining over every illustration and description. In all, Loretta Hambly had contributed just over a quarter of the examples in the book. And they varied from the legion of Roman soldiers, to a dog in its kennel, to a woman reclining on a bench with a bunch of tiny grapes in her hands.

Lillian checked the copyright page at the front of the book — decades old. Loretta Hambly was probably long dead, decaying underground, a knitted cardigan keeping her skeleton warm.

This thought reminded her of the conversation with Jasper Fletcher, the reporter from the Hexham Herald. He'd quizzed her about the potential likelihood of more skeletons being located at the farm. There was no doubt that over the centuries people had died here, and had been buried nearby, but she prayed that they weren't actually buried on her land. And the Roman Army were well known for burying their dead well away from where they lived and worked. No, Jasper Fletcher was wrong. There weren't any other bodies buried at Ithaca Farm. The skulls were... well, they were an anomaly.

Lillian tried the internet. Miracle of miracles, the publisher of the pattern book was still in business. As Harper Publishing's homepage slowly opened, Lillian searched for Hambly's name. There existed only one word to describe Loretta Hambly, and that was prolific. There were links to at least two dozen books. It wasn't hard to discern a theme between Hambly's creations — they were all firmly seated in history. There was a whole book on Roman inspired patterns. Another on Viking themed designs, including a longship with skinny brown oars. She had several books based around the Tudors and Windsors, where keen crafters could knit an entire family tree of the various Henrys, Marys, and Elizabeths if they so desired. The world was indeed a peculiar place.

With her eyes drifting shut, and the internet intermittently dropping out, Lillian gave up worrying about knitting patterns, Roman altars, and headless corpses. Sleep called. A sleep hopefully uninterrupted with half-remembered scenes of slaughter, all because of one man's greed.

CHAPTER 19
WRITTEN IN INK

Jasper never expected his story would resonate as loudly as it had. Sixteen phone messages waited for him when he arrived at the Hexham Herald, and an immeasurable number of emails. After digesting the feedback, he mused it was the one time he wished they enabled comments on the paper's online articles.

'Great article, Jasper,' John Revell gushed, his girth displacing the stack of messages from the neat pile Jasper had formed. 'Got to keep the pressure on. We can't allow her to destroy our environment and ruin it for the visitors. Good to see the mayor shares our point of view. What about the local MP? We need a soundbite from him too, even though he's a worthless piece of shite. He'll be on board, I expect, comes from farming stock, which is why he got voted in. Fat lot of use he's been, though. Spends all his time feeding from the ratepayers trough happily enough instead of serving those of us who voted him in.'

Jasper half listened to the editor rabbiting on. Complaining about the local member of parliament was Revell's favourite topic, regardless of which party they represented. Jasper had been around long enough to hear Revell gripe about Labour, the Tories, the Independents.

. . .

Still, none of his editor's opinions had ever stopped him from attending one of their political fundraising soirees — Revell was a regular in the society pages of his own newspaper. If there was free booze and food, you could count on him being there. A regular 'B' list celebrity.

'I want something on her for the weekend's edition by the end of tomorrow. Dig into her past, find out what makes the woman tick. There must be a father or husband somewhere in the picture. Didn't she crash a car? Drink driving?'

'Ah, avoiding an animal,' Jasper offered, uncomfortable with his editor's direction.

'Speeding probably. Work that in as well. The readers will love that — city folk moving in, causing carnage on our roads, and to our pastures.'

Jasper tried deflecting Revell's attention away from Lillian, but he wouldn't be deterred.

'Something juicy for the front cover. This story could be what makes a name for you, boy. You'll be the champion of rural England, protecting our way of life,' Revell said, spittle flying with his unchecked enthusiasm. 'End of tomorrow, and make it good.'

Sinking into his chair, Jasper stared at the blinking screen of his computer, a screen filled with hate-fuelled messages about Lillian's destructive plans for Ithaca Farm and the proposed sale of the Roman altar. To be fair, the words in the article weren't all Jasper's. Revell's sticky fingerprints stained the more inflammatory prose. And Jasper was prepared to wager that the fingerprints didn't just belong to Revell. He had his suspicions that Revell and his wife had their fingers in far too many conflicting pies. The sort of pies which only ever nourished the Revells, leaving crumbs for everyone else involved. Except for the mayor and her husband. They had a large slice of pie whichever way you cut it.

In Jasper's early days at the paper, before he knew which side his bread was buttered on, Jasper had pitched a story on the intricacies of Hexham's mayoral office, exposing the backroom handshakes and secret nods in council meetings. Revell had made it abundantly clear that even thinking about such an article would result in dismissal.

Revell's statement came coupled with a threat that another news-paper would never hire Jasper in any country. With that promise hanging over his head, Jasper immersed himself in stories of car acci-dents, roading woes, petty crime and the bourgeois goings-on of the local landed gentry — always good for advertising sales, he was told. But it was still a story he tinkered on in his own time, on his own laptop. Revell may come across as an incompetent oaf, but he knew his way around a computer and kept track of internet usage, including website visits. Jasper had seen more than one young intern let go when Revell presented them with their porn viewing stats, or that they'd watched, several times over, the live-streaming of an atrocious terrorist attack. So yes, Jasper kept his after-hours dossier on the mayor and her cronies off site and quiet. But this attack on Lillian seemed to feed directly into other data he'd collected about the Revell's, their tourism empire, and how far their hands were in the mayor's back pocket.

He filed away his thoughts about the mayor, turning his mind instead to the Orwellian machinations of the Department for Environ-ment, Food and Rural Affairs and their Environmental Stewardship scheme — the scheme which Lillian proposed to use in order to turn her pasture over to nature.

Click after click sent Jasper on a literal wild duck chase through wildlife management plans, protected species habitats and the issuing of licenses for the culling of badgers, bats and, he imagined, probably bears if he bothered to delve too much further. He was an experienced researcher. A journalism school graduate with two decades of experi-ence under his belt. Yet, despite all this, he could feel his life-force draining away as he tried navigating the labyrinthine prose of the sloth-like Environmental Stewardship scheme. If Lillian Arlosh managed to work this scheme in her favour, then all power to her. He couldn't work it out. In no way did it sound profitable for anyone involved except the experts. Experts who were ensconced in the First Class carriage of the government's gravy train.

He got up to make himself a weak tea, with a decent plug of milk, and considered alternative points of attack whilst the kettle boiled. The sale of the altar was one. He didn't think the average citizen could sell off the treasure they found on their own land.

He'd done plenty of articles featuring the local metal detecting club and the weird and wonderful things they'd dug up. Not that the local club was in Hexham, no one could detect this close to the wall. But he knew that they had to hand over anything of historical significance or value, and they were reimbursed for it. But what about something like a Roman altar?

Predicting a day pouring through his personal archives, he grabbed a handful of Jaffa cakes from the biscuit tin. He needed the sustenance more than the fool who'd left them by the kettle.

With his mouth full of jammy goodness, and his lukewarm mug of tea, he settled back and started trawling through his stash of old papers. The internet had its place, but there was nothing like an old story to colour a new one.

CHAPTER 20
CONVERSATIONS IN CORRIDORS

Two men blocked the supermarket aisle, oblivious to the clucking of the other shoppers. Chance had them there at the same time, next to shelves heaving with bananas from Ecuador, pineapples from Thailand, and peppers from Argentina.

And behind the shelves of plastic-wrapped fruit and out-of-season vegetables, Badger frowned. The only reason he'd stopped to eavesdrop was because he'd recognised one of the voices. The voice of his father.

'I want it stopped,' said John Revell, an empty shopping basket swinging redundantly from his arm.

'It will be.'

'Farmland, that's what the tourists want to see. Cows and sheep, tractors and farm dogs. Things they're familiar with. If she's allowed to destroy the vista from—'

'She won't be. There's enough ill feeling in the community that anything else she tries will be met with placards and farmers with pitchforks.'

The men laughed.

'And what about the permit for our newest venture?' Revell asked.

'She signed that off this morning.'

'No issues with the planning people, then?'

'Naturally, they were against it, but when your wife is the mayor, you have some sway.'

They laughed again, with Matthew Badrick, the mayor's husband, slapping his friend on the back as they walked away, talking of less controversial things, like Brexit and rebuilding the Tory party.

Over their regular Wednesday night family dinner, Badger listened to his parents dissect the intentions of the newest arrival in town - Lillian Arlosh. The conversation wasn't pleasant. Whilst Badger loved his parents, he was under no illusions that they often skirted the edges of the law. He'd been present for various discussions about the legalities of their renovations versus the pain of applying for building consents, the avoidance of parking fines, and tax avoidance versus tax evasion. He'd grown up listening to them talk freely of their efforts to save money alongside eliminating the red tape elsewhere in their lives. And sometimes eliminating that red tape extended to paying for certain privileges — which in some countries might be classed as bribery.

Badger was nothing like his parents. His moral compass was set facing a different direction. When he'd first started work as a teenager, ironically at the local grocery store, his mother had suggested that they pay him under the table tax free, claiming that it would be easier for accounting purposes. That was the first time Badger had rebelled against his parents. He didn't want to start his working life with a smear against his name. He had ambitions, and defrauding the government didn't sit well alongside those dreams.

'You seemed busy at the store today, Dad.'

'What's that?' Badger's father asked, a fork midway to his mouth.

'I wish I'd known you were going to the store. I had a few things I needed,' his mother chimed in.

'I saw you at the supermarket.'

'You should have said hello.'

. . .

'You were busy chatting to John Revell, from the Herald. It seemed important, so I didn't interrupt,' Badger offered, looking for an explanation for the overheard conversation.

Matthew Badrick shoved his forkful of chicken into his mouth and chewed, his eyes darting between his son and his wife.

'Bumped into him, wasn't anything important,' he replied, the half-chewed chicken still in his mouth.

'Did you get a chance to ask him—' Badger's mother Jane started.

'No, as I said, I only ran into him by chance. We needed a couple of things for the office,' Matthew said, interrupting his wife with a sharpened look.

Badger watched his mother slam her mouth shut and concentrate on cutting her roast potatoes into tiny, symmetrical shapes.

'Such a coincidence. I spoke with Gail Revell today,' Jane Badrick finally said, moving her food around her plate, leaving a track of minted gravy.

'And what did she have to say?' Matthew asked.

'We talked about the appalling job they're doing of the refurbishment of the Bellingham Tea Rooms. It's a historic building. Surely there's something you can do to stop it? You're the town's leading archaeologist, doesn't that stand for something? The council pays you for your advice. The way she explained it to me, and from what I've seen myself, it'll be a shell of what it was. An absolute travesty,' Jane complained, her voice rising.

Badger had doubts about the veracity of her story, and her complaints were undoubtedly more about the potential loss of income from the cottage they had at the back of their own property.

'Gail also said that the developer has some big-shot London antiques dealer coming to clear out all the old fixtures and fittings from the Bellingham building. You should be all over this, Matthew. Who knows what they're selling? Like that woman selling the altar. That stuff needs to stay in town, to give the tourists a reason to come here.'

Badger gazed at his mother as she mounted her high horse to rave about other people profiteering from history.

. . .

He fully expected her to segue into another of her favourite topics — immigrants and the lack of jobs for the locals. And she didn't fail him.

'I saw that homeless man again, cluttering the streets. I should have him reported him to the police for loitering. You'd have thought that after they closed the library, he would have gone home to his family. I mean, there's nothing else here for him. He worries me. What does he get up to all day?'

'He's harmless,' Badger argued, his patience wearing thin at his mother's racist undertones. 'He's just looking after the books until a proper home can be found for them.'

The look on Jane Badrick's face made him regret every word.

'What do you mean?' Jane pounced. 'What books? Where?'

Jane and Gail Revell had been two of the most vocal advocates for cutting the library's budget. Young people didn't use books, they'd argued. They needed the internet, and books took up valuable space and required librarians to be employed to care for them. The money for which could be better utilised elsewhere.

'Just something I heard around town,' Badger muttered, switching his attention to his meal, trying to deflect his mother's questions.

'I thought those books had all been destroyed?' Matthew said.

'Why would anyone destroy books?' Badger asked, mirroring his mother's frown.

'You find out where those books are. If they're taking up space in one of the council's properties, there will be hell to pay, and I mean that,' Jane hissed, the colour in her cheeks identical to the flesh of the meat on their plates.

'Calm down,' Badger said, 'they're books, not atomic weapons.'

'Don't you talk to me that way.'

Badger pushed away from the table, regret filling his frame. He should never have shared anything about the books in the library.

'I'm not a child anymore, Mother. Thank you for dinner. I'll see you next week.'

Back in his flat, he messaged Lillian and waited for a reply. He didn't have Apple's number, but wanted to warn her about his mother's bizarre reaction. Normally he'd have stayed out of it, but for the brief time he'd hung out with the girls, and the towering stacks of old books, he'd found a level of calmness he couldn't recall ever experiencing before. His life was one of work, work, work. Goal setting and goal achieving, with no time for reflection. No time to just sit. Their family was one of action, of doing, of volunteering. His parents sat on more committees than anyone else he knew. Which was why they had a weekly dinner scheduled in their respective diaries. It wasn't until he'd spent the time in the pseudo library that he realised he was doing something because he wanted to, not because it was expected of him.

Badger checked his phone again, still no reply from Lillian. He rang, but received no answer. It didn't unduly worry him given the patchy reception at Ithaca Farm. Despite his parent's reaction, he never once considered that they would take any action, at least not tonight.

CHAPTER 21

TEA AT THE BELLINGHAM

Lillian sipped her tea, perched on an upturned crate in the middle of a building site. Opposite her sat another woman her age, drinking from an identical mug, but seated on a scuffed leather armchair which had seen better days.

'It's going to look amazing when it's finished,' Lillian said, taking in the team of workmen scurrying like worker ants around them.

'Only if I'm alive to see it finished,' the other woman laughed, before her laughter turned into a hacking cough. 'Sorry, it's the dust. I think there's more of this old place inside me than there is outside,' she joked.

'If I had the money, I'd do the same thing to the farmhouse, gut it and start fresh. It's bloody freezing, nothing seals properly, or closes. At least the chimney company has sorted the chimney's, and got them all going. Took them most of the day. I needed it done as the insurance company wouldn't sign off on my cover until I had it sorted,' Lillian moaned, adjusting her woollen scarf around her neck, the early winter chill winding its fingers around her Antipodean throat.

'Restoring the chimneys is last on my list,' Paige Spencer moaned, flicking the builders dust from the sleeve of her jersey.

. . .

'After what I've spent on this place so far, I can't bloody well even afford a chimney sweep unless I can sell some of the stuff I found hiding about the place.'

'What are you selling?'

'A whole shop's worth of antiques,' Paige said.

'Really? Like what?'

'All of this,' she said, waving her arm around the largest room in the Bellingham Tea Rooms.

In amongst the workmen's detritus stood decades of abandoned furniture, touching almost every fashion high point from the last century. There were Art déco lamp shades stacked in bulging cardboard cartons — the glass shades varying from earthy green mints to washed out buttercup yellows. Turn of the century hat stands stood guard next to retro 1950s telephone tables complete with fire-engine red telephones, sans their long industrial cables, but still striking nonetheless. An old brass coal scuttle lay nestled against a Cold War era industrial filing cabinet, complete with paper inserts on each drawer describing the contents as Research, Finds, and Newcastle University.

'What's in there?' Lillian asked.

'Old files. I would have emptied everything into the rubbish skip, but I didn't even know it was full until they brought it down. Took two of them to lug it down from the attic. They needed access to the roof, so it had to come out.'

'Mind if I look?'

'Be my guest,' Paige replied. 'The antiques dealer from London won't want the contents, I'm sure.'

Lillian leafed through the random files in the stiff drawers, most seemingly incomprehensible — bundles of hand drawn diagrams, cross sections of earth works and what looked like drainage plans. There was a folder of black and white aerial photographs which she lay to one side, and a second folder of what appeared to be brass rubbings, like the ones she'd done as a child on a school trip to the local cemetery. She shuddered at the memory of the nightmares which had plagued her afterwards. She still remembered the details of the plaque she'd been assigned, "In memory of Charlotte Beard, killed by train, December 25, 1933."

'You're right, there's not much here other than these old diagrams and photos of the local area. Might be something among them about Ithaca Farm,' Lillian said. 'Do you mind if I keep them?'

'I doubt that they'll be any different from what you see now. The people here are very anti change,' Paige said.

'Who are you getting in to buy your things? I've got a mountain of stuff from the previous owner. Most of it probably has no value, but some of it might pay the power bill for a month or so.' Lillian laughed into her coffee.

'Believe it or not, I used a London company. It's not that there wasn't anyone trustworthy up here, it just ended up being more convenient. A good friend used them and vouched for their honesty, so I just gave them a ring. Easy. What have you got? Anything I can use for the tearooms?' Paige's face was as bright as the naked bulb hanging above the old table.

Lillian gave it some thought. 'There are some old decorative concrete statues in one of the outside sheds.'

Paige laughed. 'The very last thing I need! I need more ladylike pieces, think Victorian gilt, baroque mouldings, dainty chairs, doilies.'

'There's some god awful furniture, for sure. But who knows what's in the outside sheds?' Lillian shuddered. 'Or in the attic. There are rooms I haven't been able to face yet. They're so full. That's what happens with a deceased estate. I was left everything, including his underwear.'

'That's the story we heard, although to be honest, we all thought you were a little too keen on taking it on, and not selling it, especially with the covenant on the farm, not that that's unsurmountable.'

Whilst Lillian heard the word covenant, her mind chose not to process it, instead she just kept talking, as if the other woman hadn't just thrown a grenade under her plans. 'It's okay, I'll manage. I just have to jump through all their hoops, and dance whatever dance it is they decide is important this week, depending on which agency wants their pound of flesh. It's almost like every self-important government lackey is a direct descendent of Shylock—'

'Shylock?'

'You know, from The Merchant of Venice? Shakespeare?'

'Oh yes, pound of flesh, it makes sense now. Sadly, living here is an exercise in trial by local media, compromise and underhanded tactics to get what you want. And that's just from the local council. Add in the English Heritage bulldogs and the shaggy elk-cardigan wearing brigade who don't even want you to change the Victorian-era drinking fountains with their poisonous lead pipes. They'd rather we all suffered from lead poisoning than update anything from the golden-era of Northumberland. And all that's before we even start on the historical Roman stuff. It's a steep mountain you're climbing. And to do it alone? Well, cheers to that.'

The women clinked their mugs in a toast to doing it on their own before being interrupted by a moustached workman carrying a wooden off cut — the traditional carpenter notepad, anxious for Paige to answer an urgent question.

'I'll leave you to it. Thanks for the tea,' Lillian said, leaving her friend to deal with the latest renovation crisis. 'And good luck!'

As Lillian left the Bellingham, a van pulled up - Paige's dealer from London, and she made a mental note of the name emblazoned on the van's side - The Old Curiosity Shop. A fitting name. They would be happy with their lot today, Lillian was certain. She only wished that she had the funds to buy some of Paige's treasures, treasures which reminded her of growing up with an antiques dealer as a father. Too many years ago now, but she'd retained a love for all things old and quirky.

Her drive back to the farm provided all too brief a respite from her own woes, which hit her anew as she turned into her driveway. An unfamiliar car blocked access to the dilapidated garage, a situation made more untenable as the heavens opened and icy sheets of rain lashed the car. Tiny rivulets of water ran unchecked across the packed earth. Lillian leaned on the horn.

A guilty face appeared from within the garage. A familiar face. Lillian slammed her hand against the horn again. He didn't move other than to gesture to the rain.

At a stalemate, she manoeuvred the car as close to the house as possible, smug as her tyres threw a muddy coat over the interloper's car.

With her keys in her hand, she ran from the car to the door, scrambling to unlock the door before the rain drenched her. Jasper darted towards the open door and Lillian smiled sweetly as she slammed it shut before he made it to the front step.

Turning the lock, she leaned against the solid door, listening to the hammering from the other side.

'Miss Arlosh? Can you open the door please? Miss Arlosh?'

Lillian tried ignoring the hammering, but hiding behind the door wasn't a grownup thing to do. She could no more continue to stand behind the door than she could pretend her father was still alive. Steeling herself for whatever sensationalist headline would come from this conversation, she opened the door.

A bedraggled Jasper leapt inside, a trail of mud marking his progress as he blustered and huffed and coughed in the tiled entranceway, a large puddle spreading beneath his dripping trousers.

'Thanks,' he said, his teeth chattering.

Lillian stared, her gaze lowering the temperature of the room.

'I've left messages on your phone,' he said, trying to wipe the rain from his long face with his soaking sleeves.

Lillian shrugged. She didn't owe him anything. He'd written a hit piece about her in the local newspaper, and she was sick of playing nice to everyone, mostly men. Men from the council, men from the city, the farmers, the archaeologists, and, of course, the media. She was over being constantly dismissed because she was a woman with ideas. Lillian wasn't going to make it easy for Jasper. He was in her house, and the sooner he was gone, the better.

The tempo of the rain increased as it threw itself with ever increasing ferocity at the land, pulsing through every unwelcome gap in the windows and beneath the doors.

'Have you got some old towels? We could put them under the door? Stop any more rain getting in?' he said. 'The last thing you want is—'

'Just tell me why you're here, and then go.'

Her abruptness put a pause to his helpful suggestions.

'I'm sorry—'

'Sorry for what you wrote in the newspaper? It's too late for that. Please don't let the door hit you on your way out.'

'Look, I can understand your aversion to reporters. We can be both a hindrance and a help, depending on what you need from us.'

Lillian sniffed. 'You've done enough damage, thanks.'

'I really just want to hear your thoughts on what's been said in the media.'

'My thoughts aren't appropriate for printing.'

'Perhaps we could sit down and talk, off the record? There's stuff going on behind the scenes which you should know about. Please, Miss Arlosh?'

Lillian stared at the shivering reporter. Despite her misgivings, she couldn't help but feel sorry for him. Could he help her? Or was he after another soundbite to sink her plans? He couldn't do much more damage than what he'd already done. She had nothing to lose.

'Fine, but help me with these towels. I'm finding out how much this place is more like a sieve than a house.'

They bustled around with towels and bowls and buckets, trying to minimise the water damage from the now-apocalyptic storm assaulting the surrounding farmland. The lights flickered once, twice, before settling to a slightly dimmer version of themselves.

'I'll make the coffee while there's still power.'

'Do you have any tea? I'd much prefer tea over coffee... it's an English thing,' Jasper asked.

With the kettle boiling, Lillian waited for the reporter to begin his tale.

'It's about the altar—'

'I'd assumed that. I doubted it was about anything else I'm doing.'

'Oh, you'd be surprised. The altar features, but it's more about the whole rewilding thing. They're dead against it. And there's a concerted effort underway to stop you.'

Lillian snorted, turning to pour the steaming water into two blue-and-white Cornishware mugs.

'There's not a lot they can do about someone letting their farmland return to nature. It's not like there's a council rulebook which says, "Thou shalt not leave the grass long" or anything like that.'

She watched as Jasper shrugged before he turned his attention to a ragged notebook.

'There actually is,' he replied.

'You're pulling my leg?'

'I'm afraid not. You have to go right back to the original covenant over this land—'

'That's the second time today I've heard about a covenant on the farm. No one told me about any covenant.'

'Yeah, I had a suspicion you didn't know about that. The lawyer should have told you. Might have made you change your mind about taking it over. I can put you in touch with a good solicitor I know, London based, but don't hold that against him.'

Lillian dredged through her memories. Although a surprise at the time, inheriting Ithaca Farm was the best thing that could have happened to her. The property boasted almost pristine boundary lines, unfettered by ugly residential developments or weirdly placed commercial enterprises, like tips or fertilisers plants. The old lime quarry she could live with, which was historical now. The lower paddocks featured elegant, but crumbling, Victorian water pipes (their removal was high on her to do list). But she couldn't remember any mention of a covenant.

'Are the details in there?' she asked, pointing to his notebook.

Jasper whipped his notebook off the table and into his satchel, as if the contents were high-grade military secrets.

'Not in this notebook, no, but back at the office. I can swing by later with them?' he suggested, a smile playing at the corners of his thin lips.

This time Lillian couldn't stop a snort from escaping. Was this guy for real? Was that his pick up line? Surely not?

'Sure, I'll leave it in your hands. Let me know when you actually want to share some useful information with me. Like names, for example. Who is after me? And what is it that I'm doing that they are so afraid of?'

The reporter sat open mouthed at the table, clearly unused to being questioned himself.

'Well, um... those names are confidential. I have to protect my sources.'

. . .

'Don't spin me that line. I'm not some old lady dithering away in my dotage. Forget it. Just leave. I've got a thousand and one things to do before this place falls down around my ears, and talking conspiracy theories with you isn't one of them.'

Lillian showed Jasper to the door, all but pushing him into the rain, the distant hills invisible through the downpour. Watching him drive away, she fully suspected that he'd be back, sooner rather than later, and for the first time, the prospect of spending time in the company of another man didn't fill her with grief.

CHAPTER 22
THE CLOAK OF INVISIBILITY

Apple dawdled, the night protecting her from the evil lurking on the streets. She favoured the shadows, her evening walk almost game-like as she darted from shadow to shadow, hugging the stone walls, her movements disguised by overgrown hedgerows and entangled vines.

The scream of an engine approaching gave pause to her steps, an angry sound in the quiet night. The tiny creatures scuttled away, shrinking into burrows, retreating under rotting logs, taking wing and vanishing high into the starless sky. Apple recognised the sound. It belonged to the beast of a car the mayor drove.

The mayor, Badger's mother, Jane Badrick, had her manicured fingers in every pie in town, and it didn't matter to her whether the pie was sweet or savoury, Mrs Badrick demanded a slice, and woe betide if you didn't deliver.

Apple had once been the subject of Jane's wrath, and as such had spent the subsequent years giving the woman a wide berth. When you're the only albino in a small English town, avoiding the most connected woman in town could be difficult. Every school fair, prize giving, every community event, every public celebration, Jane Badrick was there, wielding her clipboard or microphone.

. . .

She chaired meetings, sat on the school board, attended all the parties, or otherwise arranged them and moderated the guest lists. No aspect of life in town remained untainted by Jane Badrick. And now Jane's son knew about the secret library. The risk that Badger would tell his mother terrified Apple given that Jane was the woman who single-handedly closed the doors of the town's library. And for that alone, Apple would never forgive the woman.

The car finally screamed past her. Why was Jane driving as if the Hounds of the Baskervilles were on her tail? Apple followed the tail-lights as they vanished over the hill. She hesitated, her curiosity suggesting a more circuitous route home, one which involved following the vanishing car.

Like Jane Badrick, Apple knew much about what went on in the town. And there were no meetings scheduled for tonight, the calendar unusually clear for a town counting down towards the festive season.

Slipping over the nearest fence, Apple ran across the lush farmland as she predicted the destination of the expensive car — the old library. She knew it. Badger must have said something about the books. Apple put on a burst of speed, ignoring the animal dung underfoot and the crumbling farm walls. She had to know what was happening, in case she needed to warn Pramod.

Out of breath, blonde hair slicked to her forehead, she collapsed behind a stone fence as she tried to slow her panting. She couldn't become a shadow of the night if she couldn't breathe. Apple fumbled in her bag for her inhaler, the hard plastic a small solace in the night.

Edging closer to the wall, Apple snuck a quick glance over the top. Jane Badrick stood outside the locked library door, just as Lola Cassidy pulled up in her grim looking station-wagon, more a workhorse than a status symbol, evidence that being a town counsellor didn't pay as well as some commentators spouted in the conservative newspapers.

Apple watched Jane wrench Lola Cassidy's car door open, barely giving Lola time to turn the engine off. Close enough to hear the exchange, Apple sank out of sight, lapping up the entertainment from her spot below the wall, ignoring the flood of ancient chocolate wrappers and discarded cigarette butts.

· · ·

She pulled her jacket closed as she listened to Jane screeching at the former head librarian, now head of council communications.

'You told us the books were gone. You swore in a meeting it had been taken care of. Were you lying? Do you know what happens to people who lie to me? Trust me when I say that your tenure as a council employee may be very short-lived. How does that feel?'

'Books? Is that what you called me out here? On my one night off this week, books?'

Apple could hear the woman's indignation rising. Lola Cassidy had been okay as the head librarian, pretty decent compared to some cronies employed under Jane's watch, but she was still a creature of Jane Badrick's empire.

'Are you, or are you not, hiding the library books somewhere in town?'

'Have you been drinking, Jane?'

Apple gasped, the sound traveling on the still air, but the two women standing face-to-face didn't appear to notice. Apple held her breath for a beat.

'I'm going to pretend that I never heard you say that. I'm here,' Jane said, 'because my son let it slip that you're storing the books in town.'

Eager to see the show, a sliver of Apple's head appeared above the wall, just as Jane struck a match to light her cigarette, illuminating the scene. Apple's snow-white hair shone like a beacon for a fraction of a second. A fraction of a second too long.

'There's someone out there, Jane,' Lola said

'What?'

'There's someone behind the wall watching us. Just saw the top of their hair, blonde I'd say.'

Apple froze against the wall, her heart racing. Shit. Crawling on hands and knees, she followed the line of the wall, rubbish crunching underneath her. Field mice and a wayward mole scurried out of her way, fleeing to the safety of their hidden burrows. If only a burrow existed for her to hide in as well.

'Who's there? Show yourself,' Jane called out. 'You look,' she directed.

Apple heard Jane's commands, and could only imagine the resentment on Cassidy's face, if indeed Jane had just ordered her employee to clamber over a wall to chase down a ghost.

Somewhere a dog barked, crying to a moon who refused to be seen. The moon's absence, and the dog's emotive howl were a blessing for Apple, as she caught her knee on a pile of loose stones, stuffing her fist in her mouth to halt her cry from finding its way out.

Cassidy must have climbed over the fence as Apple heard her land heavily amidst the rubble. Apple dared not look, burying her distinctive hair and skin under her arms, hoping that the deepening shadows would disguise her. The smell of the old wall was reassuring, as if the history of the fallen stones would protect her. Cassidy's footfalls were so close, the movement sending tiny cascades of pebbles around her. Surely Cassidy could see her?

Then right behind Apple's hiding place she heard, 'I must have been mistaken. I've had enough of this. I'm going home,' followed by the sound of Cassidy's retreating footfalls. 'Help me back over this wall, Jane. Think of the liability if I injure myself now.' Apple grinned into the shaped stones. So Cassidy wasn't as much in the mayor's pocket as everyone thought.

'This isn't the last of it. We should have incinerated those books, that's what you agreed to.'

'Go home, Jane. The books are no longer on council grounds, as per your directive. As far as I am aware, they were all destroyed, even the valuable ones, the ones we should have sold to fund the upgrade of the council chambers you were so keen on... So may I, politely, suggest that you let it go?'

'Mind how you speak to me, Cassidy. Remember your place, and who you have to thank for it,' Jane said, her voice full of steel.

Apple rolled over, gulping a lungful of fresh air. Night had properly fallen now, and one by one, the stars appeared, their tiny lanterns picking out the pure whiteness in Apple's hair and soul.

What an interesting development. Apple discerned trouble in paradise, as if Cassidy was chaffing under the yoke of Jane Badrick's patronage. Or was it a prison?

CHAPTER 23
FULLY CHARGED

Lillian's phone sat charging on the walnut dressing table, whilst she huddled under the covers to stay warm, almost impossible in a house with a malfunctioning heating system. And because of the leaking roof, she'd already moved the bed twice, before finding a part of the room where she wouldn't drown in her sleep. Not that sleep would come, with her mind saturated with thoughts of her conversation with the reporter and the covenants on the farm.

When she'd first moved in, she'd chosen the bedroom boasting spectacular views of Hadrian's Wall, with the historic monument appearing almost close enough to touch. The problem with this room was its sloping eaves, which shuddered with every wind gust, making Lillian fear that the roof would peel off at any given moment.

Every moan, every creak, every clatter of the remaining roof tiles set her further on edge. And somewhere, that damn dog had started howling. Or perhaps it wasn't a dog. She didn't know if wolves roamed England anymore, and hadn't wanted to ask anyone in town. Google, as usual, provided a muddle of information about reintroduction, Yellowstone Park, and werewolves. Not helpful.

Her phone chirped. Notification of a missed call. And a text, followed by another missed call, and a voice message.

Emerging from under the heavy duvet, Lillian listened to Apple's warning, her heart racing. What had Badger done?

The morning dawned with clear skies and a temperature hovering just above freezing. Damage from the storm littered the landscape — sheds sans roofs, fences down, bridges left impassable by torrents of water, and the supermarket shut because of flooding. The archaeologist's tent was nowhere to be seen, with the paddocks transformed into wetlands.

Lillian's mind replayed Apple's message from the night before. She shivered in bed, considering whether she should visit the library to warn Pramod about Badger's faux pas, or if that would inflame things.

The phone rang, Apple's name flashing on the screen

'Hey, you never rang back. Did you get my message?'

'There was a power cut last night, and my phone's only just recharged.'

'Don't you have a generator?'

'That's on the list,' Lillian said.

'You're going to need one of those before winter sets in,' Apple said.

'So I've heard,' Lillian sighed. 'Sorry I didn't ring back. So, what do we do? Did you tell Pramod?'

'He doesn't have a phone. I'm hoping to catch up with him at the cafe. Do you want to meet me in town?'

Lillian considered her day's plans, none of them urgent.

'Sure, let me grab some breakfast, and do a couple of things here. Then I'll see if the roads are open.'

After coaxing the old-fashioned wood burner into life, breakfast was her next priority.

Lillian's stomach churned — the marmalade toast and Earl Grey tea forming an uncomfortable union in her stomach.

· · ·

Despite the weather, a newspaper had still been punched through her letterbox and the Hexham Herald lay open on the table, with a photograph of Ithaca Farm dominating the front page.

'How dare he!' Lillian said, her face burning. Thoughts of murdering Jasper Fletcher, the author of the article, raged through her.

She reread the part where he quoted the mayor as saying, "Ms Arlosh seems determined to destroy the landscape which so many people rely on for their livelihoods. The thousands of walkers who hike Hadrian's Wall expect to see our famous landscape, which includes rolling pasture and healthy livestock grazing in their natural environment. They don't expect to have to navigate their way through thickets of gorse and wild pigs. Our tourism dollars will disappear as quickly as the history Ms Arlosh is selling to the highest bidder."

What was the mayor talking about? Selling what to the highest bidder?

Lillian fired up her laptop, Jasper Fletcher's card clenched in her fist. How dare he spread such dangerous lies about rewilding Ithaca Farm. She bashed out a vitriolic email, one which involved a critique of the morals of the lanky reporter, and a suggestion of whereabouts in hell he should reside.

With that off her chest, she headed into town to meet Apple and, hopefully, Pramod Sharma.

Half the cafe's patrons had their heads buried in a copy of the Hexham Herald when Lillian walked through the door. She felt the blush on her cheeks travel all the way into her hairline, and then some.

'They haven't made the connection, don't worry,' Apple said, as Lillian slid into the seat opposite.

'He's thrown me under the bus. I'm surprised there wasn't a placard-wielding mob outside the farm, calling for me to be burnt at the stake.'

'It'll blow over. No one will remember by the end of the week. I mean, how many people read the local newspaper? I bet no one does.'

Lillian's eyebrows lifted.

'It's a free paper, they only reading it because they don't have any data left on their phones.'

The two women laughed, and some of the tension left Lillian's shoulders.

'I'm just not used to being bullied by the newspapers,' Lillian said.

'This town doesn't like change very much. Give it a decade, and if you're still here, they might invite you to join one of their committees, then you'll know you've made it.'

'Talking of committees, does Pramod know about the mayor?' Lillian asked.

'He's not here yet,' Apple said. She tapped her phone. 'He's never late. He's a creature of habit.'

'Should we go check on him? Do you know where he lives?'

Apple tilted her head, the paleness of her eyes even more pronounced under the cafe's florescent lights.

'Shall I come with you?'

'It's all good,' Apple replied. 'Probably best if I go by myself—'

'Is it because I brought Badger to the library?'

'It's just better that not too many people know where he lives. People around here are funny about immigrants. And albinos. But then my family has lived here longer than almost everyone else, so they ignore me, instead of trying to run my family out of town.'

'Okay, but keep me posted. I should get back anyway. The archaeologist from the university wants to have another meeting this afternoon.'

As Lillian hugged her friend, a car pulled up across from the cafe, the driver honking the horn. They both turned to stare. Badger waved at them through the window, summoning them over.

'Is he waving at us?' Apple asked, her eyebrows raised.

Lillian hurried across the road and, with a smile, opened the side door. At precisely the same moment, Holly appeared, pushing past Lillian and jumping into the empty passenger seat.

'Thanks for opening the door, Nero,' Holly quipped, before giving a mock salute. 'You can close it now. No need to let the cold air in.'

Lillian stepped back, stunned into silence. She caught a glimpse of uncertainly on Badger's face before Holly slammed the door.

If Badger had considered ordering Holly out of his car, Holly stopped him in his tracks, almost sucking off his face by pressing her lips hard into his.

There were more important things in life than men, but still... the smile fled from the corners of her mouth.

Whatever Badger had wanted to tell her left with him, as he and Holly drove off down the High Street.

'In the immortal words of Queen Elsa, let it go. He's not worth it.' Apple said, appearing at Lillian's shoulder. 'I warned you about him.'

If he wasn't worth it, then why did it hurt so much?

CHAPTER 24

THE WOMAN FROM LONDON

After Lillian made an appointment with the London antiques dealer, she felt some of her financial worries seeping away. She wasn't expecting millions for the stuff in the house, but expected enough to cover her power bill for a few months. And by then, the altar in her field would have been sorted. Lillian crossed her fingers that there'd be a payout from the treasure fund, or whatever it was they called it. The sooner it was gone, the sooner she could get back on track with her plans. She'd give anything to see what the landscape had looked like before the Victorian improvements were made. And things had only worsened since then, with the almost complete obliteration of the natural landscape.

A hefty white van pulled into the yard, the mud splatter from the roads almost obscuring the fancy sign writing on the side - The Old Curiosity Shop. Driving the van was Nicole Pilcher, Paige's antiques dealer from London.

'Hello, thanks for coming by,' Lillian said to the woman standing on her rotting doorstep. Another thing to fix.

'What a fantastic place, it's like stepping back in time,' Nicole said.

Lillian tried not to flush under the woman's appraisal. The house wasn't exactly what the literature from the lawyer had said.

'It needs work... and that work costs,' Lillian replied, a smile touching the edges of her mouth. It was best to look for the silver lining, even if it cost a tonne of gold. Gold she didn't have.

'Renovations are the worst. They always uncover something you least expect,' Nicole agreed. 'In my case, it's usually work by Satan's second cousin once removed. The sort of tradesman who isn't up to date with his liability insurance and impossible to contact again.'

Lillian had to laugh. She'd experienced the same thing. English tradesmen were clearly as bad as New Zealand ones.

'Although in this case, I think Satan's henchmen haven't set foot in this house for a couple of centuries. Even the tap ware seems to be primordial.'

After the niceties of introductions were done, and a fortifying cup of tea offered, the women entered the farmhouse. There was no missing the gleam in her visitor's eyes as they walked through the entrance way into the kitchen. Perhaps there was more money in the contents of the house than she'd anticipated?

'You've got some lovely pieces,' Nicole said as she ran her hand over the dark oak of the hutch dresser in the kitchen.

'Almost nothing here is mine. I turned up with a couple of suitcases and a packing crate. It was... easier that way.'

The antiques dealer nodded, turning her attention to the crockery lining the shelves of the dresser.

'Do you know what you want to sell?'

'It's more a case of making space,' Lillian said.

'I can understand wanting to make it your own space,' Nicole replied. 'Paige said you'd inherited the farm, contents and all?'

'Contents and all is right. And most of it doesn't look like it's been used in years, so I certainly won't have any need of it.'

'That's completely understandable. Let's have tea first, and then you can take me on a tour to scope things out.'

'Are you driving back to London today? I didn't think to ask. You're welcome to stay?'

. . .

Nicole laughed. 'I'm here for a few days, staying in one of the Bellingham's completed rooms. I know they're not open for business yet, but Paige invited me. I think she's using me as a guinea pig, to figure out what works and what doesn't.'

Tea and biscuits consumed, they started making their way through the downstairs rooms, the antiques dealer detailing everything in a hardback notebook, as Lillian pointed out the few pieces she needed. The best thing about the exercise was that she had no emotional attachment to anything in the farmhouse. The most enthusiasm she could muster up was some appreciation for the size of the kitchen table, and the usefulness of the set of drawers in the bathroom. Apart from that, all the musty couches, layered in decades of cigarette smoke and dust, had no place in her home. The ladder-back chairs looked fabulous but were in equal parts uncomfortable and riddled with wood worm.

'I've moved a lot of things into the formal sitting room. It seemed like the best idea to keep everything contained. I felt like it was all trying to suffocate me,' Lillian said, pointing to a closed door at the end of the hall.

Lillian watched as Nicole opened the door, the ancient hinges squealing with misuse. The rasping sound of metal on metal couldn't disguise the sharp intake of breath as the London dealer stepped into the room stuffed to the gunnels with centuries of antiques from every era known to man.

'I don't think I brought enough cash with me,' Nicole said from the bowels of the room.

Lillian laughed. 'If you can get me through a few months of utility bills, that would suit me down to the ground. I just want it gone to be honest.'

She watched Nicole pick her way around the room, hands trailing over the furniture stacked back to back. She paused to lift the lid on an ebony-cased mantle clock before caressing a child's wooden sled.

'This is a treasure trove.'

· · ·

Whilst the farmhouse was old, Lillian needed a more minimalist life. There was enough on her plate without the burden of someone else's belongings.

'I'll leave you to have a good look through everything. I've got some papers I need to get onto, so I'll be in the kitchen if you need me.'

The manager of the Old Curiosity Shop didn't acknowledge her. She was immersed in a box of wooden pipes Lillian had cleared out of the various cabinets scattered around the house.

As Nicole entered the formal living room, a chill seemed to both rise up from the floor and seep through the walls, blanketing the room, tracing its icy fingers down her cheeks. She shivered, her hair standing on end. She almost stepped back through the open door to the warmth and comfort of the hall, but instead joked with Lillian about her lack of cash. It seemed to dissipate the heaviness in the room, and she took another step forward, and then another. Her breathing came easier now. It was just a change in atmosphere from the room being closed up, she reasoned with herself. Nothing more. Still, her hand brushed the tiny crucifix she wore at her throat. A christening gift from her beloved godmother.

Nicole settled into work, the otherworldly chill forgotten. This was heaven. Better than any market or car boot sale, this room alone would pay her wages for a month and restock the shop several times over. How could people bear to part with treasures like these? It never ceased to amaze her what people considered junk when in fact they were sought after antiques.

The room suffered from an overcast pall, with the light from the old-fashioned lamps barely touching the shadowy corners. Everywhere she turned, she saw profit. Profit in the shape of a copper bed pan, its turned wooden handle gleaming from decades of use. A chamberpot adorned with a decorative frog and some witty verse. Its two handles marked it as a wedding gift, and Nicole tried not to think about her former lover, her almost husband.

She knew she was better off without him, but sometimes the ache hit at the most inopportune time. Switching back to the job at hand she noted the details of the chamberpot. Only worth about four hundred pounds, its value lay more in its Instagrammability. The shop's followers would fall over themselves when she posted pictures of the verse and of the frog attempting to climb out of the piss-filled pot.

Cataloguing the room could have been overwhelming, there was so much in it, but it was a job she loved. Every day was like choosing from the lucky dip barrel at the local fête. You never knew what you were going to find. And sometimes, treasure could be found at the bottom of the barrel. Today, she didn't need to wait until she got to the bottom to find the treasure which would pay for the whole trip on its own.

'Oh,' Nicole said, her mouth a perfect 'O' in the gloomy room.

It was just as well Lillian was in the other room, as it gave Nicole time to savour her find. She was certain the woman had no idea of the value of the things in the room, which was in itself both good and bad. Bad because Nicole didn't want to scam her, but good because she could explain that the statue was valuable without letting on exactly how valuable it was. She'd allay her conscience somewhat by letting on its worth relative to everything else in the room. Maybe.

Nicole's hand caressed the pottery amphora. Late Roman, probably made in Italy, and about a metre in length. And in perfect condition. Nicole couldn't detect any chips or faults in the amphora's rim, but only an inspection under a strong light would show whether it was indeed perfect. Or, if it was a replica. It didn't feel like a replica. It had that certain roughness of the casting which oozed antiquity. With no faults, this would sell at the upper end of the market.

Nicole threw herself into the task, lost in her work until Lillian interrupted her just as she was counting the pieces of an ivory chess set to see if it was complete.

'Afternoon tea is ready,' Lillian said.

Nicole checked her watch. Time had flown. Closing her notebook, she zipped it into her satchel. So many times she'd nearly left it behind on a job, and nothing was more embarrassing that having to return to a fancy home to ask for her notebook back, especially after the potential client had turned down her offer.

'Thanks, I'm famished. I know it doesn't look like hard work, but my stomach disagrees,' Nicole joked.

The women sat at the kitchen table, talking of life in the country versus in the city, and of cities far away. And of family.

'What do you know of the family who lived here?' Nicole asked, wiping her mouth, a smear of strawberry jam sticky on her hand.

'I didn't even know they existed until the letter from the lawyer arrived saying that I was the sole remaining extended family.'

'So you know nothing at all?'

'When I arrived, it was as if the last owner had popped out for a pint. The beds were still laid, and his toiletries filled the bathroom. He must have been pretty low maintenance — still using an old cut-throat razor, and bars of carbolic soap. No aftershave or moisturiser,' Lillian laughed. 'A real man's man.'

'Have you still got the old razor? People collect those.'

'It'll be in a box in the sitting room. When I first arrived, I boxed up everything I didn't want from the master bedroom and the bathroom, and shoved it in there to be sorted later. I thought I'd sell it all online, but then I realised driving backwards and forwards to the post office was a nightmare. And that people on the internet were a nightmare. It was all far too hard, and much easier to get someone in like you, to take it all away.'

'I completely understand. It's a shame you don't know more about the family. Sometimes people like to know the provenance of things we sell. It also helps when I send certain things off to auction. The auction houses have tightened up on the chain of title. Not that that seems to be an issue here. There's a lifetime of belongings in there.'

'How much longer do you think you'll need, to go through everything?' Lillian asked.

Nicole watched Lillian's eyes stray to her wristwatch. No fancy all-encompassing internet connected watch, just a trusty old-fashioned thing that told the time.

'I can come back tomorrow if you've got things to do?' Nicole offered. Having a break might be good. It would give her time to do a little research on the things she'd already identified and had photographed.

'If it's not too much trouble. It's just that I've got to go into Newcastle, legal things. The bane of my life. There are some things the lawyer didn't quite make clear when I took over the property and now the rooks are home to roost, so to speak.'

Nicole took her leave, pleased with her decision to photograph everything as she went. She might not have finished today, but she could go over all the photos tonight and that would speed up the process tomorrow.

Nicole waved goodbye, and drove from the muddy yard. As she left, a weight lifted from her shoulders. And she couldn't help but touch her crucifix once more.

CHAPTER 25

BEGGARS CAN'T BE CHOOSERS

After her meeting at the Women's Horticultural Club, Jane Badrick slipped off her heels, replacing them with a pair of ballet flats. No one would notice, now that she was out of the public eye for the night. All she wanted to do was to drive home, have a bath, and fall into bed. She knew whose bed she'd rather be in, and it wasn't Matthew's. Oh, she enjoyed being his wife, but she also knew full well he was weak, whereas she had the power. She had all the ideas to move their dull little town forward. And what did he do? Played golf every Wednesday with the editor of the local newspaper and considered that more than enough networking for the week. If it wasn't for her, they would still be living in their postwar terraced house on the outskirts of Newcastle, and she'd still be working the reception counter at Drafford's Drapery. And despite living in an ostentatious house, with a fancy car, and plenty of time for manicures and hair appointments, she wanted more. She deserved more.

The ladies of the Women's Horticultural Club always held their meetings with servings of wine and cheese. Jane rarely imbibed with them, preferring better quality wine than the Tesco specials they served. But tonight she'd had more than one or two glasses. She remembered Pauline refilling her glass once.

Had Penny filled it again? Jane couldn't remember, but argued with herself that they were small glasses, hardly the equivalent of one of her beautiful crystal glasses at home.

Driving down the lane, Jane flicked on her high beam, the lack of street lighting as annoying as ever. The Dark Sky commitment of Northumberland was a thorn in her side, making them seem like backward savages to the rest of the country. When she was the local Member of Parliament, things would change. Jane grinned. Yes, that had an agreeable sound to it, Jane Badrick, the member for Hexham. She would be a better choice than the current musty Conservative.

Smugly ensconced in her dreams of unfettered power, Jane pressed her foot down, the powerful engine flinging her through the narrow streets. She rolled the new title around, trying out the words. They fit well. Her mind wandered to Matthew's reaction. Would he care? She'd have to tread carefully around his fragile male ego, although she'd been stroking it for years, knew which buttons to press, even though it turned her stomach more often than not these days. She certainly knew who didn't turn her stomach.

Jane took her eyes off the road to reach for her phone. When she looked back at the road, a figure stood in the middle of the lane. Jane screamed, wrenching the steering wheel hard to the left, slamming the brake.

On the still damp roadside soil, the tyres couldn't find purchase, and the heavy Land Rover clipped the stone wall, spinning the vehicle around where it clipped the wall a second time, scraping the vehicle's side, tearing the wing mirror from its bracket, shattering into thousands of slivers. The tiny pieces strewn across the road, reflecting the same number of twinkling stars above.

The airbags deployed, the powder turning Jane's dyed hair white, the revving engine obscenely loud on the empty road. Jane yanked the key from the ignition, the sudden silence a balm, and allowed herself a moment of pity, a minute to recover her senses. If she hit the man, her career would be over before it started. But only if anyone found out.

Clambering over the passenger seat, she prised open the damaged door, half falling into the lane.

'Hello?' She coughed from the stench of leaking fuel.

Silence filled the lane.

Jane picked her way over shattered glass and fragments of her near-new car. If she could drive it home without being stopped, she could claim some thief had stolen it. There would be no breath testing, no police involvement. The insurance company would believe the story of a miscreant taking the car for an illegal spin in the night. But where was the man? Her heart racing, she checked the ditches on either side of the lane. Empty.

'Hello? Are you there?'

A faint moaning.

Jane's heart sank, bile rising in her throat. *No, no, no.*

Glass crunched like ice on the road as she moved towards the sound. The temperature plummeting the closer she got, icy fingers of wind sliding over her neck and bare arms. She'd left her jacket in the car. There was no need for the extra layers with the heated seats but it shouldn't be this cold.

The figure of a man materialised in the ditch, curled into a ball, his shapeless figure providing no means of identification. What if he knew her? Jane couldn't have put into words the dark thoughts crowding her mind. Evil seeped from every pore, the scent on her skin reminiscent to that of an ancient battlefield, a foul stench hanging from her the way a snake sloughs its skin.

Bending towards the man, she shook his shoulder. Strong, muscular. Still.

'Can you hear me? Are you hurt? Can you sit up?' Her questions thick and fast, like a swarm of bees disturbed from the work, buzzing and humming, zipping faster and faster. 'Who are you? What were you doing?' Jane's face lit up as an idea bloomed. 'Did you make me crash on purpose? How dare you,' Jane said, her voice shrill, her pitch akin to that of a screaming medieval fishwife.

The man rolled to his side. Clad in a rough-spun tunic, his muscular legs were bare apart from leather sandals on his feet. Not a local accountant then.

Jane rocked backwards. A homeless man. Spinning her head from side to side, as if expecting to be set upon by his accomplices.

. . .

This must be a con. She'd read about things like this happening. Done to blackmail the witless driver.

'Get away from me,' she screamed, stumbling towards her car.

No answer from the man on the ground, although he'd pushed himself into a sitting position, his outstretched leg bent at an unnatural angle.

He muttered something unintelligible, sending Jane further away.

'Stay away!' she screamed. He would ruin everything she'd worked so hard for. The positions on boards, the trusteeships, the committees she chaired.

Jane clambered back into her car, her hands shaking as she tried sliding the key back into the ignition. The engine turned over, reluctantly spluttering into life. The enormous engine roaring like a panther on the empty roadside. With her foot on the accelerator, the car jerked forward, metal panels scraping against the ancient stone stolen from the wall centuries earlier.

Backing up, she sat panting, knuckles whitening on the steering wheel. Jane pulled the seatbelt over her shoulder, listening for the click, her decision made with no other option open to her. With no action, her life would be over.

Jane slammed her foot down on the pedal. The car lurched forward, gathering speed in the narrow lane, the tyres kicking up stones and dirt and tiny mirrored slivers of glass. A thousand reflections of the horror in her heart. She slammed into the man in the ditch.

No one would miss a homeless beggar.

Jane woke to find herself sinking into the spongy earth, waterlogged and churned up by dozens of horses coming and going. Not that she knew that. She knew nothing other than that she was cold and hungry. And angry. More than angry. Incandescent with rage.

The darkness of the night was complete. Unbroken by street lights or the subtle glow of Newcastle far away on the horizon. Another power cut.

This would never have happened if she were in parliament. She should have stood for election years ago instead of listening to her husband, who'd counselled against it. What a waste of oxygen he'd turned out to be.

Where were her shoes? Handmade by a Cordwainer in London, they'd cost a fortune. Jane checked her hair and found a handful of twigs and leaves. What the hell was going on here? How did she end up on the ground?

She checked her pockets for her phone, worried that she'd left it in her handbag or on the hands-free dock in her car. Memories slipped back, like shadows in the night. Shapeless, lacking substance. Jane tried to remember. She'd crashed, but had she walked away from her car, or had someone pulled her out? Jane ran her tongue over her lips, her signature pink lipstick long gone, and the sour taste of fermented grapes heavy in her mouth. She'd been at a meeting. There'd been a glass of wine or two. She'd changed into flat shoes to drive home. Had it only been two glasses? No, she was sure she wasn't over the limit. She knew her capacity for wine. And there'd been nibbles. Bad ones, but she'd eaten at the meeting. Terrible sausage rolls, barely cooked in the middle. They'd probably all come down with food poisoning tonight. Why was she in such a state? She'd only had it done at the hairdressers that morning. Her weekly appointment. In her role, she had to look the part, and she knew no one resented her for that. Oh, jealousy was an evil beast, she knew that.

Her heart skipped a beat. There'd been a man. A tiny gasp escaped her lips. Playing possum in her headlights. She couldn't be sure that she'd... but Jane knew what she'd done, just couldn't verbalise it. If she didn't admit it to herself, it never happened, and no one, not even the best detectives of Scotland Yard, could get her to say otherwise. She prided herself on her ability to lie under pressure. It had stood her in good stead all her life, and it wouldn't let her down now.

Jane tried orientating herself. The absence of light pollution threw her. So this is what the environmentalists had meant when they'd pushed that idiotic dark skies idea through? Begrudgingly, she had to admit that the star-filled sky was a sight she could fall in love with.

. . .

Once she stood as a member of parliament, she might reveal her support for the dark sky movement. That might win her some votes from the greenies.

A sound came from behind.

'Hello?'

No answer, but the sound stopped. If it was one of those destructive moles, she'd scream. They were as bad as the rabbits and the rabid foxes which got into the bins every week. Why on earth they'd ever voted on a fox hunting ban was beyond her.

A shuffling sound to her left. Jane swung around.

'Who's there? Show yourself,' Jane demanded. She may be in a field, her hair in disarray and missing her shoes, but she wouldn't let some homeless grifter sneak up on her without giving him a thousand barbs from her wicked tongue.

Her brave thoughts vanished as an arm snaked around her throat and a hand clamped down against her mouth. She fell to the ground, too shocked to struggle or scream. Her attacker pressed a practiced hand against her neck and the dark night was consumed by the blackest of black, as total paralysis followed.

The mayor emerged from her enforced sleep as groggy as a drunk after a bottle of rum and half a dozen vodka chasers. The soot scented air was as foreign to her as the shape of the room she found herself in. Earthen floors, brush walls, an open fire surround by polished river stones. The rustic wooden furniture against the rounded walls seemed better suited to the set of a fantasy film than the home of any Hexham ratepayer.

Jane tried clearing her throat, her lips tender against her teeth. She gagged against the metallic taste of blood. With the effort of years of dealing with incompetent people, she slowed the panic welling up. Panic wouldn't help. She needed to calm down, analyse the situation, and take control.

With her heart rate returning to normal, she studied at her surroundings with a clearer mind.

A *hovel* was the only word she could summon. A rough sleeper who had made their camp in one of the protected thickets which peppered the county. Was it that filthy librarian man who'd given her so much trouble? Was this where he lived?

At least he hadn't tied her up. She swung her legs over the side of the cot she'd woken in. Covered with a coarse woollen blanket, it looked like it belonged in a museum, not a home. Cheap camp stretchers were available at most supermarkets, so there was no need to sink to this level of barbaric living.

Jane strained to hear anything beyond the room. The fire had fallen low, the flames licking at a charred log. It would need more wood soon or it would die out. Which meant she didn't have long before whomever had brought her here came back.

The doorway was nothing more than a flap of smooth leather, and Jane stood for a moment behind the leather door, slowing her breathing as she built up the courage to look outside.

She tugged the flap aside, and daylight filled the room. It wasn't the illumination of the inside of the hovel which shocked her, but more the number of identical huts gathered outside, like round conical hats, each with a puff of grey smoke emerging from their thatched roofs.

If someone had yelled 'Action' at the precise moment, it would have felt real. But no one did. No one yelled anything. The people outside seemed oblivious to her existence. They stood in small groups, or hurried past, with bundles in their arms and packs on their backs. Horses scuffed the ground in a secure pen nearby, and murderous looking javelin-like weapons leaned against the sides of every hut.

Jane let the flap fall closed and took a step back to consider the scene outside.

She should leave. She should just slip outside when everyone was busy looking elsewhere, and make her way back to the road, and flag down the first car, regardless of what she looked like. Or was she dreaming? Jane shook her head. The sky outside had such a strange cast to it she could be dreaming. Perhaps the accident was worse than she remembered?

Her illusions were shattered when a grizzled hand flung open the flap, and a mountain of a man folded himself into the room.

Standing in front of her, his hands on his hips and a smile exposing a mouth half full of teeth, it was clear that this man was not the Indian librarian. Not by a long shot.

Jane stood her ground, refusing to quaver under the man's distasteful gaze. By habit, her hands went to her head, smoothing the blonde hair. The knotted leaves and twigs which had adorned it the night before were gone. She tugged her blouse down; the material marred by the dirt from the field, but still recognisable as silk. Jane ignored her bare feet. At least her last pedicure had been recent enough that there was no embarrassment in that department.

'Who are you?' she asked, arms crossed against her chest.

'Bricius. You honour us with your presence.'

Jane covered her confusion at the strange vowel sounds and his effusive welcome.

'Why am I here?'

The man looked puzzled.

Jane tried again. 'Why am I here, in this… this room? This village?'

'We saved you from the Roman soldiers. They would have had your head on their spikes.'

'The Roman what?'

'The invaders. We are far away from there now. It was close. But the honour of saving you is ours. The druids foretold it.'

'What?' Jane returned to the cot, her eyes watering in the smoky confines of the room, her head spinning. The assault of the man's odour, the fire, the thatch, the leather, the filthy blanket, the bare earth. The room spun around her, and it was only with a superhuman effort that Jane stopped herself from fainting. A woman like her didn't faint. Or show weakness. Regardless of the story he was spinning, she was still better than him, and the people outside this hovel, and the man knew it. Admitted as much.

The haunting sound of an eagle-like scream outside the room broke the stalemate in the room, and the man looked towards the door, uncertainly written all over his broad face.

'That sound, was it a signal? It wasn't an eagle,' Jane said. She may not know much about what was going on right now, but her husband was an avid falconer, and bird sounds she knew.

The man's face was a sight to be seen. Here was someone she could utilise.

'A signal, yes. The age of the Roman invaders is almost over. We will reign darkness upon them at dawn.'

'Yes, of course. Their time is over,' Jane said, playing for time. Time for what, she didn't know, but she had to work out a way to play this situation to her advantage. Clearly deranged, she assumed he lived in a commune, which had evaded the authorities, probably claiming the unemployment benefit, which riled her up more than anything else.

'You will ride with us, with your iron horse.'

'My what?'

'Your iron horse. We couldn't bring it. But at dawn, with you and your bast, the land will echo with the sounds of our triumph.'

Jane couldn't fathom what he was talking about, so shot him a benevolent smile and pondered her next move.

'Shoes. I'll need shoes,' she said, pointing to her feet.

Bricius slapped his head, and rushed from the hovel, once again leaving Jane on her own. Perhaps now was the time to make her escape and then close this filthy camp once and for all.

Jane crept to the leather flap and pulled it aside, ignoring the ravenous hunger gnawing at her insides. She'd kill for a wine.

The groups of people outside had dissipated, leaving one faceless man tending to the horses, and another strapping bundles of twigs together with twine.

It was now or never. Eyes bright, darting every which way, Jane darted from the entranceway, turning right, hugging the mud covered sides of the small building, her toes curling at the ground's texture underfoot. She couldn't recall the last time she'd walked barefoot anywhere, at least not since she was a child, and probably not even then. She'd been raised properly, unlike the heathen in the poorer parts of town. Hers was a childhood of plenty, with leather shoes and nannies and holidays abroad.

She paused at the back of the hovel. Not so much paused, but stopped, her mouth agape. This was not a dream, or a film set or a squatters' camp. Jane wanted to believe that what she saw was a dream, or a hallucination.

But the stones stabbing into her soft heels and the sounds of bird-calls and the shouts of men were as real as the bored housewives were at the meeting she'd attended last night. Could it only have been last night?

'Will these do?'

Jane spun around to see Bricius standing behind her, a pair of tooled leather sandals in one hand, and a lethal-looking staff in the other.

She stammered out a reply before regaining her composure and nodding at the sandals.

'Perfect, thank you.'

The man leaned his staff against the wall, and knelt before her, fitting the sandals around her feet. His touch a far cry from his rough appearance. Jane flexed her feet and took a tentative step. As comfortable as the shoes she'd lost. They'd do. They weren't the height of fashion, but she'd come to the realisation that she wouldn't be seeing anyone she knew here, not in this time.

'Are you the chieftain of this, this clan?' she tried, although realised her error as soon as the words were out of her mouth. No chieftain would ever have lowered himself to fit a pair of shoes on a woman's foot, regardless of her iron horse.

Bricius had paled, and she noticed him shaking his head. For whatever reason, they considered her magical, so she had to stop making stupid statements lest she shatter their illusion.

'Take me to him,' she demanded, and turned back to face the vast group of warriors amassed in the grassy meadow behind the round houses. More men than they had in Hexham. Hell, more men than she'd ever seen gathered in one place before, save at a football final in one of the big London stadiums.

The large man bowed his head and slipped past Jane into the melee of men swathed in sweat coated with an undercurrent of fear. The men parted like Moses parting the Red Sea. If they'd been wearing hats, Jane imagined them doffing them differentially as she passed. This was the way to be treated. This was her due. Her destiny.

'Our chieftain, Gar.'

. . .

Even without Bricius pointing Gar out, Jane would have been able to identify the chieftain in a heartbeat. The man oozed charisma and power. His bearing did more to show his level of command than his clothes, which, although they were fine, were as similar to those worn by Bricius, that they may have come from the same wardrobe.

'Ah, the witch. The druids told us of your coming, so I must trust that your appearance only brings good luck to our battle.'

Witch? For a moment Jane's memory flashed back to the English witch trials and the various iterations of the Witchcraft Act, which was only repealed in 1951, after her namesake, Jane Yorke, was convicted under the same Act in 1944 for 'pretending...to cause the spirits of deceased persons to be present'.

'You think I'm a witch?'

'But of course. You arrived on your iron horse, which refuses to budge without your power to make it so. We will return you to your beast before we begin battle, so that you may ride beside me, as the druids foretold. Do you doubt your own power now, witch?'

Jane struggled to comprehend what they meant when they referred to her iron horse, but standing on the rise with the chieftain, surrounded by men who looked up at her through hooded nervous eyes, she realised they must be referring to her car. Her Land Rover. Her iron horse. And she laughed.

Her laughter rang out across the meadow, echoing in the unsullied air, bouncing off taut leather shields and bands of silver adorning the heads of the men. This was her moment, and she would seize it with both hands the same way fate had seized her, thrusting her into this time and place. Her parents had scoffed at her history degree, pleased only when she'd married a man they considered suitable. Or above her station, as her mother had told her on more than one occasion. Although she'd been bred for just a betrothal, her mother couldn't let go of her own small island roots. After her marriage, her degree lost all relevance. An aberration her father had funded to furnish her with a husband befitting his social standing. Here she was, at the birth of England's independence, knowing the outcome before it begins, and she was going to relish every moment of it.

CHAPTER 26

MISSING

On a short walk to clear her mind, Lillian sucked in the night air. Could there be anywhere more beautiful than the Northumberland countryside?

A car screamed around the corner, its powerful engine revving higher than the manufacturer's recommendations. A solitary figure sat behind the wheel, the dim glow of the driver's cellphone illuminating the interior as the car shot down the lane, spewing stones clipped from the overgrown verge.

Lillian froze. The driver of the beast was Badger's mother, and at the speed she was going, it was more than likely she wasn't getting home in one piece. Should she ring Badger to say his mother was driving like a lunatic? She hesitated, but closed her phone. It wasn't her problem. She had enough to worry about.

As Lillian walked further down the road, there was no sign of Mrs Badrick or her car. The night was silent, and although the roar of the engine had faded to nothing, the nightlife hadn't yet ventured out. Perhaps there was no nightlife anymore? A sea of grass tended by flocks of sheep and herds of dull cattle had stripped the countryside of its unique flora and fauna, leaving a literal desert in their wake.

. . .

This is what she wanted to reverse, in her own peculiar way. A tiny drop in the ocean of climate change.

That hum again, louder this time. Lillian flashed her torch up the road, swinging it from side to side. A rhythmic cadence of feet marching in step filled the night air. Lillian shrank back, stuffing her phone deep into her bag. She couldn't face meeting any more members of the local community, especially not tonight. There must be some local Air Cadet unit nearby. She'd wait until they'd passed, then she'd ring Badger for a lift home, maybe.

The sound of boots grew louder, but the absence of chatter made the disciplined crunch sound unnatural. Lillian crouched down to avoid being silhouetted against the low farm wall.

The hum in her ears increased, as if an army of crickets had invaded her skull. Lillian closed her eyes and held her hands against her ears, grimacing as the noise invaded her head. The road vibrated underfoot and she opened her eyes, expecting to see a ragtag squad of teenage Air Cadets. But as her eyes focused, her brain tried telling her that what she was seeing wasn't real. It couldn't be real.

Hundreds of men dressed as Roman soldiers marched in unison behind the impressive sight of cavalrymen riding highly decorated horses. The staccato of their hooves guiding the army into town.

With her hands clamped over her mouth lest she make the smallest of sounds, Lillian shrank into the stubby undergrowth. The men were so close she could almost reach out and touch them. How could they not see her? She must be going mad, and others had called her worse than that. Roman soldiers on a pissy little farm road in the heart of Northumberland. Possibly a training exercise for some event, re-enactors practicing for their big day?

A shout sent a ripple of excitement ran through the soldiers, hand-in-hand with nervous chatter.

Lillian flinched at the shout, straining to see what had caught their attention as the soldier's heads swivelled in unison towards the sound. She could see nothing beyond the inky blackness.

As one of the centurions walked his horse past Lillian's hiding place, the horse's nostrils flared, and he skittered away, receiving a sullen rebuke from his rider.

The hum in her ears so loud now that Lillian couldn't hear what the rider said. She returned her attention to the soldiers filing past, some of whom appeared wounded, some helmet-less or with their arms swathed in bloody bandages.

A soldier cried out, crumpling to the ground in front of her. Followed by another, and another. Then chaos. Shouting, screaming, yelling. Their deaths were real, as real as the shoes on her feet or the earth under her.

Everywhere she looked, men were dying, overrun by an unseen enemy. A soldier, younger than Lillian, stumbled into the ditch beside her, dropping his sword and clutching at his stomach. At that moment, the slumbering clouds shifted, allowing the moonlight to illuminate the abject horror on the young man's face as realisation dawned that death waited for him on this foreign soil.

Lillian crawled towards him as he fruitlessly tried holding his stomach together.

'It'll be okay,' she whispered, reaching out for his hand.

It was only the briefest of touches, but enough for his eyes to widen. She imagined he thought he was hallucinating as she squeezed his blood-slicked hand and watched him try to speak.

'Don't talk,' she said, holding a finger to his lips, not that anyone could have heard them over the noise of the fight.

Another shout, a battle cry, with dozens of men taking up the chant, the ground rumbling beneath their cries. Lillian cowered in the roadside ditch, watching them fight their invisible foe, whilst holding the hand of the dying soldier.

The Romans were losing, men falling faster than she could count. One after another, they were stabbed and pummelled, decapitated and impaled. It seemed that their assailant had a never-ending supply of weapons, and no matter how hard the Romans fought back, nothing could save them from the slaughter.

Then the unmistakable sound of a motor vehicle barrelling straight towards the battle. The car's headlights picking out the glint of brass on the uniforms, flashes of red on the battered shields. Mrs Badrick. As she drove through the soldiers, the image shattered like a rock hurled into a frozen pond.

Jolted back to reality, the soldiers disappeared, leaving no sign of their existence. Almost no sign. As Lillian opened her hand, the hand which had been holding the blood-stained hand of a dying soldier, she found a tiny carved figure.

The figure was reminiscent of a woman, but with an overly elongated face and a distended belly.

The figure grew heavy in her hand, weighted down by the soul of the soldier. How many other lives had it seen? How many more lives would it outlive? Hers? Almost without thought, Lillian slipped the figure into her pocket and wiped the tacky blood from her hands. But regardless of how many times she wiped her hands on her trousers, or on the dew-damp grass, she couldn't wash away the feeling of the imaginary soldier's blood on her hands. For that's what he must have been. Imaginary.

Lillian looked down the lane towards the disappearing taillights of Badger's mum's car. Where had she been and why was she in such a hurry? Surely she must have seen the soldiers? They'd blanketed the road and the paddocks on either side. Lillian picked her way across the road to peer into the field beyond. The moonlight showed nothing that wasn't there before. A barren field, devoid of anything other than the sturdy inbreed sheep, snatching wary glances towards her in between mouthfuls of grass.

She was losing her mind. If she admitted as much to anyone, they'd send her to a shrink. She didn't want a doctor prying into her deepest thoughts and memories. She wanted to forget about everything she'd seen and experienced, and just go home.

CHAPTER 27

A ROLL OF THE DICE

Pramod Sharma sipped his tea and listened to the chatter swirling around the cafe. The missing mayor was the only topic on everyone's lips. Whilst he had no love for the woman and her caustic tongue and helmet shaped hair, he'd never wished harm on her.

From his corner of the Mooreeffoc Coffee Room, he overheard Gail Revell lamenting the loss of her friend, her theories of what had happened to Jane Badrick growing wilder with every passing minute.

'Her car is nowhere to be found. Only her handbag and her shoes. And I can tell you, she loved those shoes. Tods from London, hand-made. She'd never have left them. They were her pride and joy.'

'I thought they found her car?' someone asked.

'Only parts of it. The rest is probably in a container on its way to the Continent. What if they have sold her as a sex slave?'

Her audience murmured in shock, but Sharma knew, categorically, that their illustrious mayor wasn't in a shipping container on her way to the highest bidder. It was worse than that.

Shuffling from his hidden corner, he waved goodbye to the girl behind the counter before making his way out to the street, his fingers forging furrows into the ancient journal's leather cover. The journal whose words had changed since he'd last read them.

Something was wrong with the timeline. He had to go back.

Sharma double checked that the lock on the door, before weaving back through the towers of books to his bedroom.

Flexing his fingers, he rubbed at the loose flesh on his arms. The cold weather made the aching worse, and no amount of woollen scarves or hot water bottles ever chased it away completely.

The room boasted no windows or creature comforts. It had a desk — covered in piles of books, a tattered armchair — found abandoned on the side of the road and painstakingly lugged back to the church, a footstool to accompany the armchair; this he'd procured from the church itself, left tucked under a stairwell by a reverend long forgotten by the parish; and a bed — a narrow single bed topped with a pile of blankets and soft pillows. For this was Pramod's home. He suspected Apple knew, but trusted her to keep his secret.

When he'd lost his job at the local library, he'd lost his home. With no income to pay his mortgage, they had forced him to sell. But the market was sluggish, and he'd come out of the deal with little more than he'd put in, and no spare cash to rent. Like so many other men his age, he'd become homeless through no fault of his own. Being home-less and penniless wasn't foreign to him. He'd survived in the past, and would do so again, although at this age it had been harder. And then a chance conversation at a church-hosted supper club lead to the saving of the books and the saving of his life. The pastor didn't know Pramod lived in this tiny room, or if he did, he turned a blind Christian eye to the fact. But Pramod knew the hearts of men, so kept himself to himself, rarely leaving the hall at night. During the day, he happily attended to his chores using his meagre pension money, eating his main meal at lunch at the local cafe, spiriting back enough food for dinner and breakfast — food which didn't need refrigeration. The pastor may have turned a blind eye to his living conditions, but the excess consumption of electricity wouldn't make it past the parish council — hence, no refrigerator or hot showers. But then, hot showers were a modern luxury. He'd gone years without them before...

Pulling a wooden trunk from beneath his bed, he lowered himself cross-legged onto the floor. He closed his wrinkled eyes for a moment before opening the lid. The aroma of old leather and spice filled the air, and Pramod wiped away a tear as memories from the past pierced his ancient mind.

He couldn't open his eyes, not yet — the pain was too much to bear, with the scents of his past dredging up the hurt he'd buried beneath the books he lived amongst.

Unable to delay reality any longer, Pramod opened his eyes and peered into the trunk, his gnarled hands holding onto the sides as if his life depended upon it. It was true. His life rested on the contents, but it wasn't only his life at stake. There was something about the girl Apple brought. An aura he alone could feel, one he'd been waiting for. There'd been so many signs lately that time had become unreliable. His control was slipping. He still didn't understand why the gods had chosen him — a nobody. A simple carver from a small coastal village near Arikamedu in southern India.

Pramod curled nine of his fingers into his palms. The missing tenth digit was a daily reminder of the perils of his life. For it was not a life he'd chosen, but one bestowed upon him by the gods. The purpose of which he was still trying to fathom, but time was running out. Age was a weapon life was using against him. Life, or some other power only the goddess Pavarti herself understood?

He considered the contents of the trunk. Each time he travelled, he lost a little more of himself. Too far back, and he might not return. Too recent, and the travel would have been in vain. He'd spent the past week checking every history book he could find. The internet was next to useless. Fools populated the internet with flat-earth theories and moon-landing conspiracies, muddying the value of everything, leaving nothing trustworthy. The keyboard warriors would have you believe Shakespeare wrote his Julius Caesar play based on firsthand experience, or that Marilyn Monroe was living in the Rose Haven Retirement Home in Florida with Elvis. But a book, a book you could trust; peer reviewed by other experts in the field, with references and appendices. And Pramod had a mountain of them. But of course, the Romans wrote none of them.

None gave the exact dates when the Iceni attacked. It was all very well having snippets of ink tablets detailing the number of soldiers with eye infections, but the tablets never mentioned the lighting of signal fires on the night when near on a thousand men lost their lives. They didn't describe the smell of burning flesh and decaying bodies, the cries of the soldiers slaughtered in the dark, with only the crimson light of the signal fires to illuminate the scene. Nothing on the internet or in the museums or contained within the pages of a thousand thesis could accurately date the night of the attack at Ithaca Fort. Only the contents of Pramod's wooden trunk told the true tale.

Pramod gingerly lifted a carved bone cup from its resting place, its contents rattling loudly. Unwinding his legs, he slowly stood. To roll the dice now would return him to a past, where offerings to Pavarti would be of no use. It was a different god he needed to appeal to for guidance and protection. He threw his eyes once more to the article on the front page of the Hexham Herald, an article accompanied by a large photograph of an altar dedicated to Jupiter Optimus Maximus. An altar he knew intimately.

Hands shaking, he set the bone cup on the table and pulled out a second article from the trunk — a soldier's tunic, battle worn and bloodstained. It had served its former owner well, its thick leather banding saving his life on more than one occasion, except for the last time. Which is how it came to be Pramod's possession. He hesitated to use it now, for fear of being catapulted back into the maelstrom which had taken the life of the tunic's owner. A man he loved like a brother. There had never been a friendship of its equal. But desperate times called for desperate measures. Pramod had wasted so many of his chances, trying to go back to a time where he could save his friend. But now he had to return, to save more than just one man. He had to save the future.

Pramod laid the tunic on top of the newspaper and next to the cup, trying not to look at the rent in the fabric where a short sword had slain his friend. That moment replayed itself in his mind every night, no matter which century he was in, or who he was with. It was the nightmare he lived every night.

. . .

Taking up the cup, he shook it once, and tipped its contents onto the tunic, eight dun-coloured wooden dice spilling from the cup, coming to rest against the image of the altar.

Time froze.

The ancient dice showed mirror images of each other — all were sixes.

A familiar pain sliced through his head and he fell backwards onto the bed, the tunic clasped in his hands. And then? Nothing. Only the rumpled bedclothes showed any sign of where Pramod had lain. The empty room fell silent.

CHAPTER 28

THE BEATING HEART

Waking took longer every time, and Pramod struggled to emerge into his new reality. Had he calculated correctly? Was there time for him to stop the damage? He knew she did not know what she was doing, but the risk existed that she could open the world to the wrath of the Roman empire. He knew firsthand the risks and had sacrificed everything to save the world once. He would do it again.

Early winter had its clutches firmly on the land, with the wind ripping leaves from the autumnal trees, tearing at his exposed skin with its icy fingers. Pramod stumbled in the darkness, sensing more than seeing his way to the fort. He knew to keep to the shadows, hiding not only from the Roman sentries but from the barbarians who slithered about the land like the mist blanketing the floor of the valley.

Pramod smelt the settlement before he saw it, the foetid stench of open drains and hobbled livestock assailing him as he crept closer, the quiet murmurs of the Roman guards guiding him in the darkness. Interpreting their rough tongue took time. It had been too long since he'd last heard the guttural mixture of Britannic Latin.

The guards were uneasy. In different times, they would have joked with each other and played at dice as they whiled away their shift at the furthermost reaches of the empire. But not tonight.

Something had them on edge. Pramod strained for any sight or sound of danger.

As he waited, he watched for any deviation from their patrol pattern. They'd barely moved from the gateway to the village. The fort stood closed as tightly as a miser's purse, but the village had no such defences, relying on the might of the Roman army squatting mere feet away from the butchers and bakers and leatherworkers and ladies of ill repute who serviced the fort. It would be easy enough to slip into the village another way, but time was short. If he took too long, then the soldiers and the villagers would have more to worry about than one elderly Indian man limping his way into an unimportant village at the arse end of nowhere.

A shout cried out in the stillness, echoing off the heather-clad hills. The guards jumped as if attacked by a swarm of hornets.

With their attention on the inky hillside, Pramod slipped into the village, disappearing between the narrow stone buildings, stumbling on the uneven paving. He had one task to achieve, a task which would save the future. A future the girl might unwittingly ruin.

Unsurprisingly, only the guards seemed worried about the cry from the hillside. No one stirred amongst the inhabitants of the village, allowing Pramod to duck and weave through his old haunt. The last time he was here, he was much younger, and fitter and stronger, his skin much more accustomed to the biting cold of the North, acclimatised by years of servitude. Now he puffed with exertion. His sense of direction told him he had one more street to go, but since his last visit, the village had grown, spilling from its banks, swallowing the pasture and open space he remembered. Now the populace lived cheek-to-jowl, with barely any room for simple childhood games.

But the door he needed was the same. He hesitated before knocking. His sudden appearance had the potential to cause panic and confusion. But would there be dire repercussions? He couldn't be sure, but he hoped his instincts were correct and that the woman behind the door would let him in. That she'd hear him out and help him. If only for the love they'd once shared.

Pramod knocked softly. The home was used to nighttime callers.

. . .

The door swung open, and Pramod entered without announcing himself. There was no need. He was home.

'Tell your mistress I am here,' he said to the bleary-eyed man who'd admitted him.

The man disappeared, and lights appeared from deeper in the house as lanterns were lit, and they summoned his host.

As Pramod waited, he slid the door back into place, wedging the security bar into place. Unexpected visitors would be a distraction neither of them needed tonight.

'Yes?' came a voice from behind a lantern.

Pramod's nerves stayed his tongue. He swallowed. 'Metella?'

'Step into the light,' the woman said, swinging the lantern towards Pramod.

Pramod stepped forward, his aged body forgotten. In his mind, he exuded the young muscled slave he'd once been.

'Do I know you?' Metella said.

Pramod's bubble evaporated. He was nothing more than an octogenarian, only alive in this time because he hadn't lived it. No one reached his advanced years, not this close to the edge of the empire. Only the cosseted wealthy in Rome had the benefit of longevity, the few who weren't poisoned or murdered in their sleep.

'Not as you see me now. But, yes. And I know you. I know who it is you pray to in your hidden shrine. The old gods you hide from the outside world. The gods who even the druids fear crossing.'

'Who are you?'

'Someone you met in another lifetime, long since gone. Whether you choose to believe that is between you and your gods, but I have returned to warn you that soon one will come who will tear apart all that we know. All that you and I have experienced. All that you protect,' he whispered, his voice as smooth as the oil in the lamp.

If Metella had felt any fear of his words, she hid it well; her hooded eyes disguising her thoughts.

'Your riddles are too much for the night,' she scoffed. 'You speak of things you cannot understand; of things which fill the imaginations of men but which have no truth.'

· · ·

You are too old to desire what I offer, but you shall have a bed, and we will talk further when the sun has risen.'

Pramod protested. 'You must believe me. We have to stop hell from being unleashed.' But she'd vanished back into the bowels of the building, abandoning him. As he made to follow, the slave restrained him easily, his bulky hand on Pramod's shrivelled arm. How can she dismiss him so easily? The morning may not even come for them. Or if they were lucky, they would have one more day. Could they live life in a day? He felt so old and utterly useless, and the grief for his youth overwhelmed him as Metella's slave showed him to a bed, where he sank into despair, reliving the lifetimes he had lived, and loved, and lost.

CHAPTER 29
FROZEN IN TIME

The mind is a powerful but under-utilised tool, and Pramod used every fibre of his being to send signals from his brain to his fingers, urging them to move, to connect, to do anything. The rough fibres of the blanket tickled the inside of his wrist. He could feel that, but could no more move his hand than he could reach the moon.

'Metella?' he tried, his voice no louder than the wings of a moth.

No answer. From beyond the doorway came the murmur of voices, but they were too far away to hear his pitiful mewls. Pramod tried again, calling out to the only woman he'd loved.

Pramod had suspected that the debilitating headaches he suffered after every trip through time would be his downfall. They'd been getting worse, which was why he'd curtailed his trips back to see Metella, only making this last trip when the pain of missing her had consumed him more than the threat of the torturous headaches. That, and a chilling warning he'd stumbled across in the collier's journal.

Then his life changed. Nothing he'd read anywhere else seemed to corroborate the eerie warning of a disruption to time. He'd reached out to Neumegan for advice, but his friend wasn't always in this time, so he'd left a message for him and had returned to save Metella, and to save the future. But now he feared he would be too late.

Pramod Sharma watched the surrounding activity, the smoke stinging his eyes. For the hundredth time, he tried raising his hand to wipe away the smarting. Pramod couldn't move. Even wrapping his uneven lips around the warning he needed to share proved impossible. It was as though they had entombed him in a bed of concrete. Pramod tried moistening his lips with his heavy tongue, but couldn't.

In a tomb of nothingness, he screamed into the empty void, unheard by the bustling activity at Metella's brothel.

At least his ears still worked, even if time had frozen everything else. The sweet sound of female voices filtered through to his brain.

The voices came closer.

'Hello, old man.'

That voice he knew, Metella.

'What? You have no tricky words for me today? You got your bed, and now you're done with me, is that it?'

No, he wanted to scream, staring up into her painted face. A tear trickled from his eye, and Metella leaned forward, wiping it from his cheek with a perfumed finger.

'Tears? For what, I wonder? For your youth? Your lies? Get up, old man. This bed pays for the food we eat, and unless you have coin to pay for your lodgings, you can be on your way.'

Pramod didn't move, he couldn't. He tried screaming, but some foul magic constricted his throat. No, not magic, he knew magic. A stroke. Struck down by a foe far worse than any savage barbarian. There would be no medical salvation. No emergency surgery to repair the bleeding in his brain. He would die here in a brothel on the outskirts of the Roman empire.

Metella changed as understanding flashed across her face.

'Oh, you poor man,' she said, her head tilting to the side. A habit Pramod had once loved, likening her to a swallow, listening for its mate. She had once been his mate, in an alternative timeline.

'Send for the healer,' Metella ordered a nearby girl.

. . .

As the child scurried off, Metella settled herself on a stool beside the bed, rearranging her heavy skirt around her legs. Taking the old man's hand in hers, she spoke.

'It cannot have been good tidings you brought with you last night. You tried warning me of something, but what? I haven't lasted this long without heeding the omens as they appear. But last night you caught me unawares...'

Metella drifted off into her own hazy world, a world filled with broken promises and secrets whispered beneath the stars. The stars knew her heart, but what about this man? Had it not only been a week ago when she'd spent time with the seer, hearing her future, seeing it laid out at the foot of the altar? Metella cursed herself for tempting the fates. She stroked the man's wrinkled hand, tracing the lines on his palm with her nail. Lines that felt so familiar.

'You're a fool, Metella,' she whispered to herself.

If the statue-like man in the bed heard her, he gave no acknowledgment, and for that she was grateful. She would not tempt the fates again by speaking aloud her thoughts.

A fuss in the outside hallway heralded the arrival of the healer. Better than most, his patients recovered instead of dying. Most healers she knew had more success killing their patients than they did healing them, which is the only reason she ever allowed Gattus into her premises.

'A little older than your normal clients, Metella,' Gattus joked, joining her at the bedside.

'Not a client, an old friend,' Metella replied, gently squeezing Pramod's hand, to reassure him he need not fret.

'Let me get closer to him, then. The girl said he was made from marble? I thought it unlikely, as it's not yet winter, although in this country, anything is possible.'

'The girl spoke the truth, frozen like a statue, yet still he breathes.'

The healer examined Pramod, lifting his eyelids and poking at his feet. Only Pramod's increased heart rate showed any reaction to the healer's ministrations.

· · ·

'He will die unless someone cares for him. There is nothing I can do. It is one mystery of the psyche.' Gattus said. 'And, although I have seen it before, I have yet to see anyone recover. Are you sure you want to keep him here? I can have him moved and expedite his passing?' Gattus packed away his equipment, his head shaking.

Metella stood. Tall for a woman, she towered over the diminutive healer. Her anger making her taller. She would no more allow this man to order her about than she would cast out any man, woman, or child onto the streets to expedite their passing. She was a businesswoman, but she wasn't cruel. When she'd most needed help, she had received it, allowing her the success she enjoyed. She would do nothing to jeopardise that. The gods were always watching.

'No, he will stay and we will care for him, and with Ceres' blessing, he will recover.'

Metella returned to her stool by the immobile Pramod, once again reaching for his hand, paying as much attention to the spluttering Gattus as she did to the hunger gnawing at her bones. She'd known hunger and knew it would keep.

CHAPTER 30
OFFERINGS TO THE GODS

Life in Metella's brothel flowed around Pramod. Men came and went, they paid or didn't and faced the consequences, but the man still couldn't move. The girls took turns sitting with the old man, pouring out their hearts and sharing their secret desires, complaints and petty jealousies. And if the man in the bed judged them, he kept his thoughts to himself.

Metella kept to her word and had girls assigned to see to his personal needs. Some were better than others, but he experienced no ill treatment. The working girls weren't the only ones who used him as a confessional. Metella herself spent time in his room every day. She started out telling him about her challenges, and before long, she was sitting with him late at night, rekindling dreams long thought lost. And who better to share them with than a man who couldn't breathe of their existence to anyone? What Metella didn't know was that Pramod already knew her secrets.

But tonight, other thoughts filled her mind. Thoughts which didn't revolve around the expansion of the Roman empire or who wore the Imperial crown. She didn't have time for such lofty thoughts. For who was she? A harlot, who'd made her fortune on her back.

· · ·

A woman alone, who secreted coins in the cracks between floorboards before making offerings to the gods to keep her healthy. But now, tonight, she knew too much. And during her time in the viper-filled pit they called Rome, she had learnt that those who knew too much were denied the pleasure of another sunrise.

And so on the evening of the annual October Horse, everything changed as Metella pulled up a sturdy chair, adjusted the woven blanket around her legs, and moistened her lips with a fine glass of mead before sharing the heavy secret pulling at her conscience.

As she dabbed at her lips, Pramod blinked.

At first Metella thought it a trick of the candlelight, and paid no attention, but he blinked again. And for the merest fraction of a moment, it appeared his brow furrowed.

'Did you blink?' Metella asked, her voice catching in her throat as she lowered her glass.

Her patient blinked again, once, twice, three times, before parting his lips and loosening his jaw, and like a tiny bird, his mouth opened, as if he was trying to form a word.

'You blinked. Blink again if you understand me,' Metella whispered.

She knelt beside his bed, forgoing the chair, her soft hands on his face. Through all the nights he'd been under her roof, this was the first time she'd laid hands on him. His skin blending into the night, the lines on his face a map of his past.

'You heard my secret, and now that you know, there are only two options,' she said, tracing her finger down his body until it came to rest above his heart. 'First is death. Not my preference. I abhor death. Alternatively, you help me solve my issue with Rome. Before you decide, tell me why I shouldn't hand you over to the army.'

Metella watched him struggle to answer. And when his words came, they were not what she was expecting. They were at once familiar, and yet much worse.

Metella returned to her room, her heart in shreds, her breathing rapid. She wanted to pack her valuables and disappear into the night.

She was not beholden to anyone. There were girls who relied on her, and clients she valued, and those that she didn't. But she held no loyalty to them. She knew that they'd never lift a finger to help when push came to shove. Or would they? Is that why she was hesitating?

Realisation dawned too late that she'd stayed too long, and had made too many connections to abandon them when she knew what was coming.

Calling to her slave for help, Metella instructed her to fetch the darkest cloak from her chest. With help from the half-asleep girl, she slipped into the cloak and wrapped a woollen scarf around her neck, pulling the soft fabric up over her chin and mouth. It was best no one recognised her where she was going.

With the girl dismissed, Metella sank to her knees, pressing her forehead against the small altar in the corner of her room. This would be the most dangerous challenge she had faced.

'As your unworthy servant, I pray for your protection from the sword above our heads. Accept this offering,' and she placed a small figurine in the hollow at the altar's base, 'as proof of my devotion.'

Metella kissed the top of the altar, a tear spilling down her cheek, snaking its way down the stone facade before landing on the figurine.

As the cloaked Metella left the brothel and made her way towards Ithaca Fort, the clouds parted, allowing the moonlight to pick its way towards Metella's offering at the base of the altar, where it caressed the solid silver miniature of Mars, wrapping its slippery fingers around the offering, weighing the honesty of the gift.

A rush of wind assaulted the valley, making soldiers shiver and babies cry. A pack of wolves howled from the nearby hills, sending a chilling symphony echoing through the valley. Their melancholy, repeated by the owls in the trees, whose haunting cries sent the foxes scurrying back to their burrows and made the men hiding in the forest shift uncomfortably amidst their leafy beds. A chorus of whispered commands joined the wolves, but with a level of malice the most dangerous of beasts could not imagine.

CHAPTER 31

OLD FRIENDS

Metella's knuckles whitened. She had no reason not to trust Pramod's words, but she didn't want to believe him. What he'd warned her about had chilled her to the very core.

At the entrance to Ithaca Fort, Metella hid in the shadows and waited for the guards to pass. Security was lax in the absence of the fort's commander, and Metella banked on them being even less attentive given the celebrations planned for the morrow. And she was right.

Metella watched the replacement guards arrive, tired and irritable. She listened to them exchange ribald pleasantries about whose cock was the largest and whose mother was the biggest whore. The old guard slipped off to their beds, whilst the new arrivals grumbled about their shift and the coldness of the season. Metella shivered herself. Another winter in this miserable country. She'd meant to leave in the summer, but something always held her back.

During a break in their patrol, and she slipped through the unguarded gate like a shadowy wrath, the shrouded moon concealing her entrance. She stood on the cobbled road to gather her bearings. She'd been here before, on official business.

· · ·

The soldiers needed to be reminded that her girls were her stock, and that she wouldn't abide any damage done to them. And her last visit to the commander, to complain about two men in particular, had been less than a month ago.

The stench of horse manure to her right meant that the stables and the cavalry were in that direction. She turned left and clung to the walls of the buildings, counting her paces, in case she needed to escape, knowing that the darkness could turn her around faster than a flash flood.

A sound ahead flattened her against the wall. A bird swooped low to scan the ground beneath it for prey. Metella would be the prey if she didn't reach her destination without being intercepted. Raucous laughter leaked from one of the barrack blocks. Little respect shown for the men freshly returned from their watch, trying to snatch some sleep. It hadn't always been this lax. Under the last commander, the soldiers were polished brighter than the newest denarius. Guards taut and ready to respond at the slightest provocation. But not under this commander and his underlings — they were in it for themselves. No, not everyone else. One man stood apart, and it was to his room that she was trying to reach before it was too late.

The gods must be punishing him, Julius thought after he'd opened his door to find Metella in the shadows. Now wasn't a good time.

With no light from the moon, and his lantern back in his room, it was easy enough to grab Metella by her elbow and direct her down another narrow street towards the old baths. Unused since the collapse of the floor of the *calidarium*, the hot room, it had been ruled off limits to the soldiers until a proper inspection and repair could be carried out by engineers from Segontium when the weather improved. The fort's inhabitants forced to use the inferior baths on the other side of the vicus, which, not unexpectedly, had led to an increased number of altercations between the soldiers and villagers.

'What are you doing here?' he hissed from the dark.

'I come with a warning,' Metella answered.

'When we last met, you wanted nothing more to do with me. Your last words, as I recall, were a curse upon my father.'

'That was a mistake, I'm sorry,' Metella said. 'But you must listen to me. We are in danger here.'

'Here in the baths, or in general?' Julius joked, not quite grasping the urgency in Metella's voice.

'You're about to be attacked. The soldiers in the fort and us in the village. You must prepare for war.'

'As Roman soldiers are always prepared for war,' Julius replied automatically, not quite believing his own propaganda. 'Where is this intelligence from?'

'I can't tell you.'

'Can't or won't?'

'Julius, it's not like that,' Metella whispered.

'Metella, it's always been like that. I've begged you to leave, to give up your work–'

'Leaving me no means to support myself,' Metella interrupted.

'You have ample set aside for the future, as you've told me many times. And a lover you refuse to name.'

Metella objected, but Julius knew otherwise. Her profession made her an accomplished liar. And on this point her answers were always contradictory, the flush in her cheeks exposing her heart.

'Leave the army,' she said. 'And come with me, as my protector.'

'Metella, this argument is going nowhere.'

'Please, believe me. An old friend has returned from my past, our past. He is unwell, dying. But before he fell ill, he warned me of an impending battle. He has seen it.'

'Seen it how?' Julius's patience was wearing thin, thin enough that he missed the use of the word "our". The skirmish with the Iceni was of more concern than the brothel owner's irrational fears. 'I don't have time for this, Metella. I'll help escort you out of the area, as I offered the last time we spoke. I can't do much more. You are a resourceful woman who doesn't need to earn her living on her back.'

Metella held Julius in place as he turned to leave.

'My friend is a seer. I couldn't believe it was him, as I last knew him as a young man, but time does strange things here. The druids...'

Julius snorted. The druids were all slaughtered by the Romans. Someone had been speaking half truths into Metella's ears. He'd thought her better educated, but he'd been wrong about her before.

Metella had ignored his derision, and carried on talking, digging her hands into his arms as she spoke, her voice getting louder.

'My friend has seen the future. The tribes are united by a magical beast, which the druids have. They plan to attack Ithaca Fort.'

'Have you been imbibing the rot you serve your customers because I think it has muddied your mind?'

'You don't believe me?'

Julius shook his head. 'It isn't possible, Metella. The time of the druids has ended. Our gods protect this island now, and the strength of the Roman army. Thank you for your concern. Honestly, you took a substantial risk coming here tonight. It is only because the Commander is away that your entrance was undetected. But he will return tomorrow, in time for the October Horse, and the guards will not be so foolish as to allow anyone into the fort again.'

For a moment, faint moonlight filtered through the clouds, illuminating Metella's panicked face, and Julius almost apologised. The urge to trust this woman whom he'd once thought his closest friend overwhelmed him. But before he could say a word, she dropped her hands and fled into the night, without a backwards glance.

Julius waited, expecting a guard to sound the alarm, but Ithaca Fort remained silent save for the hoot of owls in the night, hunting their prey. Owls, or men imitating owls? Julius shuddered. Metella's warning sat heavily on his conscience. Who was her informant? And how could he have seen what Julius himself had seen in his own dreams? Dreams half remembered. Dreams which centred around a strange woman he'd rescued. Rescued from what? An iron beast?

His hand clasped the amulet around his neck, given to him by Metella, in the hope it would provide relief from his fear. The girl was real, somehow. And yet he could find no evidence of her existence. She'd vanished. And now Metella talked of an old friend returned. A seer. Perhaps this man knew more than Metella was saying.

CHAPTER 32

FLEEING FOR THEIR LIVES

Metella breathed into her cloak, muffling the sounds of her fear. Hidden by the shadow of the fort's wall, the guards passed by, ignorant of the woman within a cough of their reach. She'd expected more from Julius, but he was young and knew nothing of the world outside of the army, and of his sheltered life before that. His blade remained unbloodied by battle, his conscience clear. It wouldn't be long before that changed, though. It didn't need to. He just needed to believe her.

With that avenue denied her, Metella had to consider an alternative course of action, afraid that whatever she chose would have the same outcome—the death of the life she loved.

Waiting till the guards passed once more, Metella slipped through the unguarded gate, careful to keep her back tight against the stone walls, the rough blocks pulling on her woollen cloak. Crossing the unlit road exposed her to any guard who may have chosen that moment to cast his eye her way. But she was safe. The guards kept their eyes towards the dark of the countryside, looking for shadows slipping from the surrounding hills like a creeping wind.

Pausing for breath in an empty doorway, she fingered the brooch at her throat — a coiled serpent, with a red stone for an eye. A gift from a long ago lover. A secret she'd kept until he'd left without warning.

The hurt burrowing under her skin, worming itself into her soul. Festering. And now he was back, or a version of him was. An older version. The bittersweet memories of their time together, his comings and goings, until there'd just been a void. A void she'd filled with a million different men in a country far from home.

A cold fog felt its way through the street, tugging at her cloak and her memories, pushing her feet into action. They would flee after she woke Pramod. She would forgo the rest of the merchants who shared this hellhole of a home, forever soggy underfoot. She'd happily forsake the greenest of greens she'd ever seen and forget the purple-coated hills and the abundance of wildlife. It was time to say goodbye. If they ran south, now, tonight, they could outrun the fury Pramod predicted.

Metella rapped on the banded door of the brothel, stepping through when it opened at the sound of her voice. Perhaps they could reach the coast and sail home? Would that be safer than travelling south?

'Pack my things,' she ordered, slipping off her cloak, before rushing upstairs to where she'd left Pramod under the ministrations of one of the younger girls. As the guard at the door picked up Metella's abandoned cloak, the serpent brooch caught between two flagstones. The guard tugged once, twice, before the cloak pulled free, leaving the brooch wedged tight, unseen in the dark.

Upstairs, Metella dismissed the girl, a twinge of guilt settling upon her shoulders. What would become of her, and the others like her when the tribes attacked? Or would the tribesmen spare them, focussing their rage on the Romans within the stone walls of the fort? Metella couldn't allow herself to worry about the others. The gods had given her a last chance at happiness, albeit in a novel form. She'd warned the Romans. She'd done her part, as Pramod had asked. No one expected more. She couldn't give more.

'Pramod, my love, wake up.'

The man on the bed didn't move other than the gentle rise and fall of his cadaverous chest.

'I warned them, like you wanted. You must wake up. The barbarians are one step closer than they were when you arrived. We have no time left. We must leave now.'

His eyes opened and Metella's heart sang. The candlelight high-lighting the love which had sustained her despite her broken heart. She didn't understand how he'd come back, but here he was, and she wouldn't let him leave her again.

'You must find the strength to get up,' she begged, snaking her arms around his shoulders. How frail they were, where before they'd been sinuous, his slight frame disguising the strength of his intellect and wit.

Metella paused as he opened his mouth, as if he were about to speak, but nothing came out. Pramod's words had left him, just when she needed them the most.

'Try, please, for us. I can't do this alone. I've been on my own for so long, and I just can't do it anymore. Please, please get up. I need you.'

Metella sank back on the bed, leaving Pramod lying against the pillows, tears marking both their faces. She'd have to use someone else to help. The girl? She could be trusted to keep her mouth shut.

Leaving Pramod, she went to the corridor. With the night air smothering the sounds of sleep, she faltered. She believed in Pramod with all her heart. He was her one true love, and she would do anything she could to save him.

'Carmella, I need you.'

A head emerged bleary-eyed from behind a door in the hall. Her blonde hair haloed around her young head. Too young to work the rooms like the other girls, Metella kept her to help the girls with dressing and cleaning and any other odd jobs.

'Pack a bag. We're leaving. Don't say a word to anyone else or I'll beat you until sitting hurts more than my disappointment.'

The young girl opened her mouth, but Metella didn't have time.

'No questions. Pack light and then help me move the old man. We leave before dawn.'

Carmella disappeared back into her room, and Metella rushed downstairs, keeping her footfalls as quiet as possible, knowing that the building had ears. It was how she'd survived so long in business. The keeper of secrets, dripping them into the right ears, or the wrong ones, whatever she needed to grease the wheels of fortune her way.

. . .

Those secrets wouldn't save her now, not with the commander out of the fort. Him, she could twist around her finger, but she'd never needed to do that with Julius. Julius was a good boy, always doing what his mother told him. She'd just never told him who his mother was, and that it was his father who'd warned her of what was coming.

With Carmella on one side of Pramod, a bag slung across her body, and Metalla on the other, the women levered the unresponsive man up from the bed. It was easier without his eyes watching her every move, his imprisoned words trying to escape from his frozen visage.

'Be quiet,' Metella grumbled as the girl uttered a shriek of surprise at his weight. Metella had forgotten about the guard, and pulled up at the sight of the burly man, wrapped in his winter coat, two travelling bags hanging from his meaty hands.

He'd been her loyal guard for more years than she cared to remember, more years than she'd allowed to show on her face. Yes, she needed his help. Carmella performed well as a servant, scurrying around fetching combs and ribbons and wine, but knew nothing of survival. She'd been born into the brothel and no doubt expected to die in one. Of her guard's early life, she knew nothing, but he could have murdered her in her sleep and stolen all her money a thousand nights over, and yet hadn't. They both had their uses.

'Carmella, take one bag. Silas, help me with Pramod.'

If Silas recognised the name of the old man who sagged in Metella's arms, he gave no sign. Carmella groaned under the weight of the bags, but gave no complaint. Metella expected the girl was looking at this as a great adventure, instead of the flight of their lives.

'Did you empty the safe?' Metella whispered to Silas.

The big man nodded.

Metella stroked the doorframe, the slivers of moonlight painting it silver. Metella wanted to mourn for the life she'd built, for the son she'd most likely never see again, and for the girls she would leave behind. But there was no time for that. The fates had decreed that she would survive. Pramod had shown her that, coming back for her after all these years. It was up to her to seize this opportunity and reinvent herself. A wealthy widow traveling with her elderly father and faithful servants.

Metella asked Silas for a handful of coins, and laid them at the feet of the household gods.

'Protect us,' she said, stroking the carved figures.

The moon disappeared once more behind a bank of clouds. They needed to go now. In her haste to pull on her cloak and close the door behind them, Metella failed to notice the missing brooch.

CHAPTER 33

HIDE AND SEEK

Metella had had to flee for her life on more than one occasion, but this was the first time she'd felt death stalking her. She looked behind them again. The hills seemed to hold nothing but tiny drifts of snow, slowly building amidst the small copses the Romans hadn't yet decimated.

'Hurry, I can hear them.'

'Well, I can't hear anything,' Carmella said, her voice carrying on the gusting wind.

'Your voice will wake the dead. And there's enough of them out tonight as it is.'

The unlikely group picked their way through a field of grave markers honouring the deeds of men; some of whom Metella both remembered, and some she would rather forget.

There was one man she'd never forgotten, and he now lay in the handcart beside her, expertly handled by a man the size of a small carthorse and just as strong and wilful. The pain of not recognising him when he'd first arrived at her door still gnawed at her conscience.

'We must hurry,' Metella urged, checking behind them, worry etched on her face at their painfully slow passage.

The vicus beside Ithaca Fort slept on, unmoved by the fleeing brothel owner and her slaves.

If anyone cared, they hadn't bothered to ask or raise an alarm. They weren't prisoners in the vicus, merely the flotsam and jetsam of life, washed into the shadows of a Roman fort by the tides of time and chance.

The startled hoot of an owl shattered the silence. A hoot that carried on long after the owl fled whatever nightmare had disturbed it.

'What was that?' Metella froze beside a gaudy monument featuring a cavalryman impaling a barbarian warrior quivering at his feet. It was those exact barbarians that Metella now feared.

'An owl.' Carmella yawned, sleep still crusty in her eyes.

Metella ignored her. The girl had never left the safety of the vicus. Born and bred within view of Ithaca Fort, she knew nothing of life beyond Ithaca. She'd never faced a battle, run screaming from armed mobs roaming the streets, their lust for violence fuelling every thought. The farthest she'd gone was for a brief fumble in the coppice with green soldiers with more honey on their tongues than coin in their purse.

'That's not an owl,' Silas said, blowing on his calloused hands.

'What is it? A horn? Have the Roman's a new instrument?' Metella asked, shivering under her cloak, either from fear or the cold. She couldn't tell. Her instincts had only ever let her down in the past, and she vowed she'd never repeat that mistake.

'Not a horn. We should move,' Silas said, his words clipped and precise. His reputation as the antithesis of a garrulous man was the precise reason Metella employed him.

The early snow teased them as the quartet trudged through the cemetery, homages to the prowess and bravery of foolish young men surrounding them. Etched with either love or loyalty, these grave markers cared not for the dead beneath their carved facade, nor for the families and friends left behind. A memorial. A memory doomed to disappear. But for tonight, they hid those who preferred to remain hidden.

Silas pulled the cart holding Pramod, the unearthly sound hunting them across the undulating ground. Carmella's whispered terrors about evil spirits, their constant companion.

· · ·

Once past the Roman cemetery, they entered the softness of the coppice, where fallen branches and filtered snow muffled their foot-falls. The damp vegetation cushioning the solid wooden cart wheels.

Creatures of the night skittered away, chattering a warning.

Silas lowered the cart, swivelling his head towards the eerie horn. He shook his head free of the sound, and bent to lift the cart, but paused.

'Metella.'

'Shhh, keep your voice down,' Metella said.

'Your man.'

'What?'

'Your man, he wakes.'

Metella dropped her bags and rushed to the cart, to the man she'd never stopped loving.

She wiped the snow from Pramod's face with her sleeve. His skin was cold. Too cold. But his eyes were open. He was trying to speak.

'What is it? What are you trying to say?' Tears formed tiny icicles in the corners of her eyes. He'd been so indestructible and impervious to disease. His magic salves had cured her various ills and those of her girls. His knowledge of the natural world was incomparable to anyone she'd ever met. The only complaint she'd ever voiced was the unpredictable nature of his comings and goings. So many times she'd begged him to take her with him. To whisk her away from this life. Yet he'd never capitulated. Rather, he'd vanish like a wraith. Slipping through her fingers until he returned. Always without warning, lacking fanfare or any hint of rumour. An unknown quantity that she loved with her whole being.

'What's he saying?' Silas asked, shifting from foot to foot, stomping his feet against the ground.

'He's trying to talk,' Metella said, eyes shining.

'I'm cold,' Carmella complained.

Metella wondered if bringing her had been a mistake? But Pramod's warning had been enough to persuade her to bring the girl. As annoying as Carmella was, she was an innocent child.

She focused on Pramod's face, frowning as she sought to interpret his futile attempts to talk.

'What are you saying?'

It was clear he was struggling. Even in the moonlight, Metella saw the cords on his neck straining with effort, until finally, his jaw moved.

'Hide,' he said.

As he uttered the warning, the sound of the horn flooded the coppice. Carmella screamed, dropping to her knees, as two beams of unnatural light swept past, illuminating the world as if the sun had crashed into the earth.

Metella threw herself over Pramod, shielding him from the apparition screaming towards them.

'Hide,' Pramod said again.

Silas didn't need to be told twice. He scooped Pramod out of the cart and bounded past the cowering Carmella. Metella followed, dragging the whimpering girl behind her. Their belongings abandoned.

They followed Silas down towards a rushing stream, where he lead them under snow-laden branches, nature's own curtain, shielding them from the beams of light sweeping the wood.

'What was it?' Carmella whispered, her eyes wide, her teeth chattering.

'No talking,' Silas said, laying Pramod against the trunk of a willow tree, tucking the blanket around the old man's legs, before lowering himself to the ground.

Metella sat next to Pramod in near blackness, sure they could hear her heart over the rushing water.

It wasn't just the cold, the lights and the horn sending shivers through the group, it was the roaring. Louder than any waterfall or avalanche, and the pounding of booted feet. Was this the attack Pramod had warned of? But if it was, why weren't they attacking the fort?

'Soldiers,' Carmella whispered, slithering further down the bank until her feet were nearly in the stream.

'Not soldiers,' Silas spat. 'Ician sons of whores.'

They all froze, waiting out the threat, both known and unknown. And it wasn't until the sounds of nature returned to normal that Silas judged it safe to leave their leafy sanctum.

. . .

They stood on the edge of the paved road, surveying the empty horizon. Of the warriors, there was no sign. Of the beast they'd been riding, its demon footprints were writ large in the snow.

'Have you ever seen anything like this?' Metella whispered

Silas examined the tracks before the falling powder extinguished any trace.

'Druids,' he said.

'Impossible,' Metella said. 'The Romans destroyed them.'

'Druids,' Silas repeated.

Metella stared down the road. Had the danger passed? The faint sounds of Carmella whispering her concerns to Pramod reached her ears. The night now stiller than a frozen pond.

Pramod had begged her to flee with all those she held dear. There was only one other person who held her heart, and he'd refused to leave. Julius. Her son. Their son. Although she'd never told Pramod. The time had never been right. It would never be right, not now.

'We'll go another way,' she decided.

'Good,' Silas said, and lumbered through the hanging branches, returning Pramod to the abandoned cart.

'Are we going back?' Carmella asked.

'No, it's safer to carry on,' Metella said.

Ignoring Carmella's pleas to return to the vicus, they gathered their fallen belongings and continued, following Silas and the cart, ears attuned to the slightest noise.

As they traversed the bracken-covered land, Metella's mind wandered, recalling the first time she'd met Pramod, so many years ago now she could barely remember who she'd been then. But the taste of the persimmon she'd been eating at the time still lingered on her lips, even now. She could still feel the caress of the dress she'd been wearing, so light she'd almost felt naked. And he'd walked up to her, bolder than any man she knew, to ask for a bite. That was all. He hadn't wanted to buy her or bed her. He'd merely asked for a piece of fruit, to see him on his way.

At a fork in the road, Silas turned left, the wheels of the cart clattering over the stones marking the Roman Road. The sound waking Metella from her meandering through time.

'Stop,' she said. 'We're going the wrong way.'

'Safer this way,' Silas said.

'We have to go south.'

'Later.'

'But it will take longer,' Metella argued.

'And you won't be dead.'

As if he considered the discussion over, Silas picked up the cart and carried on walking, leaving Metella motionless in the middle of the road. She couldn't stand still for too long. Every inch of her body quivered with cold, especially her hand holding her cloak closed at her throat. Metella hurried after Silas, her fingers tingling, cursing him and Carmella and Pramod and the Romans and the Iceni, and even the gods themselves for putting her in this position.

It felt like they'd been walking for days when the sun pushed up through the earth and chased away the moon and the stars. The new day brought with it a modicum of hope, especially once they spied a small group of round houses, their chimneys smoking in the morning haze, and half a dozen sheep mooning about in their enclosures.

'Wait,' Silas said, lumbering towards the nearest structure.

Carmella sat on the edge of the cart, silent, her face pale.

Metella checked on Pramod, who'd fallen asleep, his breathing steady, if shallow. They'd emptied their bags, layering their extra clothing atop of the man, padding his head and covering his face, to keep him as warm as possible during their journey. If Silas had noticed the extra weight, he hadn't complained. None of them had any energy left for complaining, not even Carmella.

From the vantage point at the top of the hill leading towards the settlement, Metella watched the first door open and a burly farmer greet Silas the Roman way. After a brief discussion, Silas waved them down. Metella and Carmella lifted the cart and slowly made their way down towards the round house.

. . .

Whilst the farmer directed Silas where to store the handcart, Carmella pushed her way inside, straight to the humble fire, making herself at home, to the apparent amusement of the rest of the family who'd paused their morning routine to welcome the strangers into their home. Metella left her to it, more concerned about Pramod than her woolly-headed slave. She sighed as Silas carried Pramod through the open doorway, laying him on a pile of furs heaped by the fire.

'Thank you,' Metella said to the family as they handed Metella's little band small bowls of stew, fragrant with local herbs and a hint of sheep fat, before making themselves scarce.

'I rest,' Silas said, falling into the nearest bed, asleep before his head hit the pillow. Carmella followed him, leaving Metella alone with Pramod.

'Thank you,' she whispered. 'Thank you for warning us.' Perhaps now was the time to tell Pramod about his son. Especially when she didn't know how much longer Pramod would be with them.

Tiny snuffles came from the bed as Carmella snuggled into Silas's broad back, the two servants fast asleep, safe with the familiarity of those who have spent their whole lives living so close to one another. No, not their whole lives. Metella didn't know what Silas had done before he'd appeared at her door. He'd come with the name of her family on his lips, and a well-travelled tablet as his introduction. Metella thought that she'd travelled far enough away from her family to be forgotten by them, but not even the end of the earth was far enough to disappear completely. She'd tried not to be unsettled by it, and as the years passed, she forgot that her family had sent Silas. She was under no illusion that he was there to spy on her activities, but time made it easy to forget. Metella assumed he'd forgotten.

'What do we do now?' she asked, stroking Pramod's face, his eyes following her every movement. 'I know you can speak, my love. Try again,' she exhorted.

'Run,' he said.

It wasn't the same warning he'd given before, but it chilled her more than the snow outside, and scared her more than she'd even been scared before. The threat wasn't gone, only delayed.

CHAPTER 34

WAKING THE BEAST

Pramod believed in all the gods, and had prayed to almost all of them at one time or another. Deep in his heart, he knew the power of their benevolence and the destructive force of their anger.

It was to the gods, the old and the new, that he'd turned to for help. Praying in silence for deliverance from this frozen curse. And in return, he promised them the earth. And they delivered.

As Metella lay sleeping beside him, his fingers twitched, which lead to the flexing of his wrist and a painful cramping in his elbow as the sensation of the fresh hay tickled his aged skin.

When Metella finally woke, her tears fell freely, for Pramod was sitting up. His wrinkled hand caressing her hair, his lopsided face smiling as she muttered fervent prayers to her own gods, thanking them for his recovery. Over and over. Pramod tried to quiet her, his words half strangled, partially formed.

'My love,' she said, stroking his face.

'We can't stay—,' Pramod started saying, as Metella rained kisses upon his lips, his cheeks, his eyes, his head. 'Stop now,' he whispered, his good hand pushing her away. 'We must leave before the Roman's retaliate.'

'They won't bother us here,' Metella replied.

'They will, and they do.'

'I don't understand?'

'That's why I came back,' Pramod said, his mouth struggling with the word. 'The history books have changed. We'll die if we stay. All these people will perish.'

Pramod watched Metella process his words. His whole heart devoured her, and not for the one-hundredth time did he mentally flagellate himself for not taking her home with him. It could have been done. Neumegen had told him the story of the girl in the shop, who'd brought back her English soldier. Time hadn't derailed. He could do it now. With his one good hand, he checked the hidden pocket in his trousers, searching for the sharp corners of the wooden die. At the reassuring touch of the talisman, he fell back onto the bed, exhausted. In this state, he wouldn't be able to travel to the doorway, let alone the future. He had to regain more strength before he chanced travelling back with Metella. And this time, he wouldn't take no for an answer.

'The villagers claim that the Roman scouts could not track the Ician warriors, or their iron beast. They say that the druids wielded a spell to protect the Ician.'

Pramod frowned. The Romans wiped out the druids years ago. How could they exert their otherworldly power over the Ician without drawing the attention of the Romans? The Ician barely featured in the recognised pages of history, but here they were, playing a wild card in a bid to expel the Roman invaders. This wasn't the narrative in the alternative history he'd read. That had told a very different story, one of Ithaca Fort's commander, and his stratospheric rise to the Roman senate, a man who'd never previously appeared in any history books. History was changing. Who knew what the consequences would be?

The pious call of a raven joined the sounds of daily life outside the hovel, and Pramod felt his skin crawl. Ravens were a symbol of death, and that was exactly what he felt slithering its way across the path he and Metella were about to take.

'Metella, we have to leave. I'm not strong enough to take you home, but when I am, you will need to trust me.'

'I've always trusted you.'

CHAPTER 35
KNOWLEDGE IS POWER

'He's nowhere,' Apple cried, appearing like a wraith beside Lillian at the cafe.

Lillian could hardly carry the bags under her eyes, let alone understand a word Apple had uttered.

'Don't you care?'

'About what?' Lillian replied.

'Pramod. I've looked everywhere and can't find him. No one's seen him.'

'Maybe he had to visit family?' Lillian suggested, her brain still woozy from the night before. She'd had very little sleep, and had skipped breakfast entirely.

'You don't get it, do you? They didn't want him here, and now he's gone. Which means the library will go too, and they win, again.'

'Who is this "they" you keep mentioning?' Lillian asked. She had more important things to worry about than a missing librarian, like her sanity.

Apple was staring at her, her pale face devoid of any emotion, as blank as a school board at the start of term.

'I'd thought you'd care, but forget it. You're just like the others,' Apple said. 'He hasn't answered my knocking yesterday or today.'

'Maybe he's having a nap?' Lillian offered.

'A two-day nap? I don't think so. You haven't known him as long as I have. He always answers the door. He should be here, in this cafe, now, especially at this time.'

Lillian looked up into Apple's face, a face full of concern.

Pushing her half-eaten scrambled eggs away, she asked, 'Do you have a key to his place?'

Lillian followed Apple to the church, stepping carefully around drunken gravestones performing complex feats of gravity in the overgrown graveyard.

'How come no one looks after the graves here?' Lillian asked, pausing beside a fallen angel; an allegory for her life.

'You should ask your boyfriend's mother that question,' Apple said, before pulling open the unlocked vestibule door and disappearing into the darkened interior, returning moments later with a key hanging from a heavy metal keyring.

Apple shoved the key in the lock and barrelled through the door.

'He's not here,' Apple called out, her voice pinched tight.

Lillian squeezed through the narrow stacks of books towards Apple's voice and peered over her shoulder. Sharma's bedroom was smaller than her wardrobe.

'He lives here?'

'It looks like he left in a hurry,' Apple said, pointing to an open trunk next to a camp stretcher.

'What's on the floor next to the trunk?' Lillian stepped towards the bloody shirt and ancient beaker.

'We shouldn't touch anything,' Apple said, pulling on Lillian's arm.

'Is that blood?' Lillian asked.

Apple shook her head, but her eyes said differently. 'We should leave. I'll do another circuit around town. There are only a few places he hangs out. Most of the people here would rather see him gone.'

Lillian glanced again at the bloodied shirt before Apple harried her out of the hall. Lillian shivered in the cold, shaking her head to dislodge an unusual humming in her ears. Tonight the empty building smelled of more than old books. It carried a hint of desperation and violence and panic, triggering something in Lillian's head.

Fight or flight.

But it wasn't because of Sharma missing. There was something about the shirt, and the smell, something familiar. Scarily familiar.

'Come on. If you stand there too long, Mrs Badrick will try selling you off to the highest bidder, like she did with the old gravestones.'

Shaken from her reverie, Lillian hurried after Apple. 'She did what?'

'As well as being the mayor, she's the president of the Hexham Grave Preservation Society, and one of the first things she did was sell off the gravestones where you couldn't tell whose graves they were anymore because of how worn the stones were. People wanted them for their gardens. Imagine doing that to the Roman altars and the stuff that's on every bloody farm in the county. Don't bother answering that. Aren't you selling yours?' her face showing Lillian quite clearly what she thought of that.

'I'm not selling it, I just want it gone, so I can get on with rewilding the farm, that's all.'

Apple's silence meant Lillian added nothing further. Was there no one in town who supported her plans? Lillian could see the judgement writ on Apple's face, and the dismissive shrug of her shoulders.

'Look, it'll be faster for me to look for Pramod on my own, since you don't really know your way around yet. Ciao.' Apple vanished, leaving Lillian statue-like on the footpath, her skin prickling at the sudden abandonment.

'Hello Nero, or is it Nigel-No-Mates today?' purred a voice behind her. 'I see you can't even keep the one friend you made,' Holly said, her mouth curling at the edges, crinkling the abundance of concealer she'd applied to cover old acne scars.

'Bugger off, Holly,' Lillian said as Holly's pungent perfume wafted past, turning her empty stomach. Her patience for Holly was thinner than her grasp of reality.

'Ooh, scary words. Never mind. After the news you'll be receiving soon, I expect you to be packed up and gone by the end of the week.'

. . .

Holly strode away, her blonde ponytail swaying in time with her yoga pants-clad legs.

Lillian wanted to call her back, to grill her on what she meant, but she knew it would only add fuel to the fire. And it was at that moment that she knew she didn't want to leave this place. As crazy as it was, she couldn't leave. There was too much here she needed to understand. And besides, she had no other home, not anymore.

A group of noisy tourists bustled past, their rucksacks bulging with drink bottles and Arctic quality raincoats, their guide droning on as interminably as a second-tier politician in an election year. Lillian barely took any notice until he mentioned a battle between the Romans and the local British tribes.

Lillian fixed her gaze on the anorak-wearing man at the front of the group.

'We know very little of the battle, other than a partial sentence on a writing tablet found at Vindolanda in the 1970s. It tells us of an ambush near Ithaca Fort—'

'Ithaca Fort?' Lillian queried, pushing her way to the front. 'I've never heard of Ithaca Fort.'

'Most people haven't. Other than in this portion of a letter almost two thousand years old, it remains unmentioned in any other texts. It's generally agreed that it is a localised name for one of the minor fortlets on the wall. Slang if you like.'

'So Ithaca Farm, is that built on top of the fort?'

The guide laughed. 'Until recently, no evidence of a Roman fort or settlement existed on Ithaca Farm. The discovery last month of an altar and the cache of human skulls is an unexpected development. To be honest, some local farmer probably moved it centuries ago for reasons unknown. Time will tell. Say, are you part of this group?'

Lillian flushed. Angry at the guide, at the archaeologists, at her parents, all of them, for placing her into this position. But at least now she had a name, a point of reference - Ithaca Fort. That could well be the key to answering all her questions, to explain her visions. Why hadn't one of the archaeologists mentioned the link to Ithaca Fort? Is that why the metal detectorists were sniffing around? And the farmers, and the real life treasure hunters?

Why were they concealing the existence of a Roman fort, especially given the way the town monetised their Roman history to attract the tourist dollar? The interference of the mayor in Lillian's applications with the local council, and with the government, and all the others...

Lost in thought, Lillian pulled up outside the decommissioned town library. On a whim, she climbed the steps and turned the handle, expecting the door to be locked, but it swung open on well-oiled hinges, revealing a brightly lit room filled with brand new laptops still in their plastic-wrapped boxes.

She stepped across the threshold. Naked shelves stood shivering against the walls, their emptiness a stark rebuke against the desecrators of Hexham's library. Only dust filled the corners now, although the bottom shelves still sported faded copies of local newspapers and industry specific periodicals, their contents long since rendered obsolete by time.

'You shouldn't be in here,' came a voice from the open doorway.

Lillian spun to find Badger at the exit.

'I was...' What was she doing? 'I didn't know this building was being used for anything.'

Badger cleared his throat, a red tinge marring his cheeks. 'It's not open for business yet.'

'Open for business? I thought this place was going to be some type of information centre for the tourists. What do they need the computers for? Is this going to be an internet cafe?'

'A business hub, I think.'

'So this won't be a community space. Does everyone in town know that's what their library is going to be? Do the papers?'

'You won't find anything bad about my mother in the papers, or my father. It is what it is,' Badger said as he walked around the room, trailing his fingers over the dozens of boxes covering the desks.

'It's fraud,' Lillian said, her voice rising.

.   .   .

'Small towns,' Badger shrugged. 'Everyone just gets on with it. You have to, because you never know when you might need a favour for something else.'

'Your mother and her council have made my life hell since I got here. Even before they discovered the ruins on my farm. But she's allowed to construct a, what is it, a private business using council facilities? And no one bats an eyelid?'

'Look, it's not personal, what's happening to you and the planning permissions being pulled and all that,' Badger said. 'Thieves stole so much Roman stuff years ago, years before you were born, and decades before my family even got here, that people are afraid you're trying to sell our history by stealth. Not to mention changing the landscape and the history of the place. I know you're not,' he said, squeezing her hand a fraction longer than needed before he moved away.

'It feels personal, especially when I see what your mother is doing. I'm going to head off. Things to do, and I don't have anyone else to help me at the farm—'

'You've got me.'

'Pardon?'

'Me. I'm here if you need me.'

Lost for words, Lillian darted past him and out of the old library. She chanced a look behind her, only to find Badger's gaze following her down the hill. Lillian rounded the corner and lost sight of him.

CHAPTER 36
WHERE IS THE MAYOR?

Jasper sat at his desk, fingers idle on his keyboard. Something didn't fit. It wasn't that he didn't believe her; it was more that he did. Lillian Arlosh struck him as a woman in charge of her destiny. A woman who didn't need the world's permission to strike a path of her own choosing. So who was he to deny her one through trial by media? Yes, he was a journalist, albeit with a tinpot local paper at the arse end of nowhere, but he still had morals. There was something else going on.

'You got that article ready for me?' yelled Revell from the luxury of his glass-walled office.

Jasper held up his hand – five more minutes, and he'd have something which wouldn't send his breakfast back up his gullet. Lillian Arlosh deserved a chance before being stoned by a misguided public. He'd tried to write the article in such a way that Revell couldn't take too much umbrage at his choice of words. He hadn't written a hatchet job, although what it looked like in the print version tomorrow could be substantially different after Revell wielded his editorial axe over it.

After hitting the enter button, the article whizzed through the internet to the desk of his boss, and Jasper leaned back in his chair to wait for the eruption, but Revell's office remained oddly calm.

· · ·

Jasper glanced over his shoulder to see the man engrossed in a call of some obvious importance, as the concentration on the man's wine-mapped face was like nothing like Jasper had ever seen. He swung his chair around to watch the show. Revell's mouth hung open like the Cateran Hole as he scribbled furiously on his normally pristine desk pad.

The rest of the office had stilled as one-by-one they noticed the quiet panic on the face of their boss. A quiet which shattered as soon as Revell slammed his phone on the desk and bellowed for everyone's attention.

A crowd surged around Revell's desk. There weren't many of them, to be honest, but this was the first time Jasper had seen everyone in the glass office at the same time. It was usually just him and Revell, or Revell and Sue the receptionist, Revell and the advertising team, which only comprised Damien and Jan, or Revell and his wife (on the rare times she deigned to enter the office). Today their print manager Tom, and the Classifieds intern, whose name Jasper couldn't recall, joined them. Rona or something like that. Rhonda maybe? No. Rhema, that was it. Rhema Patel. Nice girl, more competent than the last one. Probably too good for the Hexham Herald.

'Quiet down, everyone. I've got some news.'

Obviously, Jasper thought to himself, his own pen hovering above his every present notebook.

'The mayor is missing.'

Silence. Not an exclamation, nor a giggle, nor an intake of breath greeted Revell's announcement. It was as if everyone in the room was waiting for the actual news. That the mayor, a woman whose sole purpose in life was to stop any type of progressive change unless she could directly profit from it, had gone missing, was hardly earth shattering. Jasper could think of at least a dozen gardens of aggrieved ratepayers she could be buried under. More than likely, she was at a boozy luncheon out of town and had driven off the road in a drunken haze. Not that anyone in the room would ever say that aloud.

'She's missing. This is a serious situation. Her husband is beside himself. He's shipping in police from the city. Probably from Scotland Yard too. That's how serious this is. And he's just rung us.'

'We're first on the scene, so to speak. Drop everything. Yes, Jan, even the ads. Money takes a backseat when something like this happens to one of our own.'

More like money takes centre stage, Jasper thought. Jan had already set the ads for the next print run. He'd heard Jan and Damien discussing it in the kitchenette. More specifically, they'd been discussing what would happen when the mayor saw the half page ad for the Bellingham Tea Rooms. An ad which had filled the remaining slots for that week's edition. Jasper laughed, as he realised the mayor wouldn't be seeing the ad tomorrow if indeed she was missing.

'Something funny, Jasper?'

Uh oh, he had to tread carefully here. Revell was a pushover most of the time, but his friendship with the mayor and her husband ran deep. And any negative press or comments never went down well, and almost never saw the light of day. And neither would Jasper if he shared his honest opinion of the missing woman.

'Not laughing, coughing. Sorry.'

It seemed to placate the editor, and he shot out assignments with the youthful energy of a man half his age. Jasper bore the lion's share of work, but with the welcome help from Rhema Patel.

Jasper could already predict the answers from nearly one hundred percent of the townsfolk Revell expected him to interview, "Good riddance", with an added, "That's off the record".

It would be a baptism by fire for the intern.

As the group dispersed, Jasper felt a twinge of guilt for dismissing the woman's disappearance. The look on Revell's face was one of obvious pain. The man was a terrible boss, appallingly chauvinistic and lazy, but the disappearance of Jane Badrick seemed to have hit him like the proverbial truck. Perhaps there was a backstory there worthy of its own investigation?

With Rhema the intern in the passenger seat, Jasper tried to look more decisive than he felt. Should the mayor's house be the first port of call, or the local police station?

In the end, he didn't need to decide. Two police cars screamed past, lights flashing, sirens wailing. Jasper pulled out behind them. No need to check his speed. They only had two dedicated cop cars in Hexham, and he was behind both of them.

Jasper traded wild theories with Rhema as they followed the cars. But his money was still on the likelihood that the woman had driven into a ditch somewhere, and was slowly detoxing pinned beneath her urban tractor, her coiffed hair littered with brambles, and her manicured nails horrendously chipped. Rhema – whose sister worked part-time at the nail salon in town – told him that Jane Badrick had a standing nail appointment for every Tuesday morning, rain, hail or shine. Today was a Thursday. Part of him hoped she'd ruined all her nails, a bit like the lives she'd ruined over the years.

As Jasper rounded a corner, he had to brake. The police cars blocked the narrow lane, their doors still open, examining a road littered with broken glass and pieces of car. Bingo.

'Got a camera, Rhema?'

'Yup.'

'Just start snapping until they tell you to stop. If they say nothing, keep taking photos. I'll do the talking, but if you think I've missed something, don't be stupid. Just tell me. I'm not Revell.'

'Yup.'

They climbed out of the car, Rhema clicking away on the paper's trusty digital camera. Jasper took a couple of shots on his phone. Old habits died hard. His normal assignments rarely involved a cameraperson. He'd got pretty skilled at framing shots for the paper–the usual dross, champion bakers, gardeners, taxi drivers celebrating fifty years of driving the residents of Hexham around. They'd also used that photo for the taxi-man's obituary after he'd suffered a terminal cardiac arrest less than a month later and had buried the nose of his taxi into a wall.

'Is that from her car?' Rhema asked.

'Is it the bumper of a big, expensive, flashy Land Rover?'

'It looks like it. I worked last summer for a used car dealer. I washed a lot of bumpers.'

. . .

'Then yes, we should presume so. The mayor's a big drinker, but hides it well usually. It was only a matter of time before she had an accident. No one ever talks about her drinking, but they're usually happy to something off record, at least to me. Revell would never let me write anything alluding to it, not even when everyone was trying to get the liquor licence revoked of that delinquent pub down by the bridge. Her favourite haunt, from what I've heard.'

'Oi, you two, get back,' yelled the younger of the two constables.

'Have to found the rest of the car?' Jasper yelled back.

The constable shook his head.

'A body?' Rhema called out.

'No sign of anyone, or a car,' the constable replied, before his boss told them to clear off.

'It doesn't make any sense,' Jasper replied. 'She had an accident, but drove off?'

Rhema shrugged her shoulders.

'A carjacking?' she whispered in Jasper's ear, her eyes wide.

'In Hexham? Unlikely.'

A uniformed sergeant, one well known to everyone at the Hexham Herald, emerged from the other side of the farm fence, mud on his knees and a bag of coins in his hands.

'What's in the bag, Gav?' Jasper asked. He and Gavin Bishop had been on first-name terms since they were both in single digits. Not best friends, nor enemies, more acquaintances who sometimes caught up for a beer with other lads from their extended circle of friends. It hadn't hurt Jasper's career, nor Gavin's. A bit of quid pro quo hurt no one.

'Coins. Old ones.'

Jasper heard Rhema snap off a few pics. He hoped Gav hadn't, though. Their friendship only stretched so far.

'Roman coins? Do you think they're connected to her disappearance?'

Sergeant Bishop shook his head. 'No idea. Give us a hand by backing up, eh? The Newcastle lot are on their way to do a proper scene examination...'

Jasper didn't have to be told twice.

The look on Gav's face told him all he needed to know. This was out of Gav's hands now. Anything bigger than a case of shoplifting from Tesco, and it was fired up to Newcastle.

'Hey Gav, those coins, there're some archaeologists up at Ithaca Farm. They could have a look at them for you? Might speed things up?'

'Cheers, mate. Can't see the city boys worrying about a dozen old coins.' Sergeant Bishop nodded at Jasper and Rhema before turning to the constables to oversee their scene taping skills, and sending one boy off with the bag of coins. Whether they'd been entered into an exhibit register or not didn't seem to be of any concern. Maybe it was a good thing a team from the city was being brought in.

Back in the car, Jasper waited until they were well away from the abandoned car before asking Rhema to check her photos. 'Can you see what the coins look like?'

'I can do more than that,' she said, producing a coin from somewhere in the camera bag.

'What? Where did you get that from?'

'It was on the road when I bent down to retie my shoelace,' Rhema said. 'I picked it up straightaway, I always do with coins. Gran always said find a penny, pick it up, put it in your pocket for good luck. It's a habit. I didn't realise that it might be important until after I saw the bag of coins Sergeant Bishop was holding. Sorry.'

'Don't be sorry. That's a thousand times better than a photo. Has to be connected. Did you take any pictures over the wall of the field?'

'Why?'

'I'm wondering if she disturbed some night hawkers? And they've done something with her, and dropped their hoard. It's a pretty good guess,' Jasper said. 'They've probably all descended on Hexham since the discovery up at Ithaca Farm. That's where we're going now, with your coin.'

'But won't they take it off me?' Rhema countered. 'Because of the treasure laws?'

'One coin doesn't really count. You'll have to declare it to the Finds Officer, but for one coin, they'll probably let you keep it. Just say you found it on the edge of a recently ploughed field.'

. . .

'Coins turn up all the time. Not usually a bag of them... but we'll let the police sort that one out.'

'Do you think it was the night hawkers? Will the police be cross if we put that in the paper?'

Jasper pondered her question. It was a more appealing explanation than a drunk woman wandering off after a car accident and dying of exposure somewhere in a copse of trees, which was a likely scenario. Revell would go for it, for sure.

'I think night hawkers is as good an angle as any to cover for now. They've always been a problem along Hadrian's Wall. Might raise it as an issue which needs better policing. The readers will love it. The locals hate night hawkers. Let's see what the archaeologists say when we get to Ithaca Farm.'

The site of the altar discovery was a hive of activity at Ithaca Farm. Jasper looked for any sign of Lillian Arlosh as he pulled into the driveway in front of the house.

'Are we allowed to park here?' Rhema asked.

'I know the owner,' Jasper said, climbing out of the driver's seat. 'Come on.'

Dodging puddles, the pair traipsed across the yard and past the barn, its door firmly shut. As they picked their way across the empty field, Jasper tried not to look back at the house. He had seen no sign of Lillian's car, but that didn't mean that it wasn't in the barn, hidden from prying eyes.

The archaeologists were crouched in a shallow trench, its sides as smooth as a plastered wall. Jasper had been around archaeological sites his entire career, and this was one of the tidiest he'd ever seen.

'Hey,' Jasper called out.

Three heads turned as one in response.

'We've got a couple of questions, if you've got time? Jasper Fletcher from the Hexham Herald.'

· · ·

Jasper and Rhema waited on the edge of the trench, standing away from the edge. No point getting yelled at by an agitated archaeologist. It wasn't the way to make friends.

Anson Darby emerged from the trench, his trowel tucked into the back pocket of his well-worn work pants, caked in dirt no washing machine could ever shift, regardless of the water temperature.

'How can we help?' Darby asked.

'My colleague found this coin,' Jasper motioned towards Rhema, who stepped forward, unfurling her fist. 'On the side of a freshly ploughed field. Kind of a miracle. This is Rhema Patel, an intern at the paper, and it's her first Roman coin. Well, we think it's Roman. She was hoping you could confirm. Weren't you, Rhema?'

Rhema smiled. If she was uncomfortable with the lies dripping from Jasper, she gave no sign. Definitely one of the better interns they'd had at the paper. She had the makings of an excellent reporter.

'Coins aren't my area of expertise, but I'll have a look,' Darby replied, his long fingers plucking the coin from Rhema's outstretched hand.

Jasper waited, his breathing shallow. If the archaeologist confirmed it was Roman, it didn't really move their knowledge forward any further, other than perhaps solidifying the night hawkers theory instead of a drunken car crash theory. It must have been a huge hoard of coins if the thieves had taken a hostage. He wished them all the luck in the world dealing with Jane Badrick.

'Interesting. This appears to be a gold aureus, from the reign of Nerva, one of the Good Emperors. It's in excellent condition. Looks like some poor sod just lost it out of his arm-purse.' Darby turned the coin over and over in his hand. The coin looked as if it had only been in circulation a short time. Much like modern currency. Bearing none of the wear and tear ploughed coins usually exhibited.

'It is valuable?' Rhema asked.

Jasper winced. A rookie question and one the boffins hated being asked.

'To the man who lost it, sure. And the gold has a value, but with no historical context, it gives us nothing. This one, if my memory serves me right, is more like military propaganda.'

'Still legal tender at the time, though, with the clasped hands of the emperor and a symbolic soldier. The Latin translates to harmony of the armies. A nice find. You'll need to advise the local FLO, about where and when you found it.'

'FLO?' Rhema asked before Jasper could stop her.

'The Finds Liaison Officer from the Portable Antiquities Scheme. She was here earlier. Leave the coin with me if you like, and I can pass on your details?'

Jasper could almost taste the excitement in the archaeologist's offer, and stared at Rhema, who picked up on his subtle clue.

'We're good. I have her contact details back at the paper, so we'll give her a bell when we get back. Thanks for the help. Anything new here?' Jasper asked, more because he was sure that was the question the team expected from him than any genuine desire to hear more about what they'd dug up.

The archaeologist's face flashed with something Jasper interpreted as anger, but he was quick to hide it before answering. 'Not too much today. There are some signs of this being a busy altar, with lots of sherds,' and he pointed to a muddy bucket filled with what looked like pieces of broken flint or sandstone. How they could tell they were bits of old pot would never cease to amaze him.

'No more altars then?'

'No, and it's unlikely we'd find anymore if I'm being honest with you. This was a lucky find. We'd love to investigate further, but funds, you know the drill...'

Jasper knew only too well. He'd lost count of the number of articles he'd penned, interviewing archaeologists, all lamenting the lack of investment in their field.

'Well, thanks. Do you know if the lady of the house is home?' Jasper tipped his head towards Lillian's house, crouching disapprovingly behind them, overseeing their operation.

'No idea. We're steering well clear of her. It's surprising that she's so against what we're trying to do here. Really, finding this altar could be one of the best things to happen to her.'

That piqued Jasper's attention. 'How so?'

. . .

'She wants to bring down all the stone walls. We'd love to do it for her, funding dependent, of course. If she put in an application with a letter from us supporting it, I'm certain it would get approved. But she's never asked. Just refuses us access to the site via her front yard, which means we have to park on the other side, and hike across the field to get here, with all our gear. No one is feeling very generous towards her. But she could reverse that, if she wanted.'

'I'll talk to her,' Jasper offered, before he even realised what he'd just said. 'Anyway, I'll have to go. Thanks for the help. Ah, the coin?' Time seemed to pause before Darby finally placed the gold coin in Jasper's outstretched hand.

Jasper ignored the inquiring looks from Rhema as they returned to the car and drove out of the muddy yard. As Rhema returned the gold coin to her purse, Jasper mulled over what had just happened. Anson Darby was one to watch, that much he knew.

CHAPTER 37

ALCOHOL WAS A FACTOR

Charley Scott tapped her polished boot against the oak floorboards in the Hexham Abbey's Prior's Hall. Ignorant of the original arched windows, her only thought was that she'd wished someone had lit the stone fireplace, as the place was colder than her aunt's Christmas ham last year, the one she'd forgotten to cook before they'd all arrived for lunch. The first obvious sign of her dementia, and Charley doubted her aunt would see another Christmas now that her illness had advanced so fast.

The blue conference chairs around her filled, and she acknowledged Jasper's curt greeting as he slid into the seat on her right. Too late to nab the best seat, as always, she thought smugly, her designer tote taking up a seat on her other side. You had to dress the part you wanted to play in life, although her bank account didn't agree.

With more media in the Prior's Hall than at any other time in recent memory, the mood felt festive as everyone waited for the press conference to begin. A genuine missing person, and the mayor of all people, a truly delicious set of circumstances. She'd heard a rumour that Mrs. Badrick was involved with stealing Roman artefacts and had already written a piece for a quick submission to her editor.

. . .

She'd dismissed the uneasy feeling that her informant might have fed her a lie. Everyone liked a good gossip, and there was undoubtedly some truth to the rumour.

The mayor's husband walked into the hall, tailed by two uniformed officers and an assortment of underlings. Charley hit record on her phone and waited.

'Ladies and gentlemen,' Matthew Badrick began, his voice cracking on the end of the word gentlemen.

Charley fidgeted in her chair as Badrick cleared his throat and started again.

'Thank you for coming at such short notice. As you are no doubt aware, my wife...' he cleared his throat again.

Charley crossed her legs, her toe jiggling in the air, drawing his attention. Charley froze as she realised where the mayor's husband was looking, the room silent. She uncrossed her legs and tucked them under her seat, Lady Di fashion, and wished the floor would open up and swallow her.

'My wife,' he began again, 'didn't come home last night after attending a meeting of one of her beloved committees. Personal items, and, what the police suspect to be, parts of her car, have been found on the B6318, the Military Road...' a choke closed off whatever he was about to say next, and he covered his face with his hands.

'Ladies and gentlemen,' began one of the uniformed officers.

A regular at the police briefings in Newcastle, Charley switched her attention to the Chief Inspector, ignoring the mayor's husband and his grief. Was it grief? Perhaps he was he putting on an act? Something to consider.

'I'm Chief Inspector Kevin Readdie, and I want to assure the public that we are doing everything that we can to locate Jane Badrick. Whilst the police wouldn't usually be called in for a missing person case this early, the circumstances of Mrs Badrick's disappearance give cause for concern.'

The room hummed with speculation, interrupting the Chief Inspector's flow. Like the former school teacher he was, he waited until the room quietened down naturally before continuing.

'Evidence of a vehicle crash was located on the B6318.'

'This in itself isn't suspicious, but officers have since located Jane Badrick's handbag in the ditch, along with her cellphone and her shoes at the scene. Now, it's possible that she suffered a head injury in the accident, and has wandered off. That was the initial suspicion of the attending officers–'

The assembled journalists turned as one to stare at the local police officers, the ones no longer assigned to the investigation, who sat at the back of the room, their mouths shut tight, arms folded across their chests.

'But the discovery of a cache of rare Roman coins at the crash site makes that theory less likely.'

A sea of hands shot into the air, punctuated by people yelling out questions, trying to grab the inspector's attention.

'I will answer your questions, one at a time, shortly. I have not had the pleasure of meeting Mrs Badrick in person, but I'm told she is not one to stand aside and let a crime take place under her eye–'

Snorts from the audience greeted his statement, which sent his eyebrows north, but they didn't stop his briefing.

'A theory we are operating under at this point in time is that Mrs Badrick disturbed a night hawker, or a group of night hawkers, and they have forced her from the road. What happened to her afterwards is what we are now examining. And we would like the public's help in progressing our investigation. As you can well understand, it is a distressing time for Jane's husband and son, and for all those community organisations on whose behalf she works tirelessly.'

Charley craned her neck. The son, Andy Badrick, who'd had plenty of column space alongside his parents in the past, was absent from the press conference. Interesting.

'I'll take questions now.'

The room erupted. Charley waited her turn. Someone else would ask the questions she needed answering, and she'd write them up as if they were her own. And, of course, Jasper was the first one out of the gate.

'Jasper Fletcher, Hexham Herald. Can you tell us which event Mrs Badrick was at before she disappeared?'

'A meeting of the Women's Horticultural Club.'

Jasper dived right in. 'Sorry, just one more. Did they serve wine at the meeting?'

A pin could have dropped, and people three counties away would have heard it hit the floor.

'I don't see what relevance that has to our investigation, Mr. Fletcher.'

Charley stopped breathing. Everyone knew about Jane Badrick's secret relationship with the bottle, but no one talked about it. Jasper could lose his job over this. She hissed at Jasper under her breath, but he paid her no heed, diving in with a supplementary question, fanning the flames of an underhanded character assassination.

'I understand from my sources that Mrs Badrick had had several glasses of wine before leaving the meeting.'

The shouting started again, just as the mayor's husband roused himself from his emotional breakdown, leaping to his feet, spittle flying across the hastily assembled conference tables, knocking over a jug of water.

'You'll lose your job for that sort of slander,' Badrick yelled, barging his way towards Jasper.

Charley scooped up her tote and fled from the hall. She had almost everything she needed, and more. But the last piece of the puzzle involved a nice cup of tea with her nan, a lifelong member of Hexham's Women's Horticultural Club. And then she'd have her story.

CHAPTER 38

OBSTRUCTION

After the unsettling encounter with Badger at the library, Lillian raced back to Ithaca Farm to meet the antiques dealer from London. She'd tried ignoring Apple's concerns about the missing librarian and her own fears about what had happened on the road last night, but something told her they were connected.

'Are there more rooms like yesterday's one?' Nicole asked over tea, trying to hide her excitement behind the steaming mug in her hands.

'Not inside, but the sheds are full. I don't have any use for them, so I haven't looked through them. You're welcome to,' Lillian said.

Nicole swallowed her mouthful of tea too fast, choking on the scalding brew.

In the moment it took her to recover herself, she'd formulated a plan. She wouldn't lie to Lillian, that wasn't who she was. She'd never been a deceitful child and wasn't about to start now. The worst she'd ever done was steal a stuffed toy penguin from the gift shop at London Zoo. She'd felt so guilty about that she'd made herself throw up and had confessed everything to her embarrassed parents.

. . .

They'd marched her back to the Zoo the following weekend, forcing her to confess, tears streaming down her face. It had been enough of a lesson to ensure she never strayed from the path of virtuousness again.

What she had planned wasn't really deceitful, it was a more stretching of the truth, to give her the time she needed to evaluate the collection and to consider how best to monetise it.

'I'd love to look in the sheds, if that's possible?'

'Anything's possible, I just—'

A knocking at the door interrupted them, and with a shrug, Lillian left Nicole in the kitchen to answer the incessant knocking.

Nicole sipped at her tea and flicked open her notebook, running her eye down the columns of rough figures. With this lot in the shop, she could go on holiday for a month and the shop would still strain at the seams. Heaven only knew what was in the sheds. This was almost like winning the lottery, albeit somewhat dustier and musty smelling.

Lillian returned to the kitchen, a uniformed police officer in tow, causing Nicole to choke once more on her drink.

'The police are investigating the disappearance of the mayor.'

'Oh,' Nicole said. There was nothing else she could really say. She didn't have the foggiest idea who the mayor was. Wouldn't know them if she fell over them.

'They're canvassing the neighbourhood. Seems they've found parts of her car along a stretch of the Roman Road, but no sign of her or the car.'

'Do you mind if I sit?' asked the officer, pulling out a chair before Lillian could answer.

Lillian slid into the seat next to Nicole. Nicole could almost feel the anger emanating from Lillian's body.

After running through the standard questions asking where they'd each been the night before, and if they'd seen or heard anything unusual, the officer asked if he could have a quick look through the sheds on the farm.

Lillian surprised everyone by refusing permission.

'Pardon?' said the officer, eyes widening.

Nicole almost spoke before clamping her lips shut. It wasn't her place to get involved. Not her monkey.

'Sorry, but you'll just have to take my word for it. I haven't hidden that woman's car in one of my sheds. She's the last person I'd have on my property.'

'So you know Jane Badrick then?'

'I know that almost no one in this town will cry in their tea about her disappearing.'

'Lillian...' Nicole said, spying the hungry look in the officer's eyes.

'Oh, he knows. I bet he's had his own run-ins with her as well. Am I right?'

The officer didn't answer, instead he closed his notebook and stood up, his demeanour entirely different to that from when he'd arrived.

'I'll be back, Miss Arlosh.'

Without waiting for Lillian to accompany him, he left the room, and Nicole heard the distinctive sound of the front door opening and closing, followed by tyres crunching over the loose gravel in the front yard.

'Sorry about that,' Lillian said.

'It's really none of my business,' Nicole replied, in the way English people talk when they're dying to hear the gossip, but are far too polite to pry.

'I wasn't completely honest with you about the sheds. There's stuff in one that I don't want anyone else to see. Not just yet, anyway.'

'The police will be back, probably with a search warrant. I've had a bit to do with the police and missing people, and it was a nightmare. Why didn't you let him have a look inside the sheds? If her car wasn't there, he'd have left you alone.' Nicole stopped, worried that she'd overstepped the mark. She barely knew this woman.

'I'll show you,' Lillian replied.

Nicole followed Lillian outside, the blustery wind almost knocking her off her feet. Together they wrestled the heavy shed door open, the hinges squealing in protest.

Nicole waited for her eyes to adjust to the low light. She had almost expected to see the missing car, and released a silent breath when it was clear the shed held nothing remotely resembling a car.

Lillian flicked a bakelite switch inside the door, and a weak light slowly bloomed into light.

Still, Nicole couldn't see anything worth refusing the police access to the shed, and looked at Lillian, waiting for her to unveil the big secret.

'You need to look under here,' Lillian replied to Nicole's questioning stare, pointing to a stack of dust-encrusted hessian sacks. Nicole had assumed they were covering bales of animal feed or obsolete farm equipment.

Nicole walked to the nearest cloth-covered bulk, her fear of nesting mice only trumped by her curiosity as she gingerly lifted the corner.

Nothing could have prepared her for what she saw underneath, and she stepped back, her hand over her mouth.

'How?'

'They were there when I arrived,' Lillian replied.

'Are there more...' Nicole began, gesturing towards the ghostly shapes crowding the walls of the shed.

'Yes.'

'And nobody knows that they're here?'

'No.'

'Could they be replicas?' Nicole asked, quite unable to fathom what she'd just seen in a run down shed on a mediocre farm in Northumberland.

'They're genuine. And if anyone finds them, they'll ruin all my plans. My dreams. This place will crawl with media, archaeologists, and every politician and boffin under the sun. I'll have no peace. And I can't let it happen. One altar and a handful of skulls have been bad enough. Imagine what they'll do when they find out that there are dozens more in my shed?'

'I can see why you didn't want him poking around in here. What will you do?' Nicole asked.

Lillian shrugged. 'No idea, I was hoping we could come up with something together,' Lillian said. 'But I suspect time isn't on our side.'

CHAPTER 39
A PROBLEM SHARED

The women worked together, hauling each altar piece, every single one of them heavier than Jesus himself.

'How many have we moved?' Nicole asked, wiping her palms on her filthy jeans.

'Seventeen,' Lillian said.

'It can't be seventeen, more like twenty-seven?'

'It's seventeen. I've been counting.'

The temperature hovered around zero, and plumes of their breath danced in front of their faces as they trekked across the yard into the shed and back again, with the stack of old stones never appearing to shrink.

Nicole had tried pushing all thoughts of historic sacrilege out of her mind, but every time she touched another gravestone, she'd said a silent prayer to whoever it was who'd commissioned that commemorative stone for their loved one. The inscriptions ranged from barely discernible to fully legible, but sadly her rusty Latin skills were limited to *veni, vidi, vici* and *carpe diem*, with a touch of *Caecilius est pater*.

'I wish we knew who put them here. And how long ago,' Nicole said again, accepting a glass of water from Lillian, as they both caught their breath in the freezing kitchen.

Lillian shrugged. This conversation had been going in unanswered circles since they'd started moving the collection of stones. Outside, night had already fallen. Night fell heavily in the North.

Nicole examined her ruined nails instead of watching Lillian, the silence too uncomfortable.

'You know, I can stay here if you like. Paige won't mind. The rest of Bellingham's rooms aren't ready, so I'm the only guest.' Nicole didn't really know what to do. Lillian seemed to be falling apart, pacing over to the window every half minute, looking for god-knows-what. Something or someone.

This trip wasn't panning out the way she'd hoped. She thought back to when her friend Sarah Lester went missing from the Old Curiosity Shop, and how she'd run things in Sarah's absence. She still didn't understand all the ins and outs of where Sarah had been, and she'd bitten back a thousand questions about Sarah's parents, and where exactly they were. But at least she had the experience of knowing that missing people generally reappear, at some point.

'I'm sure your friend will turn up, and the mayor,' she said, to fill the silence.

Nicole's shoulders slumped at the hopelessness of what had initially looked like the buy of the decade—the abandoned furniture and trinkets Lillian Arlosh wanted to sell, and the possibility, albeit a remote one, of adding some of the old altars into the lot. Nicole cursed under her breath as she tidied the kitchen. Anything to keep her hands busy. Her mind wandering, she barely noticed the crockery she was washing, old pieces of blue and white Spode, marked with the distinctive red back stamp, meaning the plates they'd eaten from were two-hundred years old, at least. It wasn't until they were in the drying rack that she clicked, but now wasn't the time to mention the age and value to Lillian. Not the time at all.

'Shall I make some tea?' Nicole offered, again, as the other woman paced backwards and forwards, wearing a track in the wooden floorboards.

'I don't think I could keep it down,' Lillian said.

Nicole wanted to load up the van and head home to London, but didn't want to leave Lillian on her own. The absurdity of the situation would send any woman to the solace of the nearest gin bottle.

Lillian had shown her a bedroom she could use, handing her a pile of clean sheets, and getting in an early apology for the state of the room, before shutting herself away in her own room, complaining of a terrible headache. Nicole opened the door and nearly tripped over an abandoned step ladder. The light switch failed to do anything other than make a clicking noise as she flicked it up, then down, then up again.

After hurriedly making the giant bed, noting with relief the extra woollen blankets already piled on top of the banded wooden blanket box, Nicole darted over to the humming radiator. Ithaca Farm had chilled her both physically and mentally. As she rubbed the pins and needles out of her hands, she couldn't shake the feeling that there were shadows in the past which weren't being shared.

With her hands tingling, she removed her jacket, shivering as she moved away from the warmth of the radiator. Her body screamed in protest. She hadn't packed an entirely appropriate wardrobe, not realising that winter would arrive so soon up here. Sure, she'd worked all her holidays in Germany, at her uncle's hotel, including during their long dark winters, but she'd always been prepared for that level of cold. She cursed her London approach to the cold, which really wasn't that cold at all. She'd grown soft since moving to the city.

Nicole slipped into bed, the hug of the smooth cotton sheets nicer than that of any lover. She burrowed under the covers, sleep deeply desirable after the day she'd just experienced.

As she tugged the covers up over her chin, leaving only her eyes and the top of her head exposed to the cool air, a shimmer in the corner caught her eye. She blinked, trying to refocus. A flash of banded gold light, there one-second and gone the next. Nicole tried to ignore it. She needed the sleep. It was a long drive back to London, back to the shop she managed in the absence of its owner, Sarah Lester.

Nicole had seen plenty of unexplained things in her time at the Old Curiosity Shop, and even before that, when she worked at her uncle's hotel.

You don't work in an old hotel in the mountains if you're afraid of things that go bump in the night. Life was full of unexplained occurrences. That feeling of déjà vu at the beach? Who's to say that you haven't lived that life before? Finding your car keys in a spot you know for certain you didn't leave them in. Who moved them? Was it you, or another version of you?

All Nicole knew was that what she'd experienced in London at the Old Curiosity Shop might be what was happening here. And she wanted nothing to do with it, but saw no way out of being involved. Not now that the van was heaving at the sides with the most incredible pieces from Ithaca Farm, and the promise of many more loads, including the Roman altars, if she could swing it.

The light shimmered again. You'd never see it if you didn't know what you were looking for. Nicole did, though, and that was her problem. It was evidence of the tiniest rift in time. It didn't mean the rift was in her room, but that it was close by. She recognised it because of her experience with Sarah Lester and the goings on at the antique shop. Losing Patricia Bolton to time still made her lip wobble if she thought about it too much. But those were the risks. And they weren't risks Nicole had ever considered taking. She was far too sensible. That's what her grammar school reports had all said, "Nicole is a sensible girl for her age". A comment that was neither a compliment nor a slight, but it had appeared on her reports year after year until it had become a running joke at home.

Nicole rolled over. She'd rather sleep, dreaming of her future, than risk her life to travel back in time. But someone had, and that put all of them at risk.

Somewhere a door banged in the wind, and the echos of a pack of dogs slipped in through the draughty window, whispers of cold snaking their fingers around her bare neck.

The howling echoed across the hills, reverberating off the ancient stone walls of the house, pushing its way under doors and window frames. Nicole pulled the duvet tighter around her body, trying to quash the rising panic. The dark had never been her friend. She always kept the hall light on, sometimes even the bedside light.

And in the pitch black of the room, she knew she wasn't alone. Someone else was in the room.

A window screamed on old hinges.

Glass shattered.

Her bedroom door flung open, revealing a body in the corridor, all arms and legs and flowing hair.

Nicole screamed.

And the stench. The smell following the fleeing figure was at once both of the earth and of beneath it. Reeking of decay and neglect, it assailed Nicole as she cowered in her bed.

The figure paused at her doorway, turning its eyes towards her. Eyes disguised by matted hair, his wrists bound with leather, his feet wrapped in similar strips. For a moment, the moon showed him to be just as scared as she was, until he threw back his head and his unearthly howls joined those of the dogs outside. He turned tail and threw himself out of the open window, and disappeared from sight.

CHAPTER 40

HELL

Nicole's screams had Lillian racing towards the far bedroom, only for her to see the shadow of a man in the doorway.

Skinny to the point of emaciation, with grey hair hanging like curtains down his back. The man stood with his bare feet splayed wide on the wooden floors, a grin stretched wide across his hollow face.

A supernatural chill weighed her down, slowing her steps, making it feel like she was running through honey.

Time froze.

With no warning, the man lunged for Lillian, his icy fingers plunging into her skin. Although he seemed to be nothing more than vapour and the odour of death, his vice-like grip on her arm still pulled her into the past. And into hell.

CHAPTER 41
CHEMISTRY LESSONS

Anson Darby and Ayla Raposo, the local Finds Liaison Officer from the Portable Antiquities Scheme, sat side-by-side on the industrial stools, taking turns to look through the black eyepiece of the microscope.

'I can't get over how much it looks to be newly minted,' Ayla said. 'Could it be a replica?'

'Can't be a replica. Look at the edges. And the analysis of the composition shows it to have the same makeup as the coins in the Shrewsbury horde. Someone lost it almost as soon as it was minted. Never used,' Anson said.

'I'd believe that if it was just one coin, buried deep in the dry Egyptian desert, tucked safely beside King Tut, but this came out of a Northumberland field, a field that's been in near constant use as either pasture or for crops, for the past thousand odd years. It should have been clipped by a plough, or knocked about. Tarnished, or rusted, or something. Not only that, but it's not the only one. We've got at least a dozen unused, genuine Roman era gold coins. And if word gets out about this, every metal detectorist in Europe will descend upon us like a plague of locusts.'

. . .

'No one is going to find out. All they know about is the altar and the skulls, and that hardly made international headlines. No one knows that we've uncovered the coins. I haven't even told the landowner yet.'

'You haven't told Miss Arlosh?' Ayla pushed back from the microscope to stare at him.

'I meant to, but with everything else going on, and then the police activity, I kind of forgot. I will tell her, I promise.'

'You'll lose your licence,' she said, displeasure writ all over her face.

Anson shrugged. He doubted it. They could hardly describe this as theft, because here he was, with the FLO pouring over a handful of gold coins, coins he'd found in the course of his work, which he'd immediately notified Ayla about. Stupid laws. It was a wonder any archaeology got done in England. He liked it better when they could dig where they wanted, and carry off any finds, putting them on display in private homes or clubs, unsullied by the miles of red tape which bound every archaeological dig in the country.

'Anyway,' Ayla said, her voice still full of disappointment. 'Back to the analysis?'

'Sure,' Anson said, his mind still in the past. Perhaps he should apply for one of the Middle East posts, where laws were laxer, and it was easier to make a name for himself? How he wished he'd been around in the time of Agatha Christie, when she and her second husband traipsed around Syria and Iraq, digging away using the substantial income from Agatha's books to fund their expeditions.

The pair spent the rest of the cloudy afternoon discussing the coins and their context, hypothesising a connection between the unearthed altar and the collection of coins.

'It makes little sense that there was only one altar there. There should be more. If only that bloody woman would give us permission to do a full site examination,' Anson said, slamming his fist onto the desk, making the coins jump.

'Take it easy,' Ayla said. 'These coins are in perfect condition. I won't let your temper ruin them. Remember the damage your temper caused in the past.'

'Let it go,' he said. 'It was a long time ago. Can't you just let the past stay in the past?'

Anson stood up, pushing his chair back a little too enthusiastically. 'Sorry, that was unintentional. I promise,' he said in response to Ayla's raised eyebrows.

If he couldn't keep his temper in check now, what hope did he have in trying to persuade that woman up at Ithaca Farm to let the university run a full investigation of the site? So far she'd said no to every approach, and he could feel any hope of academic glory seeping away. Some fresh blood would sweep in behind him and clean up again.

'I shouldn't have brought it up, but just try harder, huh? We have to work together, so yeah, I can put it behind me, just as long as you don't cross the line again.'

Anson nodded. Ayla was right, she always was, which made having to work with her so damn frustrating. No matter what he did, she always picked up something he'd missed, or pointed out that something he'd deemed unimportant was actually key to determining the historical importance of a find. He couldn't help it. His hand closed into a fist, but she didn't notice. She'd already turned back to the microscope. Typical. After everything they'd done together this afternoon, there she was, already rechecking his work. Redoing the analysis.

CHAPTER 42

A GIRL IN HIS BED

Lillian woke, tangled in a rough woollen blanket, clearly the cause of her bad dreams. She forced her sleep-glued eyes open, surprised her mother had wrangled the central heating system into life, only for reality to come crashing down.

This wasn't her bedroom, her house, nor her time. And the man in the corner wasn't her mother, yet he was at once both familiar and a stranger. But she wasn't afraid. Not of him, nor of her situation.

She moved, and the man at the desk turned towards her. The stylus in his hand poised above his work, concern on his face. Concern which disappeared, replaced with an inscrutable mask.

'You're awake?'

Lillian nodded, then regretted the movement, a small sound escaping from her lips. Her companion jumped up.

'You're hurt. You've had a fall. Stay down, for now.'

'I didn't have a fall. Someone hit me,' Lillian said, lowering herself back onto the cot. 'Kidnapped, I think. Where am I?'

The man pulled a stool over to Lillian. Before, the shadows had disguised his features, sketching him as an indistinct figure, a man without form. Close up, she knew him. And knew him well.

'I know you.'

'You're mistaken,' he said.

'You said that last time.'

Lillian knew she wasn't mistaken. She'd seen him before, but worst of all, she'd watched him fall in battle against a human tide of warriors, hacked to death in front of her. That was yet to come.

Lillian reached out to touch the man's cheek. Flesh. This man was real. His skin was hot to the touch. She pulled back her hand. He didn't react, save for the subtle movement of his hand touching his face where her hand had been seconds before.

'You... there's a battle coming. You should leave,' Lillian said.

He looked like someone had slapped him.

'How do you know this?'

Lillian shook her head. How could she explain?

'Metella also warned me,' he said.

'Metella?' Lillian's heart skipped a beat.

'A friend. She left the vicus before the Iceni attacked. With two of her servants and an old man. It was her I was searching for when we found you.'

'But you must remember the first time you saved me? My accident? On the road. You pulled me from my car?'

'I saw you first when Marcus found you. Then again last night when we were tracking the Iceni and their iron beast and we found your body. I thought it best to bring you to the fort,' he said, turning away to check the door. He stood for a moment, listening at the door.

'What's wrong? Why won't you remember me? ' Lillian asked, a frown finding its way onto her face.

He closed the door and stared at her. 'You shouldn't be here.'

'Well, that's obvious.'

'Your flippancy doesn't help.'

Lillian's cheeks coloured.

'I brought you here because to leave you there would have ended badly for you. Not all soldiers adhere to Rome's glorious ideals. And I would not incur the wrath of the goddess Satiada by letting those brutes have their way with you.' He gently touched a small bronze figure standing regally under a wooden arch, offerings of red holly berries strewn at her feet.

Satiada wasn't a god Lillian remembered from her Latin classes, but perhaps she was one the Romans had adopted, as they commonly did, in an attempt to better ingratiate themselves with the local population. The Romans were masters of assimilation.

'Not Mars?' she asked.

His eyes gazed into her soul.

'Women should not speak of Mars.'

'Really? You have at least a thousand different gods, and I'm not allowed to talk about Mars? At least at home we've whittled the gods down to a couple of main ones, with a few hardy claimants who jostle for power on the sidelines.'

'Do not mock the gods,' Julius said, his voice dangerously low.

'Sorry.'

'Now that you are awake, I will return you to the vicus,' he said, rechecking the door.

Lillian began protesting.

'Do not argue. You can't stay here. You go to the vicus tonight.'

Lillian thought back to her last vision of Julius, of him falling to the ground. Of the woefully outnumbered Roman soldiers defending themselves from a horde of warriors.

'I'm safer here than in the village. No one is safe. You must believe me,' Lillian tried.

'You talk in riddles. First, you mock my gods. And now you tease me with your prattle of battles and warriors. Next, you'll be predicting my demise.'

Lillian inhaled, and the temperature dropped. Sound slowed as they both froze in an unnatural tableau of fear.

A knock at the door broke the scene, and Lillian clocked the fear on his face. She scuttled to the back of the room, left dark by the candle's flickering flame.

'Who is it?' Julius called, his hand on the door.

An indistinct voice whispered back and Julius glanced towards Lillian and held his finger to his lips, before leaving the room and closing the door behind him.

Lillian sank to the floor, her feet scuffing the dry rushes covering the cold flagstones.

She could wallow in self pity and beg the gods to help her understand how she'd got here, or what her role was. She knew what she knew, and that she'd seen the future. And in that future, Julius, the man who'd saved her, would die. How soon, she couldn't tell, but his death would come at the hands of another, all linked to the men stealing the coins. She knew that for certain. But the threads that wove that knowledge together were ethereal. They fluttered in the wind beyond her periphery, like loose threads on the floor of the tailors. There, but unbound.

She stood up, her body protesting in pain, and examined the deities in their shrine. She touched them, the bronze unusually warm beneath her filthy fingers. The metal was smoother than she expected. She'd only ever seen examples of household gods in reference books, and once during a visit to the Museum of London. How perfect these were. She tried the name in her mouth — Satiada. It sounded safe. A safe name for a female goddess. Would she protect them? Lillian hoped she would, because from what she'd seen, they'd need all the help from all the gods in the coming days.

CHAPTER 43
NOWHERE SAFE

He'd been away from his quarters longer than expected, and upon his return, found the girl fast asleep in his cot.

Julius watched her breathing, the blankets rhythmically rising and falling like a solider marching in step with his cohort. Did he believe her? He had no reason not to, but her existence left too many unanswered questions. Unease perched on his shoulders, like a bird feasting on the stagnant remains of the warrior slaughtered in battle.

After he'd rescued her, she'd made a ludicrous accusation that his fellow soldiers had stolen the contents of the fort's pay chest. But he'd checked. The strongroom was intact, and the chest was as heavy as it ought to be. He should have handed her over to the guards, but something had stopped him. Was it her manner of speech? Her strange dress. He hadn't been in Britannia long enough to know the variations in the dress of the local tribes. Almost incoherent, she'd claimed to be from the future. He couldn't believe her, but in the shadows of his memory, there was a shade of something, a thought he couldn't grasp, of fantastical scenes he couldn't explain.

He'd carried her to his rooms, not completely understanding why, when she could very well be a spy for the Iceni. Yet here he was.

. . .

Julius moved away from the cot and returned to his desk, pushing aside his reports, the never ending reports he suspected no one read. From his personal chest, he withdrew his diary and sat down to record his thoughts about the girl. He'd lied to her. He had recognised her the instant he saw her unconscious form on the churned up path of the iron beast. How could he not? What he couldn't understand was their first encounter. One moment he'd been marching down the road. His patrol had paused for a comfort stop. He'd stepped away, not more than six paces, when from nowhere, two lights appeared, and a giant beast bore down upon him.

From there, it was all a blur. The beast had missed him, but there'd been an almighty crash. And once his night vision had returned, he ran to the side of the beast, only to find a woman, this woman, sitting in a chair inside the beast's belly. A chariot of a type he'd never seen before.

Perhaps he'd tell her the truth in the morning, when everything would be clearer, and she'd regained her sense. But for now, it was her warning which gave the most concern. That, and the one from Metella. It didn't pay to ignore fate when it collided like this.

The unexpected arrival of Decimus Clodius Albinus, the governor of Britain, had complicated things. And Julius could no more smuggle Lillian out of the fort than he could smuggle in a wolf cub.

Albinus had sent no word of his arrival, sending Ithaca Fort into an uproar when he'd arrived with his weighty escort and demands for the complete annihilation of the Iceni as punishment for their earlier attack on Ithaca Fort.

'The men fear him,' Julius explained. 'His skin is unnatural, like milk from the cow. Lily white, with eyes bled of all colour. Yet his own men revere him.'

'An albino?'

'As pale as the snow on the hills, but more dangerous, I'm told. Castus will do what Albinus orders, although the men are ill prepared to face the Iceni's Iron Beast. We can't even track it.'

. . .

Initially, Lillian had puzzled over Julius' description of the Iceni's strange chariot before settling upon the only explanation which made sense. Jane Badrick and her Land Rover had joined them in Roman Britain. Lillian didn't know what this meant for the fortunes of Rome, but it didn't bode well.

'I have a friend at home who is also an albino. It's a rare condition,' Lillian said, before realising that Julius wasn't listening to her. She watched him labour over his wax tablet.

'Your writing is too small. No one can read those letters.'

'No one has ever complained before. Wait, you can read?'

'Of course I can read. My military Latin is rusty, but trust me when I say people need to decipher what you've written. Make the letters larger and sign your full name.'

'What on earth for? The clerk knows me. I've been sending him daily reports for months.'

'It's not for him, it's for the future historians,' Lillian said.

Julius looked puzzled. 'You jest? This only records our numbers and provisions. There are no secrets or political intrigue. I'm not suggesting we overthrow the leadership of Rome. There's enough people doing that without me adding to it.'

'Julius, other people will read your words. Experts will analyse them and your abbreviations will be the subject of conferences lasting days with scholars from around the world. They'll publish every utterance and inference and then argue over them. They'll project words onto the walls of a museum or perhaps they'll print them every year in the tabloid newspapers. Words matter. Sign your name.'

Julius shrugged. 'I can't pretend that I understand what you're saying, but...'

He wiped his words from the tablet before labouring over his letters, forcing them to fit within the confines of the wax tablet.

'Press harder,' Lillian suggested, resting her hand on his arm.

Julius pressed his bone stylus harder into the soft wax.

'Have you finished your report?' Lillian asked.

'For today.'

'Then we need to leave,' Lillian said.

. . .

Julius shook his head. 'We've talked about this. You shouldn't be here. What would happen if the Iceni found you in the fort? You must go to the vicus.'

Lillian stood, her shadow dancing on the stone walls, a shadow hiding the fear in her face.

'No one is safe. I've told you again and again. You should have written that in your report instead of boring them with the number of soldiers with eye infections. Seriously, Julius, you're a soldier, and yet you're too afraid to recognise the threat creeping up behind you?'

'And you're just a girl, not from around here. It matters little if I believe you or not. No one else will believe the ramblings of a stranger. Sit down, please.'

Lillian swallowed, sinking onto a wooden stool, accepting that their conversation had circled back again to lack of trust. There was no escaping that Julius trusted her words as much as he trusted the beaver for military advice.

'It's not safe,' she whispered.

'There's nothing I can do.'

'The only safe place is home. Come back with me.'

Julius lifted her hand from his arm. 'How can you return, Lillian, when the countryside is full of armed barbarians, and you're hiding in the middle of a Roman fort full of Roman soldiers?'

Lillian's fingers strayed to the pocket in her jeans, the shape of the coin reassuring through the hardy fabric.

'Please go, Lillian? At least until they find the missing pay? With regards the Iceni, that's a different matter...'

'I told you who took it—'

'Yes, yes, two men, soldiers. No Roman soldier would steal the men's pay. Maybe it was the Iceni in disguise?' he added.

Lillian scoffed.

'They were Romans.'

'Get some sleep. We'll go to the vicus tonight.'

'If tonight comes,' Lillian whispered to herself as she abandoned her soldier for the single cot, pulling the fur covers up to her neck. As she fell asleep, her mind struggled with what would happen to her future if she lost her life now?

CHAPTER 44

THE TROUBLE WITH NUMBERS

Lillian hugged her knees to her chest, flinching at every violent sound outside of Julius' room. The scent from the dry rushes covering the floor tickled her nose, and she sneezed into her elbow, muffling the sound, obviously not quietly enough, as it scared a field mouse out from under the rough stretcher. The temperature in the room dropped again, goosebumps prickling on her arms, her filthy clothes no match for the Northumberland winter nights.

Lillian's thoughts strayed to what she'd seen when she'd first fallen down this rabbit hole. She'd tried telling Julius about the men stealing the coins, but he hadn't believed her. There had to be a way to persuade him about what she'd seen, or at least what she'd heard.

Lillian's head spun around. A car horn? Was that what she just heard? Shouting followed the sound. More shouting, and clamouring, and running and the clanging of metal. Lillian melted into the corner of the small room, terrified of being discovered should someone other than Julius burst into the room. She wrapped the blanket tighter around her, the grey wool disguising the white of her shirt and the denim of her jeans.

. . .

The horn sounded again, its noise more strident in a countryside devoid of the noise of civilisation, unimpeded by roaring jets or idling lorries or roaring motorcycles tearing up the picturesque country roads.

Hurried feet hammered past, and the door flew open. Behind the man in the doorway, two beams of impossibly bright light pierced the sky, and the noises of terrified men filled the room.

'Get up,' Julius said, his eyes finding her trembling form with ease.

'What's happening?'

Julius shut the door, leaning his weight against it as he seemed to struggle with his words.

'An Iron Beast is outside our gates.'

Lillian shook her head. Iron Beast?

'What are you talking about?'

Julius started gathering his writing materials and personal items, stuffing them into a pack, scooping up the tableau of household gods from his mini shrine, not recognising that one was missing, the one Lillian still held in her hands. He stopped moving momentarily to caress the top of the shrine.

'It rolls on wheels made not from wood, but from some godlike material, and it yells. It is lit by the rays of the sun, but has no heat. And the men... they're running scared. This beast rumbles down the hill, leading an army of Iceni warriors. I should never have kept you here. We must defend the fort, but how do we defend ourselves from this otherworldly beast?'

He turned his eyes towards Lillian, his pack abandoned on the stretcher.

'Did you bring this beast with you?' Julius accused, his hand straying towards the sword on his hip.

Lillian shut her eyes and shook her head, willing the nightmare to end.

'Open your eyes,' Julius demanded.

Lillian felt his shadow dwarf hers, and turned away, her cheek hard against the wall, the rough-sawn wood tearing at her skin.

'Look at me. Did you bring that beast back with you? If you did, you must know how to defeat it. How did I not think of this before?'

Lillian opened her eyes.

'Is there a car outside? Was that what I heard?'

'If a car is what you call the beast on rolling wheels, then yes. A moving carriage, like what you were in when I first saw you.'

'You remember. You said you didn't.'

'There's no time for that now,' Julius said, emptying his pack, and selecting a cloak, before smothering her with itchy fabric. 'Do you know how to vanquish the beast?' he asked.

Lillian nodded. If it was a car, then they could stop it. There was no magic involved, merely a combustion engine and fuel. But how did it get here? The same way she had?

'Don't say a word when we're outside. Women are forbidden inside the fort, so you must hide your face. Stay with me. I need you to confirm that the gods do not forsake us and that we can defeat the beast and its harlot of a charioteer.'

'There's a driver?'

'A woman leads it, yes,' Julius replied, gathering up his sword and checking his knife was at his belt.

The mayor.

Adrenaline coursed through Lillian as Julius opened the door, and they joined the maelstrom of soldiers bristling with weapons and armour.

In the distance, an unnatural light illuminated the guard towers. Light which could only come from the powerful headlights of a modern motorcar. Technology, not magic, threatened Ithaca Fort tonight.

The mass of soldiers stretched as far as the eye could see. There was no panic amongst them, just a quiet murmuring as they adjusted their armour and double-checked their weapons. Based on the bristling array of swords and spikes, shields and savage looking machines of war hooked up behind a stampede of horses, Lillian judged that whomever it was they were fighting wouldn't stand a chance.

'May Mars guide our arrows and deliver us this victory.'

Could this be the slaughter by the Ician, alluded to in the treatise she'd read, which is why Rome never recorded it? Because they weren't the victors? Her visions made sense now.

'Don't fight. Come with me instead. There's something...' Lillian struggled to find the right words. How could she tell him what she knew of the future? 'There's something wrong with your intelligence. There are more of them than you've been told. Waiting behind the Iron Beast.'

'How can you know that?' Julius asked, grabbing Lillian by the shoulders.

The mist obscuring the moonlight made it difficult to see, and Lillian couldn't tell if Julius finally believed her or whether he thought she was acting the part of a concerned lover as opposed to a genuine warning.

'As much as I don't understand your warnings, your voice tells me that what you say is true,' he said. 'Come, we must seek an audience with Castus, in the hope that he can dissuade Albinus from going into battle until we have more information.'

'Now you believe me?'

Julius cocked his head to the side, his dark eyes searching her face. 'How you know... concerns me, but the men are about to march and we are running out of time.'

They tried pushing their way through the frenzied activity towards the commander, before being stopped by the suspicious face of Marcus.

'You found the traitorous whore.'

'Now is not the time,' Julius said. 'It's urgent. We have word of the strength of the Ician—'

'Her head should be on the end of my staff.'

'She's not a spy—'

'I bet you that's what she whispers on your pillow at night. Hand her over, and form up. You're a Roman solider. Start thinking with your head instead of your cock.'

Lillian felt Julius bristle under her hand. The men poised like feral cats fighting over territory, the stench of their testosterone ripe.

'Come,' Lillian tugged at Julius' arm. 'We'll find another way,' Lillian whispered, dragging Julius away, terrified of what Marcus had planned for her.

In the melee, they fled from Marcus, hiding behind the stables.

'Please don't let them fight,' Lillian said. 'I've already lost everyone important to me. I...' What was she trying to say? She barely knew this man. This wasn't her time, or her place.

'This is my career,' Julius replied, withdrawing his hands. 'You don't know what you are asking.'

'I do,' Lillian started to shout.

'Be quiet,' he hissed. 'You can't yell like that when everyone is on edge. Waiting for a fight is like...' he half smiled. 'I can't explain it. It's like the moment you lean in to kiss someone for the very first time. You can't pull back. You're committed to the action, and if you were to pull away, you'd topple over.' Julius paused. 'I'm not explaining it very well. But that's what it's like before you go into battle. Everyone is teetering on the edge, waiting to go over. You screaming could be enough to tip them past the point of no return. They'd attack first and ask questions later, when it's too late. I no more want to lose you than you want to lose me. I'll make sure you're safe, and then I have to go before Marcus sends the guards to look for me.'

'Not the village,' Lillian begged, her voice cracking, remembering her visions.

'The fighting will be well away from the village.'

'I'll hide in the woods and wait for you.'

Lillian held her hand against her pocket, against the faint lines of her coin. Deep in her memory, the librarian's warning sparked to life. Lillian dampened it down. What did Pramod Sharma know about love?

'You could come home with me?'

The question hung in the air between them, the sounds of war barely penetrating the moment.

'I can't,' he said, squeezing her hand.

It was clear his duty took precedence over his life.

'Come, I'll see you safe before I go.'

The pair vanished like foxes in the night, darting into the woods on the perimeter of the assembling men. The cloak over Lillian's shoulders was just enough to disguise her modern clothing and her gender. They didn't stop until Julius had hidden her in a natural hollow under a willow whose branches swept the surrounding ground.

'Stay here. I will find you when it's over.'

Lillian tried to interject, as Julius held his finger to her lips.

'Nothing will happen to me. I have the might of the Empire behind me, and Mars himself. I will understand if you go home...' Julius left the words hanging.

'No, I'll wait. If you... if you don't come back, then I will go,' she said.

Another horn sounded, its mournful tone the perfect accompaniment to the prelude to slaughter.

'Knowing you're safe will sustain me,' Julius said. He held her eyes and leant forward, his lips brushing hers, pushing closer, entwining his arms around her body, for what was both the shortest, and longest, of seconds. And it was everything she'd never dared dream of, and more.

The darkness disguised their mess of emotions, but that moment was enough to tell Lillian all she needed to know. When she opened her eyes, he'd gone.

How could she face the future, knowing that he might not even be alive in the past?

CHAPTER 45
RUN, RUN AS FAST AS YOU CAN

It wasn't only Pramod, Metella, Silas and Carmella who'd fled the vicus the night the Iron Beast attacked Ithaca Fort. It hadn't taken long for the rumours to take hold, and in almost every home, on every street, people packed their valuables and ran for their lives. Fleeing in every direction other than that taken by the Iron Beast and the Iceni warriors.

The butcher hurriedly wrapped his most precious blades, forsaking every knife he'd ever cursed before. As he pulled the door shut behind him, he muttered a brief prayer to Satiada to keep the butchery safe until his return. If he returned. He'd been on the periphery of enough conflicts to know that the Romans would always protect their fort first, and the adjacent vicus if they felt like it. He hurried along the road, head down, his knives clutched to his chest, barely acknowledging the stream of villagers alongside him.

The scenes in the brothel were more subdued. Without Metella telling them what to do, or Silas yelling at them to move, they clucked like chickens, running around as if the butcher had just removed their heads with his cleaver.

Distraught that Metella had left without a word, the girls both packed and unpacked.

Opportunistic thefts by the sleight of hand rampant in the confusion. The older women knew the score. They knew what would happen to them if Ithaca Fort fell and the Iceni took control. Most of them didn't bother packing. They fled with the clothes on their back and a cape secured around their throats. Once the threat subsided, and the flood of testosterone was abated with blood, they'd return and carry on working. Fair weather whores, that was them.

The younger girls were different. They didn't know what happened after a battle. They had no experience of the blood lust fuelling the barbarian warriors. It didn't matter where the aggressor came from. Their upbringing played no part, nor their background. Men were the same the world over. Whoever won the fight celebrated the same way, with wanton destruction, unnecessary slayings and sex by force with whoever was available, be it man, woman, or child.

The villagers bleed into the countryside, carrying nothing more than fear in their hearts. Others lumbered under sacks of stock, desperate to save their livelihoods from ruin, as well as their lives. Some hunkered down in hollows under towering Wych Elm trees, waiting out the threat in the subzero temperatures. Some fleeing villagers would never leave their hiding places, dying of hypothermia, frostbitten fingers still clinging to their valuables.

A boon for generations of metal detectorist hobbyists.

The Iceni had no interest in the vicus dwelling beneath the shadow of the Roman fort. Of course, their warriors would pillage the place for anything of worth. They'd destroy the buildings, and enslave the pliable women and children, possibly some men. But their interest lay more in destroying the Romans, forcing them from the land, and out of the country. Sending them back to their gilded Roman halls.

Most of the Iceni imagined Rome as some towering gold-encrusted monolith bristling with arms and soldiers. But soldiers weakened by sun and extravagant foods. Foods which weighed them down. Wine-soaked soldiers soaked with slaves attending to their every request, growing soft off the backs of the conquered.

The Iceni knew nothing of Rome's conquests of vast tracts of the world. But they knew battle, and they'd battled this beast before, and had won. Although the Roman wolf had returned, bigger and stronger than before, the Iceni wouldn't let the wolf devour them. It couldn't, not with the Iron Beast in their ranks.

CHAPTER 46
WOMEN RULE THE WORLD

Jane Badrick's eyes glittered in the moonlight. Her normally pristinely styled hair flew wantonly in the Northumberland breeze. This was her destiny, her birthright as an Englishwoman. Behind her streamed hundreds of men and women dressed for war. Clad in leather and furs, bristling with weapons only seen in museums and on shards of decorative pottery dug up by archaeologists. The victors write the history, never the vanquished. And she was about to change history. This would secure her place in time. In the history books. And to think, she'd only ever dreamed of becoming mayor, and possibly the local member of parliament. Small minds dream small dreams. Hadn't she been told that her whole life? Her father drumming it into her at every opportunity. Yet she'd allowed her husband to derail her dreams. A man with no imagination and no drive to enact actual change. She saw it now, with a clarity she'd never had before.

Jane pushed her foot hard against the accelerator, revving the engine, sending ripples through the surging warriors around her. She smiled. The power beneath the hood of the beast, hers, and hers alone to control, to wield as a weapon.

Bricius filled the seat beside Jane. His white knuckles on the edge of the beige leather seats were the only sign of his discomfort.

Bricius may be the second in command of this tribe of warriors rising against the Roman occupation, but he was in the passenger seat and Jane was in control.

'We advance,' Bricius said, pointing towards the fort walls illuminated by the headlights.

From the back of the skittish horse next to them, the chieftain Gar shook his head. 'No. We've scared them with our show of power, with the Iron Beast,' he said, using the name the Iceni had given to the Land Rover. 'We should disappear into the night. That will scare them more,' he declared.

'No,' Bricius said. 'We're ready to fight. They're weak, with depleted numbers after our first raid.'

Jane turned towards Bricius, her icy eyes boring into his. 'You will not win,' she said. 'They will crush you. Your warriors haven't drilled for years and years. You will lose.'

'The Iceni are brave, braver than any Roman. We will defeat them, with or without the Iron Beast.'

Jane snorted. 'Then it will have to be without the Iron Beast. I will have no further part in this suicide mission.'

'The witch is right,' Gar said, pulling on the reins of his horse, turning away from the fort.

Jane slipped the car into reverse and began backing up, scattering the ragtag warriors behind her.

'We fight,' Bricius said, his hand fumbling on the gear lever.

Jane pumped the brakes, sending Bricius flying into the windscreen. Silence filled the car. Jane waited for the chieftain to intervene, but suspected he wouldn't. The Iron Beast was too much of a gift from the gods for him to ignore her instructions. She was like Cassandra, with the power to predict the future. Oh, what havoc she could wreck. Jane conveniently forgot that Cassandra's legacy was that no one would believe her prophecies.

As Bricius peeled himself off the dashboard, Jane looked towards Gar, who stared back at her before slowly inclining his head.

'We fight when I say the time is right. I have seen the future. If you continue down this track, the Romans will annihilate you and your tribe, and history will forget that you ever existed.'

'Now tell them we retreat. Melt back into the bushes. Vanish from their sights. Behave like ghosts and set the fear of the gods amongst them. Do it. Now.' Jane moved her hand to press the button for the sunroof, peeling back the shadowed glass until the interior of the car was lit by ten thousand stars.

Bricius's eyes grew wide as the ceiling above his head vanished.

'Stand up and tell them,' Jane instructed, a smile playing on her plastic face.

Bricius reached out to touch the sides of the sunroof. Jane presumed he did so to reassure himself that the night wouldn't devour him.

'Stand up,' Gar repeated, his voice harder than the steel of the dagger strapped to his leather belt.

Bricius stood, as if in slow motion, swallowing his fear, his shaking legs concealed within the confines of the Iron Beast.

The warriors fell silent, shrinking back in obvious fear of the manifestation of Bricius emerging from the solid roof of the magical beast. If they'd heard the war of wills between Bricius, Gar and Jane, they showed no sign. The power of the magic tempering their fear and confusion.

'Satiada has spoken through the heart of the Iron Beast. She wills us to return to our homes tonight. Our work tonight was to scare the Roman scum, and see,' he threw his arms towards the fort, and the motionless soldiers whose outlines they could see lining the fort's wall. 'See, they are too scared to face the Iron Beast and our warriors. We will return. Satiada has spoken. She has foretold the future, and the future will be ours. The Romans will become the vanquished.'

The warriors erupted in premature jubilation, whooping and hollering, clashing their swords and spears against the frost-bound earth and painted wooden shields. As their celebrations wound down, Jane pressed play on the CD player, and the soaring sounds of Tchaikovsky's 1814 Overture filled the air, the rising crescendo punctuated by booming canons.

Jane's smile widened at the warriors cowering on the ground, hands clamped over their ears. She gunned the engine, and spun the tyres, flinging clods of broken earth over the Iceni warriors.

She sped off down the road the Romans had so conveniently paved. A road as familiar to her here as it was at home.

Bricius sat pressed to his seat, his face as pale as the moon above them. Jane laughed and laughed. The high-pitched laughter audible even to Roman's lining the walls of the stone fort. The sound of evil.

CHAPTER 47

SUPERMARKET DELIVERIES

Jane climbed from the artificially warm leather seats of her Land Rover and stretched, the smile on her face larger than the vista in front of her. Safely tucked away in a valley still covered with ancient trees and undisturbed undergrowth, she glowed with power and promise.

'Better than fighting,' she said to Gar. 'You've scared them now, and that, my friend, is more valuable than sending your warriors on a suicide mission to attack their fort.' Jane smiled.

The chieftain smiled back, and Jane suspected it was infatuation she saw on his face.

Bricius, however, grunted, his tatty braids obscuring his eyes.

Typical man. He could have shown more appreciation for her battle tactics. She didn't have time to smooth his bruised ego or to stroke his masculinity. She'd been doing that her whole life, and look where that had got her? Eating triangle-shaped sandwiches with geriatrics who wore incontinence pants. Never again. Let the chieftain sort out his second in command.

'We angered the goddess by not sending any Romans to meet their ancestors tonight,' Bricius said, petulance dripping from his tongue.

'Is it the goddess feeding us tonight, or your friends and family who didn't just die in battle?' Jane retorted.

Gar laughed, loosening the mood, and lead Jane by the arm towards a large tent, almost as large as the downstairs footprint of her home in Hexham. After pulling back the flap, he ushered her into a smoky haze and the merry chatter of woman and men attending giant pots of food over hot coals. Certainly nothing in the pots would ever appear in the Roman recipe book attributed to Caelius Apicius. Whatever it was they were serving, it couldn't be as bad as some meals she'd consumed in her capacity at the mayor.

She commandeered a stool by the fire, but refused to loll about on furs like an actual heathen. Start out the way you meant to continue. If the stool belonged to someone higher up the food chain, then more fool them for letting her claim it. She was top dog now, unstoppable with her iron beast and her knowledge of history. Jane smiled. What a life she could lead, and one she wasn't about to squander. A vague memory of some BBC television programme surfaced. Something to do with metal detectorists and treasure. There was enough treasure on the arms of the heathens in this one tent to fund the rest of her life, and a run at becoming the local MP without drawing on her husband's money. In fact, there was very little need for her husband at all if she were financially independent. A new life beckoned.

A flurry of activity at the tent entrance drew Jane's attention. Bricius stepped aside as a weasel-like man carrying a crate broke free from the knot of onlookers and approached Jane, a mixture of fear and superiority struggling for dominance on his face.

'Your beast carried this in its bowels,' he quavered.

Jane lowered her wooden bowl.

'What is it?' she asked, her stomach constricting as she tried to remember what might be in the Land Rover.

The wiry man dropped the crate, its contents spilling at her feet. A watermelon, punnets of strawberries, rock-hard avocados, a bunch of brilliantly yellow bananas with their fair-trade stickers still attached to each half circle, a bunch of celery, vine-ripened tomatoes (pesticide free) and bags of fresh-cut coriander and dill. Her groceries, loaded into the back of her car by some nameless pimply teenager who wished he was old enough to shave.

Bricius stepped forward. 'What is this magic from the Iron Beast?'

Jane laughed and plucked the bananas from the ground, slowly peeling the skin. Holding eye contact, she bit the end of the fruit, her teeth clicking shut as she slowly chewed the white flesh. 'Fruit,' she said after swallowing. 'The Iron Beast delivers food, like a slave.'

The tent fell silent as every person stared at her. Jane revelled in the assumed adoration, passing her half-eaten fruit to the woman next to her. 'Try it,' she coaxed.

The woman's eyes grew larger than the watermelon next to her, and Jane laughed again as she imagined future shopping expeditions at the local Waitrose, and bringing back modern delicacies as bribes to her followers. For that's what she considered them to be now, followers. Minions at her beck at call, and Gar and Bricius would soon be surplus to her requirements. To the tribe's requirements.

After the excitement of sharing the fruit among the assembled tribe, and laughing at their faces as they each tried the exotic treat, they showed Jane to a tent of her own. Kitted out with furs and an almost solid looking bed, she stretched out in relative comfort, her mind replaying the events of the past few days. She could see no downside. Everything had gone as well as she expected, although there could always be improvements. What she needed now was a pen and paper, to list everything she would bring back as bribes or improvements. Her mind hovered over the addition of modern weapons. Imagine what a handgun or a hunting rifle could achieve?

Sleep came easily, and glorious dreams of golden bangles and triumphant marches up to the Roman forum filled her mind. As she slept, her plans unfurled their wicked wings. She may be the queen of this piddling tribe of heathens now, but what if... what if the glory and riches of Rome beckoned? A smile played across her face. It didn't matter who the Roman emperor was. She had the writings of Pliny and Plato, of Marcus Aurelius, and the words of Hadrian himself behind her, acting as her bibles, maps, providing a path to the highest seat in the known world. She was a powerful woman, albeit one smothered in an invisible cloak of self-importance, and there was no one who could defeat her if she chose this path. No one at all.

The early snow had settled outside her tent, and although Jane's sleep had been that of the virtuous, her immediate need was for suitable footwear. There was no way she could conquer the Roman Empire in bare feet.

She stood motionless in the doorway of her tent, waiting for someone to notice her. They would. She was a striking woman, even in the middle of a filthy campsite. Older than almost anyone there, with a full mouth of her own teeth, she knew they revered her. How could they not?

'You're awake,' Bricius said, as he emerged from the shadows of the nearest tent into the daylight, the weak autumnal sun pricking out the whorls and whirls of the tattoos covering his body. 'An excellent day to kill some Romans.'

'No, not a good day to kill some Romans,' Jane replied. 'That time will come,' she added quickly, registering the flash of anger on the face of the man. 'We must plan our attack with care, using all the power of the Iron Beast. Gar and I agreed to this plan.'

'Humph,' Bricius said, picking at his teeth with dirt-encrusted nails. 'The time is right. We've waited too long. We were ready before you arrived. My warriors want blood, not your fancy fruit. We have our own fruit here, and we have no need of yours.'

Jane felt the threat in his words. She couldn't lose him now. Despite the mystery of her appearance and the magic of the Land Rover, she appreciated that her position in the tribe was tenuous. Sure, the Romans, and the Iceni, were terrified of her so called Iron Beast. But before long, it would cease to hold their attention. A lack of fuel was her primary concern. Once it ran out of gas, or the battery died, it was no better than a hunk of sedimentary rock.

'I have other magic,' she said, fumbling for an answer, anything to sway the man's attention back towards her.

As suspected, his eyes widened, and she smiled as he took half a step backwards.

'What other magic?' he asked. 'I have not heard the druids speak of other magic.'

'It's not here. I keep it at my home.'

'Where is your home?'

Jane quickly thought about how to answer him. The best way was, of course, with the truth. 'In Hexham, at the Great Hall.' Technically true. Her office was in the room adjoined to the Great Hall.

'Then we go to your home.'

It wasn't that easy. Jane still hadn't figured out if she could get home, let alone come back again. She'd assumed, but she hadn't survived this long without knowing how to play the cards with which fate dealt her.

'I need to pray,' she said. It worked at home, so why wouldn't it work here?

Bricius smiled. At last, something his dim mind could comprehend, Jane thought.

'Where is the nearest shrine?'

The warrior lead her towards a familiar part of the countryside. Jane recognised the place, even as it was now, with no light pollution or discarded crisp packets tangled in the undergrowth. Without the asphalt roads and the overhead power lines, this was where she'd crashed her car, down the road from Ithaca Farm, swerving to miss... who was it she'd seen? Was it a soldier? Or a girl? Everything was a blur.

'The shrine, it's just beyond the rise,' Bricius said, pointing to a slight hill in the distance.

'Leave me,' she demanded.

Jane didn't need to look a second time, instantly recognising the hill as the place where Ithaca Farm now sat. Ugly in its age, a festering sore on the Northumberland landscape. A cluster of buildings and fallow land that the new owner was hell bent on destroying even further. Rewilding. She'd never heard such a preposterous idea in all her life, and she'd told her husband that.

Jane strode across the uneven ground, her feet now wrapped in strips of leather. Hardly the same as the shoes she'd lost when she'd arrived, but good enough to stop her from contracting frostbite. She'd left Bricius waiting by the tyre marks, his bulk reassuringly solid and close by, should she need him, which was doubtful.

As she crested the small hill, the hill she knew Ithaca Farm stood upon in the 21st century, she couldn't help but admire the countryside.

With nary a high-rise or wind farm in sight, the undulating hills looked better than any tourism billboard. Jane's crassness won out over nature, as she considered how good a row of holiday cabins would look on the brow of the hill, overlooking the site of Ithaca Farm and the brooding stones of Hadrian's Wall.

With no sheep or cattle to mow the grass, the altar Bricius had pointed at stood concealed within a tangle of blackthorn and holly. Traces of a flattened path lead Jane safely through the thorny arms to the colourful stone.

The altar pulsed with life under its red coat of paint, with virtuous offerings littering the rectangular base of the carved monument to the goddess Satiada.

'What can you give me?' Jane asked the altar, her eyes roaming across the scattered offerings.

If the goddess was listening, she provided no answer, silently watching as Jane knelt, out of sight of Bricius. He wouldn't understand, Jane thought, scrabbling through the offerings left on the base of the altar.

Jane brushed aside bunches of thyme, and rosemary tied together with hemp. An amphora lay on its side, its stopper long since chewed away by hazel dormice, and the contents imbibed by an army of ants and honeybees, leaving behind the faint apple-like odour of cider.

Where was the gold? Weren't these barbarians supposed to have heaped their wealth upon the laps of ungrateful gods? Well, in their eyes, Jane was almost a god, and she needed their gold more than a make-believe sky deity.

Ah. Nestled in the altar's crevice sat a leather purse, its stitching rough, but clearly good enough to hold its contents intact.

Jane tugged at the bag, ripping it from its home between the feet of the goddess Satiada. A metallic clinking told Jane all she needed to know.

With shaking hands, Jane loosened the leather knot and opened the drawstring purse. The insipid sun couldn't diminish the golden glow from within the bag. Jane's face shone brighter than the dozen coins. The gold lifting her soul up into the outer reaches of the heavens. This is what it felt like to be a god, she thought.

She needed to count the coins, in case the heathens tried robbing her. Jane wouldn't put it past any of them. Gar, she trusted, to a point, and as long as he was on her side, she knew she would be safe. Bricius was a different matter. He was proving to be a man of some intelligence, with a solid level of military acumen. He would throw her to the wolves if she looked to risk the lives of his family. But at the moment, he believed the druids had foretold her arrival. A shadowy person, she'd yet to see any sign of the druids in person. Jane hated needing anyone, but she couldn't achieve her goals without Bricius, for now. But when she returned, he was but a pawn in her game. And pawns existed to be sacrificed. Once she delivered Bricius and Gar to the Romans, and wielded her Cassandra-like power of telling the future, the commander at Ithaca Fort would have to send her to London, and from there, to Rome. Her glory was inevitable. Fated even.

Jane tipped the bag upside-down, watching as the coins tumbled from their sanctuary into her outstretched palm.

She screamed.

Pain tore at her head, striking her skull from within. Battering her eyelids, her jawbone, her lips, her tongue, until her existence was nothing more than a ghost upon the lips of the men she'd left behind.

'We've found her!'

Jane whimpered, the yelling obscenely loud.

'Over here.'

Voices washed over Jane as she curled tighter and tighter into a ball on the ground. What was that heathen doing, yelling at her? Surely he could see that someone had attacked her?

'Jane, Jane, can you hear me? Get that ambulance over here, now.'

The voices. So loud.

'Bricius, make them be quiet, they're too loud,' Jane whispered, trying to cover her ears with her arms, whilst hiding the coins from Bricius's eyes. She couldn't let him know she'd stolen the coins from the altar.

'How the hell did she get up here?' someone asked.

'Didn't we search this place already?'

'I'm sure of it. She wasn't here before. The archaeologists were up here all week, and they saw no sign of her.'

Jane kept her eyes shut, as the voices flowed over her, the harsh guttural vowels of the Northerners blending into one another, the sound more aligned to those of the Celts than anyone in modern day England could ever know.

A siren sounded, every strident note piercing Jane's body as reality struck. She was home. The coins had brought her home.

The coins! She couldn't let these men find the treasure. They were her conduit in and out of time. Each one of them was more precious than the gold they'd been made with.

Rolling onto her knees, she poured them back into their leather pouch, shaking off the hands trying to get her to stay on the ground.

'Get away from me!' she yelled, panic rising.

'Mrs Badrick, Jane, it's Neil, from the garden centre. We've been looking for you.'

Jane didn't give two hoots who Neil was, or what he'd been doing, she only knew that she had to protect her gold.

'Let me help you.'

'Get away, leave me alone!' Jane yelled.

Jane could feel the man backing away, flinching as he yelled, 'Where's that ambulance?'.

Running feet pounded the earth, coming closer, and closer as Jane drew the drawstring tight at the top of the bag, and shoved it down her top, held tight by her bra. Only then did Jane sit back on her heels, her face calm, ready to face the world. The modern world.

CHAPTER 48

NIGHT HAWKS

John Revell studied his phone. This radio silence was doing his head in. He was used to notifications pinging throughout the day and night. Tidbits and gossip and here-say were his lifeblood, his reason for coming into work every day. If it weren't for living his life vicariously through the misdemeanours of others, he would have thrown in the towel years ago, spending his remaining time concentrating on his golf swing, and leaving his bloody wife to make the money to pay their bills. For a change.

That was another thing. Gail hadn't even rung him. Her best friend was missing, and his wife was giving him the silent treatment. It was that, or she was busy with the cottages. Just thinking about the Hexham Holiday Cottages sent a sharp pain shooting through his head.

Mortgaged to the hilt, the pandemic had done nothing but add to their financial woes. Not that Gail showed any sign of worrying about that side of things, not with all the money she spent at the nail bar with Jane-bloody-Badrick.

John checked his phone again. Nothing. 'Useless thing,' he said, slamming it onto the desk, dropping his head into his hands. Perhaps Gail was checking in some guests?

It would be a miracle if she were. They'd suffered so many cancellations that he'd stopped checking the reservations book. The striking red lines made his headaches unbearable.

Jane's disappearance could benefit him... He doodled on his desk pad, and in the blink of an eye, rows of numbers were marching down the page. Numbers crossed out, rewritten, circled. No matter which way he looked at it, the missing woman would be a boon to his bottom line. She'd been a thorn in their side for so long, it had been impossible to staunch the wound. Gail wouldn't hear an ill word of her friend, and John needed Jane's connections for the paper's survival. Or at least that's how he'd been operating. The only thing he needed her for now was to sell more papers. And for that to happen, she needed to stay missing, and not turn up in a ditch somewhere. That could come later.

Revell rang Jasper, ordering him into the office, regardless of his employee's rostered morning off, knowing full well that he wouldn't complain. Jasper was a good operator. He did what he was told and didn't curl his lip at the more mundane aspects of the job. Not like Charley Scott, lording it over them all up in Newcastle. She'd used them. After everything he'd done for her. As soon as she got a better offer, she'd packed up faster than a Tory minister, escaping a mob of angry miners. John monitored the bylines in all the local papers. You never knew when a former intern might prove useful. An intern like Charley might have the inside scoop on Jane's disappearance. Those city types usually did. It wouldn't surprise him if she slept her way to scoops.

With a calming breath, he rang Charley Scott's number, pushing all thoughts of his crumbling financial situation out of his mind.

Jasper finished brushing his teeth, and checked his hair in the mirror, smoothing an overgrown mop in need of a trim. He fancied dropping in to the Bellingham Tea Rooms for a coffee and scone before a quick trip to the barber. Then work. One rostered morning off a month was one perk of the job.

. . .

The frontage of the Bellingham Tea Rooms were obscured by a phalanx of white vans, emblazoned with the logos and web addresses of the various tradespeople — electricians, plumbers, plasterers. Any parking warden worth their salt would have a field day. Jasper edged his tiny car into a minuscule gap, not even bothering to lock the thing before sauntering into the cafe inside.

Paige had done an excellent job of both restoring the period features of the once grand building, whilst bringing it into the modern day at the same time. They should have finished the renovations the previous year, but, the pandemic. Everything was now described as pre-pandemic, or post-pandemic. There was no in-between.

As Jasper stood in line, he kept half an ear on the surrounding conversations. It never ceased to amaze him how much tradies knew. They may look busy fixing the pipes under your sink, but they're still listening to your phone calls, your arguments, and judging the daytime television you're bingeing, or the porn still playing on your laptop. And today was no different. The only topic of conversation was that of the missing mayor.

Answering a phone call from his boss on his morning off was never a good idea, and today was no different.

Abandoning his place in line, Jasper hightailed it back to his car, speeding the short distance to the 1960s building housing the Hexham Herald. For a town filled with exquisite historic buildings, the newspaper filled the ugliest in town. Squat like a nuclear bunker, the orange-toned brick walls always made him think of Trump. And the building had just as much class. With gold lettering above the entrance, the whole thing now resembled a throwback to the 80s when John Revell had first bought the building for his fledgling newspaper empire, an empire which hadn't grown further than Hexham's city limits. Even walking through the doors, Jasper sometimes fancied that he could smell fully leaded fuel and the stench of a thousand cigarettes.

'You took your time,' Revell called from his glass enclosed office as Jasper made his way inside.

Jasper desperately needed a restorative coffee before facing his boss, and his stomach growled in anger at the implied haste in Revell's command.

'I've been on the phone to the city,' Revell said, his tongue curling around the word city as if it were a dirty word. 'They let slip that the police think she stumbled across some night hawkers, disturbed them, and then things turned nasty.'

Jasper nodded. That was his information as well. Although every time he tried imagining Jane Badrick involving herself with some lowlife night hawkers, it just didn't sound like the woman they all knew and despised.

'You went to that meeting the other night, right? The one with the metal detectorists? They might know something. Go interview them. We might get the jump on the city people. That'd put their noses right out. I told them I'd share whatever we uncovered, but I didn't say when.' John Revell tapped the side of his bulbous nose.

'Sure thing,' Jasper said, closing his open notebook, the page unmarred.

'And ring me the second you hear anything. The entire team's working on this,' Revell gushed, as if they had a staff of dozens instead of the handful that only just filled a booth for their Christmas drinks at the Twice Brewed Inn every year.

Dismissed, Jasper returned to his desk, rolling his eyes at the questioning looks from Rhema and Jan, huddled together at the advertising desk.

Damien was more direct. Sidling up to Jasper's desk, he wasn't backward in coming forward to ask Jasper what their leader knew about Jane's disappearance.

'Night hawkers,' Jasper replied.

'Hmm, they've always been a problem round here, but I shouldn't think that they'd be up to kidnapping anyone. Not when they can just ship their stuff off shore to sell it. A quick jump over the Channel, a dealer who doesn't ask questions, and Bob's your uncle, the money's in the bank,' Damien said, fiddling with the stained straps of his denim overalls.

'True,' Jasper said. 'And they'd have to be stark raving mad to kidnap her,' Jasper laughed. If Revell noticed the mirth, he showed no sign, remaining hunched over his desk, the phone pressed tightly to his ear, his fountain pen furiously scribbling on his blotter.

'What was she doing on the Stanegate, anyway?'

'Coming home from a meeting,' Jasper replied. He should have recorded what Revell had said. Something about a committee meeting? Women's Knitting Club or Gardening Club or something inane like that. It would come back to him.

'My wife goes to those meetings, and to bookclub. I always have to take her and pick her up. They like their wine, those ladies. They dress it up like they're all important, creating solutions for the community, but in reality, it's a good old booze up once a month. If they didn't serve wine, my wife would never set foot in any of the meetings. Have you ever been to a book club meeting?'

'No.'

'Me neither. Ladies only. Liquored up, all of them.' Damien laughed. And continued laughing all the way back to his desk, where his rolling chortles sent the papers on his desk fluttering to the floor.

The juxtaposition between the alcohol free meeting of the Hadrian's Heroes Metal Detecting Club and the apparently booze-filled meetings of the Women's Horticultural Club couldn't have been clearer. Not that anyone else would ever mention it, but ladies who did good things in the community were usually the ones who got away with literal murder.

'Come on, Rhema,' Jasper said, grabbing the camera bag and his satchel.

'Pardon?'

'We're off to interview some metal detectorists. The scourge of Hexham.'

'Oh,' Rhema replied, grabbing her coat and handbag from the back of her tatty office chair.

Jasper worked the phone, chasing down the various members of the Hadrian's Heroes Metal Detecting Club. The club's president couldn't have been more helpful — the possibility that night hawkers might have kidnapped the mayor appeared to be the most exciting thing to have happened to the club since their inception in 2008.

And thus Jasper and Rhema found themselves outside the Harley Garden Centre, where they found a bespectacled man in a dark green apron hopping from foot to foot, his excitement palpable.

'That's him,' Jasper said to Rhema, killing the engine. 'Clifton Beaufort, president of Hadrian's Heroes.'

'Mr Beaufort, thanks for taking the time to meet with us at such short notice,' Jasper shook the man's hand. 'This is Rhema, our intern.'

'Lovely to meet you, Rhema. Clifton Beaufort. One of the Somerset Beauforts, but don't hold that against me.' The joke rolled off his tongue as if he'd made it a thousand times before.

'Is there somewhere we can talk?' Jasper asked, conscious of the flow of ancient humanity staring at them as shoppers walked in and out of the garden centre. This was definitely the place to run any election campaign if you were trying to secure the pensioner vote.

'Of course. We have a lovely cafe inside, with a quiet table down the back. Most shoppers don't like it because it's next to the kitchen.'

The trio made their way inside, eyeballs following them every step of the way. They lived in a small town, and small towns were prone to small lives, which meant anything remotely new or exciting became amplified the same way football chants reverberated around giant stadiums the world over.

Settled at the sticky table, Jasper tried marshalling the exited club president, but the man was a box of over-hyped squirrels, his imagination running wild with theories, each one more outlandish than the one before.

'Mr Beaufort—'

'Clifton, please.'

'Clifton. What can you tell us about night hawkers?'

'Oh no, I don't know any. No, none. I've heard of some, but I don't know any personally. Scum of the earth. They give us detectorists a bad name. And they contravene the code of conduct of the National Council for Metal Detecting. None of our members would ever conceive of breaching the code. Goes against everything we stand for.'

'Right. But you must have heard rumours? Stuff turning up on the open market? Strangers hanging out at your weekend digs? Or someone asking unusual questions at the local rallies?'

Clifton Beaufort removed his glasses and cleaned the lenses with a corner of his apron, appearing to give Jasper's question some serious thought.

'There's always new people turning up, but they don't hang around long. Detectoring isn't an easy hobby,' Beaufort said slowly. 'You can see it in the green hands. They think they're going to find the next Fishpool hoard. But most of the time they find diddly squat, maybe a 10p piece if they're lucky. So they give up.'

Rhema cleared her throat, 'What about people who just watch?'

'Just watch? What, you mean people who watch us using our detectors?'

Rhema nodded.

'Well, there's always a crowd at one of the big rallies. We hold them a few times a year as a fundraiser. I told Jasper about it at the meeting he came to last week. Last month, we raised nearly £500 for the local judo club—they needed to replace their mats. Shocking state they were in.'

'So, can you remember any chatter about people who didn't look like they fit in? People are always gossiping. I've been to one of your rallies.'

'You have?'

'With my grandad, he belongs to North of the Tyne.'

'They're a good club. Very professional, not as old as us, though. Well, yes, I suppose you're right. The lads were talking about those re-enactors, you know, the ones that dress up in Roman kit. Usually they're in an enormous group, organised like. But there's these two lads, older looking. They kept to themselves. Foreign maybe? Only saw them once, but the lads reckon they've seen them skulking around near Ithaca Farm. Not that you're allowed to detect up there. Shouldn't be too hard to track them down. They all know each other that lot. Weird, if you ask me.'

'Ithaca Farm?' Jasper clarified.

'That's the one. The old man would turn in his grave if he knew what that woman had planned for his farm. It's criminal, rewilding. Never heard such a thing in my life, and I work in a garden centre.

This is farming land and it should stay farming land. Rewilding. That's about as wild as someone kidnapping the mayor.'

'Well, thank you for your time. It's been very helpful,' Jasper said, snapping his notebook shut, giving Rhema a sly nod.

'Yes, thank you,' Rhema parroted.

'Say hello to your grandad from me,' Beaufort smiled. 'It's a good club he's in, but if he ever wants to leave the dark side, we'd be more than happy to have him join Hadrian's Heroes.'

Jasper and Rhema left Clifton Beaufort chuckling at his own humour, and climbed into the car. Jasper ramped up the heater as they started defrosting. The internal temperature of the Harley Garden Centre cafe felt similar to that of Antartica, bone-chillingly cold.

'This feels like we're in an episode of the Twilight Zone,' Rhema said through chattering teeth.

'How are you even old enough to know about the Twilight Zone?'

'The latest season had my favourite actor in it, Kumail Nanjiani.'

'How many seasons are there?' Jasper asked.

'Four, I think, and a movie. But don't you think it feels like that? With everything that's going on?'

'A bit,' Jasper said, flicking through his notebook.

'Roman re-enactors, missing people, night hawkers, religious shrines centuries old. It's like, don't mess with the dead or they'll come back and haunt you. Oh, and all the rewilding stuff. Don't forget that. Mix it all up and you've got a whole fifth season of the Twilight Zone just like that.'

'Do you know anyone in the re-enactor scene?' Jasper asked.

'I'm not that old,' Rhema pouted. 'I don't even know who you'd ask. Someone up at the Roman Army Museum, maybe?'

'Maybe,' Jasper replied. 'I might head to Ithaca Farm and have another look round.'

'Haven't you already been up there?'

'Yeah, when they first uncovered the altar. And again when I tried interviewing Lillian Arlosh.'

'I heard from my brother that she's a bit on the weird side. Keeps claiming to have seen a Roman soldier. That sort of thing. See! It's definitely the Twilight Zone now. Do you want me to come with you?'

Jasper considered her request for a moment. The girl exuded all the youthful enthusiasm only someone her age had, but he needed a different vibe for revisiting Lillian.

'What time does your brother finish work?' he asked.

'Normal time. Why?'

'Do you think you could ask him about the visions the Arlosh girl had?'

'Sure, you'll drop me at home, yes? Saves me busing home in this weather.'

The weather had turned to sleet, a stark reminder that the winter snows would be on their doorsteps sooner rather than later.

CHAPTER 49

MORE TO THE STORY

Badger thumped his fist against the wall of his childhood room, over and over. There was still no sign of his mother or her car, other than the parts of her car the police had collected, and her shoes. And they wouldn't even let him help. Said he'd only get in the way. *In the bloody way*. That's what his father had said to him, to his face.

Badger fell onto the single bed, cradling his wrist and staring at the ivory ceiling. Ivory. The entire house was ivory. He didn't miss this bland bedroom. At least his new flat had some character, some life to it. Badger vividly remembered his mother comparing dozens of paint samples and arguing with the interior designer over one particular shade of ivory. Both the painter and interior decorator had warned it would look yellow given the small windows upstairs. But his mother knew best. She always did. And now his childhood bedroom ceiling looked like it belonged to a pack-a-day smoker. He hated it almost as much as he hated his mother. He hated everything about this town. But he especially hated his bedroom ceiling. He would have been better off waiting at the pub for news, instead of returning to his parents house and hanging out in his old room.

Wiping a reluctant tear away, Badger remonstrated with himself. He didn't hate his mother, but he didn't like who she'd become.

Or how she trampled over everything good in the town. Hexham was full of good people doing good things. Just getting on with life, and yet his mother had made it her mission in life to bend everyone into mini clones. If she had her way, the entire town would be the same colour as his ceiling. But that wasn't a reason for someone to hurt her. She was still his mum.

Badger checked his cellphone again. No messages. Just a blank emptiness stretching into nothingness. It summed up his life, or lack of. Not even a message from Lillian. He tried her number again, but with no joy. The call went straight to her messages, again. He returned to glaring at the ceiling, cursing his parents in equal measures. His father for being so weak and his mother for being so strong.

He'd always known his place in this world. The son of the mayor and her ever so talented husband. The kid with the one mother who attended every school meeting, who volunteered at every election, at every community cleanup day, the annual charity food drive. The woman who put her hand up for every Christmas parade and Easter service. His mother practically lived in church halls and in the society pages of the newspaper. He had the one mother who was never home. And when she was? Well, then she'd be planning her next conquest. The annihilation of whoever had slighted her at the last meeting, the last fundraiser, the last charity drive. Her capacity for harbouring a grudge, for exacting revenge, seemed indefatigable. And he hated her for it. He hated the friends he'd lost, the teachers who zipped their lips shut around him, the adults who gave him a wide berth, or who treated him with kid gloves, lest he reported back to his mother. But despite all that, he loved her. Or felt that he should love her. It was complicated.

A heavy knock sounded at his door.

'What?'

'Andrew, the police are downstairs. They want to talk with you.'

Badger frowned. Why? He could barely recall the last time he'd seen his mother. Maybe at dinner a couple of nights ago? The woman was almost never at home. He held the uncomfortable opinion that having a child had been Jane Badrick's biggest mistake.

'Andrew, now,' his father's disembodied voice commanded.

Badger scooped his phone off the floor and wrenched open the door.

One look at his father's face, and Badger's face softened. His dad looked like complete shit, as if his mother's missing car had run him over and then dragged him through the hedgerows.

'You doing okay, Dad?'

Matthew Badrick shrugged, his eyes downcast, as if examining the boots on his feet for the first time.

'She'll be pissed when she gets home and finds out you've been wearing your work boots inside.'

Sure enough, a trail of dirt littered the hallway, contrasting with the white wool carpet Jane Badrick had slathered the house in, with no consideration given to her husband's job as a consultant archaeologist, with the obvious consequences of muddy boots, dirt-encrusted overalls and windbreakers covered with ancient muck.

'It'll be our secret,' Matthew said, his lips lifting a fraction. 'Come on, the police want a quick chat downstairs.'

'What about? I've already told them everything I can remember about mum and her plans. I haven't remembered anything else.'

'It's not about your mother,' Matthew said, the smile vanishing. 'It's about your friend, the one ruining Ithaca Farm.'

'Lillian, what about her?' His phone had four bars of service and was almost fully charged, but with zero missed calls or messages.

'The police will explain, although they're wasting their time. My guess is that she's finally realised she's not cut out for country life, and has hightailed it back to wherever she flew in from. And now the police are wasting their time searching for her instead of for your mother, who should be their priority. I mean, she is the mayor of this town.'

Badger leaned against the doorframe. Stepping into the room was akin to walking into the lion's den without a whip. The sitting room bulged at the seams with his mother's friends, his father's colleagues, and even more police. It looked like a meeting of the local Neighbourhood Watch group, which, of course, his saintly mother had run when he was barely even old enough to walk out the front gate without holding her hand.

'Andrew?' the uniformed constable asked.

'It's Badger.'

Badger's father interrupted. 'Everyone calls him Badger, it's a nick-name. I got called it myself at university, we've the same hair, you see.'

'We're...' the police officer started, before looking at her colleagues. 'Sorry, I'm here to ask if you've heard from Lillian Arlosh in the last twenty-four hours?'

Badger knew enough about the police to recognise that the young woman was a constable, probably fresh out of police college, and was feeling judged by the audience of more senior officers and a collection of some of Hexham's more notable citizens.

'Do you want to talk in the kitchen? There's more room in there,' Badger suggested.

They moved into the kitchen, with Badger indicating a ladder-back chair for the constable.

'Beautiful saucepans,' the policewoman said. Rows of gleaming copper pans hung from the rack above the kitchen island. 'They must be amazing to cook with.' A poor attempt at trying to put him at ease.

'They're not used for cooking, they're just for show,' Badger said. 'Mum enjoys collecting valuable things for show. Saucepans, antique furniture, friends, you know, that sort of thing.'

'Right... Um, well, I'm just here to ask about Lillian Arlosh. I understand that you two are good friends?'

'We are. Why?'

'Her colleague reported her missing, so we're following up with her friends.'

Badger checked his phone. Still nothing.

'Has she rung you?'

'What? Oh, no. No, she hasn't. I've been trying to get hold of her all night. And today...' Badger stared at his phone screen, his thumb hovering over the call button. The list of outgoing calls long and singu-lar. Calls to Lillian, all unanswered.

'Do you mind if I have a look?' the constable asked.

Badger handed over his phone, reduced to examining his nails, bitten to the quick and stained with old soil.

. . .

The constable scrolled through the call log, recording in her notebook the number of calls Badger had made, and the last one he'd received from Lillian.

'This last call? Can you tell me about that?' she asked, pointing to one call which had lasted a couple of minutes.

'It wasn't really anything. Just your usual call,' Badger said, scratching his head. He couldn't remember the bones of their conversation. It hadn't seemed extraordinary at the time. 'I can't remember. There's so much going on... sorry.'

'That's okay. Look, here's my card,' she said, sliding over a business card. 'Call me if you hear from Lillian or if you remember anything else. And I'm really sorry about the situation with your mother. I'm sure everyone is doing all that they can to find her.'

'Thanks,' Badger said. 'Shouldn't you also be looking for Lillian? Or doesn't she matter?'

The constable shifted in her chair, a blush creeping up her face.

'People your age are slightly different—' she started.

'So you're not looking for her then? Typical. Oh, it's all good to look for her Majesty. What's another missing young woman? Off on a bender. Is that what you think?'

Badger's raised voice brought his father into the kitchen, along with Chief Inspector Kevin Readdie, who stepped forward, his hands outstretched as if trying to diffuse the situation.

'Now, calm down.'

'Don't tell me to calm down. You lot should be out looking for my mother, instead of lazing about here. But it's not just my mother who's missing, is it? No. Another woman is missing as well, and none of you care. Well, I do. I'll look for her myself.'

'Sit down, son,' Readdie said.

'I'm not your son, I'm his,' Badger said. 'Fat lot of good that is, though, isn't it? He doesn't look too worried about his missing wife. My mother. Are you worried, Father? Or are you trying to decide whether this will help her reelection campaign? Well, I'm off.' Badger bolted for the kitchen door, slamming it shut behind him. Someone had blocked his car, so he grabbed a random pushbike someone had left outside.

Badger took off, pedalling like a competitor in the Tour de France, anger coursing through his body. None of them cared. His father put on a good show, but that's all it was. And as for the police. As useless as a two-legged stool.

He tried not to imagine what they were saying about him back at the house. Unhinged. Stressed about his mother. A good son, but a handful. He'd heard it all over the years. All excuses for the fact that he'd lived most of his life being cared for by a succession of nannies and babysitters, whilst his parents lived their ever-so-important lives. Christ, his parents even owned the flat he lived in, which was the only reason he could afford the rent given his sporadic employment history. He should have worked harder at university instead of partying as hard as he had, and suffering the mortification of returning to Hexham, his tail between his legs. Maybe he should try university again? He couldn't wait to escape somewhere far, far away from Hexham, and the inter-twined tentacles of his parents.

The bike took him to Ithaca Farm, where he found the place seem-ingly deserted, apart from a van parked in front of a shed. Abandoning the bike in the weeds around the door, he knocked, before trying the door handle, so used to barging in when Seb's grandad lived here.

'Yes?'

Badger stopped short on the threshold.

'Oh my god, I'm so sorry. I knocked, and... well, habit really, sorry. I should have waited. My friend's grandfather used to live here, and I came over all the time, avoiding my parents. And oh god, now I'm rambling, sorry. I'm Badger. I heard about Lillian, and I wanted to see if she'd come home yet? The police came to see me and...'

Badger gave up, closed his mouth and waited for the woman in front of him to march him off the premises. But she didn't.

'Thanks for coming. Lillian mentioned you. I don't think she has too many other friends, so it was a short list I gave to the police. You, and Apple and someone called Jesha. I haven't met them. And I haven't heard from them. I'm Nicole Pilcher, from London.'

'Can I come in?'

The woman nodded, and Badger walked into the house, although house wasn't really an apt description, it was more like a time capsule.

Everything he remembered about Seb's grandfather stood just as he remembered. The old church pew, cast out of St Giles Church after someone had carved twenty-seven giant penises on the back one Sunday, too deep to be sanded out. It hadn't bothered William Arlosh, who gave it pride of place in the entranceway. Even the old elephant foot umbrella stand remained in the corner, still jammed with various umbrellas and shooting sticks. An uncomfortable relic from another era.

'How do you know Lillian? Are you a relation?'

'It's a weird story, but I'm an antiques dealer. I manage the Old Curiosity Shop in London. But I'm also a friend of Paige at the Bellingham, and she suggested that Lillian use me to clear out some of her stuff. From what I can tell, there's no one else in Lillian's family.' Nicole shrugged. 'So I'm staying until someone says otherwise, or until Lillian comes back. Anyway, come on through to the kitchen. It's the only warm room in this entire house.'

Badger followed Nicole into the fug of the kitchen's warmth. He hadn't realised how cold he was after his frantic cycle. As he stood warming his hands by the fire in the ancient hearth, he listened as Nicole relayed everything she knew about Lillian and her whereabouts. He couldn't help but think that she was leaving something out, but couldn't place a finger on what.

'Do you think it's got anything to do with what's out there?' Badger asked, pointing to the gazebo covering the ruins, and the archaeologists.

Badger watched the other woman's cheeks colour. *Weird.*

He had another theory, one which involved his mother. A theory which made his stomach roil and his skin clammy. That was a hunch he didn't want to give voice to. Not yet.

'I wonder,' Nicole replied, staring out the window. 'Have they spoken to that archaeologist from Newcastle?'

Nicole and Badger picked their way across the field, hailing the man knee deep in mud.

Badger stood back as Anson Darby climbed out of the hole, seemingly taking a great deal of care over the placement of his feet and hands.

Badger explained the situation to the archaeologist.

'I'm sorry to hear about Lillian. But I don't possibly see how I can help? We're not allowed any access to the house or yard, and I haven't seen her lately.'

Badger had heard his father talk about Anson Darby, how he'd been the up-and-coming bright star at the university, once voted most likely to discover the next Hadrian's Villa, but in recent years, Darby's name wasn't spoken about so reverently. More damaging was that his father barely spoke of him at all. The archaeological world was small in this part of England, and almost everyone knew everyone, or at least knew of everyone, and where they were in the pecking order of funding. Anson Darby was closer to the bottom than the top.

'Badger thought that maybe someone had taken Lillian because of the altar,' Nicole said.

'I didn't exactly say it like that,' Badger muttered.

'Sounds unlikely,' Darby replied, tucking his trowel into his belt and smoothing back his hair. 'There are always people abnormally interested in finds like this. Yes, of course. But why would they take Lillian? If anything, I'd be more worried about them accessing the site after dark, wielding shovels with wanton abandon, damaging whatever else may be down there.'

'What if they thought she knew that there were others?' Nicole said, staring at the archaeologist.

'Other what?' Darby asked, head to one side.

'Other altars?'

'Other Roman altars?'

'Yes, those or funeral stones?'

'You mean funereal statuary? She knows where there are more?' Darby's voice cracked.

'No, no, that wasn't what I was saying. I... I was just...,' Nicole stuttered.

'Are you saying that there are other altars?' Darby asked, his voice full of excitement.

'I don't know what she was saying. Look, I've got to get back to the house,' Badger said, his eyes following Nicole's hurried steps back to the safety of the kitchen. *What did she know?*

Even with his back to the archaeologist, Badger could feel the excitement emanating from Darby. Or was it greed? What wasn't Nicole sharing with him?

Everything Seb's grandad used to say was making more and more sense. As unlikely as that seemed. But it didn't matter which way he looked at it. Either his mother, or his girlfriend, were in deep trouble. *Girlfriend?* Badger hadn't realised until now the strength of his feelings for Lillian.

Nicole Pilcher needed to tell him everything she knew.

CHAPTER 50

THROUGH ADVERSITY COMES FRIENDSHIP

'What else can I do?' Apple sat on a stack of coffee table books, a stack so high her feet were dangling above the dusty floor.

Apple hadn't wanted to invite anyone else into the inner sanctum, but she'd exhausted every avenue she could think in her search for Pramod Sharma. The man had vanished. So here she was, stuck with Jesha Martin, who hadn't stopped picking up almost every book and putting it back down again, in a slightly different spot.

'Can you stop that?'

'Stop what?' Jesha asked.

'Moving the books,' Apple said.

'Oh, sorry, it's just been so long since I've been in a library that I almost forgot what they looked like.'

'Sorry, I'm just really worried about Pramod. And no one seems to care.'

'We could ring the police,' Jesha suggested.

'Hmm, but they're all focussed on Mrs Badrick. They will not give a toss about an old homeless dude,' Apple said.

'I thought you said he lived here?'

'He does, but not officially, although I think the church knows. Maybe? I don't know.'

'So his stuff is here, then?'

Apple nodded.

'Have you gone through it looking for clues?'

'I'm not Nancy Drew, but I had a quick look. I didn't want to go through his personal things. He doesn't really have much.'

'Let's go,' Jesha said, jumping up and knocking over a stack of Stephen King novels.

Apple tried to hide her frustration. Jesha had been the least offensive option available. She'd tried getting hold of Lillian, and then Badger, her first choices, but neither of them were answering their phones.

Winding through the aisles of books, the two girls made their way to the tiny room Pramod Sharma had been using as his bedroom. Neat to the point of obsessiveness, there weren't that many places to search for clues. The bed was an old army cot which had probably last seen service in the Vietnam war. A small open bookcase sat next to the bed, stacked full of historical books on the Roman army's invasion of the British Isles, each book bristling with annotated notes in a foreign language.

'Where was he from?' Jesha asked, flicking through the books beside Sharma's bed.

'I assumed India, but then I never asked. It didn't matter,' she said. 'It doesn't matter,' she corrected. 'Does it matter where he comes from? I mean, to you, does it matter to you?' Apple asked, her voice sharp.

'No, I just wondered what language these notes were in. They all seem to be about the history from around here. You know, stuff about Vindolanda, and Corbridge, and all those places. Wonder why he was reading up on it?'

Apple had to shake her head.

'I miss actual books,' Jesha said, stroking the pile before moving to examine the stack of books on the windowsill.

After that announcement, Apple started reconsidering her opinion of Jesha Martin. People were surprising.

'These are all about Roman history too,' Jesha said, turning the pile spine out for Apple to see.

Apple glanced at the books, but turned her attention to the only other personal looking item in the room, apart from the blood stained tunic, an old wooden trunk open beside the bed.

'Help me with this,' she directed, pulling the trunk further into the middle of the room, the tin corners scraping across the floorboards, leaving tiny furrows marking its passage.

The girls began pulling things out of the trunk, piling them haphazardly to the sides, where they joined sawdust and a wayward sewing needle, still threaded with a smidge of white cotton.

'Why would anyone keep all this stuff?' Jesha asked. 'For Halloween?'

The once full trunk now stood nakedly empty, disgorged of its treasures. It bore no markers of who its owner was, or had been. Its former contents told another story. One full of imagination and tragedy.

Apple sat back on her heels to contemplate the mess that they'd made. And the meaning behind the mess. She was well read, and smarter than average, but even she was at a loss to explain how what looked like the entire contents of the Hadrian's Wall Gallery of the Great North Museum was in the travelling trunk of a homeless man who looked after the forgotten books of Hexham in an old church hall.

Everything they'd pulled out looked brand new, as if it had come directly from the factory. Apple counted at least three daggers with ornate horn handles, a complete replica Samian ware bowl in perfect condition. A wooden ladle, a small collection of household deities, a wooden dice, a cup made from metal, and a small brooch in the shape of a bird of some sort. And a heavy woollen cape, roughly spun and the colour of fog.

'What's all that for? Dress-ups?' Jesha asked, hefting the cloak over her shoulders and spinning around.

'Take that off,' Apple said, grabbing it from the other girl. 'There's nothing here which says anything about his past.'

'What about that green stone thing?' Jesha asked, pointing to a heavy stone wedge wrapped in oilcloth that she'd left on the bed together with a lonely sterling silver soup spoon and matching fork.

'I don't know what that is,' Apple replied, 'but unless it's got a forwarding address on it, it's not any help, is it?'

Jesha shrugged. 'Looks like something my nan bought when she was in New Zealand.'

Apple spent a moment staring at the stone peeking out of its oilskin wrapper. Just a trinket, a tourist novelty. 'There must be something else. Are there any labels on the trunk?'

The two girls checked the sides of the trunk, then flipped the lib back over, sealing away everything that they'd returned to the trunk.

'There,' Jesha pointed.

A buff coloured tag hung from the clasp on the top of the lid.

Neumegan, Auckland, New Zealand, it said, in a faded spidery script, barely legible.

'I thought his name was Sharma. Pram Sharma.'

'It's Pramod Sharma,' Apple said. 'I've never heard of anyone called Neumegan.'

'Sounds German or something, yeah? Is this his stuff then and Pram was looking after it?' Jesha asked.

'I think we've done all that we can now. I should call the police.'

'You think? I mean, they're busy looking for Badger's mum and the rewilding girl. Three missing people would probably blow their mind.'

'Wait, what do you mean, "the rewilding girl"?'

'You know, Lillian. Didn't you get a message about it?'

Apple checked her phone. Other than the unanswered messages to Lillian and Badger, and the one to Jesha, the window remained empty of any other messages. 'No, I didn't get any messages. What's happened to Lillian?'

'Don't know. The police somehow had my name because they thought we were friends. I mean, we chatted a bit, but we're not really close, not like you. Why didn't they ring you? I don't think they're that worried. Just asked me if I'd seen her around over the past couple of days. Which I hadn't. There's no way I'm traipsing all the way out to Ithaca Farm. I'd rather go to Newcastle any day of the week. Have you seen her?'

'Have you got the number of the officer who rang you?'

'I'll text it to you.'

Apple's phone pinged with the contact.

· · ·

'It's probably best you go, just in case Pramod comes back and sees that we've been through all his stuff. I'll tidy up. And can you not say anything about this place to anyone? It's just that these books were all meant to be incinerated. On Jane Badrick's orders. The shit will really hit the fan if word gets out. Too many people know about it already.'

'A secret library! I love it. Your secret is safe with me. Just as long as it's okay if I pop by now and again to grab a book or two. I'll bring them back or exchange them for some of mine. I think I've read everything on our bookshelves at home, at least twice.'

Apple couldn't believe her ears. The girl was a Rubik's Cube. You never knew what she'd surprise you with next. 'Sure, and thanks for this. Thanks for today.'

Jesha left with a hefty Salman Rushdie book, and a couple of LJ Ross's, all of them well read. Apple locked the door behind her and slithered to the ground, phone in hand. How should she report Pramod's disappearance? Maybe he didn't want to be found? Maybe he'd gone off like her old cat, Tippy, to die somewhere quietly, with no fuss? Or maybe, just maybe, all three disappearances were linked? But how?

The constable settled into the corner of the worn couch and fixed her eyes on Apple. 'You say that you're Lillian's best friend?'

'That's right.'

'I didn't have your name on my list.'

'Lillian hasn't been here that long. She's not really friends with anyone else in town, apart from me and Badger.'

'By Badger, you mean Andrew Badrick? And he's Holly Corben's boyfriend. Is that correct?'

'Yes, and yes. No, sorry. No, that's not correct.'

'Which part isn't correct?'

'He's not Holly's boyfriend anymore. They broke up.'

'Over his friendship with Lillian?'

'You should probably ask him about it. Or Holly, she hates Lillian.'

'Hate is a strong word,' the constable said, pen poised.

'Can you remember high school?'

'Yes.'

'Then I bet you can remember how some girls were absolute bitches for no reason? That's Holly Corben, a complete bitch.'

'You said in your call that you wanted to report another missing person, though? You mean Jane Badrick?'

'No, Pramod Sharma.'

'The elderly man in town? How do you know he's missing?'

'I haven't seen him for three days now.'

'That could be because you've been busy with your friends, and you could have missed each other. Ships in the night and all that?'

'I don't have other friends. Other than Lillian and Pramod Sharma. And I haven't seen either of them for three days. Don't you think that's strange? How long has Mrs Badrick been missing? The same amount of time?'

'I know you're worried about your friends, but it's unlikely that they're linked. But we'll look into it, I promise. Did Mr Sharma mention anything about a trip? Can you remember?'

'No. No trip, no family, no mention of anything, other than he'd see me the next day, like normal.'

'Like normal? Sorry, I'm confused. You saw him every day? Why?'

The library was fast becoming one of the worst-kept secrets in.

'At the old St Mark's church hall. We'd meet there every afternoon. I help him with the books. And people come to borrow books, and to donate them, and I help sort them. The church knows all about it. No one uses that hall for anything. So now it's a sort of repository, but for old books. Books no one else wants or needs.'

'A library,' the constable said. 'Here in Hexham, I never knew.'

'No, that's kind of the point. We didn't want too many people to know, mainly because of where all the books came from.'

'And where was that?' the constable asked.

'The Hexham Library. We saved them from the incinerator. The incinerator that Jane Badrick had condemned them to.'

. . .

'Ah, we can't get away from the connection with Mrs Badrick. You have been very helpful, thank you. If you think of anything else, here's my number,' she said, passing over a business card. 'I'll see myself out, thanks.'

After being dropped off at Ithaca Farm, Apple picked her way across the muddy yard. Old bits of farm machinery leaned drunkenly against barn walls, rusting their worth away. Free range chickens scattered, squawking their distress as she dared encroach upon their territory. And somewhere beyond the buildings, a pack of dogs howled into the gloom, the pregnant clouds threatening to drown the rolling hills in another dusting of premature snow.

Apple knocked on the door, knocking her shoes against the wrought iron boot scraper at the door. She paid no attention to its design, using it like she would any other boot scraper, as a tool to disgorge gravel and grit, mud and muck.

Badger answered the door.

'I tried ringing you,' Apple said

'Sorry, I was with the police.'

'Me too, just now. Any word?'

Badger shook his head.

Apple stood in the entrance hall, taking in the faded visage. Old world charm is how design magazines would describe it. Her mother would call it dust collectors. She'd call it fascinating. 'I can't believe she has so much stuff.'

Badger looked around. 'Nah, this all belonged to Seb's grandfather. She inherited the house with everything still here.'

'Wasn't there some rumour about the old man having a few screws loose? He used to see things, and make up stories about being a soldier? Like, not a soldier in the war with the Germans, but a Roman soldier, or something like that.'

Badger nodded.

'Hello?' Nicole appeared, a mug in her hand, her face as white as the snowflakes now falling outside the grimy window.

'Ah, hi, I'm Apple, Lillian's friend. I thought I should come and see if I can help?'

'Have you heard from her? From Lillian?'

'I spoke with the police and gave them as much information as I can remember...' Apple tapered off.

'Come through to the kitchen, it's warmer, and there's cake.'

'Cake?'

'Apparently, she bakes when she's stressed,' Badger explained.

Sitting at the kitchen table, Apple was taken with the decidedly boringness of the kitchen compared to the entrance hall. Standard pots and pans adorned the hanging wooden rack. Plain crockery languished on the hutch dresser, interspersed with the odd piece of more gravitas. Two cardboard boxes lay stacked in the corner, covering a broken window panel.

'This cake is lovely,' she said, more to break the silence than in any actual love for the dry sponge cake her mouth rebelled against.

'Can you hear those dogs?' Nicole asked, staring out the window, her hands pressed against the glass. 'Why are they barking?'

Apple shuddered as a grainy image of dogs tearing into the body of her friend formed in the shadows of her mind. Her whole life she'd always jumped to the worst conclusions.

'We should check, shouldn't we, Badger?'

Badger looked like a deer caught in headlights, but drained the dregs of his tea and stood up. 'Yup, let's go,' he said.

The snow dampened the noise outside, making everything sound hollow and far away. Identifying the direction of the dogs proved almost impossible. They'd fallen silent as soon as Apple and Badger had stepped outside.

'You don't think...' Apple started.

'No, not at all.'

'Yeah, but why can't we hear them now?'

'No idea. Do you want to check over by the altar first? The archaeologist bailed as soon as the snow started. I watched him go.'

The pair stood at the side of the trench, staring at the slash of dirt, all sharp angles and planks of wood. A pile of stones stood to one side, and the gap in the fence yawned wide.

'My dad was going on about the benefits to nature of rewilding,' Apple said.

'I've been reading about it since meeting Lillian,' Badger said. 'I get what she's trying to do. Even just this small gap is making a difference. Look.' Badger pointed to a hedgehog, snuffling its way in the gloom through the new opening in the stone wall.

Apple held her breath as the creature teetered on the brink of the trench, before it thought better and scurried around the edge to the safety of the open field. 'That was close.'

'That's just one hedgehog. Imagine the lives of all the other creatures without these walls.'

'So you're recommending that we dismantle Hadrian's Wall now?' Apple asked.

'No, what I'm saying is that I understand what Lillian is trying to do here, at Ithaca Farm. It didn't always have these walls. In the scheme of life, they're pretty new, and nature can do without them.'

'I can't hear any dogs now, can you? Do you think she's out there?'

Apple wasn't sure if he meant his mother or Lillian. The saddest part of her uncertainty was that she assumed he meant Lillian, and not his mother.

The pair turned around, each walking several paces in different directions, surveying the ground. Churned by the stomping boots of the archaeologists, and the earlier media scrum, there was no telling if dogs had been in the area or not. Everything looked pretty much as it always had. Lush green grass, old cow pats and sheep pellets, and along the base of the remaining pasture wall, clumps of Shining Lady's-mantle bristled, their serrated leaves looking far deadlier than they were.

With the light almost gone, Badger and Apple returned to the relative warmth of the kitchen, well aware that with each sweep of the clock's hand, Lillian's disappearance, and that of both Badger's mum and Pramod Sharma, turned more ominous.

CHAPTER 51

WHEN PASTS COLLIDE

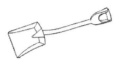

Anson leaned against the freezing window of his tired flat in Maidens Croft. He should at least be living in a semidetached. He deserved something a damn sight better than this. He'd worked so hard, for such a long time, and this was all he had to show for it? Look at what Lillian Arlosh had inherited, a whole bloody farm, complete with Roman ruins and a stunning farmhouse surrounded by views people would kill for. And she was just going to let it go back to nature?

And what was that woman going on about, other altars? If he could find them, discover them, then his career would be made. The altars and the coins. He'd be a living legend, just like Howard Carter, the man who'd discovered the tomb of King Tutankhamun.

Damn it. He had to know.

Anson ripped his coat from the hook on the back of the door, slamming it shut on his way out. The sky boasted the mottled greys of a tortoiseshell cat, and looked just as unpredictable. Another storm approached, which didn't bode well for the site. Even Ayla had suggested leaving any further excavations until early spring, although she would say that. It wasn't her university position teetering on a funding knife-edge.

The skies opened, and not even the fastest setting on his windscreen wipers could move the sheer volume of water. Syria, and its sunny weather, looked more and more appealing. Anson was oblivious to the fact that Damascus itself suffered from rain and snow.

Anson gunned his engine. This job was too much. Too many hoops, too many idiots, and too many do-gooders, like Lillian Arlosh. Her harebrained idea of rewilding Ithaca Farm took out the award for the most stupid. What did she think was going to happen? That they'd all be singing kumbaya and hugging saplings she'd never live to see grow taller than your average horse? Madness.

Pulling into the yard at Ithaca Farm, he could barely see through the sheets of water running down his window.

Anson sat in his car, fuming. The Arlosh woman didn't deserve her share of the funds if they declared the coins as treasure. He could put that money to much better use at the university, among other places.

Gritting his teeth, he opened the car door, and dashed across to the house, where he hammered on the door before turning the handle and letting himself in, again.

Shaking himself off, he called out, 'Hello?'

No answer.

The place still looked exactly the same as it did last time, and from the time before that when he'd begged William Arlosh to let him dig at Ithaca Farm. He'd been turned down then as well. Bloody farmers and bloody environmentalists. Why couldn't they understand how important it was to uncover the history of the place?

With the rain trying to hammer its way through the roof, it wasn't a surprise that they couldn't hear him, but that never crossed his mind. Instead, he ploughed through to the kitchen, noting that the heating was on. It certainly made a difference, especially compared to the last time he was here. They must be nearby.

After spying some paperwork on the kitchen table, he idly turned the pages — all applications for environmental grants. The greenies were hard at work spending the government's money.

. . .

If he'd studied climate change at university instead of archaeology, he could bloody well do what he liked in the fields of Ithaca Farm, with buckets of cash. That much was becoming clear. The figures on the applications were for sums higher than his entire department operated under in a single year. Where was the equity in that?

Leaving the papers, he returned to the entrance hall and looked up the stairs. The mess of the broken balustrade had been cleaned up, but the handrail hadn't been replaced, leaving the top of the stairs looking like a child missing its front teeth. He wouldn't risk going back upstairs, not again. No one was going to be storing old altars upstairs. If they were here, they would be downstairs, or outside in the sheds. He'd come here about the coins, but as soon as he'd driven into the yard, the mud splashing the sides of his car, the pot holes sending judders through the chassis, Nicole Pilcher's words crowded in upon him. He knew she'd meant that there were other altars. He knew it in his gut. And like a dog with a good bone, he wasn't about to let it go. Not now, not when his entire career rested upon this discovery.

The door opposite the kitchen was shut, just like it had been on his two previous visits.

Anson reached out and turned the tarnished brass handle. The door swung inwards, releasing an arctic chill, sending shivers through his body. In the dim light, Anson could only see a room filled to the brim with bric-à-brac and furniture, some shrouded in dust blankets, others stacked haphazardly around the room. In one corner, a stack of artwork leaned drunkenly against the wall. He turned to find the light switch, the old bakelite switch cold to the touch. Nothing happened when he flicked it. He tried again, and was about to try for a third futile time, when he turned back towards the art.

It had taken several seconds for his mind to decipher what he'd just seen. The pelting rain against the curtained windows had added to the noise in his head, drowning out the logic. Those weren't frames.

Anson ignored everything in his path. Nicole had been telling the truth. His assumptions were correct. There were other altars, and they were here, in Lillian's house. She knew about them and had told no one. The bitch. What a discovery this would be, and it was all his. How he would claim it was of no consideration yet.

He knew that he'd stumbled across the find of the decade.

No one cared about treasure hoards. They usually had no context. The public loved them though, and they got feet through the doors of museums faster than you could say King Tut's Curse. But true archaeologists such as him would rather have a beautiful detailed inscription on an altar or a burial stone which told a story. That's what moved archaeology forward. Let the detectorists keep their coins, or sell their stolen treasure to unscrupulous scrap metal merchants for cash, and bugger the loss to history.

He stretched out his hand to caress the nearest stone and almost cried as his fingers slipped into the deep grooves of a carved inscription. There must be at least half a dozen here, in this room. Were there more? Anson didn't care if every citizen of Hexham disappeared like Lillian, as long as they stayed out of his way long enough for him to... To what? What was he planning on doing? Rescue the altars? How would he claim them then? How would he explain their provenance? He could rebury them. All of them. Tonight.

CHAPTER 52

A VISITOR FROM OUT OF TOWN

Lillian couldn't stay hidden, not with what she could hear. Her knowledge of the history sat on the hazy side, but the Iceni could be scaling the walls now, slaughtering the Roman soldiers. Murdering Julius.

The rush of running boots had stopped, replaced with eerie echoes of shouts and the retreating sound of a horn. As the last notes faded, Lillian felt the faint tingle of memory, but brushed it aside. This was her world now, a world she had to survive.

For any normal person, finding a way home would be a priority. But she didn't just want to go herself. She wanted to take Julius with her. And to do that, she needed to find her way back to where it began. Back to the strongroom, where they stored the soldier's pay. And she'd never have a better opportunity in this melee.

From her hiding hole, Lillian struggled to get her bearings. In the dark, everything looked identical. She scurried across the fields, keeping as close to the edge of the road as much as possible.

A soldier flew around the corner, the moon highlighting the terror on his bearded face.

Lillian flattened herself against an oak tree, but he paid her no heed, increasing his panicked pace as the horn sounded again.

It wasn't from any instrument Lillian recognised. Only one thing made that sound: a car horn.

Lillian stumbled as her mind grappled with what she'd heard, scraping her legs against the dressed stones of the fort's walls. She wasn't alone here. Somewhere outside was someone like her. But not a friend.

Limping towards where she thought the strongroom was, Lillian ignored the pain from her shredded shins, oblivious to the blood dripping from the scrapes. There would be time for that later.

The clouds parted, the white moon and stars illuminating the bricked archway of the steps leading down to the strongroom. It appeared unguarded, at least for the moment.

Lillian hesitated. The horn drawing her attention away from her task. She looked to the sky, where far above her, the kneeling form of the Hercules constellation guided her forward, encouraging her to vanquish her fears, the way Hercules vanquished Draco.

Leaving the pull of the strongroom, Lillian pushed forward towards the top of the wall, walls bristling with Roman soldiers, their cries snuffed out by the sight holding them captive somewhere beyond the wall.

She had to see, to be sure of what she'd heard. Then she'd find a way home.

Pulling her cloak tighter around her body and face, she limped up the nearest staircase, trying to look like she belonged, oblivious that she stood out just as much as the beast beyond the wall. But no one cast any glances her way, their attention drawn by the parallel beams of light spewing from the monster's mouth.

As Lillian stepped from the ladder onto the buttress of the wall, the wind caught her breath at the sight of a Land Rover driving in erratic circles beyond the reach of the archers who'd nocked their arrows but stood motionless and silent.

The driver gave a last burst of the horn, and someone appeared in the open sunroof — a warrior, his visage a cacophony of tattoos, with wild hair and his arms cluttered with clinking bangles.

He shook his fists towards the Romans before the Land Rover sped off, scattering the hundreds of similarly tattooed warriors in its wake.

As if coming out of a trance, Lillian fled down the ladder, the hood falling from her head in her haste. Her bloody footprints marked her trail, but still no one followed. No panicked shouts of warning chased her escape, and she slipped down the worn staircase into the blackness of the strongroom. Her hand reached into the pocket of her jeans, her fingertips brushing the golden coin laying within, and the world exploded.

The pain came in waves. Crashing and banging with sulphuric undertones and glints of piercing light, with unrelenting noise. Pulsing, and echoing, and shouting, and filling her mind with scenes from a movie or snippets from lives previously lived. How could she still be alive?

'Lillian, can you hear me?'

The light grew sharp and Lillian jerked away. She struggled to cover her eyes. What was happening?

'Lillian, wake up. You're safe, you're in hospital.'

The hospital?

'Lillian, it's me. It's time to wake up,' Apple said.

Mum? Lillian tried to open her eyes, but the light was too bright and the noises too loud. All the beeping, and talking, and the sound of trolley wheels clattering over the linoleum together with the clinking of steel instruments and the rustling of clothes. Clothes made of microfibers and wool blends, and polyesters and nylon.

A hand stroked the side of her cheek, and her mother's faint perfume wafted across her. Chanel No. 5, the perfume her father always bought her mother, every year, until he didn't.

'Mum?' she croaked.

'Hey, beautiful girl, you're back. Welcome back to the land of the living. You had us all so worried.'

Through a squint, Lillian looked around the room. It wasn't her mother. Of course it wasn't. But for the most fleeting of moments...

It was Apple, standing next to the bed with Badger and a nurse.

. . .

Behind her friends were two uniformed police officers, milling uncertainly in the doorway.

'What happened?' Lillian asked, her throat dry, the words no more than a whisper.

'That's what the police want to know, and us too, but you rest. Talk when you're ready,' Badger said, his hand stroking Lillian's cheek. 'That's the only part of you that isn't grazed,' he said as he leaned forward to plant a gentle kiss on her cheek.

'Grazed?'

'I think that's enough for her now.' The nurse shooed everyone out like mosquitoes on a summer's eve.

Lillian closed her eyes and tried rolling away from the light. The excruciating pain telling her that that wasn't a good idea.

'It feels worse than it is,' the nurse said. 'But give it a week, and you'll hardly notice it. It's mostly superficial. I can only hold the police off for so long before their pestering wears me down. So try to sleep now, and I'll tell them to come back tomorrow, yes?'

Lillian would have nodded if the pain in her head wasn't still loitering at the base of her skull.

'Can you turn the lights down?'

The world beyond her eyelids dimmed, and the nurse must have closed the door, as the sounds grew muffled. A sort of peace descended and Lillian tried to make sense of what had happened. And to decide whether coming back, back to now, to the modern day, was what she wanted.

Her coin? With a start, Lillian struggled to draw back the covers to check her jeans. Her heart sank. They'd dressed her in a lightweight hospital gown, the type which gaped open, leaving your rear for the world to see if you ever ventured from the sanctum of your bed. Had they thrown her clothes away? Perhaps the whole thing had been a dream? She hoped it was. A tumour eating away at her brain, causing hallucinations. That was the only excuse which made any sense.

One additional person loitered near the Lillian's bed — Jasper Fletcher. He'd avoided catching the eye of the police by slumping in the visitor's chair in an adjoining cubicle. The inebriated patient filling the bed hadn't objected to Jasper's existence, and merely continued groaning theatrically about her broken foot.

From his vantage point, Jasper heard the police discussing how an antiques dealer from London had almost run over Lillian's body on the old Roman road, swerving to miss her, and ending up in a ditch, before calling for help. That must be the woman staying at the Bellingham, thought Jasper, jotting down notes, his shorthand illegible to anyone but him.

Jasper watched as the doctor ushered everyone out of Lillian's room before closing the door and turning to talk to the police. He'd had to reposition his chair to catch their conversation. 'Quiet,' he said to his cubicle companion, who'd started up again. The man obliged theatrically, bringing his nicotine-stained finger to his lips. Jasper caught the tail-end of their conversation. Grazes, bruising, no suggestion of sexual assault. A Roman coin found in her pocket.

A Roman coin? Jasper helped himself to his companion's glass of water, the plastic cup crumpling under the distracted grasp of his hand. Surely this all tied in with the story of the night hawkers and the disappearance of Jane Badrick? He had to get back to the office. Whether Revell liked it, this story had to be run.

Waving goodbye to his new friend, Jasper emerged from the cubicle, but hesitated. A stranger was standing outside Lillian Arlosh's room. A tall man, dark hair, an old-fashioned overcoat almost brushing his ankles. For the briefest of moments, the man's hand reached for the handle, before deciding against it, and the man strode away. Jasper only caught the reflection of his face in the window. A long face, with sad eyes covered by wire-rimmed glasses. No one he knew. Perhaps this was the elusive Mr Arlosh?

Jasper rushed to catch up with the man, but at the junction of the corridor, he'd disappeared. Jasper stood, turning in circles. How had he missed him? Unless the man had run like Beckham for a goal, he should have been able to catch him before he reached the exit.

· · ·

Outside in the icy night air, life resumed. Cars coming and going. An ambulance backing into the ambulance bay. Nurses stood smoking on an elderly patch of lawn, shivering in lightweight cardigans and stomping their feet as they indulged in a habit which would eventually see them admitted themselves as patients in the not too distant future.

Still no sign of the stranger.

Jasper punched in a number on his phone and stomped his feet, emulating the puffing nurses. Christ, it was cold. 'Hey, it's me. Yeah, I'm at the hospital. They found Lillian Arlosh... yeah, I knew it wouldn't take long. They found her on the road, battered up, and get this... with a Roman coin in her pocket. I need you to find out whatever you can about that coin. Can you do that? Use your feminine wiles for me? Cheers.' He rang off. Life as a journalist was very much, I'll scratch your back if you scratch mine, lark. Everything was a quid pro quo.

With a final futile glance around the carpark, he climbed into his car, and not for the first time wished he'd upgraded to a model with seat warmers, and motored to the office. This story wouldn't write itself, and if he didn't get it done tonight, one of the big papers would scoop him, and he needed this story. It could well be his ticket to a new car, a new flat and a job with a proper newspaper.

CHAPTER 53

A PIE AND AN ALE

In the shadows of an empty room at the end of the hospital corridor, Henry Neumegan leaned against the window and watched the redheaded journalist climb into a car and pull out of the carpark. He still shivered every time he saw someone risk their lives behind the wheel of a motor engine. Of course, he'd been in them before, but only as a passenger. Getting into an accident as a driver would create too many questions. Trains were his preferred means of travel, first class, where possible. He had no need of aeroplanes.

The girl was his primary concern. What did she know? How far back had she travelled, and more importantly, how? Pramod Sharma was nowhere to be found, as normal. But he'd wait. The man usually turned up. Both of them were getting too old for this lark. Like a silver-plated tea set, the gloss had worn away from the edges. There were pros and cons of every life he'd lived. He appreciated hot water on tap and modern medical advances, but the slowness of life and the complete absence of network television and keyboard warriors were the key attractions of the past couple of centuries.

An alarm pierced his reflections, and he turned away from the window. Somewhere in the building, someone was having a worse day than the girl who was suffering from mere scrapes and bruises.

Hardly life threatening in the twenty-first century. Topical antibiotics and sterile bandages would take care of any infection. He always took back a tube of the stuff, decanting it into a ceramic pharmacy pot and burying the evidence. Caution was a requirement in the life of a time traveller.

Judging it safe to leave, Neumegan slipped from the hospital room, and took the stairs to the exit. With the journalist gone, it was easy enough to hire a taxi waiting at the rank, its running engine keeping the heater pumping.

Neumegan directed the driver to the Twice Brewed Inn, mumbling in response to the driver's drivel about the latest Tory party challenge and the problems of Brexit coming home to roost. He'd predicted the impact of Brexit based on his vast experience in most other centuries. There were many historical examples which, if the politicians bothered learning from, could easily have solved the housing crisis, the immigration debacle, the shortage of doctors, nurses, teachers, trained mechanics. But no, politicians knew best. But history repeats, just ask the Egyptian Pharaohs. Ask the Roman Senate. Ask George Washington or Elizabeth I.

'We're here, mate,' the driver said, pulling into the unsealed parking lot of the Twice Brewed. 'You tried the steak pie here? My missus says it's the best in the whole county.'

'Thank you for the recommendation. It's the weather for pie. Nothing like pie and gravy,' Neumegan agreed, tipping the man generously. 'Is there any chance you could return here tomorrow, at midday?'

Neumegan's generous tip disappeared into the driver's pocket. 'Of course. Midday it is. Back into Hexham, or somewhere else?'

'Hexham first, to see if a friend has returned from his travels, then into Newcastle.'

The driver looked as pleased as punch at the prospect of such a decent fare, his smile answer enough for Neumegan.

'Tomorrow then, cheers.'

Neumegan stepped cautiously through the light dusting of snow. Whilst living in Auckland, he'd only seen snow once, and it hadn't settled.

. . .

The snow in Northumberland was a different beast altogether. And he could only hope that his friend had prepared appropriately for his trip back in time.

After ordering the steak and ale pie, and a pint of bitter, Neumegan mused about the ease of time travel now. You could order anything you wanted online, instead of trawling estate sales and antique stores. Those platforms had their place, but if he wanted to dress like an American rancher circa 1870, his costume and coins were only a click away, and posted to wherever he liked in the world, sometimes within twenty-four hours. Sharma was the same, although age had caught up with him the last time he'd seen him, just after the great fire in Auckland's Queen Street, and the strange coincidence of the young London antiques dealer appearing in his pawnbroking shop — Sarah Lester, now another dear friend, whom he'd entrusted with his secret.

Interrupted by the service of his food, he returned to the modern day and to his fellow diners. People watching, wherever he was in time, fascinated him. People were the same wherever and whenever he was. Sure, some customs were different, and cultures, but mostly, people wanted to be loved, and to spend time with their loved ones. Diners sitting alone attracted him. Why were they eating alone? Were they travelling for business or recovering from a marriage breakup? Or were they finding themselves? That seemed to have become more popular, especially after that book by Elizabeth Gilbert came out, although he mostly observed that phenomenon in India and Italy, not so much in Northumberland.

He watched a familiar woman arrive alone, a book clasped to her chest. The pale girl from the hospital. Lillian's friend. In what seemed like no time at all, the waiter appeared at her table carefully balancing a pie and chips and what looked like a glass of lemonade. She barely glanced at her food as she ate, her attention totally drawn by the words on the page.

Neumegan slid his eyes past her to the next table — an older couple, both with jovial faces, the man waving his hands as he illustrated some important point, the eyes of his companion crinkling in amusement. Then a group of ruddy-faced hikers, five of them with an empty seat in the middle.

A subdued gathering, and not the sort of weather he'd expect to see hikers out in. As he watched, the waiter delivered six pints of beer, and the five middle-aged men raised their glasses to toast the empty seat. Ah, a memorial to a lost friend.

Neumegan understood their pain. He'd said goodbye to too many people over the years. Some through death, and some because of his preference for living in the past. Time played funny tricks, and it didn't always pass at the same speed. That had thrown him in the beginning. There'd be times where he'd been away for months, but only a smudge of a day had passed at home. He'd aged, but the world had waited for him. Now his trips back were short, and he'd stopped time travelling home a long time ago. It was easier for everyone that way.

'Another drink, sir?'

Neumegan nodded to the waiter. 'And the dessert menu, please.' If their sweet offerings were as good as the pie, he'd be a fortunate man.

His eyes strayed back to the albino woman and her book. He had a bag of books upstairs in his room — an assortment of leather-bound first editions. Early on, he'd realised that bringing valuable items from the past, and selling them in the present, was the easiest way to fund his 19th century lifestyle. He exchanged whatever funds he'd raised to buy gold sovereigns — the most useful currency in his preferred time of 1860's Auckland, New Zealand.

'Sorry, sir, but we've run out of crème brûlée, can I interest you in something else?'

Neumegan watched as a waiter walked by, carrying what he assume to be the last brûlée. 'The berry sorbet, thank you.' His taste buds agitated as he observed the Lillian's friend crack through the thin layer of caramelised sugar, mixing it with ice cream before taking a mouthful, her eyes never once leaving her book. He had to know what she was reading. From here, it looked old. It most certainly wasn't a Lee Child, or the latest Stephen King, or one of the popular Andrene Low thrillers he'd seen in every bookshop window in Hexham. No, it was old, leather-bound, with tissue-thin pages and even from his table, he knew it would have a specific smell modern books could never achieve.

. . .

There was something about the thin folio, and the way she was holding it. Fate had a funny way of twisting timelines together, as if for her own entertainment.

'Excuse me?' Neumegan said, approaching the table. 'So sorry to bother you, but I've been watching you read, and after debating with myself, I have decided that I must know what has held your attention so firmly throughout your meal.'

Neumegan had been mildly concerned that she'd take offence, but she laughed at his query.

'Oh, I doubt that you've heard of it. I don't think it's ever appeared on the best-seller charts.' She inserted a stained receipt to mark her page, closed the book, and passed it to him.

The cover felt warm in his hands, the burgundy leather well worn, the gold lettering slightly faded. He could just make out the wording, *Tamerlane and Other Poems by A Bostonian.*

'May I?' he asked, indicating whether he could open it or not.

'Of course.'

Neumegan's hands were shaking, but he was doing an admirable job of controlling himself. The front page showed itself to be a tea-coloured title page, repeating the name of the publication and that of the author. A publication date of 1827 stood proudly under the printer's name, a company long since lost to time. There was no contents page, only a short preface with the famous line, *Nos hæc novimus esse nihil*, and then the first poem titled *Tamerlane.*

'Who is the author?' Neumegan asked, his voice catching, as he lowered the tome to the table.

'It doesn't say,' the woman said. 'Although I looked it up on the internet, and I think it's a copy of Edgar Allan Poe's Tamerlane.'

He couldn't breathe and his head grew heavy, the room seemingly devoid of oxygen. Neumegan closed his eyes to wait for the room to stop spinning, for the ground to solidify.

'The internet said that there were only twelve surviving copies,' she added

'There are thirteen, and this is the thirteenth copy,' Neumegan said. Being this close to the book only confirmed his suspicions.

· · ·

'Printed by Calvin Thomas himself, although there's no plaque commemorating Calvin and the location of his excellent printing press, only a chain of coffee shops and high-rises. Boston was far more pleasant in 1827. Thomas was young, I...' He'd almost told her how he'd bought it from Calvin as a favour, to help the young man out. 'I gave this copy as a gift to a friend of mine—'

'To Pramod Sharma?'

'Yes, how could you... How do you have it?'

'We're friends. When he went missing, I searched his room and found it in his trunk. I was expecting you, but I wasn't sure when you'd arrive. I'm guessing that you must be Mr. Neumegan? Your name was also in his trunk, but I couldn't find you online. Just like I can't find Mr. Sharma. You are both shadows. Everyone has a digital footprint, but you don't, unless you include one entry in the WWI Online Cenotaph at the Auckland War Memorial Museum? You're old, but you're not that old.'

Neumegan had no words, his mind still reeling as he held the Edgar Allan Poe publication he'd once given his friend. It had taken him years to discover Pramod Sharma and their shared ability. Friendship soon followed. But now this girl had Sharma's book and was worried about him. That wasn't good.

Before he had time to ask more, he blanched, and turned away, bending to stuff the book into his satchel.

'Is everything okay?' she asked.

'Have they gone?'

'Who?'

'The police. They just walked in?'

'I can't see any...' she said, 'Oh.'

Two officers rounded the corner, notebooks in hand, scanning the room, chatting to diners, smiling and nodding.

'They're still here, talking to the diners,' Apple said. 'Why the worry?'

Flames brushed Neumegan's cheeks. 'My ID is hardly current,' he said, and watched the realisation dawn in the girl's eyes.

Apple laughed until he hushed her.

'Shush, you're bringing attention to our table.'

'Hardly,' she said. 'They're more likely to wonder why we aren't having an animated conversation than inquiring too deeply about our mirth. Just pretend we're old friends, catching up by chance.'

By the time the police made it to their table to question them about whether they'd seen any sign of the mayor and her Land Rover, Neumegan reigned supreme at the other side of the table, boring the young officers with his gushing enthusiasm for the brûlée and the convivial atmosphere of the pub.

After the police left, Apple smiled into the dregs of her lemonade, as Neumegan summoned the waiter and ordered a double whisky.

'Dutch courage?' she asked.

'Something like that.'

'May I ask a question?'

'Of course. I'm sure you have plenty,' Neumegan said, sipping his drink.

'How out of date is your identification?'

Neumegan appeared to consider the question. He and Sharma had kept their lives as much under the radar as humanly possible in this electronic age. You could achieve so much with cash, although recently that had become more difficult with the latest pandemic changing the way retailers operated. But this girl... this girl seemed trustworthy.

'It wouldn't look out of place in the Imperial War Museum.'

'I'm impressed,' she said. 'Is Pramod the same as you?'

'Yes, but he'd never leave Poe's book behind. There are some things we always travel with.'

'There were other things in the room,' Apple offered.

Neumegan waited for what he knew was about to come.

'A cup of dice and a Roman tunic.'

Neumegan choked on his tea. Only a great calamity would have sent his friend back to such a dangerous time, and now he feared he'd never see him again. Because, Neumegen knew that Sharma would do whatever it took to protect the timeline, including risking his own life.

CHAPTER 54
VISITING HOURS

'Did you hear? They found the mayor's wife, up by Ithaca Farm.'

'No! Was she alive?'

'Screaming like a banshee.'

'Shame that they found her alive.'

The pub erupted in laughter, as the group of boomers downed their ale and laughed into beards devoid of oil or aftershave, their shirts straining at the buttons, and their underwear well past its use-by date. The same scene replicated itself all around Hexham and the nearby villages. Jane Badrick was no saint, despite how she portrayed herself. Her going missing, and staying missing, had been the highlight of dinner conversations for miles. If she'd remained missing, her reputation would probably have slowly morphed into something more saintly. *Remember the lovely party she put on for the Olympic Games? Were you at that wonderful dinner she hosted for Christmas when she arranged a real reindeer for the children to pet? Oh, and who could ever forget the work she did for the Horticultural Society? She had greener fingers than I could ever hope for.* Oh yes, death is almost always the great redeemer of questionable reputations.

Badger wasn't at home when they located his mother.

. . .

He was sitting outside a hospital room in town, sipping a lukewarm can of soda, lost in his thoughts. He'd ignored the last three phone calls from his father, but had answered the fourth, certain that it would be the worst news. It wasn't. And now he sat outside the hospital room of the girl who lived at the farm where they'd found his mother, delirious and obstructive, refusing any offers of aid. His father repeating what the police had told him. Badger believed it. His mother could have been held captive by Saddam Hussain himself, but if the situation didn't suit her narrative, she wouldn't have shared one iota of information about her ordeal.

'She's awake. You can go in now if you like?' a nurse said, emerging from Lillian's room, leaving the door open.

Badger stretched and peered in towards the bed. The geometric patterned curtain half concealed the bed, but he could see Lillian's face, and she was smiling at him.

'Hello,' he said, walking into the room, a stupid grin on his face.

'Hi.'

'Enjoy your trip?' he asked.

'It could have been better,' she replied, a faint smile ghosting her face.

'Do you want to talk about it?'

'Not really.'

Badger pulled the hard visitor's chair closer to the bed and sat down. He wanted to hold her pale hand, laying ever so close on top of the branded hospital sheets.

'Thanks for looking after Nicole,' she said.

'Apple was there too. She looked after her way more than I did.'

'It was a surprise finding you here, waiting for me,' Lillian said.

'To be fair, it was easier hanging out at Ithaca Farm than waiting with my father for any news. Besides, Ithaca Farm is legendary.'

'Why?'

Badger shrugged. 'Lots of rumours, but everyone remembers Seb's grandad talking about fending off the Northern barbarians. Kind of just thought he was talking about Scottish football hooligans or something. I never paid too much attention, although me and Seb had great fun playing with all his swords and stuff. Are they still there?'

Lillian didn't reply. She'd turned away from him to stare out the window.

'Hey, did I say something wrong? Sorry.'

'No, it wasn't anything you said. Just... I don't think Seb's grandfather was mad at all.'

'Ah, you never met him, remember?' Badger said.

'True, but I know what he must have been going through,' Lillian said, finally turning to look at Badger.

'What makes you say that?' Badger almost didn't want her to answer. A creeping sense of dread washed over him as he watched her struggle with her words. Holly's laughing taunts of calling Lillian Nero dredging up memories he'd long since buried. Memories of playing with swords and daggers, and hiding in sheds amongst old gravestones stacked in rows. Seb's grandfather had never minded, only ever asking the boys to keep their games within the confines of the farm, and to swear on their mother's lives never to touch any coins. His only rule. Never touch the coins. And Badger had never thought to question that one rule. Why should he? He had an abundance of pocket money, not that there was anything to spend it on in the countryside. He had everything he needed right on his doorstep.

'Can we leave it? They're sending me home tomorrow, so shall we talk about it there? Remember the last time I was here, when you pulled me out of the rubble? And Holly saw you, and basically ended any sort of normal life I might have been able to have in this town?'

Badger remembered, and not for the first time, cursed ever having thought Holly Corben was anything more than an obsessive airhead, with a large cruel streak running through her to rival that of the emperor Caligula.

'Sure, I understand. I'll... I guess I'll see you tomorrow then.' Badger was halfway to the door when he spun around. 'Oh, and they found my mum, too. Up at your farm, near your altar. So it's all good news. Apart from her car. They haven't found that.'

Lillian waited until Badger had left before allowing his words to take purchase in her mind. It took a while, her brain was still fuzzy. Dehydrated, they'd said, plugging her arm with a needle hooked up to a drip. And she tried to remember if she'd had anything to drink or eat while she was... what was she? Away? Abroad? Existing in another dimension. Her life had turned into one long series of The Twilight Zone, but without the omnipotent narrator, the one who ensures everything makes sense.

They'd found Badger's mother. Excellent news for Badger and his father, Lillian allowed. But what she knew of Jane Badrick outside of her family role wasn't good. The town library being the largest black mark against her. Then there was the way she'd made life difficult for her plans to rewild Ithaca Farm.

A phrase niggled in the recesses of Lillian's mind. A car? The sound of a car's horn? Was it Jane Badrick's car?

Lillian gasped. It had to have been. Both were missing for a similar amount of time. She knew she'd seen a car from the top of Ithaca Fort. Although absolutely nothing made sense, least of all seeing Jane Badrick's car in the middle of a Northumberland field surrounded by Celtic warriors, whilst Roman soldiers prepared to defend the fort.

Staring at the ceiling, Lillian knew one other thing. She'd left Julius there. Alone. To face what could only be certain death. For that's what she'd witnessed in her vision that very first night. She had to get back. She had to save him. Lillian hoped that Badger would understand.

CHAPTER 55

A SOLDIER'S LOT IN LIFE

Decimus Clodius Albinus stood motionless behind the desk, his pale knuckles resting on the polished surface. Titus Caelius Castus stood behind him, his florid face a picture of abject misery.

Julius shuffled backwards, his movements small and cautious.

The other men filling the space coughed, heads either hung in shame, or held defiantly up, as if to say, it's not my fault, it wasn't me, blame the others, look at me I'm the only competent one here.

Leather tunics rustled. One man scratched his arse, the sound of his nails against his skin enough to drive his nearest neighbour into a quiet rage, who elbowed him hard. A muffled curse.

'A demon you say,' Albinus said, his moist lips barely moving. 'A demon beyond our walls? What are you? Roman soldiers, or the spawn of barbarian whores, raised on tales spun from the cursed lips of the vanquished druids?'

The men adjusted their positions, feet growing tired, stomachs rumbling, eyes gritty with lack of sleep from the horrors of what they'd all seen. The horror that the governor so vehemently denied the existence of. Denial which had gone on for more than the three hours since he'd returned from his tour of Vindolanda, only to find Ithaca Fort in disarray.

'This demon is docking you all one denarius for dereliction of duty. Every single last one of you cowards. Now get out of my sight, and I will not hear one more word of an Iron Beast or a demon under the control of the barbarians. Out. Julius Aurelius Stertinius, you stay.'

The men scattered like leaves in the wind, each of them casting one last glance at the sacrificial lamb standing motionless in the centre of the room.

'I believe you to be a sane man, Julius, and not given to moments of delirium. So please tell me, what happened in my absence? Was it the drink? Did the men imbibe too much while I was gone? A poisoning of the food supplies? For these are the only suggestions which make any sense.'

Julius couldn't answer. His fingers strayed to the amulet hanging around his neck — a winged phallus. Although he suspected his *fascina* would not protect him from the wrath of the governor of these cursed isles.

'Well, man? Answer me.'

'I can only say what I saw with my eyes and heard with my ears. And it was not of this world,' Julius replied, entwining his fingers around the leather cord of the phallus.

'I ask nothing less of you.'

'What the men say is true. It was an iron beast, on the blackest of wheels, with a voice like a bellowing cow, and possessed by Pluto himself, but in the form of a flaxen-haired harridan. I know nothing more other than our arrows bounced off the beast and it showed no sign of injury. And then it vanished. There was no time to give chase...'

'No time? We are the Roman army, guarding the border for the Emperor. We have nothing but time until they recall us to Rome.'

'By the time the men had recovered their wits, the beast had vanished.'

'The truth sets you free, yes?'

Julius could do little more than hang his head, his cheeks aflame. His head bobbed almost imperceptibly. It was true; the soldiers had embarrassed themselves with their superstitious fear, but sharing that fact hadn't made him feel any better.

. . .

Bile rose from his stomach, bringing with it his breakfast, and Julius coughed as the regurgitated mutton caught in his throat. Fear paralysed him all over again.

'This beast must be easy to track. If our men can track a thief on foot, then finding a wheeled carriage should be easy enough to accomplish.'

'We've tried,' Julius said. 'The barbarians obscured the tracks. We can find no sign of the beast.'

Albinus released his grip of his desk, and Julius fancied he could see imprints of the man's fingers in the wood. He braced himself for the governor's next words, holding his hands behind his back to hide the nervous shaking.

'Try harder,' Albinus said. 'I'll not have the men sharing this story any wider, or we'll be the laughingstock of the Empire. This is not to appear in any official record, understood?'

'But the scribe has already recorded the event,' Julius said.

'Destroy the record. Burn it. I want no mention of this getting out, although it's probably too late. We'll face that issue if it arises.' Albinus sank into a campaign chair, the leather creaking under his weight, disturbing the greyhound at his feet, brought with him from Rome. The hound, Lelaps, took more exercise than its master, who'd given up all forms of exercise, other than of the horizontal type.

'Is there anything else?' Julius chanced.

Albinus gestured towards an oak chest beside the desk, about the size of a mole. 'That needs to be locked away in the vault.'

The vault usually only held the soldier's pay and the legion's standard. It was unusual to store anything else in there. Julius almost asked, but the marble cast to Albinus' face stopped him.

'Of course, I'll see to it now,' Julius said, hefting the trunk, staggering under the unexpected weight.

'It belongs to my wife's family,' Albinus offered, but turned away, adding no further information.

'Is she joining us here at Ithaca Fort?' Julius asked.

'Finally, yes,' Albinus said. 'I have persuaded her that her place is here, regardless of how she feels about it. The chest, Julius.'

· · ·

Julius vacated the Praetorium, his mind running through ancient memories, his arms aching under the weight of the mysterious chest.

As Julius approached the vault, he nodded at the men guarding the entrance, surprised that they'd been put on duty at the same time. Known troublemakers, he'd personally directed that the two of them be kept on separate duty details to avoid any further problems. This was Marcus' doing. He'd been making it a regular habit, interfering with rosters. Why, though?

Navigating the steps down into the vault, Julius mulled over Marcus' intentions. Those two guards shouldn't be on duty together. It was a recipe for disaster.

Julius unlocked the vault, automatically checking the placement of the standard. Standing proudly, as it should be. The pay chest sat solidly in the centre of the room, its lock engaged. After placing the governor's trunk to the side, Julius ran his hands over the iron bands on the lid. Smooth, complete with intricate carving, the trunk was a work of art in its own right.

Curiosity got the better of him, and he tried lifting the lid, but the box was locked. It was just as well, he thought, readjusting the chest's position on the table.

Just as Julius turned towards the stairs, a golden glint caught his eye. The flame from the oil lamp wavered as he bent towards the glimmer.

Julius knew what he was seeing, but didn't want to believe what danced in the light. A coin. One golden denarii. There was no earthly reason for a coin to be on the ground. Unless... unless someone had been into the pay chest.

The key to the pay chest lived in Julius' leather belt, a belt he had never removed apart from during his brief visits to the baths.

With his heart hammering through his rib cage, Julius slid the toothed key into the lock, turned it, and opened the iron-banded chest.

Rows of linen bags stood to attention, bulging at their base, squatting like pregnant gods.

Julius didn't need to count the bags, there were no voids in the chest.

But still he chose a random bag, the spluttering oil lamp masking the shape of the bag. Fair light would have shown its uneven form was more akin to bubbles of sea foam than bags of coins.

The bag felt wrong. And logic told him what his heart refused to believe. Kissing the amulet at his neck, Julius opened the bag, allowing the worked river stones to tumble from their cocoon. The clattering masking the shattering of his peace.

Bag after bag spewed its contents onto the floor of the vault. Not a single denarius appeared. The commander and governor needed to be told. There was only one course of action open to them, and that was to find the thieves and the coins. Before the legion found out.

The girl had been right. And now Marcus' reaction to seeing Lillian in the fort on the night of the second attack of the Iceni made sense. She knew who'd stolen the coins. And Marcus knew who'd seen him.

CHAPTER 56
THE WOMAN RETURNS

Jane Badrick begged the use of the nurse's phone. Better to delve into the dark web on someone else's device. No stranger to this part of the internet, it didn't take long to find what she was looking for.

She'd had a taste of true power and hungered for more. Returning to Gar and his tribe was now her only goal. And to do that, she needed a key to the past. Fortunately, her long years of attending graduations and university dinners offered her unparalleled access to the staff and vaults of Newcastle University, and if her little spies were correct, Anson Darby would give her what she needed.

She sourced another item through the nurse's phone. The sort one couldn't easily buy in England. In Texas, yes, guns were as common as white bread and mayonnaise. But not in England.

Jane smiled, as she imagined the outcome of a well armed Iceni against the might of the Roman army, until she betrayed them in order to get what she truly wanted. Entrée into the upper echelons of Rome.

Gold and glory. Oh, what a wonderful time she would have.

To Be Continued...

Ithaca Lost - Book #2 in the Ithaca Trilogy

ITHACA LOST

Can one woman stop the power of Rome breaking through the thin veneer of time?

With treasure seekers and archaeologists swarming over Ithaca Farm, Lillian struggles to regain control over her life. The ancient Roman festival of Saturnalia is approaching, giving her one opportunity to return to the past to warn the Roman soldier Julius of the treachery threatening his life, and her future. But she isn't the only modern day traveller trying to slip back in time...

Mayor Jane Badrick has spent all her money on the dark web, gathering together an arsenal worthy of an army, a Roman army. And with her at the helm, history is about to change.

A sweeping saga of friendship, love, and the corruption of power.

THE FORGER AND THE THIEF

Five strangers entangled in the forger's wicked web, each with a dangerous secret, and an apocalyptic flood threatening to reveal everything.

A **wife** on the run, a **student** searching for stolen art, a **cleaner** who has lined more than his pockets, a **policeman** whose career is almost over, and a **guest** who should never have received a wedding invite.

In a race against time, and desperate to save themselves and all they hold dear, will their secrets prove more treacherous than the ominous floodwaters swallowing the historic city of Florence?

Dive into a world of lies and deceit, where nothing is as it seems on the surface...

REVIEW

Dear Reader,

If you enjoyed *Ithaca Bound*, I would love it if you could please leave a rating or review on your favourite digital platform. Or post about it online, or even ask your local library to order in a copy for others to enjoy.

Thank you.

Kirsten McKenzie

CAST OF PLAYERS
THE ITHACA SERIES

Lillian Arlosh, owner of Ithaca Farm

Andy 'Badger' Badrick, Friend of Lillian
Matthew Badrick, Badger's Father, Archaeologist
Jane Badrick, Badger's Mother, Mayor

John Revell, Editor, Hexham Herald
Gail Revell, wife of John Revell
Jasper Fletcher, Reporter, Hexham Herald
Sue, Receptionist, Hexham Herald
Tom, Print Manager, Hexham Herald
Damien and Jan, Advertising team, Hexham Herald
Rhema Patel, Classifieds Intern, Hexham Herald
Lorna Milroy, BBC London Reporter
Charley Scott, Newcastle Reporter

Darren Saunders, Lawyer
Seb Arlosh, Friend of Badger's
William Arlosh, Seb's Grandfather
James Losh*, 18th century ancestor of William Arlosh

Lola Cassidy, Councillor
Jesha Martin, Friend
Apple Collings, Friend
Holly Corben, Girlfriend of Badger
Paige Spencer, Bellingham Tea Rooms Proprietor
Anson Darby, Archaeologist, Tyne River University
Ayla Raposo, Portable Antiquities Scheme
Sergeant Gavin Bishop, Hexham Sergeant
Chief Inspector Kevin Readdie, Newcastle Inspector
Clifton Beaufort, Hadrian's Heroes Metal Detecting Club
Graham Ryan, Hadrian's Heroes Metal Detecting Club

Nicole Pilcher, Antiques Dealer
Pramod Sharma, Librarian
Henry Neumegen, Pawnbroker
Loretta Hambly, Creative

Julius Aurelius Stertinius, Roman Soldier
Marcus, Roman Soldier
Darius, Roman Soldier
Gaius, Roman Soldier
Titus Caelius Castus, Commander of Ithaca Fort
Metella, Brothel Keeper
Carmella, Metella's Servant
Silas, Metella's Manservant
Gattus, Healer
Caelius Apicius*, Roman Recipe Book Author
Decimus Clodius Albinus*, Governor of Britain

Gar, Ician Chieftain
Bricius, Ician Warrior

Satiada*, Celtic Goddess worshipped in Roman Britain
Meditrina*, Roman goddess of health, longevity and wine
*Genuine historical figures

BOOK CLUB DISCUSSION QUESTIONS

1. What was your favourite part of *Ithaca Bound*?
2. Who would you have aligned yourself with in Roman Britain?
3. Which scene has stuck with you the most?
4. Would you want to read another book by this author?
5. What surprised you the most about the book?
6. *Ithaca Bound* goes back 1,900 years. Where and when would you like to time travel to?
7. What is one question you have for the author?
8. How would you have survived at *vicus*, the Roman village next to Ithaca Fort?
9. Which characters did you like best? Who did you like least? And why?
10. If you had to trade places with one character, who would it be and why?
11. How likely do you think it is that someone like Mayor Jane Badrick exists, and would behave the way she did?
12. How did the setting impact the story? Would you want to read more books set in this world?

ACKNOWLEDGMENTS

This book has been a long time coming, seemingly almost as long as the Romans ruled Britain!

I want to acknowledge the incredible real archaeologists I've met whilst volunteering at Vindolanda Roman Fort. Of course, everything in *this* book is made up, so parts of it will undoubtedly be historically inaccurate (sorry Andrew). But the spirit behind this fictional story is a homage to Andrew, Marta and Penny, as well as Sonya and Colin, and all the incredible volunteers from the Magic Corner, and the heart racing 2017 crew! I could name you all, but then I'd probably miss someone, but I will specifically mention Lucy and Joe (the best digging siblings ever), Sam and Claire, Jackson and Tracy (the Canadians), the two Emilys, Hannah (thanks for being such a great friend to Sasha), Steph, Gary, Graham and Norman, Anthea, Pete, Lizzie and Megan and Brian. As I said, there are too many of you! I love you all.

Thank you to Mark Richards (and his wife Helen for keeping him on task), for the original illustrations in this book. You are a genius.

There will be a second book in the series, out for Christmas 2023. I promise... And then a third book to complete the trilogy.

Thank you once again for reading *Ithaca Bound*.

ABOUT THE AUTHOR

Kirsten McKenzie fought international crime for fourteen years as a Customs Officer in both England and New Zealand, before leaving to work in the family antique store. Now a full time author, she lives in New Zealand with her family and alternates between writing time travel trilogies and polishing her next thriller. Her spare time is spent organising author events and appearing on literary panels at various festivals around the world.

Her historical time travel trilogy, *The Old Curiosity Shop* series, has been described as *"Time Travellers Wife meets Far Pavilions"* and *"Antiques Roadshow gone viral"*. Audio books for the series are available through Audible.

Kirsten has also written the bestselling gothic thriller *Painted*, and the medical thriller, *Doctor Perry*. Her last thriller, *The Forger and the Thief*, is a historical thriller set in 1966 Florence, Italy, with some ghostly links to *Painted...*

She is working on her second time travel trilogy, which begins with *Ithaca Bound*, and features many of your favourite characters from the *Old Curiosity Shop* series.

Kirsten lives in New Zealand with her husband, her daughters, and one rescue cat. She can usually be found procrastinating online.

You can sign up for her newsletter at:
www.kirstenmckenzie.com/newsletter/

Printed in Great Britain
by Amazon